WALL STREET RAIDERS

To my wife, Flora and my son, Shane

Thank you for your love and support!

Tim

Thanks for your support.

Black Street II
Prologue

Old School slow jams played in the background as I laid in bed next to this chocolate beauty. In the middle of the night I awakened and sat up to make sure I wasn't dreaming that she was really here with me. I ran my hand across her bare back gently, and moved it slowly toward her bare backside. Caressing and enjoying the feeling and sight in the dimly lit room. I felt slight shifts in her body as my hand made its way around her body, letting me know my touch pleased her. For her to be here with me after all that had taken place was a dream come true. My serenade opened the door to let me back in, but would she allow me to stay? A question only time could answer. The hurt and pain I caused was unforgivable. I had been cold, irrational, and unforgiving for no good reason. Kendra was the prize all men desired, and who my mother spoke about.

We were in a presidential suite at the Waldorf Astoria hotel on Park Avenue. The one bedroom suite on the 60th floor had English Manor décor, with a plush king size bed, a sitting room with a flat screen HDTV, marble bathroom, and a kitchenette. The days were filled with passionate love making, soul searching conversations, movie watching, snacking, and a rehashing of moments passed. Kendra desperately needed to know- what were the driving forces that separated us and made me walk away from her so definitively. Answers were hard to come by, well good ones. I struggled to answer her questions realizing a little soul searching was needed on my part. There were some hard questions I had for myself, and if I couldn't look in the mirror and answer them truthfully to myself, then I wasn't the man I thought I was, and I wasn't becoming the man my mother could be proud of, or the man Kendra could commit to.

Late nights in the hotel as Kendra slept, I found myself facing the bathroom mirror asking the hard questions to myself. Was Black Street a good idea? Did I practice racism in trying to accomplish that goal? My distrust of Emmy to work on the trading desk, was it solely because of her interracial marriage? And, did her relationship effect my decision to walk away from Kendra knowing she was almost a part of an interracial marriage? What about Ted? My attempt to take his book away from his nephew Stephen, was that an act of betrayal after all he had done for me? Even Timothy crossed my mind. Did he really sell me out or did he just do the right thing? The questions kept piling up as I stared in mirror. It got to a point where the questions were plentiful, but the answers were dormant. When it became too much, I retired back to bed beside Kendra seeking comfort, reassurance, and affection which she never denied me. Kendra had the best qualities that a man could ever want in a woman, a wife.

It was there in the midst of darkness, I knew, I wanted her to be my wife. Was I the man she wanted as her husband? After all I put her through, could she forgive me and look past my shortcomings to see my true potential. From the depths of my heart hope was high, but the reality of her pain was evident. Despite the phenomenal time we were having I detected Kendra's struggle to come to grips with my inexcusable reaction and behavior to the revelation of her previous relationship. I felt time was my enemy. I didn't want to leave this room if it meant Kendra and I would just go back to dating, living in separate homes, spending some nights together, and just talking on the phone to her nights. The commitment and sanctity of marriage is what I desired with Kendra and settling for something less was not an option. What did I need to do? Answer the hard questions.

After the third day in the hotel, Kendra needed to get back to work. She said, jokingly I was the only one without a job. It was a good joke, and I needed the levity at the time. There were the burning questions I needed to answer for myself. It left me in a mood of awkwardness at the end of the three day getaway. I knew she had to get back to her business and that her customers just might send an APB out on her as a missing person. Kendra opened up her boutique in Harlem six days a week like clockwork, and if she wasn't in the store personally, friends or family covered in her absence, but this time the spontaneity of my request for her to join me at the hotel left her unprepared. I told her, I would be staying in the hotel an extra day just to think through some things. She understood and said she'd call and check on me later. My last question I posed to her before she departed.

"Are we okay?"

"For now, "she replied quietly.

Her response was not very reassuring as I didn't think it would be. Once she left, the soul searching began. I made myself a morning bath sat in it for over an hour just thinking and pondering the questions before me. Still I wasn't ready to answer, so I dried off, made my way to the front room where Kendra and I didn't spend a lot of time, but upon inspection was very nice room. I took comfort on the very soft leather couch residing in the middle of the room and turned on the flat screen television mounted on the wall. I did a little channel surfing before coming up on an episode of Sanford and Son. This sitcom was timeless. It was one of my mother's favorites; she liked it so much she bought the DVD's from the first four seasons. Anytime my mother was stressed, she would go work out then come home and pop in a DVD of Sanford and Son just to laugh. I would sit with her a lot of times and our laugh fest would last from one to two hours depending how many episodes we watched. This particular episode of Sanford and Son, Fred was working on the taxes for their junk business, and Lamont was uncomfortable in the way Fred was going about it. So, Lamont questions his father. Fred then declares to his son. "Black folk have the same right as White folk." "What right is that" Lamont asked? "To cheat on their taxes," Fred said in response. I chuckled and laughed through the whole episode, but when it ended, I realized my pro blackness had been bred into me since my youth.

My mother always tried to seek out black contractors for work on our home and to work with her interior design business. She always said if we don't support black businesses than who would? Recycling black dollars thru 8-12 businesses was a huge theme in the community I grew up in which emphasized dollars making its way through the local community economy before it left the community. This in turn would support small businesses in the community, create jobs, increase taxes generated from the community which in turn would get the attention of government officials to increase services. So, for my first question about Black Street, right or wrong my heart was in the right place. I wanted to create opportunities for African Americans in a place that traditionally overlooked our talent – no apologies for that. Now, how I went about creating those opportunities brought me back to a lesson learned long ago. Two wrongs don't make a right! I did discriminate against those non-African American candidates even though it was in effort to right historical wrongs. As Ted tried to point out, my efforts were more of a political statement to show Wall Street up than to realistically correct inequities in the hiring practices of Wall Street.

To affirm Ted sentiments brought me face to face with my ego. My ego was the culprit, my true driving force. Evidenced by my attempt to steal Ted's book, rescind Emmy's offer without consulting with Tim, pulling Betty over to be my HR rep, run-ins with Junior, and just in my general management style as Managing Director of the fixed income desk at GPG. What I realized was the very character trait that allowed me to get the Management Director position on the fixed income desk and turn it back to the number one desk at GPG was the same trait that threw my career in a downward tailspin and forced me to leave my MD position before I was ready. My ego really didn't serve me well with Kendra either. Her engagement to a white man wasn't the driving force that separated us, but the fact that any man had held such an intimate position in her heart before me was all ego. The fact that it was prior to her meeting me didn't matter, I wanted that place in her heart to be for me and me alone – past, present and future, and when I found out that it wasn't, my ego couldn't take it, so I thought it best to jet!

It was mentally draining to face and tackle those questions calling my character into question, but I stripped down to my essence, free of ego and the chip that resided on my left shoulder. I ended up in the bathroom mirror once again.

"What are you trying to prove?" I stared into the mirror. "Better than that, who are you trying to prove it to?"

The answer was staring back at me in the mirror. Why? Why did I feel the need to prove my own self-worth and the worth of African Americans to myself? Did I feel a need to measure up; measure up to who and why? Is it that I believed that Wall Street was the measuring stick? This was getting a little too deep. I put a halt to it! There was no way all questions would be answered by the time I left this hotel, but the satisfaction of coming to grips with my ego or just recognizing the role it played in my life thus far was progress, and I was happy to walk away with that. My first step was to make amends with those that I could make amends with for my past transgressions.

The next day, before I checked out of the hotel, I made a call to Betty. She was still at GPG. I asked her to meet at the coffee shop where we had our first meeting. To say she was surprised to hear from me would be an understatement. I could hear trepidation in her voice. I hadn't talk to her since the mediation hearing. I heard from Charles and Darrell she was removed from being the HR representative for the fixed income desk. They hadn't talked to her, but the interim managing director –Walter had relayed the information. It seems Junior didn't stay true to his promise to put Timothy as managing director of the Fixed Income Desk, typical Junior!

I arrived at the coffee shop on Wall Street around 10am. There sitting in the back corner in the same exact seat as our first meeting was Betty- her back to me. As I approached and plopped down in the seat opposite her, she was startled and I laughed, but I could see immediately she had been crying –eyes watery, runny nose, and handkerchief in hand. She was clearly unnerved!

"Betty what is wrong?" I put my hand out to console her. She withdrew her hand from the table. "Come on Betty." I pleaded. "I'm here to apologize and try to make amends for what I put you through."

"Apologize." She responded quizzically. She sat back in her seat and blew her nose, then continued. "I am the one that should be apologizing to you."

"Why would you say that? I was the one not forthcoming with my entire vision for the trading desk. I should have shared with you my intentions of an all-black trading desk during our first meeting, and then allowed you to choose if you wanted to be a part of that vision. I took that opportunity away from you by not being honest, and I am sorry I did."

"You were a little deceptive in your approach, but I knew you were up to something from the very first meeting – more than you let on. So I knew the risk, but I was thankful for the opportunity. I accept your apology, but I still owe you one."

"I don't see why."

"I knew they had turned Timothy, and I kept quiet about it." She said as she waited for my reaction.

"At that time Betty you were in survival mode, and you had a young son to look out for. I do not and will not hold that decision against you. Self-preservation is the first rule of nature."

She stood quickly, so I stood. She hopped around the table crying and gave me a hug which caught me off guard. We both nearly fell to the floor. As we embraced she spoke. "What you did with that trading desk –giving more African Americans opportunity to work on Wall Street, bringing back the desk from the depths of destruction, and shaking the Wall Street elite to its core was nothing short of a miracle. "

"Thank you – you have no idea how much I needed to hear that at this time."

Betty and I sat back down and continued to chat for a while. Her duties had been regulated back to almost nothing, and she was seeking job opportunities elsewhere. I gave a brief update and my priority of mending my relationship with Kendra. Time slipped away and Betty had to get back to the office, we pledged to stay in touch, and then said good bye.

It felt good to clear the air with Betty and apologize. I am glad she didn't harbor any ill feelings against me and surprisingly she thought she owed me an apology after all I put her through. It indicated to me that she was a true friend and cared for me. It took true character for her to reveal to me she knew of Tim's betrayal. At the time, my mind was elsewhere, so even if she had told me, I don't think I would have heard her, nor would it have change the outcome.

I sat there in the coffee shop reflecting on the past. My conversation with Betty stirred up some uncomfortable feelings about Tim. Tim and I had a history clear back to our undergrad Ivy League days. When his betrayal became evident at the mediation, the last thing I thought, I would ever do was speak to him again. Not because of all the help I had given him to become a better salesperson and the opportunity as an economist, but just that we were friends and he sold me out, nothing more. My thoughts were, if you can't count on your friends, who is left? Maybe the measuring stick I was holding was one he couldn't measure up to and that was a mistake on my part. My friendships with Big Mike, Charles, and Darrell transcended to one of family. Although they didn't agree with all my decisions one hundred percent, they supported me. They knew what was in my heart, and family knows what's in your heart. I found myself dialing Tim's office number at GPG.

I asked Tim to meet me at the coffee shop, without hesitation he agreed. About twenty minutes later Tim came walking through the door. He looked around until our eyes met, and he quickly made his way to the back of the coffee shop where I was seated. I stood as he approached. The greeting was awkward. No, pound or dap just a traditional handshake suffice for the moment. We both took a seat.

"How've you been?" I asked.

"I've been better." Tim answered.

"How's the wife and kids?"

"Good.....How have you been?"

I thought for a minute and then returned. "Good." I shook my head affirming. We both were silent looking at each other, hesitant to talk about the two ton elephant that was sharing this coffee table with us. I took the initiative. "Tim, I called you just to say to you face to face I am sorry for betraying your trust." He was silent but listening intently. "I should have shared my vision for the trading desk, and given you the real reasons for rescinding the offer to Emmy. I should have given you full disclosure, and we could have had an honest debate about your feelings and the decisions I was making that directly affected you."

"Hey man, I appreciate you coming to me like this, and to tell you the truth, you've been heavy on my mind. I accept your apology. I hope you can find it in your heart to forgive me for betraying your trust. Believe it or not I didn't sell you out because of the managing director offer, but because I thought it was the right thing to do. I believe in equal opportunity for all. I should have gotten off your train way before it got to its final destination. When I revealed our plan to the Mackeys, I didn't leave out my part and my support in what you were doing. The offer was enticing, but I knew the Mackeys',there was a slim to none chance of getting that managing director position, and just for the record I didn't want to hire Emmy to pick up on her."

"Tim, we've known each other since undergrad. I know we see things from different lenses, but what drew me to our friendship was your honesty and morale character. You have a good heart, and I put you in position where you had to compromise some of the principals you live your life by, and for that I'm sorry. I don't know if my ego ever became bigger than my vision for the desk, but I understand it was a real possibility. As for Emmy, I never believed you had ulterior motives other than professional aspirations for her. I just said it to cover up my real reasons."

"Did you really rescind her offer because she was married to a white man?" He asked.

I thought about the question for a minute before I answered...... "Yes and no." Puzzled at my response Tim queried me further with his eyes. I explained. "At that time we were under a microscope and with Junior breathing down my neck, I was a little paranoid. My first interview with Emmy left me a little uneasy, her pro blackness and straight talk about Black Street, to say the least, was unsettling. I was impressed with her candidacy as you were, but when I met her husband, I jumped to the conclusion she was a plant by Junior. So, my rescinding her offer was more of a paranoid reaction to her being a plant then any objection to her husband, but her husband is what prompted the decision." Tim eyes studied my every word which still had him questioning me. I tried to elaborate further. "Tim the decision was unfortunate. I made some assumptions about Emmy based on her conversation and her choice of a mate. And, if truth be told given the same set of circumstances, I would make the same decision."

Tim smiled surprisingly. "How do you do that?"

"Do what?"

"Make something that was obviously wrong sound okay, and do it with such eloquence it makes me sympathize with your position."

"I'm just telling you the truth."

"That's why you were so successful. You are the best salesman I have ever encountered. It's just not about selling a product or service, but it's really about selling yourself. Once you get people to buy in on you, then the rest is easy. Now, I realize why I didn't leave the desk when you revealed your plan about hiring an all-African American trading desk. I never believed in your plan, but I believed in you!"

It made sense what Tim was saying. Maybe the others- Big Mike, Darrell, and Charles felt the same way. Maybe I leveraged our friendship to get them to go along with my vision for the GPG trading desk. I don't think it's something I did intentionally, but my mother had always told me that I had a magnetic personality and that it would serve me well in the world of business. Tim and I finished up our conversation. We shook hands and I promised to stay in touch.

I took the subway home after my meeting with Tim. While riding on the subway, my mind shifted to the last person I thought there needed to be reconciliation with. Ted, he was still on his trip around the world with his wife and wouldn't be back in the state for at least six months. Ted was my mentor and friend, and was responsible for me getting the managing director position. We ended badly. Our disagreements stem from the direction of the desk and his turning his sales book over to his nephew Steven. After my attempt to take the sales book back through some covert strategies that back fired, I realized I should have let Ted retire and leave his book to who he wanted. He had done so much for me and he was a true friend and mentor. I should have acquiesced to his wishes and left well enough alone, but my ego stuck its head up once again and led me down a path I regretted.

I arrived home to Big Mike, Darrell, and Charles all lounging in the television room channel surfing and checking out ESPN highlights. It was Charles and Darrell's first day GPG free. They handed in their resignation the day after I was forced to resign from my position as managing director. Once the word circulated around GPG of my resignation, Junior wasted no time in dismantling the desk by swapping personnel from other trading desk within GPG forcing professionals from Black Street to swap profitable and productive books for less than profitable books of business. Most saw this as unfair, but Junior justified it by saying the way in which the desk was assembled was not fair. There was no concerted mass exodus on the part of the remaining professionals of Black Street because Junior gave no time to organize, and replaced Charles and Darrell immediately with friends he knew that worked on Wall Street. Junior executed some of his own covert operations to retain 75% of the books built under the Black Street umbrella.

I took a seat beside Big Mike on the couch and helped myself to some of the snacks on the center table.

"I thought you would be back earlier." Big Mike spoke.

"Yea, I took the time to go down to Wall Street and speak to Betty and Tim."

"What the hell did you do that for? Big Mike retorted while Charles and Darrell sat up.

"I felt I owed Betty and Tim an apology."

"Apology?" Charles questioned.

"I can see an apology to Betty, just because of the position we put her in, but Tim?" Darrell joined in.

"Yea, we don't owe Tim anything; fucking sell out!" Big Mike shouted.

One thing stood out in our conversation about my apologies to Betty and Tim, Big Mike, Darrell, and Charles always referred to us, never singling out that I owed the apologies. These guys continued to reaffirm what I already knew; we were more than friends, we were family. When one of us was in trouble, all of us were in trouble. I really appreciated their friendship and the brotherhood we shared. I felt I owed them an apology the most. No matter the mistakes I made and my tardiness in revealing my true vision for the trading desk at the time, they stuck by me and gave me support. I took them for granted and didn't give consideration to their reactions or how my vision and decisions affected them. So, that's what I did, I apologized!

"There's no need for that Shane. We all respected your vision and understood what its purpose was, and truth be told, we admired you for the courage, which gave us the courage to follow and support your vision." Darrell said.

"I'm down with you like AC Collins was down with OJ." Big Mike added.

"I think I'm going to cry." Charles said jokingly.

We all had a good laugh.

"But, what I want to know is, what the hell are we going to do now? Darrell and I know you and Big Mike have something up your sleeves, but Big Mike will not even give us a hint. We don't ever have to worry about him dropping a dime. He keeps his lips tighter than the security at Fort Knox." Charles said.

"I'll let Big Mike tell you." I yielded to Big Mike to reveal what all his overseas travelling was about.

"I was soliciting international investors for Black Street Capital."

"Black Street Capital?" Darrell queried.

Big Mike excused himself and went to the office upstairs without saying a word. Darrell and Charles looked at me.

"Patience."

Big Mike returned and placed some documents in front of Darrell and Charles. Darrell picked the papers up and a big smile came over his face. Charles quickly took the papers and I could see his eyes moving at a rapid pace reading through the papers. He could not hold back his excitement.

"Goddamn it! We got our own company." Charles exclaimed.

"Yea, Shane set up "Black Street Capital" an investment company where all of us are equal partners owning 25% of the company each."

"Was this part of your plan always- for us to go out on our own? Darrell asked.

"Yes, I never thought Black Street would stand, but I thought I would have more time to transition the trading desk we built at GPG to our own company "Black Street". The previous managing director of the fixed income showed me the blue print, when he organized the mass exodus of talent from the trading desk to his own business venture. Big Mike and I just needed a little more time and we could have crippled GPG to the brink of no return, and that ass hole Junior would have deserved every bit of it."

"Ah man, the Mackeys would have committed suicide. Brilliant Shane, so your plan was to take everyone with you?' Charles asked.

"Yes!"

"Not, to be critical, but we own 25% of what? How much capital does Black Street Capital have?" Darrell asked.

"We have just less than half a billion in capital."

"What the fuck did you just say?" Charles questioned.

Big Mike repeated. "Half a billion."

"How in the hell did you guys pull that off? Darrell asked.

"Big Mike did a hell of a job getting investors!" I said.

"Shane was a big part of the success. I arranged video conferences between potential investors and Shane, and he laid out the vision for Black Street Capital, and the success of "Black Street" the trading desk had vibrated throughout international markets. Quiet as it's kept, a lot of investors were trying to seek us out, and when they heard about a startup opportunity with Shane for Black Street Capital, they were jumping at the opportunity."

"We are about to blow up!" Charles declared.

"Where did you set up the video conferences? Inside GPG?" Darrell asked.

"No, we rented video conference rooms at different office spaces on Wall Street. And, since we were operating on international hours the conferences took place before or after market hours." Big Mike replied.

We continued our question and answer session about Black Street Capital. How five million of the capital was our equity in the company which I put up personally. How all the investors were limited partners with no management authority in the Black Street Partnership, and all of us were General Partners with management power. The company Black Street Capital was the Holding company with equity of five million, and the Black Street Partnership had five hundred million in capital. Everyone was happy with the organizational structure, and was ready to go. What type of financial operations we were going to undertake? Our mission statement was simple, but not telling in our purpose: Black Street Capital provides financial value through capital markets domestic and international. This statement was vague enough to warrant questions from its ownership. "Are we going to be a brokerage and underwriting company similar to GPG? Are we going to start a hedge fund? Are we going to be financial consultants? The answer was no to all these questions.

"Leveraged Buyouts!" I said.

"Corporate Raiders?" asked Darrell.

"Yes."

"You mean arbitrage?" Charles added.

"Yes, buy and sell companies."

"Aahh… Shane I don't know about arbitrage. "Darrell rebutted.

"What is the problem with arbitrage?" I asked.

"I liken that financial business to a seek and destroy mission."

"Why do you have to put it that way? We will be looking for undervalued companies that have more value in its parts than it does as a whole."

"I didn't mean any offense. I just think we can do better."

"Arbitrage is the only way we can get the returns that our limited partners require of us."

"What is the required return on investment?" Charles asked.

"Twenty five percent." I answered.

"In this market environment twenty five percent will be a difficult return to attain. There are only two financial businesses that will be able to get double digit returns. One is a hedge fund and the other is arbitrage." Charles said.

"Thus arbitrage."

Darrell gradually moved in agreement with us. Arbitrage has always had a villainous taint against those who indulged in these types of financial transactions, but I didn't concern myself with the perception of others. My main focus was making money, and returning the required twenty five percent to investors. We discussed our next moves -office space, personnel, equipping the office, and a business trip to our largest investor base: Africa. Everyone lit up when I suggested a trip to Africa, none more than Big Mike. He had tasted the motherland and thirsted for more. Charles, Darrell and I had never been, but the thought of going was more like a pilgrimage or rites of passage. As Big Mike tells it, if you are a black man, before you leave this planet, you must take a trip to Africa. It is a life changing experience, and gives you a renewed sense of self and history.

These guys were chomping at the bit, raring to go, but before the tip off for Black Street Capital, I had one pressing issue that needed my immediate attention.

"Okay enough business, how did it go with Kendra?" Big Mike asked.

"Couldn't have gone better! That's my girl, and I'm going to ask her to be my wife!"

"Wife? That is a big step, you sure you want to make it?" Charles responded.

"Absolutely!"

"You got a ring?" came from Big Mike.

"Need to get one."

"Then, what are you waiting on; don't put off tomorrow what you can do today. You are going to make her one happy lady. Congratulations!" Darrell said.

"She hasn't said yes yet." I said.

"Ain't no sista turning down rings these days." Charles said.

"I know that's right." Big Mike joined in.

I knew Kendra loved me. There was no doubt in my heart she would be my wife, but her time for healing was short. The last couple of days had been a special time. Two days, was that enough time for her to fully forgive my past transgressions? I would soon find out, because these guys jumped up faster than me to get their coats and hit the streets in search of a ring for Kendra.

I knew exactly where I wanted to go. Kendra frequented this jewelry shop in Harlem owned by this Jamaican sista, Carmen. She was caramel brown with dread locks down her back, heavy Jamaican accent, five six, and always well dressed in ethnic custom fitted dresses or attire from the Kendra line. All her jewelry was handmade, and she was the most popular jeweler in Harlem. When we walked through her front door, she gave us all the warmest greeting. I had come here a couple times before, but never really paid too much attention to her. Kendra and Carmen used to go on and on like two sisters that haven't seen each other for months. So, my attitude, I must confess, wasn't the best and part of that wall I built up toward this sista was jealousy. Anyone that was friends or communicating with Kendra on a deeper level, I saw as a threat. We didn't hang out too much with her friends, and when we did, my shield prevented them from getting too close. I thought if Kendra saw my discomfort, she would distance herself from her friends. Even though this sista experienced my awkwardness towards her, her greeting was still warm and sincere.

"Welcome, how you brothas doing today?" Carmen asked.

"Good." We all spoke in unison.

When she saw me, she smiled and walked toward me. "Shane let me talk with you." She took my arm and led me over to a corner of her shop. She sold much more than jewelry, her shop was filled with art –paintings, pencil sketches, statues, and other esoteric artifacts. She sat me down on an earth tone suede couch huge cushions comfortable enough to sleep on. I sat down and looked up toward my boys, they had these smirks on their face, but they all were clearly interested in what she had to say to me. "Shane, the serenade you laid on my girl Kendra was nothing less than phenomenal. You showed all of Harlem how much you love my beautiful sista, and there were young black men and women observing this moment and seeing just how beautiful black love is, and how a man should treat his woman… like a queen. By the way you are a good beggar!" She laughed.

"I wasn't begging." I responded. "I was serenading as you said."

"You were begging!"

"Fellas, was I begging when I serenaded Kendra." I shouted.

"Hell yea!" They yelled out.

I laughed and Carmen laughed. "There is no shame in doing what you need to do as a man to get your woman back. You had the balls to admit you were wrong, you made a mistake and you were willing to make amends. There are not many men in this world that could or would do that –their egos would not allow it, and I was surprised yours allowed you."

"Surprised me too."

I think my response surprised her; she was silent just observing me, looking into my eyes searching for the real Shane. I didn't blink, looking directly at her. After a few moments, she broke the silence and rose to her feet.

"What brings you into my store today? Is there something I can help you find?

"I'm looking for a wedding ring." I responded.

Carmen sat back down beside me with excitement. She hugged me without words, embraced my hands and raised me to my feet. She led me to her jewelry counter in the back of her shop as my boys followed behind me.

"Shane, I want to show you something. I don't have this particular ring in the shop, and I probably would have never ordered it because of its price, but it is custom made and one of a kind. It's not a diamond, but the stone is from the mother land and rare, and Kendra will love this ring."

Carmen pulled out a jewelry magazine opened it to the exact page as if she had it bookmarked. The ring wasn't traditional in the least, but it was stunning. Carmen described the band of the ring as a mix of gold and platinum which gave the band a golden yellow color; it matched the stone centered on top the band. Although the stone was eye catching, the design of the band was what really made the ring standout- it twisted up toward the top and crowned to allow the stone to rest atop of it. This ring was truly fit for a queen, my queen Kendra. The reaction from Darrell, Big Mike, and Charles was immediate and definitive.

"That's the one!"

I couldn't have agreed more. "What's the delivery time on something like this?" I asked Carmen.

"I can order it today, but I should tell you this particular ring is about two hundred and fifty."

"Two hundred and fifty dollars that's not bad at all. I thought you were going to get hit for way more than that." Charles said.

"It's not two hundred and fifty dollars my brotha, its two hundred and fifty thousand dollars."

Big Mike almost choked; he had to back away from the counter. Charles and Darrell had their own versions of grumbles, but I didn't flinch. Price didn't matter. I pulled out my black card and handed it to Carmen. She smiled. Once she charged the card, I told her just to give me a call once the ring arrived. Ready to leave, Charles lingered, and then gave me a look like he wanted to take a shot at Carmen. So, we left him there.

As we walked through the streets of Harlem, Big Mike, Darrell, and I discussed the ring, then the topic shifted to possible locations for the headquarters of Black Street Capital. There was only one location I thought would be appropriate for the type of operations we were going to conduct – Wall Street. Big Mike and Darrell agreed. Before we knew it Charles joined us on our journey back to the house. We all just stared at him, prompting him to give us the details.

"Ah she struck a brotha out."

"I didn't think she was going to give you any rhythm". Big Mike said.

"What do you mean by that?" Charles asked.

"Just that you weren't her type."

"Type?"

"Yea, you know a Rasta man."

"I would have to agree. Carmen loves reggae music and a couple of times I've seen her with a man. They both were Rastafarians." I added.

"Well, why didn't you tell me that?" Charles demanded.

"What did you want Shane to tell you, that she wouldn't go for a little short chubby Kat like yourself?" Big Mike joked.

"Fuck you Big Mike, but Shane could have warned me that she liked bum Rasta's."

"Charles, I'm not going to tell a man what I think a woman's type is. My motto is if you see something you want, go get it. A woman's type should never even enter your mind, if it does, then you have doubt, and that makes you weak. Weakness makes you prey not a hunter, and your true nature is to be a hunter."

"What the hell are you talking about Shane?" Darrell joined in.

"I simply talking about self-confidence, and eliminating doubt."

"Shane's right! I could tell Carmen appreciated the confidence in my approach, but said she was involved with someone. I asked her, was she engaged? She answered no. So I asked her out for dinner.

She laughed, and said she could see why Shane and I are good friends."

"Now she thinks we all are ego maniacs." Darrell said.

"So what, I don't give a damn about what anybody thinks." Big Mike sentiments were the same as mine.

Our conversation about ego and self-confidence continued, until we ran into my friend and savior from my first potential beat down in my drunken state, Ice.

"Shane, what's happening?" Ice shouted out. He walked over.

"Ice, what's happening?" We gave each other a dap.

"Man, you are an icon in this community after what you pulled in front of Kendra's place."

"Yea, that was a little crazy, but necessary."

"Hey a man got to do what a man's got to do!"

I introduced Ice to Darrell, Charles and Big Mike. They'd heard me talk about Ice, but they had never met him. Before we parted ways, I pulled Ice close and thanked him for his intervention in the bar that day. When he left, Charles made him the butt of a joke.

"Was that a pimp? Haven't seen one of them in quite some time."

"Ice is cool man. He saved me from an ass whipping before I got the beat down from Kendra's date."

"You mean somebody else wanted to beat your ass before Kendra's date?" Big Mike asked.

"It was three of them, and they looked far more dangerous than Kendra's date."

"Shane, you need to take some self-defense classes and start a workout program. Matter of fact all of you need to start working out. You guys have put on some weight while I've been gone."

"A workout program sounds good. Could you put one together for all of us?" I asked.

"Done!"

We made it back to the brown stone and we all went straight upstairs to the office and continued are strategy discussions for Black Street Capital. Before I knew it the sun was setting and there was a knock at the front door. Charles ran down to see who it was. It was Kendra. The first words Charles uttered to her were confusing to say the least.

"Congratulations!"

"Congratulations on what?"

Charles realized that he was about to let the cat out of the bag, so he tried to clean it up. "I was just congratulating you on getting back together with Shane."

"Where is Shane?"

"Shane." Charles shouted. "Kendra."

A light shined inside my heart when I saw her. She ran to me before I could get to the bottom of the stairs. She gave me the warmest hug and kiss a man could ever desire from a woman he loved.

"Get a room!" Charles shouted. Big Mike and Darrell echoed his sentiments walking down the stairs.

Both Kendra and I laughed.

"What's in the bags?" Big Mike asked.

"Oh…I brought some Jamaican food." Kendra responded. A couple of chuckles were let out by the fellas. "What's so funny? You guys like Jamaican don't you?"

"Yea, lets' eat." Charles declared.

Kendra and I made our way to the kitchen. I set the table, and she served the food. We all ate dinner together. The conversation was good. I always admire Kendra's easy way with people. She engaged everyone at the table, and when she was talking to one person, you had her undivided attention. The topic eventually got to Black Street.

"What's the next step for Black Street?" She asked.

"Africa," Big Mike said.

"Africa?" She looked directly at me. "You are going to Africa?"

I shook my head yes with a smile.

"I want to go!"

The fellas looked at me, but I never took my eyes off Kendra. "Done!"

Kendra seated across from me at the head of the table, leaped up, ran over, and jumped on top me sending us both to the floor.

"I love you." She said.

"I love you too." I returned.

Africa

We secured office space for Black Street Capital on Wall Street. The space was located in Mid-Manhattan, Trump building on the 81st floor. It lent itself to one of the most beautiful views of the New York sky line. The space had a reception area, private offices, and a three thousand square foot trading room surrounded by glass windows that extended from the floor to its fifteen foot ceilings. As soon as you walked in this room you felt that you were on top of the world, and given the arbitrage business we were venturing into, a feeling of invincibility would go a long way.

We only needed limited staff and our plan was to tap into some of our colleagues from GPG who were a part of the "Black Street" desk, but we decided not to assemble them until we returned from our trip from Africa. The anticipation for our trip to Africa continued to build for everyone. Big Mike's praise of the people, the culture, and the food gave everyone a sense of hunger to experience it for themselves. No one more anxiousness and excitement about the trip, than Kendra. She told all her friends about the trip including Carmen. When I went to her shop to pick up the ring, which was even more impressive than its picture, she was excited for Kendra and the idea of traveling to Africa.

The day was upon us to travel to Nigeria. We flew out of JFK into London and from London straight into Nigeria. Upon our arrival the sky in Nigeria was grey, overcast, but the weather was warm and humid. The airport wasn't as modernized as the ones in the States and London. In comparison it was drab and dingy. The paint was faded and the carpet worn out as were the seats in the airport, but the one thing that stood out was the people. They were beautiful – vibrant, vivid, animated, tranquil and calm at the same time. As we walked through the airport, we quickly realized they knew us. There was a sense of coming home, but seeing that things had changed since we've been gone or that we had changed so much that there was a silent discomfort, but not enough to cause damage, nothing a conversation of re-acquaintance would not cure.

We were met by one of Big Mike's friends when we arrived, Boompai. He became Mike's driver while he was in Nigeria. He stood about 5'9, dark skinned, thin framed, in his early forties. Boompai was dressed in traditional attire, green and gold with matching hat. He had the most genuine smile and welcomed us to the motherland graciously.

"Welcome back my brother" he greeted Big Mike, and embraced him.

"Thank you my brother, and it feels good to be back," Big Mike replied.

Boompai looked around Big Mike, and greeted us with the same kindness. "Welcome."

"Thank you" we responded.

He walked to each of us and gave us a personal greeting. After we collected our luggage, Boompai led us out to the parking lot where there were two white vans, Toyota's version of the VW beach van. His son was driving one of the vans and he the other. Big Mike, Kendra and I rode with Boompai, Darrell and Charles rode with his son. As we exited the Lagos airport and entered the city toward downtown the traffic was thick. Most cars on the road were small foreign late model with faded colors. There were a lot of vans used as taxis, eight to ten people riding at once. Everyone drove aggressively and they used their horns proactively or should I say leadingly. The best words to describe the traffic in Lagos, was controlled chaos. There weren't any distinctive traffic lanes and stop signs and signals were far and few between. Boompai and his son maneuvered through the traffic magnificently, there was a couple of close calls…too close for comfort for most of us Americans, but as we stayed in Lagos we found out that was an almost everyday occurrence when driving in Nigeria-close calls.

We arrived at the V, our hotel, located in the heart of downtown Lagos. If we hadn't flown over eighteen hours, I would have never realized we left the states. This Hotel had all the accommodations of an upscale western hotel. First class and the service was top notch. While the hotel staff was mainly Nigerian, most of the guests were westerners' visitors as were we. I did feel a sense of pride and comfort to see all these black people managing and operating this immaculate hotel from the janitor to the manager. For me to feel this way must be some kind of commentary about my American experience. Is it that I had never seen this in America? Yes, for the most part I had never seen a large meticulous operation of business or commerce solely operated and managed by African-Americans. Sometimes when I travelled to different cities in the States I did see more African-Americans at work in different capacities, but nothing in unison where we all were working for a common goal.

I think my vision of "Black Street" trading desk was not only for the benefit to provide opportunity for African-Americans, but it was for my own therapy, to dispel any myths about us not being able to work together or that our cooperation as a group would result in an inferior product or service. I felt my trip to Africa was more than just a business trip to meet with investors. Kendra really was tuned in to what was going on around us. We had just gotten settled into our room which was small, but elegant -plush carpet, leather couch, flat screen TV, king size bed, kitchen with every amenity. Kendra embraced me tightly.

"What's wrong? I asked.

"I'm overwhelmed. Do you know what I mean?"

I understood exactly. We were on a sojourn back to the mother land from whence we came. Something spiritual hit us both, and we sat in the quietness of our room embracing each other, taking in the moment. It was like nothing I had ever experience. Almost like an out of body experience. Big Mike and the others came by our room to ask if we wanted to get dinner. I declined and returned to Kendra on the couch, not wanting this moment to end with this woman God has seen fit to give me a second chance with. I was not going to squander this opportunity.

Later that night while Kendra was asleep, Big Mike, Darrell, Charles, and I met in the lobby with Boompai who not only was our driver for this trip, but translator, guide, cultural teacher, and ally. We talked at length about our investors, their expectations, personalities, political connections, economic resources and reputations. The upcoming meetings with investors were more of a formality. All documents and contracts had been signed and notarized already, but to put faces with all the players in Black Street Capital" would be invaluable. It would give the investors a sense of belonging to something bigger than the investment.

One of the investors', whose reputation wasn't the most stalwart, was our single biggest investor with one hundred million in capital invested. Boompai reported he had a big ego and at times could be difficult to take. Big Mike said he was the most anxious of all the investors to invest with us. His name was Jakar. Jakar had interest in oil, construction, and trucking in Nigeria. He had attempted to become an American citizen, but was denied more than once. I remember him from a video conference Big Mike set up. He had many questions, and was not only the biggest single investor, but was one of the first to submit his money into the trust that had been set up for Black Street Capital. I had forgotten his face, and some of our other investors, so this was the perfect time to get reacquainted. It was getting late, we retired to our rooms, and Boompai went home with instructions to pick us up 8:00 am the next morning. Our first meeting was with Jakar at 9:00 am in his downtown Lagos office.

The next morning we arrived at Jakar's office about fifteen minutes before 9:00 am. We were welcomed by his receptionist, a thin dark complexioned Nigerian girl in her early twenties. We waited in the lobby while she let Jakar know we had arrived. Shortly he made his way to the lobby and greeted us with excitement. I didn't realize how big a man Jakar was. He stood about 6'3 and weighed in around 250 pounds. His hands felt raspy and callus like worn out crumbled sand paper when I shook them, his face had some scars, but he was well groomed. Jakar was a fast talker reminded me of a con man. He did have a warm smile, but it didn't seem genuine. I still didn't have any reservations about Jakar. I knew his angle and his motive. It was simple –American citizenship. With successful business partners in America he knew he could at least get a visa for visitation, if we lobbied on his behalf which I didn't have a problem doing for him.

After greeting us in the lobby, Jakar guided us to a large conference room and told Boompai to stay in the lobby. Waiting in the conference room were several business men along with a government official of Nigeria, the Ambassador Folajimi I recognized from an internet picture we saw when Kendra and I were researching Nigeria. Once we entered the room everyone stood and Jakar did all the introductions leaving me for last. When he introduced me, everyone clapped and Folajimi came forth.

"Shane Jackson it is an honor and pleasure to meet you my brother, welcome home!" he hugged and embraced me, hugging me in the traditional African way, an embrace to the right and then the left`.

This room full of influential businessmen and the ambassador took us all by surprise. We were caught off guard, but we were quick on our feet, and embraced these men as they welcomed us. "Such a greeting for us is an honor, and to be here in our homeland welcomed is heartwarming – thank you!" I announced.

Jakar directed us to have a seat at the conference table, and everyone else took their seat. Jakar was seated at the head of the conference table at the far end, and the Ambassador was seated at the foot of the table near us. We were seated to the right nearest the Ambassador and everyone else filled the seats around the table. Much to our surprise the discussions and conversations that pursued were focused on Black Street, the trading desk on Wall Street, not Black Street Capital. The questions were abundant ranging from what was the inspiration for Black Street to how we pulled such a feat off in a predominantly white male dominated industry. I was forth right in answering all their questions, Darrell, Charles, and Big Mike added good information on strategic management and operations of Black Street. We all were in sync, because by now there were no hidden agendas by any of us. We had hashed out any difference we had in private about Black Street the trading desk and Black Street Capital the business venture. We were a hell of a team!

During the question and answer session, Jakar did not say a word, but he was intensely observing, especially me. He was studying me, my responses, my body language, my tone, and my verbal language. Then, just when the conversations started to die down after about an hour, Jakar spoke.

"Shane did you ever fear for your life?"

"Fear for my life?" I answered with a question.

"Yes, in your efforts to create a trading desk with all black professionals did you ever fear for your life?"

"Why would I fear for my life?"

"How old are you Shane?"

"Thirty."

"You are still a very young man my brother even more the reason why there should have been fear in your heart, but as some would say your youth served you well, because you failed to realize the dangers around you. If you had, you might have stopped your pursuit of Black Street."

Jakar lost me! What dangers was he referring to, and what did my youth have to do with anything? The look on my face told him I didn't understand.

He continued. "Shane, you developed one of the most profitable trading desk on Wall Street, and on top of that you made a political statement by staffing your desk with all African-Americans – that combination makes you a threat."

"Threat to whom?" Darrell asked.

"America."

"What?"

"Why did you seek capital from Africa for your new venture, Shane?" Jakar asked.

"I knew Africa was rich in resources and knew we could gain more capital per investor than if we were to focus in the states within the African-American community. And, at the time I didn't want anyone to know we were raising capital for Black Street Capital, so I opted to look for money overseas,"

"No matter within the borders of the United States or outside of them, you still focus on the darker people, why?"

"Opportunity, it's just that simple. Creating opportunities for black people where they have been traditionally locked out."

"That is a very noble deed. But, make no mistake you are on someone's radar, and now you have reached across the seas, there's no way you haven't gotten someone's attention."

Folajimi chimed in. "You will be watched and tracked until your intentions are revealed."

"Our only intention is to make money!" Big Mike expressed.

The Folajimi continued. "So you say…….., but if your intentions reach beyond making money to one of policy change, empowerment of your people, over throw of your government….

"Whoa!!! Let's step on the breaks here. No one has those thoughts. We are businessmen looking to claim our piece of the American dream……that's it!" I said.

"I believe you have no intention of overthrowing your government, but you are looking to improve the opportunities of black people around the world, and that my friend may be a threat to some." Jakar replied. "Through your new business venture Black Street Capital you will soon have more money than you have ever imagined..." He didn't know I had a big imagination. "And with that money, if used wisely, will bring you great power. If power is used to connect black people around the world economically and politically, then mark my words – you will become public enemy number one!"

There was a silence around the conference table. I looked in the direction of Big Mike, Darrell, and Charles on each side of me. We all were confused and didn't really know what to make of the conversation taking place. I looked at the Ambassador, and he shook his head in agreement with Jakar. I thanked them for their time and their wisdom, because I didn't want them to think I didn't value their words. We all shook hands, and Jakar took me aside.

"My intent is not to alarm you Shane," he said in a low voice. "It is to merely make you aware of the road ahead – you are young man with vision and purpose. What you did on Wall Street was monumental, and powerful people have taken notice. I also don't say this to scare you, but only to plant the seed of preparation, so you are prepared for whatever they throw at you."

"Who are they?" I asked.

"The people with power and influence over governments, agencies, and people."

"I need names!"

He changed the subject that instant. "Shane I would like to invite you to dinner at my home; you and your lovely girlfriend."

But I was persistent. "What about the names?"

"We can talk more once you come to dinner. I will be in contact with a date and time." He shook my hand and walked over to the Folajimi, Charles, Big Mike, and Darrell followed.

"What did he say to you?" Darrell asked.

"Nothing more than what he said at the table, but he did invite me to dinner at his home."

"When?"

"He said, he would contact me with a day and time."

"All of us," Charles asked?

"No, just Kendra and I."

"That was an unexpected and weird exchange." Big Mike exclaimed.

"Who you telling!.. Let's head out."

We said our goodbyes to everyone, and met Boompai in the reception area of Jakar's office where we had left him. With puzzled looks on our face, the first words from his mouth were "Are you alright?" We responded somberly "Yea". Silently we all were thinking the same thing about what Jakar said. Was it believable? And, if it was believable, what should we be doing to protect ourselves?

We had a few more stops to make that day with other investors, so we forged ahead keeping our appointments, but all day we were haunted by Jakar's words. The rest of the day went as we expected, uneventful- shaking of hands, exchange of pleasantries, and getting more acquainted. We got back to the hotel late afternoon. Kendra was in the room reading through some books about Nigeria; she had researched places to see in Nigeria.

I didn't want to concern her about the conversation with Jakar, so I just entertained her thoughts about sightseeing and exploring African culture. Her excitement about being on the continent of Africa was contagious, and my excitement grew as the list of things to do and see grew. I contacted Boompai for his input on the places Kendra and I wanted to see. He came to our room later that night to discuss transportation and the best places to see from our list. I also wanted to have a private discussion with him on some preparations I needed his assistance with.

I queried Boompai about places in Nigeria that one would consider paradise. His first and only words were Victoria Island. He describe the island as a slice of heaven with bluest of waters surrounded by powered white sands, custom made villas on the shores and the finest in dining restaurants Nigeria had to offer. I asked Boompai to make some special arrangements for me on Victoria, for the day after tomorrow.

Kendra and I joined Charles, Darrell, and Big Mike for dinner later that night. Everyone had a great time together. We were family. She was like a diamond amongst mere coal; all attention was on her. Onlookers and passer-byers would gaze upon her beauty and smile; her pink linen dress accentuate her dark skin, her dread locks-jet black drew out her big brown eyes, and when she stood up, let's just say all hell broke loose – mumbles and grumblings from all directions. Her curves although conservatively covered were undeniable. As the dinner progressed Kendra inquired about our meetings that day.

"I've been so anxious and excited about seeing all the sites Nigeria has to offer, I forgot to ask you how your meetings went."

"I've been thinking about what Jakar said since we got back to the hotel. That was the strangest conversation I have ever been a part of; what about you guys?" Charles interjected.

We all just stared at him, and then he looked at all of us and caught on that this wasn't the appropriate time to discuss Jakar. "Oh,..My bad," He was silent after, but Kendra would not let that stand. She looked directly at me.

"What happen with this Jakar person?"

"Just an investor that was rambling on about something nobody understood." I tried to dismiss it by categorizing it as nonsensical.

"Well what exactly did he say?" she inquired calmly. She sensed my hesitation. "Shane, we are back together right?"

"Yes!" I said emphatically.

She placed her hand ever so gently on the back of my neck and rubbed me softly which sent a warm tingly feeling down my spine and relaxed me. "Charles, Big Mike, and Darrell are your close friends and partners, and I would never interfere with that, but I should be your best friend, your closest partner and confidant."

"You are! When it comes to you they don't even matter."

There were grumblings at the table. "Hey, I know the point you trying to convey to your lady, but damn, isn't there a better way of putting it?" Big Mike commented.

The laughter and smiles commenced. "You all know what I mean. You guys are family and brothers to me, but Kendra's my lady, and when I lie in bed at night with the weight of the world on my shoulders it will be with her not any of you. So, therefore she is correct about being my best friend and my closest confidant. "

"Right to our faces!" Charles retorted with sarcasm.

"So, what did this Jakar character have to say?" Kendra submitted the question once again.

"In short, he said what I accomplished on Wall Street in creating the first all-black trading desk has put me on some people's radar."

"That's good isn't it?"

"Not according to Jakar, he says the people who may be watching me don't have my best interest at heart, and maybe fearful of my intentions with Black Street Capital."

"Who are the people that are threatened by you?"

"He wouldn't say directly, but I surmised it's some type of US government agency CIA or FBI."

"I think Jakar is off his rocker!" Charles exclaimed.

"I don't think he's crazy at all. If he is, he's crazy as a fox." Big Mike joined in.

Both Darrell and I noticed a change in Kendra's demeanor, so we tried to change the topic. "What's for dessert? I asked.

"Yea, dessert!" Charles joined in.

"Are you worried Shane?" Kendra asked in a concerned tone.

"No and neither should you!" I leaned over and kissed her on the cheek and whispered. "By the way you look beautiful in that dress; can't wait to take it off you."

"Why wait?" she whispered back in my ear.

At this time the waitress was at our table taking dessert orders. "I think we are going to take our dessert to go, matter of fact, send it to our room!" I rushed Kendra up from her seat and proceeded to the elevator to go up to our room.

I heard my boys yelling out. "Good night to you too! Great having dinner with you two! "Then I hear Charles say, "I need a woman out here in Africa. Let's find a party! Where's Bommpai?"

Kendra and I vanished to our room for the rest of the night. The restaurant in the hotel did try to deliver our dessert, but either we did not hear the room service or we just didn't care. Later that night they did accommodate us with fresh fruit and wine which we enjoyed in the comforts of our bed.

****

The days that followed we squeezed in just a few more meeting with investors and reserved the rest of the time for the sights of Nigeria. The sightseeing was more than a typical tourist experience. I think we all felt a spiritual connection to Africa, its culture, its people, its food, and its land. We took in the traditional sights- slave ports, beaches, and other popular tourist destinations. The special trip was to the Yoruba market and the Osun River. Boompai described the market as a place where people of the Yoruba faith come to find materials for their prayers and rituals, and the Osun River as an Orisha in the Yoruba faith that is responsible for the creativity and colorfulness of this earth. Boompai was a great guide and enriched our experience with his wealth of knowledge about the history and idiosyncrasies of the different cultures in Nigeria.

While in the Yoruba market, we ran into Jakar much to our surprise. He greeted us warmly.

"Greetings my friends!" He said with an outstretched hand for me to shake.

"Jakar, I thought you lived in Lagos?" I replied taking his hand into mine to shake.

"I do, but I have a home here in Oshogbo. This city is my place of birth." Then he looked in the direction of Kendra. "This must be your lady friend who made the trip with you?"

"Yes!" I introduced them. "Kendra this is Jakar, Jakar this is my girlfriend Kendra." Kendra extended her hand for a handshake, but Jakar went in for a hug, she obliged. While they were hugging I gave Kendra a playful quizzical look, she couldn't help but laugh. "She is beautiful Shane, regal; she looks Nigerian. I bet, if you traced your family ancestry, they come from Nigeria possibly Yoruba."

"I'll have to do that, I do feel a strong sense of comfort and belonging here!"

"It is not uncommon for one to travel to the motherland and feel a strong sense of their roots.... I told Shane, I wanted to invite you two to my home in Lagos for dinner. How about this weekend?"

Kendra looked at me. "Yes, I think that would be fine." I responded. I noticed he was still holding onto Kendra's hand, so I gave her another antic stare. She chuckled once again.

Jakar briefly addressed the others and went on his way. Once out of sight, I pretended to scold Kendra about Jakar holding her hand.

"Why did you hug that man and why did you hold that man's hand after he greeted you?"

She played right along. "I don't see no ring on this finger, so I'm free to hold or to hug anyone I please."

Oohs and aahs followed from the crowd – Big Mike, Darrell, and Charles.

"Ain't that something; you're my lady, and I can't control who hugs and holds your hand."

"Like I said, ain't no ring on this finger" displaying her ring finger.

"Yea, ain't no ring on that sista's finger," Charles interjects.

I see this was a no win situation, so I acquiesced and conceded the point. We wondered around the market some more before we headed home. On the drive home Kendra cozied up to me, attempting to lay her head on my shoulder, but I used my shoulder to push her off. She pushed me back and then we laughed. She took my arm and wrapped it around her and snuggled in close to my chest and fell asleep. I whispered "I love you." Almost too soft to hear, she replied with two words. "I know."

The next day our plans were to go to Victoria Island, just Kendra and I. It was quite a long drive, but Boompai said it was worth it. I had no intention of coming back the same day. Boompai had rented a Villa right off the beach for me and I rented a small villa for himself on the Island, so he could chaperone us while we were there. Once we got to Victoria it was just as Boompai described, beautiful, tranquil, and the nearest thing to paradise I've ever seen. Kendra was equally excited. She prompted Boompai to stop the van, before I knew it; she was out of the van running towards the beach, towards the blue waters that was filled with white sand. I followed after her in hot pursuit. When I caught up to her, we both fell in the sand and rolled around in that moment of bliss. I couldn't have been more turned on! Once we stopped rolling around we laughed and she attacked me with the warmest kiss. Kendra really knew how to show her appreciation, and I knew how to reciprocate.

Boompai shouted to us on the beach from the board walk, he yelled that the villa we rented was just down the beach about a half mile.

"You rented a villa for us out here?" Kendra asked.

"Yes, I thought it would be nice to lounge out here for a day or two."

"You thought right!"

"You want to walk to the villa."

"Yes!"

I yelled to Boompai that Kendra and I would walk along the beach and meet him up at the villa. He went back to the van and took off. Kendra and I held hands and took a casual stroll down the beach.

"I've never seen anything so beautiful." Kendra said.

"It is amazing."

We took off our shoes letting our feet sink into the san as we walked. She led me toward the water where we sauntered through the warm low tide. "I don't know if I'll ever be able to repay you for this experience."

"Why would you think you needed to repay me?"

"I guess, I don't mean that literally. I'm just having the experience of a lifetime, and I'm thankful."

"I'm thankful you came along. You have elevated this trip from just a business trip to one of cultural enlightenment. It's been a humbling experience seeing some of the historic slave quarters before they were shipped to the Americas. Going into the townships and seeing the culture and people has been a life changing experience. I think everyone of African descent must make a pilgrimage to the motherland; it gives each of us a new found sense of identity."

"I couldn't agree with you more. I could see myself living here!"

"Really!"

"Yes, absolutely!"

"I can't say, I would like to live here. The jury is still out on that one. I would miss Harlem, friends, and family."

"I would miss them too, but you could always go and visit or they could come to visit you."

"Ah… you may have a point, but I still think it would be a hard transition for me. Something about the African-American culture keeps me close to its heart and soul.

"No, I don't discount our own culture, but it all stems from here – Africa." Kendra ran down the beach with water kicking up behind her. I ran after her, we fell and tumble in the water this time. Luckily we were only a hundred feet away from our villa. We both saw Boompai on the balcony of the villa waving. I picked Kendra up and threw her over my shoulder. I carried her off the beach up to our villa where Boompai met us.

"Here is your key. I opened up the windows and patio doors, so the ocean breeze could make its way through the villa. I'll give you a chance to clean up and relax, and then I will come get you for a bit of sightseeing."

"That sounds like a plan." I responded.

Boompai left. Kendra and I entered the villa. It was angelic, made of clay and oak wood. It was the perfect complement to the beach. The walls were as white as the sand on the beach, the floors had dark stained oak wood laid throughout, except the kitchen and bathroom had earth tone ceramic tile. The space was wide open, it felt like a loft, but it did have separate rooms, but the rooms had no doors just a sheer cloth covered their entrance. The patio had wooden doors that opened up to the beach. Kendra and I dripped water through the villa as we admired its beauty.

"We better get dried off and showered, so we can be ready when Boompai comes." Kendra said.

"We have plenty of time before Boompai comes knocking on that door." Then I gave her the look. The beach water had left her clothes clinging to her body, accentuating her every curve, and making me unable to keep my eyes from her.

"Oh, you want to have some fun before Boompai comes back?"

I shook my head no. “No….there are beads of water from your neck down to your feet, I want to suck each and every bead of water from your body front and back.” I said. “Then if there’s time for some extracurricular activity, so be it! Does that sound like fun to you?’

“That sounds more than fun.”

“My sentiments exactly.”

And, that just what I did to her for the next hour. She was sweeter than chocolate ice cream.

Kendra and I showered and dressed. Not to my surprise, but to Kendra’s surprise the kitchen refrigerator was full of food. Boompai had arranged for someone to go to market and stock the refrigerator with fresh fruits, vegetables, juices, and water. We had just enough time to eat a snack, before Boompai knocked on the door to pick us up.

We set off in the van with Boompai taking in some incredible sights, but the highlight was a festival taking place on the Island. There was food, drink, cultural dances, and a parade. We ran into a friend of Boompai, an elderly woman dressed in a purple and green traditional dress and hat. She was short in stature; her back was curved just from the ware and tare of living, dark skinned with marks across both cheek bones, reminiscent of a tiger’s claw. Boompai told us she was a wise woman, but some think she is a little crazy. Her name was Abasiofon.

“So, you two are from America.”

“Yes.” I responded.

“First time in Africa for you and your wife?”

“Uh…, she is not my wife.” I said shyly.

“Are you kidding? You look like husband and wife, you look like kindred spirits.”

Kendra and I both just looked at each other with a smile and then look at the elderly woman.

Abasionfon took Kendra’s hand. “Don’t worry my dear; you will be married to this fine young man before you leave this continent.” We both were taken back by her prediction. “I am a high priestess and license to perform marriage ceremonies." She then handed a card to Kendra. "I will talk to you soon."

I looked at Boompai; he looked back at me with dismay, and mouthed the word "Crazy".

I said nothing after the old lady departed our company, neither did Kendra. We walked to the car in silence and Boompai drove us back to the villa. There was an awkward feeling on the drive back. We wondered if the elderly wise woman knew something that we didn't, especially something so intimate to our own experience. When we stepped out of the van, we could hear African music coming from our villa. Kendra walked to the door, opened it to a four piece band playing out on the patio. A table was set up in the middle of the main room leading to the patio. There were flowers and champagne, and two young ladies standing by in the kitchen. Kendra was pleased.

"You are full of surprises, this is lovely." She kissed me on the cheek.

The band continued to play as we entered the room, and the two young ladies showed us to the table as if we were in a fine dining establishment. The sun was setting on the beach. The yellow radiant sunshine filled the villa providing a natural illuminant that couldn't be matched by a thousand candles. My timing was perfect. Our first course was a mango salad which was delicious and our conversation got more interesting moment by moment.

"I knew you were romantic, but you really have out done yourself!"

"Top the serenade?"

"The serenade was a redeemable moment, but this is just icing on the cake."

"You're right....... I should have never let you go." I said in regretful tone. "I was never so lost and out of sync in my life. You are my balance, the air I breathe, the beat of my heart, the rhythm to my spirit, and I can't live without air or a beating heart, and I won't attempt to." I stood, took two steps toward Kendra, then dropped to one knee. Kendra breath quickened, water filled her eyes. I pulled the ring from my pocket, opened it, and presented to her. Her eyes bulged, she began to shake and fiddle around in her seat. "Kendra Sampson will you do me the honor in being my wife?" The instant she launched from her chair into my chest wrapping her arms around my neck sending me backwards to the floor with her on top of me kissing me passionately. Once she came up for air, she answered.

"Yes, Mr. Shane Jackson, I will do you the honor of being your wife" then she let out a scream. "Aahh!"

As she lay on top of me showing her happiness through her kisses, I felt some movement in her pelvic area, slow and subtle at first, then it progressed to very deliberate with purpose. She was aroused. "You want me don't you?"

"In the worst way, I've wanted you since your clothes were all wet clinging to your body." She said in low sexy voice.

I looked to my left and then my right. The two girls were back in the kitchen kind of snickering, they were young, and the band continued to play, but had a voyeuristic look about them. "Unless we want to put a show on for our guest, then we better get rid of them." Both Kendra and I stood up. Kendra took the lead.

"Okay everyone listen up. We want to thank you for the beautiful dinner and music, but it's time to go."

"You haven't had your main course." One of the young ladies said.

"Yes, you are right, so just leave the plates on top of the stove, and we will get to them later. Now hurry up time is of the essence."

I walked to the door to let our guest out. The two young ladies exited with smirks on their face, but not before I tipped them for their help. The band quickly followed them, and one of the members patted me on the back in envy. I returned the pat in agreement. Once everyone exited, Kendra ran and jumped me again. This time legs straddling my waist and arms wrapped firmly around my neck. As soon as she started to kiss me, she stopped.

"Where's my ring?"

I had to think, I searched my pockets, no ring. "Where in the hell did I..........." then looking down where Kendra flattened me on my back, there the ring was sitting in the open box shining just as brightly as the sunset. Kendra spotted it too! She leaped off me to get to her ring. She sat in amazement.

"It's beautiful....it's the most precious thing I've ever seen and that I have ever received in my life." Tears swelled up her eyes again.

I scooted beside her on the floor admiring the ring. "Your friend Carmen said you would love the ring."

"You got this from Carmen?"

"Yes, she's quite the salesperson."

"That's my girl...... Would you do me the honor of putting the ring on my finger?"

"It would be my pleasure." I took the ring and placed it on her finger. She held it up just admiring the design and the stones shining like stars in the sky.

"Oh man....you did me good." Kendra expressed, then silence overtook her and it seemed she was deep in thought. She took a deep breath and spoke. "I want to get married her in Africa."

"Huh......."she took me completely by surprise. "What.... you trying to make that old lady's prediction come to fruition?"

"I'm just telling you what's in my heart."

I paused and studied Kendra. I really had no real objections to marrying Kendra in Nigeria, but it all felt a little unreal with Abasionfun predicting what Kendra was suggesting. I initially just chalked it up to her picking up on the chemistry between Kendra and me, but it looked like it had more substance to it. "I will marry you anywhere you want, but do we have time to it do here and now?"

"Yes! Darrel, Big Mike, and Charles are here. We can fly our parents out, my brother, Carmen, and some other close friends."

"Where would we have the wedding? There's a lot of planning that needs to go into this right?"

"Shane, we are here at this beautiful villa and the most gorgeous beach anyone could ever dream of. We can have it right here!"

"You are serious aren't you? I thought you might want something grander."

"There's nothing grander, than this place and with the addition of family and close friends, it couldn't get any grander for me."

"Okay lets' do it!"

Another Lambeau leap and I was back laid out on the floor. Only this time there was no stopping us. Our love making was more intense with a lot more tenacity which took me by surprise. I hate to admit it, but I had a hard time keeping up with Kendra. She was putting it on a brotha in a way she had never done. I had to stop her in mid-stream.

"You've been holding out!" I said.

She laughed.

"That's crazy! What other tricks you got up your sleeve," I continued.

"You'll find out on our wedding night!

"You've got to be kidding me. Any more than this and I might not survive our wedding night."

"Ah….you'll be alright young blood" and she patted me as if to say hang in there.

We took our lovemaking to higher heights. My rhythm became steady and in unison with her body and breathing. I kept the rhythm until she changed hers, then I would transition to match. We were in sync; it was a one of kind experience. It was the truest form of love making –two people in a physical realm taking each other to a higher level of experience and pure ecstasy. Finally with our bodies exhausted and damp, we fell asleep.

Boompai arrived that morning to take us back to Lagos. Kendra wasted no time filling him in on our intentions to get married on Victoria Island, and using the villa for the reception and our wedding night. She wanted him to contact Abasionfun to reside over the nuptials. Bompai offered to assist Kendra with the planning of the wedding, and became our designated wedding planner. Kendra had a list of things that needed to be done in one hours' time with Boompai's help they made things happen. I fell asleep in the van on the way back to Lagos. When we arrived back in Lagos, Boompai had reserved the villa once again, arrange for us to reserve a section of the beach for our ceremony, and had a caterer lined up for the reception. Kendra had informed her parents, Carmen and a few friends, and booked them all flights to travel to Nigeria by week's end.

When we entered the hotel about mid-day, Charles, Big Mike, and Darrell were all in the lobby contemplating where to eat lunch. Once we saw them, Kendra did not hesitate to show her ring off. They congratulated both us, but didn't make a big fuss about the ring, Kendra was taken back.

"You guys don't like the ring?"

"Yes we like the ring. We were with Shane when he bought it." Darrell said.

"You didn't tell me they went to Carmen's with you to get the ring."

"I didn't?"

"No you didn't, but I should have known."

"Yea, you should have known he wouldn't make a move without us knowing." Charles interjected. "And speaking of Carmen, how's she doing?"

"How's Carmen doing?" Kendra looked at me.

"Yea, Charles took a swing when we went to her shop, and she threw a slider right passed him."

"Temporary setback no fault of her own, she didn't realize who was standing before her."

"Didn't realize who was standing before her, and just who are you Mr. Charles?" Kendra said jokingly.

"A man that is about to be a king. We all are about to be kings!" Charles transitioned to a serious tone. "If you thought what we did at GPG was big, wait till we are up and running Black Street Capital." Then Charles turned his attention to me. "Yesterday, when you and Kendra were in Victoria, some of the investors paid us a visit.....man I'm telling you. They are mesmerized by us, hanging on our every word, as if they are adoring fans. I've never felt anything like it. They see it in us, what we've seen in ourselves from the very beginning of our experience together at GPG, but too humble to articulate it. We are giants amongst mere midgets!"

"Giants amongst midgets? Someone has the big head today."

"Kendra, I know what Charles just said sounds egotistical, big headed, or whatever would categorize it as, but he is just being truthful. We are going to do some impactful things, and the world will best sit up and take notice." Big Mike joined in.

"I don't doubt for one second you all are very special men with the potential to have a lasting impact and impression on society, but let it not be one of self-gratification."

"We are bigger than that! Darrell commented.

"Yes, I think so too. And, I'm in agreement, great things are ahead of us, but I always knew that. I'm glad you guys realize it too. Now we must harness this energy we are getting from here and carry it back to the States and use it to take Black Street Capital to heights never seen before by a financial company." I said.

"I just want you all to let your heart lead you not your egos."

No one commented. Charles, Darrell, Big Mike and I just looked at each other. Then, I grabbed Kendra and pulled her close. "My fiancé, soon to be my wife, I can't wait until you are all mine."

"You don't have long to wait." She replied.

"When is the wedding?" Darrell asked.

"Saturday." Kendra responded.

"This coming Saturday?' Charles asked.

"Yes!" Kendra replied.

They all looked dumbfounded.

"Lets' eat I will fill you guys in at lunch," I responded.

We ate lunch inside the hotel, Boompai joined us and I filled the fellas in on the plans for the wedding. Boompai and Kendra continued to work their cell phones making arrangements.

Later that night Kendra and I returned to our hotel room. I notice she was a little nervous and became very quiet and recluse. I thought it was just a case of the premarital jitters, and she realized the moment would be upon us in just a few days. I took a shower, then lounged on the couch in my robe catching up on world news and markets. Kendra was in the back room fumbling around with something. She walked to the kitchen, looked at me sitting on the couch, hesitated and said nothing, returned to the back room, until she made another appearance standing nervously to my left about ten feet away.

"I don't want to sign a prenuptial agreement." She declared.

I chuckled and smile. "Is that why you are walking around here silent and looking unsure?"

"I didn't know your thoughts on it……..everything is moving fast, and I didn't want it to pop up without you knowing my feelings."

"Did you think I was going to ask you to sign one?"

"I wasn't sure."

"Really!"

"I wasn't sure."

"Kendra when I asked you to marry me, it was mind, body, and soul. Money never factored into that equation for me. I want us to be together forever and start a family. There is nothing more valuable than family. Family to me is priceless. So, to put your mind at ease, it never crossed my mind to ask you to sign a pre-nuptial agreement. What's mine is yours from this day on, and I wouldn't have it any other way. "

Tears flowed from her eyes. She jumped on the couch and put her head in my lap. "You still have a few days before what's yours is mine." She laughed.

"When you accepted my proposal and put my ring on your finger in my mind from that day forward you were my wife."

She gave me a kiss, and soon after fell asleep in my lap as I continued to watch the news.

****

All the arrangements were set; Kendra and Boompai did a wonderful job in the short amount of time before the big day. A section of the beach and the villa were reserved, Kendra's parents and brother were flown in along with Carmen and friends- her bride's maids. The caterers were set to serve for the wedding and the reception. My mother flew in, whom I hadn't seen for several months, but I made it a habit not to let a week go by without talking to her, so we stayed in contact frequently. She was well informed about what was taking place in my life. I lost contact with a lot of my mentors -Mr. Roberts, Mr. White, and Ted, but the one that remained through it all was my mother.

The wedding day was more beautiful than I had imagined. The weather couldn't have been better which made the whole scene on the beach angelic. There were more guests than we invited. The word of my wedding spread to my investors in Black Street Capital, so they attended with family and some friends. Since the wedding took place on the beach the available space was really unlimited, and all attendees stood to witness Kendra and I exchange wedding vowels. An atrium was placed on the beach, made of iron, draped in white ribbon and flowers. Kendra was stunning in a long white linen dress. Her dreadlocks were pulled back in a bun held by a white laced ribbon. Carmen and the other bridesmaids were all dressed in white linen dresses. My groomsmen and I were all dressed in linen, cut in traditional African attire –loose fitting long shirts hanging below our knees; relax fitting matching pants, and sandals. Charles, Big Mike, and Darrell were in all white, and I had white pants and a dark golden shirt. I didn't have a best man; I had best men which they all graciously accepted.

Kendra and I exchanged vows with our feet firmly planted in the sand, the warmth of the sand filled our toes, and the moment filled our hearts. Tears were contagious that day. It started with Kendra moved to Carmen, then Kendra's parents, my mother, and finally me. Charles stepped forward and nudged me to stop with water works. I turned ever so slightly toward him.

"I can't help it. I'm marrying the woman of my dreams." I tried to whisper. When I turned back toward Kendra, she jumped into my arms and kissed me. "She hasn't pronounced us man and wife yet."

"I knew you were going to be my husband, when you walked in my shop for the first time with your mother."

Women are always five steps ahead of men. That's just the way it is. When you think you are doing the choosing, you've already been chosen.

At the end of the ceremony family and guest came up to congratulate us. Food and drink were set up just a few feet away along with tables and chairs for the reception. There was a five piece band playing African rhythms. The guests drifted toward the reception, while the wedding party and family took pictures on the beach. Afterward we joined the reception for food, drink, and dancing. As we socialized Jakar asked to speak to me in private for one moment. With Kendra's approval I granted him a private moment.

"You have a lovely bride and you are very lucky man!"

"Thank you," I said gazing over in the direction of Kendra as she caught my gaze and smiled.

"She is to be your number one confidant from this day on," Jakar stated. "Just a little advice from a man who knows."

"I appreciate the advice and will take it to heart."

"Shane, we didn't get a chance to have our dinner together, but I just want to clarify my words. My intention was not to scare you or to give you the impression I was talking out both sides of my mouth. My words were probably not chosen carefully enough. Shane you are a man with a vision. All men with vision can be perceived as a threat. The potential for you to gain power and influence are great, so the combination of money, power, influence, and vision can be baleful for people that are adversely affected by your vision."

"What makes you think my vision will adversely affect others?"

"Given your history it is an absolute certainty! It's your wedding day, go back to your lovely bride. We have plenty of time to talk."

"I'll be flying home in a couple of days."

"We have phones in Nigeria…" He laughed and pulled me in close for a hug. "Call me anytime my friend."

I returned to Kendra's side, but Jakar's words weren't easily dismissed. I felt there was some validity to what he was saying, and that his words were from the heart, but today was our day. We danced on the beach with each other and family and friends. Everyone wanted to dance with Kendra! She was captivating in her linen dress. To be in her presence made you feel privileged as though she was the African Queen Nefertiti.

While Kendra was occupied with family, friends, and admirers, I had a shared moment with Big Mike, Charles, and Darrell.

"You got a good one Shane." Darrell said.

"Yea, I got lucky."

"She is fine!" Charles joined in.

"She's regal, a real woman," Big Mike added!

"Make you think, what does she see in me?"

"Yea, I often wondered that," Charles said, we all laughed.

"Hey, I saw you dancing with Carmen," I said to Charles.

"Yea, a brotha just planting some seeds to see if they'll grow."

"If you water and nurture those seeds, they are sure to grow." Big Mike added.

As they chatted it up about Carmen, I looked over the guest in attendance. Jakar was socializing and chatting it up with the Ambassador. I caught the eyes of Kendra laughing and once again she gave me that million dollar smiled. It was arousing checking out my lady from a far; seeing her interact with others and just being blissful. As I continued to peruse the crowd one gentleman stood out. I didn't know him, but I didn't know a lot people at the wedding. He was dressed in traditional African attire, but the clothing on him was out of place. He had a short haircut – real simple, stood about 5'9, middle aged, but no signs of graying. I didn't know why this man had stolen my focus; I continued to study him. He was husky, but not fat. He mingled amongst certain groups and looked comfortable and blended well. The kicker was he didn't look African, he looked African –

American, and I knew all the African-Americans at the wedding personally.

Boompai approached and diverted my attention away from the gentleman. “Is everything okay?” He asked me.

I hesitated. “Yea….Yea….Boompai do you know that guy over there!” When I turned back to where the guy was standing he was gone. I gave the guest a once over and didn’t see him anywhere.

“What man?”

“Ah,..Never mind, I don’t see him any longer.” I started to think Jakar’s words were making me a little paranoid.

“You okay?” Big Mike asked.

“Yea,…Yea…. where’s my wife? Hey I like the sound of that! Where’s my wife!” I bellowed out once again. Kendra looked up came over to me and gave me a hug. She felt good in my arms. I picked her up in the cradle position and carried her through the crowd of people as they parted to make a path directly to our villa.

Takeover

Back in the states we all were eager to get started with Black Street Capital. We had our office space on Wall Street, and while we were in Africa the office space had been equipped with a trade room and all the private offices came pre-furnished. All we needed was to add personnel to help with the analysis and trading once we found a company worthy of our investment. For the trading and financial analysis we reached out to some of our colleagues that worked at GPG with us. We had four of them in mind that we thought would be perfect fit in the mission of Black Street Capital.

There was Vernon Clarke, heavy set, stood about 5'9, medium complexion, and was Charles's right hand man when it came down to trading strategies at GPG. Next, was Clyde Washington, about 6'0 tall, dark complexion, Ivy League educated; somewhat arrogant and sometimes not the most likeable person, but his analysis on financial and markets were tops. The added bonus with him was that he had a trading background, so he could be used for trading purposes too if needed. There was some resistance to Clyde when his name was recommended, but we all decided the value added outweighed the personality shortcomings. Dexter and Maria Andrews were the last two. They met on the trading desk at GPG, and about three months later were married.

At the time we all thought they had jump the gun, because they were total opposites. Dexter had more of sheltered life, his experiences were limited, he reminded me a lot of Tim – courteous, high moral fiber, and an introvert. Maria on the other hand was from Brooklyn. Her mother abandoned her at fifteen. She had a short life in the world of prostitution, until she turned her life around by returning to school and getting her GED. Attending a community college and transferring to NYU, she received her Bachelors of Science in economics. I admired her drive and determination. She was sassy, but above all she was a good reader of people. Maria had the ability to see through all the bullshit and get down to the essence of a person, and that quality shined through in her financial analysis. Maria was very attractive, light complexion, long brown hair, five foot seven, and a sexy figure, her father was African-American and mother Puerto Rican.

Pressed for time, we called them all in for interviews at the same time which turned out to be not much of an interview. We all gathered in the trade room.

"We called all of you here to offer you an opportunity to work with us here at Black Street Capital. We are familiar with your talents and feel each of you would be a good fit." I started off. "Black Street Capital simply put is an investment company. We will look for investments in companies with five hundred million in market capital or more. Our mission is to look for undervalued companies where the parts are more valuable than the whole. We will buy and sell these companies for a profit." I paused. "I have only one question to all of you. Are you interested in working with us?"

"Yes! They all said in unison convincingly.

Then there was a "Hell Yea!" coming from Maria. "We've been waiting for you all to come back to get us. We knew you all had something brewing and everyone was speculating about your next move. You have some doubters and haters out there, but I never wavered. A lot of us know what kind of operation you run Shane, and no one's turning down a job offer from you!"

"I couldn't have said it better!" Clyde confirmed.

"I appreciate those words of support, but now Big Mike, Charles, Darrell, and I are all equal partners in Black Street Capital. So, it is us as a team who are bringing you guys on."

No objections from any one.

"Since we don't want to seem like pushovers in our hiring process, there has to be some kind of test or requirement for hiring you all. We have decided on something; it is definitely unorthodox, but we feel it's a true measure if you will fit in here or not…..Everyone line up at the other end of the of the trade room." Charles announced.

They all looked at each other, but none of them hesitated. They lined up at the far end of the trade room next to the entry door.

"All right, this is a test in rhythm and pulse. When you participate in financial markets you have to be able to put your hand on the pulse of the market and find its rhythm in order to make good decisions." Charles continued.

We lined up two on each side making a path down the right side of the trade room; Big Mike and me on one side, Charles and Darrell on the other.

"First up is Mr. Vernon Clarke." Charles called out.

Vernon stepped to the forefront. Charles hit play on the remote and the office system blasted out James Brown –"Say it loud, I'm black and I'm proud –Say it loud, I'm black and I'm proud." We started two stepping and clapping our hands and before we knew it Vernon had busted into to some moves reminiscent of a pop locker. He moved with ease and perfection in his Brooks Brothers' suit. Moving his hands and body in ways you'd think a man of his size couldn't do. He hopped and jumped his way down through the soul train line. It was an incredible performance, spectacular. We all were amazed at how talented of a dancer Vernon was, we couldn't contain our enthusiasm and excitement. We practically tackled the guy when he finished with pats on the back, hugs, pushes, jumping on his back, and any other thing we could do to show our appreciation of his dance performance. Charles cut the music.

"Welcome to the family Soul Train! I declared loudly. Everyone cheered, and Soul Train became his nickname.

"Next up, is Clyde," Charles said, then he pressed the play button on the remote. James brown kicked in loudly "Say it loud, I'm black and I'm proud. Say it loud, I'm black and I'm proud."

Everyone in the whole room was breathless when he danced his way down the soul train line. He crip walked the entire time. When he finished, I was lost for words, but Darrell wasn't.

"Can you tell me how an Ivy League educated man knows how to C-Walk?"

Clyde laughed. We learned later that he was gang affiliated in his youth, but made a change when his SAT scores were through the roof, and he got a full academic scholarship to an Ivy League school.

"Welcome to the family C-Walk." I announced, and that became his nickname.

"You're next Dexter." Charles directed him to come to the forefront of the soul train line, and then hit the play button. "Say it loud, I'm black and I'm proud. Say it loud, I'm black and I'm proud."

Dexter didn't have a good start. He was timid, stiff, awkward, and lacked rhythm.

"Stop the music!" Big Mike shouted. "Dexter, what the hell are you doing? Are you listening to the beat or the words, because you are off beat?"

"Hell Dexter looks to me like you're dancing in between the beats." Charles said.

"Shit Dexter, I wouldn't even call that dancing!" I joined in.

"Leave my baby alone." Maria came to her husband's rescue. She walked over to him at the end of the soul train line and gave him a very intimate kiss."

"I think, I got wood." Charles interjects.

"What the hell man!" Darrell, Big Mike, and I all questioned Charles.

"You are going to shut us down before we get started." Darrell stated.

"Ah… don't sweat that. I know how y'all roll, and that's what I like about all of you. You keep it real." Maria responded.

"Well, with that lets welcome white-chocolate to the family." I said. Everyone cheered. Hugs and handshakes ensued.

"Next coming down the soul train line Maria," Charles announced, and then he hit play. "Say it loud, I'm black and I'm proud. Say it loud, I'm black and I'm proud."

Maria was cool with it, she moved slow and smooth, moving her hips ever so slightly, gliding her way down through the soul train line to cheers from everyone. I couldn't think of a nickname for her so I just announced. "Welcome to the family Maria." She raised her hands in victory and received hugs from everyone.

****

We were properly staffed; there was work to be done. Our investors were patient, but I wanted to hit the ground running. I had my eye on a textile company with its corporate offices in Idaho, but all its' manufacturing was in Mexico. I remembered the company from my GPG days. I worked with underwriting to redeem all their outstanding debt (bonds), and took the company public. World Textiles was a simple operation that manufactured textiles and shipped their products back into the U.S. Cheap labor and low overhead was the key to their fifty percent profit margins. World Textiles owned four ships to transport product from the coast of Mexico. At the time they went public I remember asking myself what stock investor would be interested in a company like this, and why would they want to go public, instead of selling the company straight out.

I found out that the company was family owned and there were some older members that did want to sell the company outright, but some of the younger members wanted to keep the business, and Junior convinced them the best way to pay out the older members was through an IPO. I remember questioning Junior at the time on the wisdom of an IPO for this World Textiles, and true to form he retorted with disdain. "Keep your mouth closed about things that don't concern you." Right then I knew it was a set up – Junior and GPG was setting the company up to be taken over by a bigger fish, one that needed some manufacturing operations in Mexico, but at the time I still couldn't figure out what the real catch was. Knowing how they play on Wall Street there had to be more to it than just some synergy in terms of manufacturing or lowering overhead cost with cheap labor.

I wanted to dig a little more into the company and see what I could find. I filled in everyone on the particulars about the company and how it came to be on my radar. I delegated the market cap valuation to Charles, C-Walk, and Soul Train. I wanted details on trading volume, float, shareholders, stock outstanding, and Directors of the company. I left the fundamental analysis for White-Chocolate and Maria. I wanted them to dig into the financials of World Textiles and dissect it like a frog in a biology project. I wanted the true value of all the assets liabilities on the books absent any accounting tricks. I had Big Mike focusing on setting up a dummy corporation, so when we started accumulating shares of the company, no one would know it was Black Street Capital. Darrell and I worked the phones using our contacts to gather any information we could about World Textiles – material and non-material.

Within two weeks the intel came in on World Textiles. Charles and his crew reported back- two hundred and fifty million in market capital, five million shares outstanding, float about hundred thousand shares, and daily volume small- not worth mentioning. Shareholders were majority family members and some individual investors, not many institutional investors, but GPG held about four percent of the outstanding stock, just enough to have a position in the company without having to report it to the SEC. SEC required six percent ownership before there was a requirement to report your holdings to SEC. My suspicions were raised when I found out about GPG stock ownership in the company, but they weren't confirmed yet because none of the market information came back with anything significant that would point to any hidden value. Charles believed the trading value of the company was priced right given its industry and the size of the company.

Dexter and Maria came back with the fundamental analysis of the company based on its revenues, assets, and liabilities. World Textiles according to their analysis was worth just under three hundred million, the company was poorly managed, but with new competent management in place they would push the value upward to just over three hundred million. There wasn't anything noteworthy.

All things equal, the market and fundamental analysis were indicating the market was properly reflecting the true value of the company. I noticed some real estate holdings in Puerto Rico on the balance sheet and upon questioning Dexter and Maria my suspicions increased.

"Those sections of land in Puerto Rico, what's the story?" I asked.

"They were lots purchased by World Textiles, before the Mexico deal came about." White-Chocolate responded.

"The land was supposed to be developed and used as a manufacturing facility, but with NAFTA and other incentives the Mexico deal made more financial sense for the company." Maria injected.

"How big is this land mass?"

"Just about five hundred thousand acres."

"Five hundred thousand!... Really?."

"Yes, but its dead land, almost worthless. "

"Why is that Maria?"

"From the reports we're getting, the practical use is limited without a significant capital investment, and given the education level and average wages earned in the surrounding areas, it would have been a much greater investment on World Textile's part."

"So, it was the capital outlay that scared them?"

"Given the management of this company, I think they got cold feet in taking on a project of this magnitude, and they decided on a 100 year lease term in Mexico in a facility already equipped to handle their manufacturing needs along with a cheap labor force." White-Chocolate rejoined.

"Everything you both are telling me makes sense, but my suspicions are running wild. I want to further investigate this land ownership by World Textiles."

"Why?" Maria asked.

"Because I think there's more there than meets the eye."

"What do you want us to do? White-Chocolate asked.

"I want Maria to fly out there to do some snooping around." I looked directly at Maria. "Go out to the location and look around, look for something out of the ordinary. Go into the surrounding areas, talk with some of the people, find out about the political climate, and about the people with influence .....You think you can handle that?"

"Of course!"

"Can I go with her?" Dexter asked.

"I prefer you don't. I think Maria will be able to navigate better on her own and get people to be at ease with her presence quicker. I hate to say it, but people still are on edge about black men, especially black men they don't know."

White-Chocolate agreed. Maria caught a flight out to the Puerto Rico the next day.

****

It didn't take long, about two days into her trip; Maria called into the trade room.

"Shane line 1, its Maria." Charles shouted.

White-Chocolate looked up. I gestured for him and Darrell to pick up line one with me. We all sat at one long trading desk that was in the center of the room. "Hey Maria, I have Dexter and Darrell on line too. What did you find out?"

"Your suspicion about this land here was right. The first thing I did when I landed was charter a small plane to come out and survey the land. There is an oil exploration pump smack dab in the middle of the land pumping for oil for all to see."

"How can that be?" White-Chocolate asked.

"The land is huge and massive, and it is far off the beaten path. Not too many people would think or have a reason to survey the land from the air."

"Precisely!" I joined in.

"I had a chance to talk to a few of the locals and it seems most were anticipating employment opportunities with World Textiles and was devastated, when their plans changed to Mexico. They got renewed hope when they were told there would be other opportunities through another company moving here."

"You get the name of the company," I asked?

"Let me see my notes...... I think the name was Titan."

"Titan industries?" Darrell questioned.

"Yes."

"That's a GPG's client." Darrell stated.

"They are one of the biggest oil exploration companies in the world." I rejoined.

"Oh shit, this is huge!" Darrell declared.

"Maria, who told the locals about Titan Industries?" I asked.

"According to the people I've talked to it was a local politician named Raul Espinoza."

Someone from the outside lobby was ringing the bell, and I knew it was the lunch we ordered. I asked White-Chocolate to go and get the sandwiches we ordered. Once he left I continued the conversation with Maria and Darrell. "Maria I need you to find out all you can from this Espinoza. We need to know what the exploration has turned up to this point; any laws or regulation about oil exploration that might hinder an operation, and a time line for Titan Industries to be fully operational. Now, Maria the only way you can get this information is to get close to Espinoza. Are you comfortable with that?"

"Maria hold on," Darrell said! He put his line on hold and told me to do the same. "What are you asking Maria to do?"

"I'm asking her to get the information we need to validate our assumptions about this land."

"But, what are you asking her to do to get it? We are not pimps," He whispered.

White-Chocolate walked back in the trade room with the sandwiches, then asked was Maria still on line one. "Yes" I said. He picked up the line and talked to his wife. Darrell and I got up from the trade desk and walked outside the trade room towards one of the private offices. We were followed out by Big Mike and Charles. Big

Mike was the last to make it into the room, and he closed the door behind him.

"What's going on guys," Big Mike initiated?

"Maria has uncovered some significant information about this land holding that World Textiles has on its books. This new information has the potential to take this deal through the roof." I said.

"How much through the roof?

"My guess .....With the information we have now- four to five billion."

"Holly shit," Charles interjected! "So, we stand to make three to four billion off this deal?"

"Yes! And, I have asked Maria to secure and validate more details about the land, and in pursuing this information I requested her to get closer to her source."

"And that is the issue." Darrell rebuffed.

"What's the issue?" Big Mike asked

"Well, the issue is two-fold. Is it fair for us to ask Maria, a married woman to compromise herself in the pursuit of this intel? Second, we asked her in a covert way."

"What do you mean in a covert way?" Big Mike asked.

"We did it behind the back of White Chocolate."

"Okay, let me clarify my request of Maria. First, when I asked her to get closer, I meant to befriend Espinoza, maybe even flirt with Espinoza, to use her personality and charm to persuade him to share what he knows, nothing more than that."

"I don't see anything wrong with that." Big Mike replied.

"Me either!" added Charles.

"Okay, I will go along with that, but initially I wasn't sure, so I think it prudent to speak in clear terms of what we are asking her to do. I don't want to leave any room for misinterpretation."

"Agreed!" I responded.

"What about White Chocolate?" Big Mike asked.

"What about him! We are going back and forth about nothing. White Chocolate knows his wife. Whatever she does or doesn't do, is between them. We have concern where there need not be, and let's not forget Maria used to give blow jobs for a living!" Charles said animated.

"Hey that's not needed! Respect! Maria is a part of our Black Street family." I clarified.

"Yea Charles, why would you say *something* like that?" Darrell added.

"I'm sorry for putting it that way, but I guess my real point is, she has real life experiences, and some of those experiences good and bad has made her who she is today – a bad ass bitch! And, I mean that in the most complimentary way! I know for certain, she knows exactly what Shane asked of her and she doesn't have the slightest reservation about getting information by any means necessary."

"What does that mean?" Darrell retorted.

"We all know what that means. We all are grown ass men here, and from our collective experiences we know what it takes to make it on Wall Street. So you can try to sugar coat it all you want, but with three to four billion at stake, she needs to get that information or we sub her out with someone else."

"Maybe that is the answer. Have Maria contract out a professional, to get the information and feed it to her." Darrell said.

I didn't think Darrell's idea was good, it had merit, but at this time Maria was perfect for the job. Charles was right her collective life experiences made her strong and savvy. I was counting on her street smarts to know where to draw the line in getting intel from Espinoza, and her financial expertise to know if he was feeding her bullshit. As for White Chocolate, again I was in agreement with Charles. What goes on between husband and wife is between that man and that woman. I thought Darrell was correct on full disclosure to White Chocolate. So, my plan was to cover all concerns in one fell swoop.

We all exited the office and walked back into the trade room. Soul Train and C-Walk eye balled us. We all returned to our seats on the trade desk. White Chocolate was still on line with Maria. Darrell and I picked up the line along with Charles and Big Mike. Clarifying our desire of Maria in her quest for additional information was awkward, but I pushed forward detached of emotion. I used the same words, I used in the private office -charm, persuade, flirt, befriend, to describe my wishes of Maria. White Chocolate gave a quick look in my direction as I was explaining myself, but said nothing. Maria as I anticipated didn't have the slightest hesitation in accepting the assignment. She ended the conversation with "You can count on me." I knew I could. I disconnected from the line as did the rest. White Chocolate didn't say a word; he returned to his seat on the trade desk and continued to work the rest of the day. As far as I was concerned, it was a done deal.

We didn't hear back from Maria for a few days, and when she called, it was a brief conversation about the progress she had made, but nothing of material significance. It wasn't until two weeks later that she hit pay dirt and phoned in the news around 6:00am in the morning. We had been anticipating this call, so everyone picked up the line including Soul Train and C-Walk.

"Shane your suspicions about this land have been validated. I have empirical evidence the oil exploration pump on the land is owned and was installed by Titan Industries. They have already researched drilling rights, and have plans for erecting a massive oil exploration plant with the potential of employing up to three thousand employees from the surrounding towns."

"Jackpot!" Soul Train said.

"There's more… from their initial exploration results the site has the potential to pump 25million barrels of oil a day!!!

"Are you kidding? That means its potential exceeds the capacity of some small Middle Eastern countries like Libya and Iraq." Darrell interjected.

"It gets even better. It looks like the Mackey's hands are all over this deal. They have manipulated World Textiles, led them to the Mexico deal, kept them in the dark about the land potential for oil exploration out here, and they are the ones that low balled the valuation of the land."

"Is there a timeline?" I asked.

"Yes, in the next few months Titan will finish up testing the oil well. Espinoza is clearing out all the red tape and has all the political heads lined up in support of Titan Industries. It's going to be a cake walk for them."

"Is there any other pertinent information we need to know." Charles asked.

"No, that's it for now. There are some smaller detail things, but we can go over that once I'm back in New York."

"Okay, good work. There will be a ticket waiting for you to fly out tomorrow morning." I said.

"Thanks, I will see you guys soon. I love you honey!" Maria exclaimed.

"I love you too! " We all responded, and everyone had a good laugh even White Chocolate."

Once we ended the phone conversation with Maria. We mapped out a plan to accumulate shares of World Textiles. We planned on using the dummy corporation Big Mike had set up to keep the Mackeys from sniffing us out. Darrell and I made contact with our banking financiers; the ones we knew had no relationship with GPG, for obvious reasons. We laid out what we saw as the financial fundamentals of the deal. This deal was strictly a takeover and liquidation, and even the most conservative estimates of return were a doubling of our money in six months to a year. We felt we needed about five hundred million in capital to buyout the company, a premium over the stock price was to be expected in a takeover situation. We had two hundred and fifty million from private investors and we needed an additional two hundred and fifty million from our banking contacts. Given the potential returns and the short turn around period, we secured the other two hundred and fifty needed from three banks and two more private investors in the states.

Once the money was transferred to our account, it didn't take us long to accumulate the six percent of the outstanding stock of World Textiles and file with the SEC. Once papers were filed with the SEC we were on GPG's radar, but given the dummy company we set up there was nothing pointing to us. We knew of a few inquiries by GPG about our dummy company just from conversations with friends on Wall Street and other players, but no one had the slightest idea it was us. We contacted the family members which owned the controlling interest in World Textiles to set up a meeting in their corporate offices located in Idaho. We asked for discretion because of their relationship with GPG, and they were happy to accommodative our request.

Big Mike, Darrell, Charles, and I all flew out to Idaho to meet with the family. When we made it to the corporate headquarters, located in an industrial building complex, we were greeted with reservation. Everyone was polite, but the site of four men of color all in expensive suits wasn't an everyday occurrence. Some made it seem like this was their very first time seeing black people in the flesh. The family members were waiting for us in their conference room, and we were escorted by a young lady who looked like a junior executive. Once we entered the conference room, all of the family members looked surprised, but warmed up to us once the meeting started. We were straight forward in our presentation which Darrell handled. We made it clear, we wanted to buy their controlling interest in the company which was by our estimation about eighty five percent, then came the questions.

"If you were to take over the company what are your plans for it?" One family member asked.

"Would you move the headquarters?"

"What would happen to our employees?"

We hesitated in our answer because we weren't prepared to answer those types of questions. Our focus for the last few months was strictly the financial aspect of the takeover. Darrell looked at me, then Big Mike, and last Charles. I spoke. "We will buy your company, break it up and sell the parts, and anyone else who approaches you about buying your company and tells you something different is lying!"

They all looked at each other. There was silence until a middle aged woman with reddish hair, pale white skin, dressed casually in clothing that resembled hiking attire spoke. "What's your offer?" I could tell by the way she was dressed and her demeanor she didn't make it to too many office meetings.

"Seventy five dollars a share." I responded. I was willing and ready to go all the way up to one hundred dollars, but I saw no need to go there initially.

"Wholly shit! Those god damn Mackey's didn't offer that........" the brunette responded, but was nudged by a family member.

"How much did the GPG offer?" Big Mike asked.

Now they hesitated, but then the brunette spoke with conviction. "Sixty dollars per share!"

"Well my offer is good for today only. I can have the papers drawn up today and have the formal offer for your shares in this office by morning." I came back.

There was more hesitation on their part, "We need time to think about it." one of them said.

"Well you have until the end of the day. We are staying at the Hyatt in Downtown."

We all stood and shook hands. As we made our way out the conference room and toward the elevator, the brunette caught up with us. Once we entered the elevator, she entered to, and when the doors closed she spoke.

"Why seventy five dollars a share and not sixty dollars a share?" She asked.

"I'm sorry, but your name escapes me." I said

"Nancy."

"Nancy, to put it bluntly, GPG is low balling you on the price, and to be perfectly honest by our estimation the true value is closer to eighty five, but we need to leave ourselves a cushion in order to make the deal profitable for us."

"Why would GPG low ball us?"

"They have a client waiting in the wings ready to purchase your company, sell the parts it doesn't need and keep parts that have synergy with their operations. This client is a very large and powerful corporation from which GPG makes lots of money. So, by giving you a lower price, it adds more juice to the deal for their big client."

"What's the name of the client?"

"I'm not at liberty to reveal that." She looked at me suspiciously. "Look, we are businessmen looking to make a profit off this deal. If I reveal all my information to you, what's to stop you from going back to GPG and using the information as leverage to boost the price? I've already given you enough information to do just that, that's why my offer is only good for today. When we leave, the offer leaves."

"What happens if we decline your offer?"

"Then, take the sixty dollars per share offer from GPG, and we will move on to our next deal."

We made it down to the lower lobby. She studied all of us, then said "eighty five dollars a share, we have a deal." She extended her hand toward me and we shook on it. I didn't question her authority to make the deal with us, but given her bluntness in the meeting I felt she could influence the others to agree to the eighty five.

When we made it back to the hotel, we used their teleconference room to set up a mini-office to coordinate with the law firm we contracted out to draw up the legal documents for the takeover of World Textile. Big Mike took the lead on reviewing all documents required for this deal. Charles kept tabs on the market along with the others back at headquarters in New York. Darrell and I did our due diligence in lining up potential buyers for the different parts of World Textiles. By the end of the day we had heard from Nancy with the good news of the family accepting our offer. Big Mike was satisfied with the contract terms thus far that would bind World Textiles to SCJ LLC (which was the dummy corporation we set up).

The next morning we met in the conference room at World Textiles headquarters. Signing the contract went relatively smoothly. The family had attorneys there representing their interest and Big Mike represented ours. There was a clause in the contract that allowed for a due diligence period of 90 days allowing us to examine the books and any other necessary documents and agreements, that we felt were pertinent to the operations and value of World Textiles. There was no objection to the due diligence just the length of time allowed for it, but in the end we came to an agreement. The last thing I wanted was to be rushed through this critical part of the process. Since I wanted a firm off Wall Street Marcus Anderson to conduct the due diligence, I knew we were going to need more time because of travel. Once all the documents were signed by both sides we set up a timeline and schedule, and the contact people to begin the process.

We flew out the next day, and the Marcus Anderson firm flew in the next day along with White Chocolate and Maria. They were the leads on this effort of discovery, and the best people for the job. I also felt they needed this because I could see the tension building up between the two of them ever since Maria got back from her assignment in Puerto Rico. I knew the assignment would be a cake walk, so I put them in a nice and romantic suite where they could spend some quality time.

It didn't take long before GPG sniffed out "Black Street Capital" as the culprit that snatched their World Textiles deal from under their nose. The calls started the morning we arrived back in New York. The first call was from Junior.

"Can I speak to Shane Jackson?"

"Speaking."

"You son of a bitch, do you know who you just fucked over.....do you?"

I kept calm as usual, and as usual the calmer I got, the angrier Junior got. "I'm not sure to what you are referring when you say I fucked over someone."

"Fuck you Shane....Fuck youuuuuu!"

"Hey Junior," he was silent. "Are you still dating that blonde I met in the elevator with you, when we first met?"

"What's it to you asshole!"

"Well,.... I'd rather fuck her than you." then I hung up the line. When I hung up the line, Darrell looked directly at me.

"Junior huh,.... You are going to drive that guy crazy."

I didn't hear back from GPG the rest of the day. The next morning I got a call from Mackey Sr.

"Shane, can we have a sit down?"

"Of course Mr. Mackey."

"Is tomorrow good, about an hour after the opening?"

"Sure."

"I'll see you in your office tomorrow."

"Okay."

The next morning the Mackeys arrived along with two other suits. Since we still didn't have a receptionist, they had to ring the bell in the lobby, and I had C-Walk greet them and escort them to the conference room where we had refreshments set up.

All of us took the meeting –Big Mike, Charles, Darrell, and I.

We didn't exchange pleasantries, the conference room was tense. Mr. Mackey introduced the two suits senior executives at Titan Industries. They both were middle to late fifties, heavy set with ill fitted suits for their physique. They look none too happy with us and were clearly controlling their anger.

"You are stealing from us and we don't take too kindly to that!" One of the Titan executives said.

"Well, if you feel that way, there's no reason for this meeting. You might want to just contact the authorities to get involved." I responded.

"I didn't mean literally, I meant it figuratively."

"Yea, smart ass!" Junior interjected his two cents. Mr. Mackey extended his hand across the forearm of Junior resting on the conference room table and patted him softly.

"Shane, we realize you have done your homework on World Textiles and you see an opportunity for profit here, but we have been working this deal for a few years now and we all feel you're piggy backing off all our hard work." Mr. Mackey expressed.

I didn't say a word, neither did my partners. We let Mr. Mackey continue.

"There is a bigger picture here beyond money. Titan Industries is a global company that can take World Textiles international and provide access and opportunity to markets like no other company. The personnel at World Textiles will become a part of the Titan family which will improve the opportunities for them. Having said all that we are willing to compensate you for your efforts in acquiring World Textiles at a hundred and fifty dollars a share, you will more than double your investment – none of your investors will be disappointed."

"I agree Mr. Mackey, no investor would be unhappy with that kind of return, but I'm looking for a greater return than that." I responded.

True to form Junior did not disappoint. "Are you fucking nuts?" he shouted.

Now the two executives from Titan Industries gave Junior the evil eye.

"No, I don't think I'm nuts Junior." That title Junior didn't sit well with him, he looked cross. "Hear me out then make your judgement. Our offer is eighty five dollars a share for the remainder of shares held by GPG. The same offer we gave to the Waltons, and on acceptance of that offer by GPG we are willing to sell World Textiles, the entire company, to Titan Industries for three point seventy five billion."

"Are you shitting me?" Junior retorted.

At that dollar price the Titan executives and Mr. Mackey knew my homework reached all the way into Puerto Rico. "If Titan doesn't want the entire company, then I'll take three billion for the land in Puerto Rico, and I will sell the rest of the company to the highest bidder." My last statement let them all know we knew what was taking place in Puerto Rico.

The two executes looked at Mr. Mackey, and nodded in the affirmative toward him. Darrell and Charles both pushed my legs with theirs underneath the table. We had them, they knew it and we knew it. We were looking at three point four billion in profit off an investment of only three hundred and seventy five million. Now that was a return on investment. Mr. Mackey rose from his seat and said. "We have a deal." He extended his hand and we shook on it.

"I will have the agreement drawn up in the next few days and have it sent over to GPG, for your review."

"Sounds good Shane!"

When we all left the conference room no one was talking but Mr. Mackey and Me. We lingered behind a moment before heading for the lobby. He spoke in a low voice.

"Good Job Shane, this is quite the accomplishment for your first deal. I think it will be quite the feat to top this one on your next." We reached the elevator. He shook my hand once again and patted me on the back, then joined the other three in the elevator.

Once the elevator doors closed, we were fully aware any celebration could be heard down the elevator shaft, so we walked back into the trade room announced the deal and there were daps and hugs all around. Maria and White Chocolate were missing from our small celebration in the trade room, but Soul Train gave them the good news by phone. We decided not to do any real celebrating until the deal was complete and the money was in the bank.

It took close to six months before the deal was completed, and most of that was just contract negotiations. Each party trying to protect their interests and accounting for any contingencies that might come up after the deal was signed. We really had three deals in one, so we took every effort to ensure all agreements were iron clad tight. We had recourse where we were concerned, and the recourse for the other parties was limited when it involved their interests. We double checked and tripled checked everything. The smallest of details were not overlooked, and I have to give most of that credit to Big Mike. His eye for detail was second to none, his legal background proved to be invaluable.

Once we got the call about the wire of three point eight billion hit our account the celebration began. The feeling was surreal. We were like adolescents going to Disneyland for the first time. We had heard about it, dreamed about it, imagined being a part of that experience, and now we had arrived. We had champagne delivered to the trade room. We toasted to our success and all the efforts of everyone to make this deal happen. Once the initial elation died down a little, I sat back at the trade desk and called Kendra.

"It's done three point eight billion just hit the account."

"Congratuations baby! I love you."

"I love you too!"

"How do you feel?"

"Weird, like I'm occupying a time and place that doesn't exist."

"What do you mean doesn't exist?"

"A space that is unfamiliar.... I hope, I know how to act."

"Don't scare me baby!"

"No, no, you don't ever have to worry when it comes to you! My feelings and actions toward you will always be loving and caring, and if given a choice between money and you, there would be no choice, only you!"

"I'll meet you at home for some real celebration. What you think about that?"

"I like that, but I promised the others we'd hit Julian's in Harlem for some drinks. Why don't you join us? We can walk home together and start the real celebration."

"Okay see you at Julian's, I might be a little late. I have to shut down the shop."

Kendra hung up, and then Big Mike grabbed me, practically pushing me out the door. We caught the subway into Harlem having the grandest of times and picked up a couple of party goers on the way who just wanted to be a part of the celebration. We didn't know them, we met them along the way and they joined us. When we arrived at Julian's, I noticed a brand new hat shop right next door. I was intrigued by hats something about them, they felt sophisticated, fun, and reminded me of days passed when every gentleman wore a hat. I wandered over to take a look. To my surprise there was Ice behind the counter. Was he robbing the place? But he didn't look nervous when we entered. He greeted us and welcomed us in.

"This yours Ice?" I asked.

"Yea man, I opened up just a few weeks ago."

"It's a nice shop man!

"Thanks, just trying to go the legit route for a change."

"That's all right! Well you found a customer in me. Show me what you got."

"Alright Shane, let me see. Are you looking for casual look or something more?"

"Something I can wear with my suits to work."

"Okay, you want to go Mad Men style? Okay you about what, six three, one ninety."

"Yea, just about there. I've been getting my work outs on with my boy Big Mike."

"I think Fedoras would suite you well. There are all kinds of fedoras, but the ones that will compliment your body type are over here."

Ice led me over to some very fine top of the line hats. He wasn't dealing with any cheap brands, and each one he suggested, I tried, I loved. Those hats were sharp. Everyone else started shopping and trying on hats. I ended up purchasing five brims from Ice, and Big Mike, Charles, and Darrell followed with three each of their own. The other guys purchased a couple each as well. We asked Ice to hold our purchases while we went next door to celebrate. He congratulated us and said he would join us later.

We left Ice's shop and went to Julian's where we had drinks, appetizers, and some Cuban cigars that Big Mike furnished for everyone. We sat in booths adjacent to each other and reminisced about our time at GPG, and the audacity I had in pulling off an all-black trading desk.

"No one could believe your ass Shane. Everyone thought you were the Messiah coming to deliver all us lost souls in the finance world. That opportunity and experience was a one in a million, and everyone on that desk knew they were a part of something big and historical. When they disbanded the desk, others were being picked up by other Wall Street firms at a rapid pace. My honey and I turned down offers because we knew you were going to come knocking, and knock you did, on our first deal, we hit the ball out the park. What did I tell you baby." Maria turned to White Chocolate and gave him a good one across the lips.

I was humbled and secretly elated by the compliments they kept dishing out. I was at a loss for words so I simply sat in silence and took it all in. Ice joined us and shared his story of how he met me, which everyone enjoyed. Big Mike, Charles, and Darrell took it all the way back to our days at Jordan. Without them, there would be no me, and I thanked them all for their friendship and belief in me. While the conversations continued, I checked my watch for the time expecting to see Kendra walk into Julian's at any time. Julian's was crowded; the place looked to be at capacity. I set back and sipped my drink and puffed on my Cuban cigar. I was squeezed in between Charles to my right and Maria to my left in the booth. Word had circulated that we had just closed a billion dollar deal and there were no shortage of people coming up to congratulate us. As people were hovering all around us a patron caught my eye. He was standing at the bar in a conservative suit with the same non-descript look, much like the man I saw at my reception. I was stunned. He never looked my way, but I would have sworn it was the same guy. I became alarmed and Maria noticed.

"Shane you okay?"

I didn't answer. I kept my focus on this guy who stood at the bar.

"Shane…" she nudged me to draw my attention. "You okay?"

"Yea..yea…" I turned back to refocus on the man at the bar and he was gone. I tried to move quickly out of the booth to find him by pushing Charles. "Let me out. Let me out." I urged him.

He moved hurriedly, but was puzzled by the urgency along with Big Mike and Darrell. "What's your hurry?" They all asked.

"I'll be right back." I moved through the bar rapidly, got to the spot where I saw him, he was gone. I made my way out the front entrance and looked down the street and saw just a few people who couldn't look anymore different than him.

This was my second sighting of this guy, and I was confident my mind wasn't playing tricks on me. Now my concern grew and my mind drifted back to the words of Jakar, and what we just accomplished at Black Street Capital. Maybe his words had more substance than I wanted to believe. I stood outside Julian's with my thoughts, and then Maria walked up from behind and startled me. I jumped.

"Shane are you okay?"

"Yea."

"Who are you looking for out here?"

"Kendra, she's supposed to meet me."

"You sure, you're okay."

"Positive!"

Maria stood there observing me almost studying me, so I asked her was she okay.

"I wanted to talk with you in private, and I hadn't had the opportunity since I got back from Puerto Rico, and we were so busy with World Textiles."

"What about?"

"My assignment in Puerto Rico."

My heart quickened, this was a conversation. I didn't think I would have to have, nor did I want to have. Maria face was looking seriously somber. I tried to lighten the mood.

"Hey we are supposed to be celebrating."

"Right now I'm not in the mood to celebrate. I'm in the mood to have a discussion with you.

We took a seat on a wooden bench to the left of the bar, but she stood back up quickly. She paced a little, and then she stilled herself in front of me looking directly into my eyes, studying me without words. It felt like she was trying to penetrate and look deep within me, attempting to see my essence- my soul. Was it one of compassion she saw, understanding, sympathy, or a plain self-serving an empty man? The moment was awkward, but my cigar comforted me. I took a long slow drag, which confused her because it made me appear nonchalant, cold, and unappreciative. When she finally thought she recognized who was before her, her eyes swelled up with water and the tears followed. I stood to comfort her, but she slowly pushed me away. I handed her my handkerchief.

"Did you ask me to get closer to Espinoza because of my past experience?"

"Yes."

She studied me again. " She spoke quietly. "You knew I would do that for you didn't you?"

"I thought the odds of you doing it were in my favor."

"You are an arrogant fuck,......I guess the traits that make you successful cut both ways and make you an asshole too." I had no response. She continued. "You know I got mad love for you Shane. I see you, I see your faults, your shortcomings, your ego and arrogance, but I also see your passion, motivation, your drive, and your loyalty for those you care about. I thought you cared about me."

"I do care about you Maria." I said sincerely. "I didn't mean to hurt you or put you in a position that would compromise you. I truly thought from your experience…you could handle the situation without having to result to any physical intimacy."

Again she cried. I knew right then that something physical took place between Maria and Espinoza. I tried to hug her, but she pushed me away once again.. I never thought……" I couldn't finish my sentence. "Does White Chocolate know?"

"No, and he must never know. This is between me and you. I don't want anyone else to know. Please Shane, do not tell anyone. I'm trusting in you!"

"You can trust me this goes no further than here."

Even in this heart wrenching moment, Maria's capacity to make light of this darkest moment amazed me. "Shane I think in a previous life you were my pimp and I was your bottom bitch." She chuckled.

"Put them on the main road; teach them how to change clothes. I know ya heard of that," I rapped!

We laughed. "You owe Dexter an apology."

"What?"

"You heard me. You owe Dexter an apology.

"For what?

"For disrespecting him the way you did. You came on the line and asked his wife in front of him to get closer to a man without consulting him first. I know you got balls of steel, but that was a cold move. That was a street move – total disregard for the feelings of others. Like I said some traits cuts both ways." Shane I love Dexter, and you made him feel less than a man with your request of me. I had my hand in it too, but it's time you mend fences with him.

"Not going to happen." I said calmly.

"What?" She was beside herself and couldn't believe the nonchalant way I refused to apologize to her husband. "You selfish egotistical son of a bitch."

"Hey, whatever is going on between you and white-chocolate is between you and him, and has nothing to do with me. When it's all said and done, we are all adults and we all made our decisions with full disclosure of information. "

Maria just looked dumfounded. "Fuck you Shane!" She pushed me out of way and made her way back into Julian's.

As I stood outside, I thought for a person who just made three billion dollars I sure didn't feel happiness at that moment, but that changed when I saw Kendra walking up the block toward me. She was a sight, a lady, from her walk, to the way she dressed, it was how she carried herself, and it was who she was.

"Hey Mr. Good bar!" She hugged and gave me tender kiss, not too much to cause a scene but just enough to let me know I was loved.

"Hey babe, I'm glad you made it" As I embraced her. I felt comforted by her familiar scent of jasmine. I wanted to go home. "I'm ready to go home."

"You are so bad, I just got here. Where are the guys?"

"Here they come." They all spewed out the door of the bar smelling of alcohol and cigar smoke in a festive mood.

They all greeted Kendra and she congratulated everyone on the day's success like only she could with utmost sincerity and kindness. Once things settled down I grabbed Kendra and pulled her close to me.

"What are all you guys doing out here? I thought the celebration was inside?" I asked.

"Well we seen you and Kendra out here, and thought we'd bring the celebration outside." Darrell responded.

As we all stood outside and socialized Maria mean mugged me the entire time. The disdain in her glare toward me became evident to Kendra, and made both of a little uncomfortable. So, I decided to call it a night after about 15 minutes mingling.

"Hey guys, Kendra and I are going to head home for our own little private celebration." I announced.

"The night is still young." Darrell exclaimed.

Kendra quickly co-signed our departure. "I need some quality time with my husband. You have had him long enough with this World Textile deal."

No one had a rebuttal to that statement. We said goodbye then began our walk home, while the others walked back into Julian's.

On our walk home Kendra did not hesitate to bring up the stare by Maria. I told her the entire story from beginning to end even the part about something happening between Maria and Espinoza. I know I promised Maria not to tell anyone, but I really believed that was a promised not to tell anyone amongst our Black Street crew which I fully intended on keeping. When I finished telling her the full story her reaction was one of surprise and disappointment.

"Oh Shane! I think you do owe them an apology."

Again I questioned for what, and as best she could, Kendra tried to lay it out for me, but I wasn't buying it. My mind set was we were all adults responsible for our own decisions. Kendra let it go and just gently kissed me and told me she loved me.

Kendra was in a league all by herself, she was my escape, my love, my friend, my companion, my confidant, my comfort, my support, but best of all she was my wife. It felt good to have someone down with you no matter your shortcomings or flaws. They still loved you deeply and wanted the best for you. Kendra was that for me, and I for her. But, what I wanted when we got home was pure fun, and that's just what we had, fun. The celebration could not have been more special than to spend it making love to a woman who truly had my heart.

"You think we can celebrate like this each time I complete a billion dollar deal!" I asked as we lay in front of the fireplace naked with just a blanket over us and a bowl of popcorn with two glasses of wine by our side.

"We can celebrate like this when you complete a one dollar deal!

Mo Money

A few months had passed and Kendra wanted to organize a dinner party for some close friends and family at our home. I invited everyone from the office, and Ice. My circle of friends didn't really go beyond my work place except for Ice. I had been seeing him more frequently because of the addition of hats to my wardrobe. I fell in love with having a distinguishing look of a hat atop my head along with my suits. Kendra like the addition and complimented me on the look. Others in the office followed suit with the hats. It quickly became the calling card of a "Black Street Capital" professional man. One day Big Mike and I were walking through Harlem after work and group of young ladies coming out of a restaurant asked if we work for Black Street Capital. After our deal with "World Textiles" we made a name for ourselves. We had write ups in several periodicals and magazines, including the New York Times and Wall Street Journal. The real pride came for all of us when we made the cover of Ebony and Black Enterprise. The articles in the black publications were much more flattering in their description of our accomplishment. Some of the others almost painted us as money grubbing corporate raiders only out to make a buck. One magazine even compared us to drug dealers, in our prowess, and determination to get the World Textile deal completed. After reading the article I vowed not to give another interview to any publication.

We had become recognizable throughout our Harlem community by adults and children alike. It was a good feeling to see kids in the community looking up to us, hearing them say they wanted to be like us when they grew up – not a drug dealer, pimp, or hustler, but a business person working in the finance capital of the world. I had no idea our presence would have such an impact just by making Harlem our home. Charles, Big Mike, Darrell, and I lived in the same community not more than two blocks away from each other in any direction. We became the closet things to celebrities in Harlem.

Kendra and I had discussed leaving the community and moving more upstate into a rural community away from the city, but we both agreed Harlem was home. Given our increased financial wealth we could have easily afforded a much more swanky home with all the trimmings, as a matter of fact, we could have had a few of those homes, but Kendra didn't get caught up into accumulation of material things to justify our existence. I loved her for it. My goal and desire was to make her happy, and give her options and opportunities she wanted from life. There was nothing really beyond our means, and I let her know that!

"I just want you baby." She replied. "Well,….. I do want to start a family."

"Okay, you scared me for a moment."

"Ah baby, I will always want you, but I just want to make some additions to our family."

"Additions, meaning plural."

"Yes plural, more than one."

"How many?'

"With all the money we got, why worry about a number. We have enough money to give fifty kids a good healthy life."

"You don't want fifty kids do you?" I asked seriously

Kendra laughed. "You are crazy! No, Mr. Jackson about four or five would be perfect."

"That's a pretty big family."

"Yes, it's on the larger side, but I know- I will be a loving mother and you a loving father. I want to have your children and raise a family with you."

I hadn't thought about such a large family, but when I did give it some thought it felt right.

The party began around seven pm. Kendra had the place looking festive with plenty of food and drink. It was a relaxed and casual atmosphere; everyone mingling having a good time. I stayed on the periphery like the Mile Davis "Birth of Cool" album playing in the background. Kendra was the perfect hostess, and I helped where she needed me. Those who hadn't seen or talked to me in a while came up to congratulate me on the World Textile deal and the success of Black Street Capital. Big Mike and Charles were having a good time with some of Kendra's lady friends. I would have to say Kendra's friends were quite an attractive group.

Big Mike and Charles had been hitting the New York night scene pretty hard and consistently since we closed the World Textile deal. We had noticed a significant change in Charles since the closing of our first deal. He was never one to lack confidence, but his bravado and style had kicked up a notch. Even Kendra noticed the change in Charles. She had mentioned his attention to more detail in the suits she made for him, and his style had become flashier. His approach and the way he spoke to others could be condescending at times which we had to correct him on more than a few occasions. But, when it came to Carmen he was like a kid at the first day of school trying to impress his teacher. Carmen was a stalwart. She was good woman, independent, free thinker, and very pretty. In a lot of ways she reminded me of Kendra.

Charles told me he had gotten to know Carmen a little better in Africa at the wedding. He confided that he thought she was uncomfortable with his height and weight. He began to work out after work with the rest of us. Charles was about five foot seven and while he wasn't fat, he wasn't in the greatest of shape either. Carmen was about five nine and worked out religiously. He knew there was something there he wanted to build on. He was going to make every effort to make his feelings known to Carmen. By the looks of what I was seeing at the party they were getting along well. She was laughing and touching him, a good sign.

Big Mike on the other hand was not limiting his conversation to just one of Kendra's lady friends. He was just enjoying the moment. His maturity shined through, not coming on to anyone in particular, but just making a connection with all. Very sincere and polite in conversations his tact was admirable. He towered over everyone with his six foot five frame. The women were jockeying for position to get near him. Big Mike had become more settled and comfortable with his future since his assignment overseas at GPG, and once Black Street Capital was launched. He had been the foundation on which we built our business. His worth had climbed tremendously in our takeover strategy; his legal mind lent itself to detail and anticipation of any obstacles we may encounter in taking over a company. I wasn't more proud of anyone than I was of Big Mike. He above all was really thriving with our acquisition strategy, but only Darrell still remained somewhat distant about the direction.

At the party Darrell didn't mingle as much. He helped Kendra and I in making our guest feel welcomed and in particular he helped Kendra. As I was talking with some of our guest, I glanced up and saw Kendra and Darrell laughing in the kitchen. They stood shoulder to shoulder leaning up against each other laughing. I knew Darrell and Kendra had become close since they met. Darrell would constantly tell me I was a lucky a man to have Kendra in my life, but never with envy, but rather with pride of my choice and a sincere hope for our happiness. I knew he stopped by her boutique after work at times to chat and hangout. Sometimes we would go together, but what I saw in the kitchen no matter how innocent, didn't feel right to me. I said nothing because I knew Darrell loved us both, and we were close, and above all I trusted my wife. I didn't want to be or act like a jealous husband.

Some of our guests got on the topic of social responsibility. This topic seemed to peak everyone's interest, I was sitting on the couch surrounded by others standing and sitting around in the front room. Kendra came around and sat next to me on the couch. Darrell and the rest of the Black Street gang were to my right standing. I thought the conversation was interesting – people gave their perspectives and opinions on community, giving back, literacy, and our youth of today. I didn't have very much to say, I just listened, until one of Kendra's friends Vernon (which I had met when Kendra and I were dating) pulled me off the sidelines and right into the middle of the conversation.

"What about you Shane, how do you feel about community or is your only concern making money," asked Vernon? He was in his mid-forties, born and raised in Harlem, and avid community activist. He stood about five ten in height, dread locks with specs of gray throughout with matching salt and pepper beard. Thin framed, dressed in light earth tone clothing, he looked the part of an educated bum.

"No, I believe in community."

"What do you believe about community?" He came back.

"I'm in agreement with most of the sentiments here about a united and cohesive community."

"But how are you adding to or helping build that unity or cohesiveness?" he said in a demanding tone which had an overtone that I wasn't doing shit in his eyes. "I never see you in the community volunteering your time, teaching our youth, or giving to those who are less fortunate than you. Don't you think a responsible community conscious man should do more than just reside in a community? He should live in the community! I mean to contribute in way that I just described! I don't see that coming from you in no way shape or form!"

His tone irritated me, then I thought how does this man, a guest in my home, have the gull to question me about how am I contributing to my community's growth and prosperity, and on top of that insinuate all I care about is money. I looked at Kendra sitting beside me as if to ask her what's up with her friend. She said nothing. It seemed she was waiting to hear my response along with him. Did Kendra share his impression of me? I wondered, and felt alone and attacked in my home where my lioness wasn't helping protect the home front. Now, I was mad, but instead of cursing and throwing Vernon out of my home. I took a philosophical approach. "What one hasn't heard, a lot of times is not seen."

"What the hell does that mean?" he said sarcastically.

Before I could respond, I heard a female voice shout.

"Shut the fuck up you fake bum Rasta wanna be. Obviously you don't know Shane, because if you did you would never come into his home and disrespect him the way you are doing; you old ass nigga!" I knew the voice, but it wasn't coming from where I had expected it to. It was Maria and there was fire in her eyes. I was surprised given the slight tension between us in the office ever since the Puerto Rico incident. White Chocolate tried to control and pull back his wife, but she was having none of that. She stepped directly to Vernon and continued her fierce defense of me. "What Shane meant was if people don't hear about what you're doing to help your community; they make the assumption that you are doing nothing. So, as a person in is this community, let me tell you what Shane has done for me and others. He has given me and others the economic opportunity to participate in an industry traditionally overlooking our talents. He has given us access to what many say has made America great –Capitalism."

"Young lady I did not mean to offend Shane or you, or to be disrespectful in his home." Vernon responded timidly.

"All of us here know what the fuck you meant. Don't back down now you sorry mutha fucka! I heard y'all talking about all the money Shane has, and how he doesn't give back to the community. My husband and I heard you and some of your little friends over there." She pointed them out. "Let me tell you this. The multi-billion dollar deal we just completed that everyone has been congratulating Shane and us on; the legal firm used was black owned, the back office operations and consulting firm was black owned, and even though only a small portion of the money came from black owned banks all the clearing and banking operations went through black owned banks. Now you tell me if he is giving back to his community."

Vernon was silent.

"Just like I thought, you wanna be niggas, always want to point fingers at what you think somebody ain't doing according to what you think should be done. If your thing is feeding the homeless and volunteering time on a hot line, then do it. Just because a person is not doing what is visible to you doesn't mean he isn't doing anything. You stupid mutha fucka!"

Vernon stood up off the couch and as a reaction to his movement, White-Chocolate pulled Maria back and took her place, then I stood and stepped forward along with Big Mike, Darrell, Charles, Soul Train, and C-Walk, surrounding Vernon front to back. Kendra quickly grabbed me. Vernon sat back down with his hands up.

"I apologize, if I offended anyone. That was not my intention, and I surely wasn't standing to physically threaten our sista, but just to embrace her for her passionate defense of Shane. Clearly I don't know this man as much as I thought, and I apologize to him and Kendra." Vernon said.

Calmer heads prevailed. Kendra backed everyone up from around Vernon. I sat back down on the couch and everyone else returned to their original space in the room. Once order was returned to the room, I sat quietly in thought while all eyes were upon me. My focus was Kendra and there was disappointment in my eyes, she knew it. I finally spoke.

"Let's change the topic."

Then I stood and made my way to the kitchen followed by all of Black Street. There were rumblings in the kitchen of throwing Vernon's ass out of my house, but I told them it wasn't necessary that he apologized, so as far as I was concerned the issue was dead. Big Mike and Maria were the hottest. They wanted his head on a stick. I suggested all of them go home and we would talk on Monday in the office. Thanking Kendra for her hospitality, they each left shortly.

Once they left, I went upstairs to my bedroom not saying a word to our other guest or Kendra. I went to bed feeling down trodden. Most of our remaining guest didn't see my retreat upstairs, and I heard chatter of my whereabouts. Not ten minutes passed before Kendra entered the bedroom.

"Vernon's really sorry about what happen. He would like to apologize to you in private." She said.

“No, it’s not necessary. Let him enjoy the rest of the night, but after tonight…I don’t want to see him in our house again, and for that matter, I don’t’ want to see him again.” I said calmly.

“But, he is a good friend of mine.”

“I never said you couldn’t be his friend. I just said he’s not a friend of mine, and I don’t want to see him. If it is your choice to still spend time and remain friends with Vernon, it’s your choice. I choose not to be around him.”

“Shane, Please!” she pleaded.

I didn’t respond. My mind was made up and no amount of pleading on her part was about to change my mind. She exited the room and closed the door behind her. I turned on the television to the world news. I quickly dosed off. After about an hour Kendra returned to the room. She nudged me ever so slightly. I awoke slowly, sat up in the bed, adjusted the pillows to give myself a cushion on my back, and I leaned back against the headboard. Kendra sat beside me on the bed.

“Are we okay?” She asked.

“Do you feel the same about me as your friend Vernon does?”

“Vernon has tremendous respect for you, and you know how I feel about you. I think you are a great man headed for great things!”

“He sure has a funny way of showing it, and you…..I was just taken back.”

“Vernon can be overly passionate in his arguments and rude at times. I guess I’m used to him; it never dawned on me that it would upset you so much. Usually my friends have passionate disagreements, but still part friends”

“I felt attacked in my own home, and even worse, I felt abandoned by my wife.”

“Abandoned?” she questioned.

“Yes abandoned. Vernon attacked my character and when I looked to you to help in my defense, you didn’t stand with me. It almost seemed you were in on the attack with him-instead of siding with me, your silence sided with him.”

“How can you say that to me?”

"I'm judging you by your action or your lack of action. It took Maria to put Vernon in check."

"I'm sorry, I didn't curse him out for you." She said sarcastically.

"It's not about cursing him out, but doing what's in your heart, protecting those you care about when they are under attack, coming to their aid........

"I didn't know you needed protection," She said defiantly.

"You still don't get it. It's not about me needing protection, but about you standing by me! You know this conversation is becoming more disappointing than Vernon calling my morale character into question in my own home. Let me ask you a question. If someone came into our home or even better, if we were in a social setting, doesn't matter where, and someone called your morale character into question, how do you think I would react?"

"I don't know." She answered somberly.

"Really?"

"You'd probably take their head off."

"I would rip their heart from their body and stomp the damn thing into the ground. If I was not in agreement with you, we would have that conversation in the privacy of our home, but never for public display."

She was silent. Slowly I think my perspective dawned on her. I continued. "One thing in this marriage I demand is loyalty. If we don't have that, we have nothing. I don't want to sleep with, be with, or be around anyone that is not loyal to me."

"I am loyal to you, and you should know that!" Her eyes watered.

"I thought I did, but it didn't feel that way tonight."

"Does my loyalty include ending my friendship with Vernon?"

"Do I need to answer that question?"

"I guess not." She rose from the bed slowly. "I'm sorry I disappointed you today. " She then, walked into the bathroom and took a shower.

I didn't think I was unreasonable in the conversation. I wasn't asking of her or telling her anything that if the tables were turn, I wouldn't expect of myself. Loyalty was number one for me in any relationship love or business. I was not willing to compromise on this with anyone including Kendra. I loved her more than life itself, but if her loyalty was questionable, that would be a bit too much for me to stay in our marriage. In stark contrast Maria's loyalty was unwavering. Despite the tension between us she still was in my corner ready to go to battle with anyone whom she saw as a threat to me or Black Street that was reassuring.

I rose early the next morning and left Kendra in the bed sleeping. I was the first in the office which gave me some alone time to reflect on the conversations of last night. I still felt anger toward Vernon. He was out of line. My thoughts about Kendra's non-action were clouded. I was questioning her loyalty which I never expected to do. Once those thoughts entered my mind, it wasn't long before the scene with her and Darrell flashed through my mind once again. Was this just friendship or something more? My anger started to cloud my judgement. Finally reason and sanity took a hold of me – one of my best friends and my wife…., my wife Kendra, not possible. I knew I had to come back from the edge before I jumped off. I knew deep down Kendra was loyal and if she perceived a threat against me, she definitely would defend me.

As I sat there with my thoughts, Big Mike entered the trade room.

"You alright?" he walked toward me and took a seat in the adjacent seat from me.

"Yea, just thinking some things through in my head."

"Yea, it got kind of crazy at your home last night. What was up with Vernon?"

"Don't know, but he will never be invited back into my home."

"I don't blame you. He was way out of line. Maria really went after him."

"Yea, she's the mother of Black Street Capital."

Big Mike just shook his head in agreement, then stood, patted me on the shoulder, and walked out of the trading room into one of the private offices leaving me to my thoughts.

I understood Big Mike was just giving me some space to deal with my thoughts. About a half hour later the rest of the troops came marching in the trade room. Everyone was in a festive mood, recounting the events of last night with excitement and detail. Maria was hailed the heroine. She acquiesced to somewhat of a shy role in the face of all the accolades. As I watched her reaction our eyes met, and there was an unsureness and nervousness in her eyes and body movement. She quickly looked away without acknowledging me. I understood her discomfort. All this was quickly broken up when Big Mike re-entered the room.

"What's our next move?"

Everyone looked directly at me!

"Mo money, mo money, mo money, and mo money!" I stated as I chuckled.

Everyone cheered, but the voice of reason broke up the cheering session.

"Really Shane? Is it going to be another buy and fire sale in the name of money?" Darrell expounded.

"Darrell, you have objections to making money?' I asked.

"No, I don't have any objections to making money, but to what end. Are we just gathered here in the name of money?"

"What else is there Darrell?"

"There is a lot more! We can build something, let's not just buy and sell to our hearts delight, but let's build a viable business entity that can participate in this great economic society."

"What is it that you want to build Darrell?"

"I want to build a legacy of business and commerce. I want us to own, hold and leave assets for future generations to manage."

"You want to start a mutual fund?"

"No, I want us to own a company where we have products that we innovate, manufacture, and deliver domestic and internationally. We have the expertise to run an international company. Charles you have the accounting, Big Mike you have the legal, I have the marketing, and Shane you have the financial."

"It makes sense Shane." Big Mike added.

I looked at Big Mike surprised. He returned the look, looking for understanding. I turned to Charles. He shrugged as if he was indifferent.

"What about us?' Maria broke the silence.

"I'm talking a multi-billion dollar international company that will have operations all over the world. All of you will have your pick of top executive jobs managing some aspect of the business."

"Sounds good to me!"

All eyes were on me. My thoughts were back on the words of Vernon last night. "Are you just concerned with making money?" Now, I questioned Darrell. Did he feel the same way as Vernon? Had he talked to Vernon or for that matter to Kendra about me just wanting to make money? The feeling from the morning returned, but more profound and penetrating this time. I needed to leave, I needed some alone time, I rose up without a word grabbed my bag and headed for the door.

"Hey man you okay," Big Mike asked?

"Yea…yea, just leaving for the day. If anyone of you needs me, hit me on my cell."

"Ay Shane, I didn't…………." Darrell began.

"No worries, you're just making me think. I will see you all tomorrow." And I left the office.

I didn't head home. I went to central park. The air was crisp and cool, and I just walked through the park alone with my thoughts. Did everyone think I was greedy including my wife? I always thought some greed was good because it kept you hungry and non-complacent, but it wasn't my intention to be overtaken with greed, and I have always been about giving back. It was the reason for Black Street initially- to create opportunity for those historically that had been denied. Wasn't that giving back? As Maria said, using black owned businesses and contractors in the operations of Black Street Capital, wasn't that giving back? Darrell wanted to build something. What the hell did he think Black Street Capital was- a five and dime store? My blood rose, more than it did last night from Vernon's attack.

I didn't like the feeling so I tried to clear my mind by just walking and not thinking. After about an hour I found a bench and sat. I watched people for the next hour, couples walking through the park, joggers, people walking their dogs, and cyclers riding through the park. I took in the beauty of the park, the green grass, the autumn leaves, and beautiful multi-colored trees. I fell into a tranquil sleep, until I was awakened by my cell phone vibrating in my coat pocket. It was Kendra.

"What's up Babe?" I answered.

"I was worried about you. Called your office and they told me you had left. Where are you?"

"In central park."

"What are you doing there?"

"Sleeping."

"Sleeping? Shane that is dangerous."

"I just needed to get some of my thoughts together."

"Thoughts about what? About last night……I told you, I'm sorry about last night and that won't ever happen again!"

"Do you think I'm only concerned with making money?"

Silence, then she chose her words carefully. "Money is not your only driver, but it is your major motivator."

"And that is a character flaw?" I retorted without letting her finish her complete thought.

"I didn't say that!"

"Then what are you saying? Making money is wrong?"

"No, there are just other things to aspire to other than to make money. Don't you think producing something and leaving a legacy has value."

"I see who's been in your ear." My phone buzzed. It was Darrell. "I got another call coming in I have to take."

"Shane!"

"We can finish this conversation at home later. I got to take this call."

"Okay." Kendra hung up the line.

"This is Shane."

"Shane, Darrell, you good."

"I will be."

"I got Jakar on the other line. He wanted to congratulate you on the World Textile deal."

"Okay, put him through."

"Okay, I will talk to you later, uh?"

"Yea."

Darrell put through the call from Jakar.

"Mr. Jackson, congratulations!"

"Thank you."

"You have done us all proud. Everyone here is thankful for your rewards."

"I'm glad everyone was satisfied with their return on investment?"

"Satisfied doesn't describe their feeling, more like ecstatic. Great job." Jakar tone changed from congratulatory to business. "What is your next move?

"Not sure,... There has been some debate about our next move."

"Is there dissension amongst you?"

"No, but there is disagreement.

"Disagreement is healthy, but can be difficult amongst partners. Is this disagreement about leadership or ideas?

"Ideas."

"So, I would assume the disagreement is about direction."

"Yes."

"Not knowing any details, I would say that sometimes in order to be a good leader; you have to be a good follower. This will be my last comment about this subject and I hope you take this one to heart. Sometimes we are pushed into greatness by the people around us."

I didn't reply. I was thinking about his words and how relevant they were to my life at this time. Vernon questioning my community service, Darrell pushing to do more than just make money, Kendra echoing those sentiments, and Maria, prompted my silence and Jakar to change topics.

"Shane I want you to look into some security for you and others."

'Security, why?"

"You've made a lot of money on your first deal, beyond the expectations of most, but not mine. . You are on the radar my friend."

"I see. I think I might take that suggestion to heart."

"I have one more topic to discuss with you before, I let you go."

"Yes, what is it?"

"I would like to come to the U.S. to visit on a Visa. Can you help me with that?"

"I'll see what I can do. I don't believe that will be a problem. I will put Big Mike on it right away, and we will be in touch."

"Thank you Shane, and once again congratulations."

Our conversation ended. I wasn't surprised by Jakar request for a visit to the states, and I think part of his purpose in investing in Black Street Capital, was gaining access to travel to and from the states, I had no problem with helping him. I viewed Jakar differently, I wanted to keep in close contact with him, more now than ever since the two episodes with this unidentified stranger I encountered in Africa and the States. More and more his words started to resonate with me. I had become more aware of my surroundings and the people in and around my general proximity. I hadn't reached the point of paranoia, but awareness, which would require me to take some precautions.

Time had slipped away; it was past 3:00 pm. I made my way home. Kendra was waiting by the door when I opened it. I was startled by her presence. She hugged me right when I walked through the door, and held me tight.

"I don't' want us to be at odds. Whatever you decide I will support you 100 percent. Never to worry because I will always have your back." She kissed me very tenderly. "We have more pressing issues anyway."

She grabbed my hand and led me to the bedroom. As I glanced at her walking in front of me I realized she was dressed in a very sensual outfit – white lingerie with short see through coat giving a perfect rear view of the thong underwear and her glistening dark tone skin. I gestured for her to make a three hundred and sixty degree turn, so I could get the full preview. She obliged much to my appreciation. I loved her dark skin and I loved her ass.

"The time has come for us to start working on that family we talked about," she said with a big smile.

"I'm with that!" Before I knew it she leaped into my arms and straddled my waist with her legs. The rest of the night was a blur. There were flashes in my mind of making love in the bed, and out of the bed, on the bedroom dresser, standing upright against the wall, bathroom sink, and finally in a bubble bath filled tub where we lay in bliss.

"Okay, I need you to be home by 6:00 pm every day until we accomplish our goal." Kendra said.

"I'm good with that!" I wanted to start a family as bad as she did.

We lay in the tub washing each other's body for quite some time, until hunger got the best of us. We agreed she would clean up the bathroom, and I would go downstairs and cook dinner, so we did.

We had a quiet dinner together, and soon after I dropped in a DVD of Sanford and Son. We watched several episodes filling our home with laughter.

More Problems

I arrived the next morning still mulling over conversations had about the direction of Black Street. Truth be told I wasn't feeling better about the situation and felt conversations had taken place without my presence. Big Mike and Charles didn't seem as surprised as me when Darrell articulated his vision for Black Street. Although Kendra and I had very romantic night, I still think she had questions about my motivations for Black Street, but as she said we had more important things to focus on which was starting a family, and I was all in for that.

Darrell arrived in the office shortly after me. As usual we greeted each other in the tradition of brotherhood way with a dap and a hug.

"How you doing?" Darrell asked.

"I've been better."

"Hey,... -

Just then Big Mike and Charles walk in the trade room.

"What's happening fellas? Charles declared.

Both Darrell and I were silent. We glanced at each other then back at Charles and Big Mike.

"Lock the door" I called out to Charles.

Charles walked and locked the front door. We all stood facing each other in the middle of the trade room. I started the conversation off.

"When I envisioned Black Street Capital, my vision was of an investment company on Wall Street. I've never desired, wanted, or needed anything else. Wall Street is the finance capital of the world, and I want to be where the action is. Capital markets are the heartbeat of the American economy. I like the pace of the markets, the hunt, and the competition. I thought you all were hunters like me. I've always wanted a career on Wall Street, and that's what I have, and I have no interest in owning a company settling in running and operating it on a daily basis.

"I am a hunter like you Shane, but owning something and leaving something in place for my kids is very appealing. Charles responded.

"You don't have any kids!"

"I'm talking about the future.

"Shane that is appealing. "Big Mike added.

"Got damn! Ya'll made up your minds?" I responded.

"We talked yesterday and decided that this would be the direction for Black Street." Darrell added.

"Yesterday?"

"Yes."

I thought to myself, and these are the men I call brothers. I was heated. I did everything to contain myself, but I had to let it be known the betrayal I felt at that moment.

"So behind my back you conspire to take the company in different direction than its original intent. I guess that's what I get for starting Black Street Capital and making my so called brothers equal partners only to be stabbed in the back."

"It wasn't like that!" Darrell rebutted.

"You don't mean that Shane! We are your brothers. Charles added.

Big Mike was shocked by my words the most. I think my words actually hurt him. "I can't believe you said that! If I hadn't heard it myself, I would have never believed you said it."

"Well believe it! And, as of this moment I'm out! I will get our accountants to cut me a check for my share of the equity in Black Street Capital, and I will go follow my dream, and leave the other bull shit to you all."

"You are not serious!" Darrell responded.

I walked out of the trade room to the amazement and astonishment of the others. Where was I going this time? Didn't have a destination in mind, I just wandered around Wall Street for about a half hour until it struck me to pay Ice a visit just to cool my jets and possibly purchase another brim. I took the subway to Harlem and walked directly to his hat shop.

When I entered he was busy, but no matter how busy he was Ice always took time out to greet me.

"What's up young blood?" He shouted from the back of the store where he was helping some customers.

I nodded my head to respond to his shout out. He strolled up to the front of the store gave me a dap and a hug.

"What are you doing here this time a day Shane?"

"Taking the day off just to smell the roses."

"Well where's Kendra? You shouldn't be smellin those roses by yo'self."

"She's at her shop, so I'm rolling solo today."

"Shit,.. sometimes a brotha needs to roll by his lonesome just to get his thoughts together. Go ahead kick back and let me handle this customers and will rap a taste after. So, that's what I did. I kicked back and checked out Ice's inventory, picked out two hats –these two much more casual than the others I purchased, read some magazines he had laying around the store, then finally settled into oversized leather chair to relax. After about 30 minutes the store cleared out, Ice locked the door behind last one to leave, came and took a seat a cross from me in the other leather chair. He handed me a cigar, lit mine then his.

"So what's happening young blood?"

I paused and looked at Ice, took a deep breathe, then spoke. "When you look at me what do you see?"

Ice looked surprised. "I don't see a brotha that cares what others think about him, so I'm surprised at your question. What is really going on young blood?"

"A difference of ideas at work."

"Between you and your homeboys?"

"Yes."

"What is it that they want?"

"Legacy."

"And you?"

"Money!"

Ice shakes his head ever so slightly moans in understanding. "Let me ask you this; are your homies older or younger than you?"

"Older."

"When man gets older, he starts to care less about filling his pockets with cheddar and more about leaving his mark in this life time. Your partners have reached that point in their lives. You haven't gotten there yet, but see you still young. You still want to hunt and catch prey."

I shook my head in agreement.

"You ever asked yourself why I stopped you in the streets that day, and asked you about the purchase of those tickets for the theater."

"You needed to sell the tickets."

"Yea, I did need to sell them, but I stopped you specifically because of where you worked and because I saw the hustler in you. When I talked to you a saw myself in you –we both were hunters." Now, ask yourself why I'm not on the street corners no more hustling.

"I figured you got tired of them streets."

"True, and I thought that was the main reason, but as I reflect back on those street hustling days. I wanted more. I wanted to leave my mark in a good legitimate way. Some might say a hat shop is not much of a mark, but its mine and one day can be left to my children."

"Didn't know you had children."

"Yea, got a daughter. You will meet her one day soon. She will be working her part-time as she does her college thing."

"I look forward to meeting her."

"Yea, she's a beautiful smart young sista. This hat shop allows me to give my daughter a job opportunity to make money while she makes her way through college. I couldn't have done that on the streets, at least not legitimate work. And, if that is part of the mark I leave, then this is something I can hold my head high about."

"That's good stuff Ice."

"The best stuff."

I shook my head in agreement. We chatted about another fifteen minutes, then I let the hat shop headed for Kendra's boutique which was about 20 minute walk from Ice's hat shop.

I walked through the doors of Kendra's boutique and to my surprise, and maybe it should not have been a surprise there was Darrell standing in the back of the boutique talking with Kendra. They both looked startled and concerned when I walked through the door. They actually took a step back from each other. I walked toward them.

"What's up Shane?" Darrell asked.

"Nothing."

"Where you been babe?" Kendra joined in.

"Walking."

I looked at Darrell, and then I looked at Kendra. Darrell looked uneasily as did Kendra, and my demeanor wasn't helping the situation. I wasn't angry, but clearly irritated.

"Hey, I need to get back to the office." Darrell announced.

I didn't acknowledge him. I kept my eyes on Kendra.

"Shane lets talk later."

"Yea."

"Talk to you later Kendra."

"Okay, Darrell thanks for stopping by."

Darrell walked out of the boutique. My stare told Kendra I wanted an explanation about Darrell presence in here.

"Shane, Darrell's concerned. He said you quit Black Street today. "

She was looking for a response, but I didn't give her one. I just kept looking at her.

"Why are you looking at me that way?"

I still didn't respond.

"The last time you didn't talk to me we ended up apart for months, and it all most ended us. Do you want to go through that again?"

Silence.

"I don't believe you sometimes. I love you, but Shane your ego is too much to take sometimes."

I left the boutique, and Kendra did not try to stop me. She was exacerbated. She was now reliving the days of old when she we apart because of her previous relationship with a white man. Uncertainty in her eyes was strong.

I walked home numb. I got scared. Was I repeating my same behavior that lost me Kendra before? One thing I did realize, I was a bad communicator, when things got difficult to face, I clamed up. I didn't have answers for my behavior. I just know, I felt alone and betrayed by everyone close to me including Kendra. I felt she should have told Darrell she didn't want to hear it, and whatever I had decided she was behind him 100%! Was that too much to ask of your wife? Instead she questions me indirectly about my decision to cash out of Black Street as if I had lost my mind. I didn't like that.

****

Kendra and I walked pass each other for the next two weeks in our home as if we were perfect strangers. The baby making plans were on hold as far as I could tell because no intimacy was taking place at all. She wasn't making love to a brotha, hugging a brotha, kissing a brotha, or even feeding a brotha. For the first couple days we were sharing the same bed, but we practically slept on the edges of the bed on our respective sides. I got fed up with pretending to sleep together and started sleeping in one of the guest bedrooms.

I was getting up each morning dressing to go to work, leaving out the house, going to Wall Street, reading the Wall Street Journal in its entirety, and sitting in a coffee house for hours on my laptop looking for companies as possible takeovers. The days weren't at all exciting because I didn't have my crew by my side, but I figured I'd hire a new crew just as employees and not equity partners. I ran into few Wall Street players when I was in the coffee house, but all were too shy to ask what I was doing there. I started to think if I really was going to leave Black Street; I needed to find office space for my new company, so that's what I did. I started looking for office space. This went on for the entire two weeks Kendra and I weren't speaking.

One day after my foe work day I made it home and something felt different. It hit me when I walked through the door. I called out to Kendra, but no answer. I slowly walked around the house and no one was home as far as I could tell, but when I made it to my study in the back room there behind my desk was my mother.

"Mom." I said.

No response, now I knew where I got that from. She just looked at me with disappointment. She shook her head in disappointment, and then spoke.

"Sit down son."

I did as I was told. I sat across from my mother facing her sitting behind my desk. She didn't look angry, but concerned. I know Kendra must have given her a call, and requested her visit for the purpose of talking to her son. Since Kendra was nowhere in sight, I knew this conversation would be one on one between my mother and I. It was good to see her, but I wish it was under better circumstances. She started her talk off with one word.

"Purpose,… we all must find our purpose in this life, and no one, and I mean no one can tell you what that purpose is. It's something that comes from within, but I can tell you what your purpose will use. It uses your god given talents and gifts. This is your journey and no one else's. People can and will have suggestions and opinions about the path you choose to travel, but at the end of the day it is your choice. You must find for yourself, your destiny. You are burdened with that task for your life. "

"Son you have surrounded yourself with good people, Darrell, Big Mike, and Charles are the salt of the earth. They mean you no harm, but just like you they are searching for their purpose, and it may not align with yours and that's alright. You all are men, and if you choose to go your separate ways doesn't mean those friendships die with the business relationship."

She paused and looked to me for understanding. I nodded that I indeed understood her message so far. She then continued.

"Kendra is good woman and only wants the best for you, but as I told you, I have told her only you can determine your destiny. She may have input as your wife, but you are commander and chief of our own ship, and the course you set to sail must come from you. Now know this, if you sail off course, it's okay. You are smart enough to correct your course if need be, and all of us must respect and honor your decision even if we don't agree with it."

I understood the message my mother was conveying clearly, and I agreed with her, but my only concern was that I never really thought about my purpose or destiny beyond working on Wall Street. My talents were clearly money and finance. How to use those talents to fulfill my purpose hadn't really occurred to me beyond what those talents really lent themselves which was making money. Just in my last two weeks of preparing to transition from Black Street I did some soul searching and played with the idea of a deeper purpose to my life beyond just making money. Thinking of Kendra and I starting a family weighed heavily on my mind, and the legacy I would be leaving for my kids.

Kendra and my mother meant the world to me, and I wanted to make them proud. To disappoint them would be a heavy burden on my heart. I didn't care what many people thought of me, but I did care about what they thought. I desired to be a good man, so Kendra could say with pride I have a good husband, and my mother could say I raised a good son.

I conveyed my concerns to my mother." I don't know what my purpose is."

"And that's okay. Your journey will reveal it to you in time….Let me ask you a question."

"Go right ahead."

"Is okay for you to help someone else reach or find their purpose in the process of finding your own?"

I knew exactly what she was getting at. "Yes."

She nodded her head in agreement, stood up, came from behind the desk and gave me a hug. It was a warm greeting that I needed at the time. Doesn't matter how old you get a mothers hug is always comforting and healing. We talked a little more. This time the conversation was lighter, and then I asked.

"Where's Kendra?"

"She's gone out so we could talk in private. She said she would bring some dinner back for all of us."

No sooner than my mother finishing her sentence, Kendra walks through the door."

"Hello." Kendra called out.

I walked out from my study alone.

"Hey stranger."

"Hey..Mr. Goodbar."

I smiled. Those words felt good hearing them from Kendra. I approached, she approached and we embraced. The heavy emotion of our two week in house standoff was released through our embrace. As moments passed the grasp of each other became more intense, and wasn't broken until my mother enter the hallway.

"I'm hungry."

Kendra broke away. "Yes Ms. Jackson, I have the food right here. I hope you like Chinese food."

"Yes, that sounds good."

"Lets eat in the kitchen." Kendra said.

My mother and I followed Kendra to the kitchen. Our conversation was upbeat over dinner mostly catching up with mother and trying to convince her to move to New York.

Darrell's Plan

Kendra told me that my Black Street crew was waiting on me. They hadn't made a move since we last spoke. They were awaiting me move to liquidate my equity share of Black Street. When no movement on that front ever occurred, they knew my decision wasn't final. So, they wanted to give me all the time I needed to sort my thoughts out. It seems that Kendra was in constant contact with them, specifically Darrell. I don't know how I really felt about that, but I knew it would be addressed in its own time.

I was anxious to get back to the office, so arrived Monday morning early I thought before anyone else had, but as I entered the trade room there was Darrell sitting deep in thought. He stood with a smile as walked I toward him.

"Shane, it's good to see you."

"Good to see you too." I had no idea if Kendra called him and gave him a heads up or not, but his demeanor indicated uncertainty.

"So what's happening man?"

"Well, I given your idea some thought about a buy and hold strategy, and at this time I can support that strategy."

"Aw man! You don't know how happy am to hear that. You had us all worried."

"I was worried also."

We gave each other a dap and hug.

Charles, Big Mike, and the others entered the trade room. At the sight of Darrell and me talking, they all gravitated to us.

"Are we all good?" Big Mike asked.

"Yes, we are good! Darrell has showed us the way to our future!" I answered.

"Okay, what's the plan?" Charles asked.

Darrell looked at me and I gave him the floor to lay out his plan. I knew from the passion he displayed yesterday he had something specific in mind. I also knew sometimes in order to be a good leader one needed to know how to follow. Darrell said two words that would change the course of all our lives.

"Blue Sky!"

Darrell described Blue Sky as in international, integrated energy company that operated in several business segments. The company explored, produced, refined, supplied, and transported petroleum. Blue Sky had about a million and half shares outstanding that traded at seventy dollars a share putting its market capitalization around one hundred billion dollars. Shared looks went around the room. Once we heard the number one hundred billion, even I entertained the thoughts of too big. In order to establish a majority position in Blue Sky we needed north of fifty billion dollars that was a tall order for anyone seeking a leveraged buyout. Our resources and banking relations were strong, especially since the World Textile deal, but fifty billion was enough to give any financier or investor reason for apprehension.

Darrell had done his homework, the majority stock holders in Blue Sky were the Shaltz family and Red Shaltz was the CEO and Chairman. Red Shaltz represented five generations of the Shaltz family who founded Blue Sky Oil Exploration from a single exploration mine in Texas, to an international business over the next five generations. But, over the last decade management has been less than stellar under Red Shaltz. Red Shaltz's nick name was Big Red. He was six foot three and weighing two hundred and sixty pounds. Silver gray hair surrounded the perimeter of his head from temple to temple Big Red resembled a throwback to the icons of the American economy. Despite his appearance, the word was he was a gentle giant and had a very likeable character, but his attempt to diversify the company into unrelated fields had stifled the growth of the company and drained its cash position which had translated to 25 billion of market cap lost in the last decade. Given the trajectory of the stock price over the last five years Blue Sky could be looking at another 10 billion dollar loss in market cap in the next three years. Stock holders had been jettisoning the stock like a jet dumping fuel.

With the poor performance of the stock and his other business ventures not paying dividends Big Red had been suffering from depression, blaming himself for the poor performance of the stock and the loss of net worth for shareholders. Blue Sky from all market pundits was a perfect takeover target by one of the larger oil exploration companies. However most were wary because no one knew the extent of Blue Sky's woes and felt the bottom hadn't hit yet, and most wanted Big Red to come with hat in hand asking to be taken over. Previous generations of the Shaltz family had been tough business men, some say even treacherous. Big Red's stubbornness was his downfall, He wouldn't divest from his latest losing venture into technology which disturbed the rest of the family and made them restless in the face of their shrinking wealth. The family had started to line up against Big Red and was ready for a sell. To credit Darrell's research, he had information about the family already consulting GPG about selling the company, and Big Red flipping his lid when he found out.

There was dissension in the family that controlled fifty five percent of the company. Darrell was more optimistic about Blue Sky's future than most. He pointed out despite the misadventures Blue Sky's core business was still profitable, and he felt with our connections in Nigeria we could expand Blue Sky's operations to the continent of Africa easily. Darrell felt if expansion into Africa went well, instead of a hundred billion dollar company, Blue Sky would be a two hundred billion dollar company. He was talking double in market value, and his time horizon was about ten years.

I liked everything I heard from Darrell and was intrigued by Blue Sky. This deal would take a lot more research and work on our part, but everyone seemed to be excited by the possibilities. We decided to move forward with more research and analysis. I broke down the team along the same lines as I did with World Textile –Big Mike, contracts and legal, White-Chocolate and Maria – financial analysis, Charles and Soul Train, C-Walk – market research, and

Darrell and I would talk to potential financiers and investors, and map out an overall takeover strategy of Blue Sky.

****

For the next several months we did nothing but work on Blue Sky. Sixteen hour work days became the norm. Once we started dissecting the company it was much larger than we first thought. We needed help; our group was too small to do a proper and thorough analysis of the company. Instead of contracting out a consulting company I decided to bulk up Black Street with additional personnel, and the only person I could think of for getting the best professionals was Betty. I offered her a job as Director of HR at Black Street Capital. Her first day was emotional for us all. When she entered the trade room, a homecoming commenced. Everyone greeted her and welcomed her to Black Street Capital. Betty hugged each of us and thanked us for the opportunity.

"No reason to thank us! You are partly responsible for all us coming together. If it wasn't for your eye for talent, we would have never known Soul Train, C-Walk, Maria, and White Chocolate. We need you to work that same magic you worked when we built the Black Street trading desk. The only difference now, it's for Black Street Capital." I said.

Tears fell from her eyes. "This is the second time you save my career from the depths of despair. I don't know what to say, but thank you. I mean that from my heart. I thank you, and my son thanks you." Betty quickly gave me the tightest hug, and then released me. She left the trade room and went into the office we had set up for her amongst the private offices outside the trade room.

Betty had us fully staffed within two months. We rented additional space in the building and ended up with twenty five full time employees. I told Betty once we acquired Blue Sky, she would take the director position of Human Resources over the entire company. She was shocked and overwhelmed.

It wasn't until we had fully separated out each of Blue Sky's business segments and fully understood the business, products, market, and financial structure that we took a position in the company. When we did, it didn't go unnoticed and it wasn't our desire to enter the room quietly. We took a six percent position which required registration with the Securities and Exchange Commission. A two billion dollar stock purchase into a publicly traded company got the attention of everyone on Wall Street. After that purchase our phones were inundated with calls from media and request for interviews to talk about our intentions in taking a position in Blue Sky – our reputation preceded us and the word on the street was our intentions were to do the same with Blue Sky, as we did with World Textile, we did nothing to dispel the rumors. Our standard response companywide was no comment, nothing more nothing less.

Blue Sky management, especially Big Red didn't appreciate the implications of us taking a significant position in the company. He adamantly denied the company was up for sell, and he was well aware of Black Street's accomplishments with World Textiles, and vowed the grandest of fights if our intentions were to take over and liquidate the business his family built with five generations of sweat. Other family members were muted in their responses to the media, just saying they were not in the know and as far as they were concerned the company wasn't for sale. The media continued to hound us with phone calls, but could not penetrate our standard mantra. Then a call came into my direct line on the trading desk. It was Mackey Sr. He wanted a sit down, but he wanted it informal over dinner. I agreed to the meeting the next night at a little Peruvian restaurant in upper Manhattan. We both agreed to bring our wives.

Kendra and I hadn't been out to a restaurant in several months because Kendra was very picky about what she ate given she was six months pregnant with twins. We had been home bodies since we got the news of her pregnancy. We both were excited and nervous about the new additions to our family. Like every expectant couple, we were excited about having babies in the house and nervous about keeping them safe and healthy. We removed every potential impediment in the house we thought was a potential hazard while Kendra was pregnant, then baby proofed the house right after. It took some convincing on my part to get Kendra to agree to a night out, but once I told her who we would be having dinner with and why, she agreed.

When we arrived at the restaurant Mr. Mackey was already seated with his wife. The Hostess led Kendra and I to their table. Both stood and gave us a warm greeting. Kendra's pregnancy made the introductions much easier and comfortable. Mr. Mackey had never met Kendra, and I had never met his wife. Mrs. Mackey was taken by Kendra and her pregnancy.

"Is this your first?" She asked.

"Yes, they are our first."

"They?"

"Yes, we are expecting twins?"

Mr. Mackey looked at me and gave me a pat on the back. "Congratulations Shane! A man is not complete without a family." He shook my hand.

"Thank you!

Kendra and I sat down, Kendra next to Mrs. Mackey and I next to Mr. Mackey. Mr. Mackey and I left the women to their own conversation mostly about the baby- Kendra was not lost for words when it came down to talking about her pregnancy and Mrs. Mackey seem to be truly excited at the sight of Kendra's pregnancy.

Mr. Mackey and I started off our conversation with small talk about some of my old colleagues at GPG and some other executives on Wall Street. He first told me about Ted having to come back and baby sit his book after travelling with his wife around the world because his nephew Steven proved to be more incompetent then first expected. How Emmy – the young lady whose offer I rescinded turned out to be a real asset for GPG and how she had moved from sales to an underwriting team at GPG. According to Mr. Mackey Timothy fell into his old ways once I departed from GPG. I knew right then without any explanation from Mr. Mackey that he threw Tim back into sales and away from his strength –Research. He never mentioned me hiring Betty away from GPG, and he never mentioned his son Junior. After the small talk he wasted no time getting to the meat of the matter.

"I see you have taken a significant position in Blue Sky. What are your intentions?"

Mr. Mackey pulled no punches! He was a savvy veteran and obviously had an interest in Blue Sky. He knew my intentions could only be one of two things, money through a buy and liquidate strategy or a buy and hold. Any misdirection or misrepresentation would be seen right through, so I laid my hand on the table.

"Buyout."

"With the intentions of a sale?"

"Not this time. My interest is more purposeful?

"How so?"

"Instead of just being a broker in this economy and making money, I have a desire to be a player in the world economy- a part of the business commerce and political landscape."

He just looked at me, almost studying me as if he didn't recognize who was sitting beside him. He nodded his head in the affirmative to say he understood. I continued.

"I found a couple of things out about myself while working for GPG. I was motivated by trying to create opportunity for other African-American candidates, but more than anything else my driving force was money, and now I desire to be more. I never really understood, no matter the progress I made at GPG, why my mother always expected more? She never articulated what that more was. I think she wanted me to find that more on my own, and Blue Sky is that more for me."

No words still from Mr. Mackey. He put his hand on my shoulder, and said in a soft tone. "I understand." He paused, took a sip of his wine. "Titan Industries has interest in Blue Sky, but you drew first blood while they were still digesting the World Textile deal. They are prepared to offer you five times the stock price plus and an incentive which would cash you out a little over One billion dollars to relinquish your shares in Blue Sky to them. "

In my old mindset I would have closed the one billion dollar deal before I left that dinner, but even that amount of money couldn't move me from my new found vision.

"Not interested." I said calmly.

"From our little chat here I didn't think you would accept the offer, but I had to put the offer out there on my client's behalf."

"Understood."

For the rest of the dinner Mr. Mackey did not mention business again. We enjoyed the company of our wives, drank a little more wine, and had some desert. It actually was a pleasant evening, and I got to see another side to Mr. Mackey that I think very few discover about him. He was very charismatic person in his own way, warm and caring toward his wife. He had a world view on issues, conservative, but compassion for those who were less fortunate.

Kendra and I parted company with the Mackeys after dinner. Our driver in a black Lincoln Towne car was waiting for us outside the restaurant. On the drive home Kendra cuddled close to me. "I enjoyed the dinner and the conversation. I would have to say Mr. Mackey was not as I thought."

"I've known him for some years now, and he is not as I thought either."

We both giggled. Kendra snuggled closer and fell asleep on the ride home.

Changes

We continued our pursuit of Blue Sky. We had some informal conversations with Big Red over the phone which weren't at all cordial. He was more than irritated with our courtship of Blue Sky and vowed a fight to the end. And, what complicated our takeover of Blue Sky even more was the bidding of Titan Industries for Blue Sky. Titan stepped up their pursuit of Blue Sky, and they had deeper pockets than us, but what evened the playing field for us temporarily was the reluctance of Big Red to sell Blue Sky to anyone. He managed to keep the family together with the not for sale mantra, but there were cracks in the armor from the beginning and those cracks were getting wider.

Black Street and Titan had accumulated a fifteen percent interest in Blue Sky. The street was buzzing about the competition between Black Street and Titan to take over Blue Sky. They were calling it "The Battle for Dominance". Dominance was the appropriate word to describe Blue Sky because its market share was the largest amongst all oil exploration and refineries in the world. Blue Sky had deeper pockets than Titan and could hold off any hostile takeover for an eternity, but some of the family members wanted out and there in lied their weakness. Our strategy was to hammer at that weak link until it broke. Titan took on the same strategy.

Given that Titan was already in the oil business, all the bets were on Titan to win out. Our pockets weren't as deep as Blue Sky's or Titan's. Our investors and partners would not be in for a long protracted fight, and we might be forced to sell our shares in Blue Sky, take a profit and payout the proceeds to our investor base. This potential scenario wasn't out of the realm of reason. We still hadn't secured all the financing needed to take a controlling interest in the company at fifty one percent. We were currently fifteen billion dollars in with reserve just short of another ten billion. Darrell and I were working tirelessly trying to get the financing in place, but the street made it hard with all the publicity betting against us. Banks became squeamish to commit to any more than they already had and our private investor base was already to their limit. Our options were dwindling, but we forged ahead never succumbing to the notion we would not succeed in our takeover of Blue Sky.

Darrell, Charles, Big Mike, and I never took our eyes off the prize and never changed our state of mind for success. As we continued to personify success without a doubt, it resonated with all around us, and fed into our purpose and mission of buying Blue Sky. No one complained about the hours or the work load. Black Street had become the ideal work place for African Americans, so if someone wanted to leave, he or she knew there were fifty qualified professional black men and women waiting to take their place. Betty would get daily inquiries about job opportunities at Black Street.

Black Street was now recognized as a powerful player on Wall Street, and with power came change in all of us. We all walked and talked with just a bit more confidence and arrogance than usual. But, Charles took it to a new level. Charles had always been somewhat of a comic, but some of his jokes to the others in the trade room had become mean spirited and condescending. He also became a skirt chaser, late nights at the hot spots – restaurants, bars, night clubs, and strip clubs. One day Charles arrived at work with the same suit, shirt, and tie he had on the previous day. He looked worn out and suffered from a mild hangover. I wasn't close enough to him this particular morning to smell him, but others were.

"You smell like pussy!" Soul Train exclaimed.

"I smell like your mama's pussy, you fat fuck." Charles retorted.

"You smell like some sour pussy. Like you got a hold of a bad piece, you might want to get checked out!" C-Walk added.

There was a roar around the trade room and didn't sit well with Charles, especially when White-Chocolate almost fell out of his chair with laughter. It didn't take long for Charles to single him out.

"Look who's laughing a mutha fucka who has the finest wife on Wall Street, but she walks around here like she ain't been fucked right in years. You little dick mutha fucka!"

There was nothing funny about Charles' comments, and White Chocolate reacted violently charging toward Charles only to be intercepted by Big Mike. Charles stood up surprised at the reaction of White-Chocolate.

Maria calmed down her husband and led him back to his trading desk. She looked at Charles in disgust." You bastard," She yelled!

"Charles, let's talk." I said.

I led and Charles followed me out of the trade room followed by Big Mike and Darrell. We went inside one of the private offices and closed the door.

"What the fuck was that all about?" I asked Charles

"What? I was just having a little fun."

"Fun? That was not fun what happen in there!" Darrell said sternly.

"We joke a lot in there, but you crossed the line, and what was that little dick crack about?" I rejoined.

Charles was quiet.

"Damn man, what happen?"

Charles took a breath. "One day after work, Maria and I went for drinks at some little hole in the wall bar not too far from the street."

"Where was White-Chocolate?" Big Mike asked.

"He was travelling with Shane and Darrell when they made their first presentation to the Blue Sky Board of Directors….. Anyway Maria and I were throwing them back and the alcohol took its effect. She talked about how White-Chocolate was coming up short in the bed –I'm talking short in size and duration, and how she has to use dildos and shit to get herself off."

"Get the fuck outta here!" Big Mike couldn't believe what he was hearing. "Did you hit it?"

"No, I wanted to, but she wasn't having any of that. But I do know who she wants to give it to."

"Who?" Big Mike asked.

Charles raised his arm slowly pointing in my direction.

"Ain't happening!" I blurted out quickly and firmly.

Just then my cell phone rang. It was Kendra. "Hey, what's up?"

"It's time." She said calmly.

"Time?"

"My water broke."

"AAAAHHHHHHHHHH!" I yelled in joy. "Is your mother there with you?"

"No, Carmen is here and she will drive me to the hospital. I will meet you there.

"Okay babe, I'm on my way!"

I hung up the phone and my three buddies were staring at me.

"Kendra's having the babies. She's headed to the hospital now"

They all yelled and jumped on me in the office. We all fell over onto the floor in joy. We picked ourselves up from the floor and ran out the office like elementary students running out of class for recess. As we rushed into the elevator 1, someone was getting out of elevator 2 walking toward our receptionist. I didn't pay much attention because my mind had already left the office.

When we arrived at the hospital, they had already taken Kendra into labor. I had to clean up real quick and put a hospital gown over my clothes to join Kendra in the labor room. When I entered, she smiled but was in obvious pain, but she still looked beautiful. Carmen was there with her, but left when I entered the room. After three hours of pushing, sweat, and pain, Kendra delivered our baby boy and girl –Miles and Monique. They were healthy and vibrant. At first sight of my babies, my heart melted, and I knew how blessed I was. Just as I felt when I married Kendra, I desired to be the best husband I could be. Now with my twins, I desired to be the best father I could be for my children.

After the doctors cleaned and checked out the twins, they handed them to Kendra and me for some private time before they let anyone enter the room. I had my family and at that moment nothing was more important. Kendra looked at me and Monique and then to Miles and tears streamed from her eyes. I sat next to her and Miles with Monique.

"I love you! You did it Kendra. There's no way I can repay you for our two blessings." I gently kissed her on her forehead.

After about fifteen minutes, visitors entered the room. It was Kendra's family members – mother, father, brother, and cousins along with Carmen. I left the room to celebrate with my boys. When I walked into the waiting room, they were there all smiles with cigars in hand. We didn't light them, but we celebrated like frat brothers crossing over the burning sands!

"Bring me the boy! Uncle Mike got a lot to share with my nephew."

"Damn, Shane you got a wife and kids. You've come a long way since our days at Jordan. I just want to say, I got love for you, and I'm glad I'm a part of your life, and I'm proud and happy to call you my brother."

"I feel the same way Charles, but do me a favor."

"Anything!"

"Make it straight with White-Chocolate and Maria."

"You got it! Can you do me a favor?"

"Anything" I repeated.

"Can you hook a brotha up with Carmen?"

"You need me to hook you up? I said surprisingly.

"Yea, he needs some help when comes down to that sista. In her presence his swag disappears, and his tongue betrays him. It's a pitiful sight." Big Mike said.

"I'll put in a good word."

I looked over toward Darrell and tears had swelled up in his eyes. "You good?"

"Not to be condescending, but I am proud of you! You have a beautiful spirited woman and now you have a family. God has truly blessed you, and I couldn't be happier for you."

I stood and gave Darrell a dap and a hug. The celebration continued until a nurse came into the waiting room and told me Kendra had requested our presence. We headed to the room to join the rest of the family to share in the birth of my children.

*****

I took the next two weeks off, to help take care of my kids and assist Kendra in her recovery. Even though I wasn't in the office Darrell gave me daily updates on our progress. Charles, Big Mike, and Darrell came by to visit after work and assisted where ever they could. Darrell made the most visits. He really had taken to my family and had been there for Kendra and I, assisting with errands, cleaning up, and helping watch over the kids. One day Darrel came by as I was on my way out to go to pick up groceries. He stayed with Kendra and the kids while I went out.

As I made my way to the store I decided to go by Big Mike's house. He lived only two blocks away. Big Mike had bought a brown stone. I hadn't been there very often, but I was with him when he closed the deal. Once I pulled up in front of his home, I got out of my car and knocked on his door. He didn't answer, but I got the distinct feeling someone was watching me through the peep hole. So, I spoke out.

"Big Mike, open the door it's Shane."

No response, I stood there for a few seconds then walked down the stairs leading down to my car.

As I got to the bottom stair, Big Mike's door opened and there stood a woman in the door way about five foot seven, brown skin sista, short cropped hair cut dyed a reddish brown, and she was wearing form fitting jeans and a white blouse. She was very attractive.

"Shane?" she asked.

"Yes." I answered.

She took a couple steps back in the doorway and gestured for me to come in while she held the door open. I walked back up the stairs and entered Big Mike's home as this woman closed the door behind me.

"Is Big Mike home?"

"No, he has gone out to the store?"

"If you don't mind me asking, who are you?"

"I'm Adriona, Big Mike's girlfriend."

"Girlfriend?" I questioned.

"Yes, it may be surprising that Mike would have a girlfriend, you and the rest of his friends know nothing about, but I know all about you all. He does nothing, but rant and rave about all of you."

"How long have you and Big Mike been together?"

"About a year."

"A year!" I uttered. I was puzzled why would Big Mike not even mention to us he had a girlfriend. It was as if he was trying to hide her or was he embarrassed by her. She was a beautiful woman, any man would be proud to have under his arm. "I don't understand why….do you live here with Big Mike?"

"Yes, for about six months now. I'm really glad I got to finally meet you. Hopefully, soon I can meet your wife and your new baby girl and boy.

"Mike told you about Miles and Monique?"

"Yes, he so proud to be an uncle to your kids."

"My kids are fortunate to have him as an uncle."

An awkward moment of silence came between us. She was hesitant to speak her next words, but they revealed her meekness. "I don't mean to be rude, but Mike will be back soon. Is it okay if I asked you to leave?"

I paused, looked at her and fear and trepidation filled her face. "Yes, I understand." I replied.

She opened door and there stood Big Mike grappling for his keys.

"What's up Big Mike?"

He was surprised. I could see he was clearly disturbed by my presence in his home standing next to Adriona.

"What's up Shane?" A muted response, his eyes went directly to Adriona. Her eyes and head were dropped downward to the floor.

Big Mike walked in, gave the bags in his hands to Adriona. She took the bags into the kitchen.

"Shane lets go into the parlor."

We walked into the parlor which was just off from the kitchen. I could see Adriona nervously putting the groceries into the cupboards and refrigerator. Big Mike didn't offer me a seat. He stood across from me in the room anxious and nervous.

"What are you doing here?" He asked in an irritated tone.

"What?... Man I came by to see if you wanted to go to the store with me to pick up some groceries for the family. I knocked on your door and met Adriona. She tells me she's your girlfriend."

"How long you been here?"

I didn't understand the line of questioning. What was I doing there? How long had I been here?

"Big Mike this is Shane. Why are you asking me silly shit?"

Just then Adriona entered the parlor.

"Mike it's not his fault…." She uttered.

"Not my fault, what the hell is going on here Big Mike?"

He turned from her to me angrily, then back to her. "Go upstairs I'll deal with you later."

Without another word Adriona went upstairs. Big Mike turns back to me. "Shane I'm going to have to ask you to leave my home."

"Leave your home? Did I step into the twilight zone? Did you fall and bump your head. What the fuck are you talking about Big Mike?"

"Shane, leave my fucking house!" He turned and went upstairs.

I was dumb founded by Big Mikes behavior. I watched him storm up the stairs, then heard him slam his bedroom door, and he began to berate, reprimand, and accuse Adriona of the most asinine things. I crept up the stairs to have a closer listen.

"Why did you let him in my home?" he yelled.

"I wanted to meet him." She replied in a pleading voice.

"Why did you want to meet Shane?"

"You talk about him all the time, and how much you love him as a brother, and how he helped you change your life around. Why wouldn't I want to meet the man, who has had such an impact in my man's life?"

I moved closer to the door to clearly hear their exchange.

"Did you fuck him?"

"What? Mike you can't be serious asking me that type of question."

I hear a loud thud against the walls, and the walls shook!

"Just answer the fucking question. Did you fuck Shane?" He asked in a tormented voice.

I knocked on the bedroom door. "Big Mike let me talk to you."

"Shane, I told to leave my fucking house." I heard footsteps pounding toward the door, and before I knew it Big Mike flung the door open and grabbed me by my shirt and coat, then commenced to push me up against the wall. "Why can't you do as I wish in my own house man?"

I could see Adriona standing in the room terrified. I pushed back which enraged Big Mike, and he began pushing me harder against the wall. He was much stronger than me so, he was winning the pushing contest. With my back against the wall I tried to reason with him.

"You are not making sense man. Why would you accuse her of such a thing? Why would a thought like that even cross your mind concerning me?"

"Shut up Shane! I asked you to leave and that is just what you'll be doing."

I heard Adriona scream, "Mike don't." The next thing I knew Big Mike swung me around to his left one hundred and eighty degrees and my legs hit the stair case banister which knocked me off balance, then everything went black.

****

When I awoke from the darkness, I was in a hospital bed with the top of my head wrapped in bandages and Kendra by my side. Darrell and Charles were in the room too. My head was pounding, and I didn't feel like myself, my mind was hazy, something was missing. I surveyed the room, Big Mike was absent. My first words were to Kendra.

"What happen to me?"

"You don't remember?"

I paused to try and think, but my mind was blank as a fresh white sheet of paper. "No….I don't."

Darrell left the room.

"We don't really know, but it looks like you had some sort of accident over Big Mike's house. He called the ambulance to bring you to the hospital, then he called us to meet you guys hear. Baby, you don't remember anything?"

I shook my head no. "Where are the kids?"

"Carmen is watching them at the house."

Darrell came back into the room with the doctor. He asked everyone to leave the room while he examined me. He checked my motor skills, check my blood pressure, my heart, then asked me a series of questions. I answered best I could given my condition. The doctor called Kendra back into the room.

"Your husband has suffered a concussion. He has a temporary loss of his short-term memory, it may return in time, but it's not guaranteed. He doesn't show any signs of brain damage or internal bleeding in his cranium."

"Thank god!" Kendra responded.

The doctor continued. "His cat scan came back clean. He will need plenty of rest for the next few days, and then he should be back on his feet close to a hundred percent."

"Thank you doctor." Kendra shook his hand.

When the doctor left the room, Darrell and Charles came back in. Kendra filled them in on what the doctor had said. They both let out a sigh of relief.

"Where is Big Mike?" I asked.

"He's all torn up over this man. He is out in the waiting room. He will be relieved you are going to be alright. I'll go out and bring him in." Charles left to get Big Mike.

I was tired, dosing in and out of consciousness. Kendra and Darrell sat silently in the room, Kendra by my bedside and Darrell on the couch at the other end of the room. Big Mike entered the room with Charles. Big Mike walked on the other side of the bed opposite Kendra.

"How you doing?" He asked.

"I'm going to be alright. Thanks for looking out for me, and calling the family."

Big Mike was hesitant. "Yea…yea." He shook his head up and down. He then stepped back and took a seat on the couch beside Darrel.

I fell asleep. They released me from the hospital the next day. I was happy to get home and was anxious to see the little ones. I worried about scaring them with this big bandage across my head, but I think they were too small to really notice the difference in Daddy's appearance. For the next couple of days I rested and played with my baby girl and boy. Just as I started to come into my own, I got a visit from Darrell and Charles with some disturbing news.

Public sentiment had started to turn against us in our bid for Blue Sky because of my head injury. There had been all kinds of preposterous stories circulating about my health; ranging from I had suffered brain damage to I was in a coma. We quickly hired a PR firm to handle the negative publicity, and they arranged for me to do a series of interviews so the public, investors, and board members of

Blue Sky could see my health was not of concern. Interviews were set up with all the major networks and some business news networks. The interviews went well and we were able to squash the unfounded reports. I returned to work to a warm welcome. It felt good to be back, and I felt reenergized.

Big Mike was the only one who seemed uneasy around me. He greeted and welcomed me back, but there was a bit of nervousness in his demeanor. I wondered why. Why would he show signs of discomfort, when he is around me? I didn't dwell on it too long; I kept my eye on Blue Sky. We still needed to secure the additional financing to buyout Blue Sky. Darrell and I were working on it feverishly. We wanted to talk to Jakar. I had secured a Visa for him sometime back, but he hadn't taken the opportunity to visit the states yet. When we called and asked him to come to the states for a visit, he was more than happy to oblige.

A Visitor Arrives

It was tumultuous times for Black Street, just as Jakar was arriving in the U.S. Titan Industries was ramping up their pressure on the Blue Sky family members to sell their controlling interest, and there were signs that their persuasion was starting to break the ranks from Big Red. The deciding factor was money. Titan was willing and ready to give all stock holders a twenty five percent premium above market value. With our financing in question there was no way we could compete. Morale was low around the office because we were losing the battle. Darrell and I knew we needed a miracle to pull this off, but first we needed to get the financing in place.

We put Jakar and his two associates in a five star hotel in Manhattan provided them with a car and driver that escorted them to any place they desired to see. Jakar called me on the trading desk.

"First class all the way my brother! I love it! We have been treated like kings since arriving here."

"I'm glad you are happy with the accommodations."

"So, when will I see you my brother?"

"After market hours today, we'll have your driver bring you over to the offices on Wall Street and give you a tour. Then dinner if that's okay."

"That sounds fine Shane, see you later. I think my associates and I will take in some more sites.

"Enjoy."

I hung up the phone. I happened to glance downward and noticed a letter in between my desk and Darrell's that had slid down on ground. I use my letter opener to reach the letter and slide it out. On the envelope Shane Jackson was written, nothing else. I opened the letter and it read.

"Hello Mr. Jackson, my name is Brendham. It is important that we talk. CIA and FBI are watching you."

Had Jakar words been given life? I wanted to know who this Brendham character was. I asked around the trade room about who left this letter on my desk. No one knew. So, I went out to the reception area to ask the receptionist if she knew about this letter.

"Yes, I put it on your desk."

"Who gave it to you?"

"A man, I don't remember his name, but it was the day you rushed out of the office when your wife went into labor. The gentleman asked for you by name, and I told him he just missed you. He left the letter, and I put it on your desk."

I was silent, who was this Brendham and what did he want from me? Was it just to tell me I was being watched by the government?

"Did I do anything wrong Mr. Jackson?"

"No, not at all thank you." I walked back into the trade room deep in thought. Darrell was the first to notice my state of mind. He walked over to where I was standing.

"You alright Shane?"

Big Mike and Charles noticed Darrell and I standing by the trade room door. They both walked over.

"What's up?" Charles asked.

I said nothing, just gestured for them to follow me out of the trade room. I went into a private office. They followed.

"Close the door behind you."

I handed them the letter.

"What the hell is this?" Charles asked.

"What does it mean?" Darrell added.

"Don't know." I answered. "This was handed to our receptionist the day Kendra went into labor. She put it on my desk, but it slipped between Darrell's and my desk. I just discovered it today."

"There's no number or contact information. Was there a card in the letter?" Big Mike asked.

"No."

"What the hell are we supposed to do with this?" Charles asked.

"I think we wait for this Brendham guy to contact us."

"Do you think this has anything to do with the arrival of Jakar?" Darrell asked.

"The letter was delivered more than a few weeks ago, so the timing doesn't match. But, the words of Jakar are more profound now that we have received this message."

"Why would the CIA or the FBI be watching us? We are just businessmen." Charles exclaimed.

I was deep in thought.

"What are you thinking Shane?" Darrell asked.

"Well, my mind is still cloudy about some past events, but I do remember seeing a stranger at my wedding in Africa."

"There were a lot of strangers at your wedding in Africa." Charles stated.

"Yea, you're right, but his guy I saw wasn't African. He was African-American."

"How did he look?" Big Mike asked.

"Late fifties, salt and pepper hair, medium build and height. He had a narc look to him, someone trying to fit in, but couldn't. Then I thought I saw this same guy at Julian's when we were celebrating the World Textile deal."

"Why didn't you say something to us?"

"I wasn't sure, because when I went to go confront the guy, he was gone. And, I didn't see him again after that."

"Man, this is getting weirder by the moment. What are we going to do?" Charles asked.

"Wait."

"Looks like your memory is coming back about certain events, what about your accident at Big Mikes House?" Darrell asked.

"What the hell? I told y'all that was an accident and you can't let it go." Big Mike barked out.

"Big Mike, Kendra is concerned about what took place. She's not getting any answers from you, and Shane doesn't remember.

Whatever took place landed Shane in the hospital, so there is concern."

"Yea, what happened Big Mike? You guys get drunk and were horsing around?" Charles rejoined.

"No," Big Mike said agitated!

"Aye y'all leave Big Mike alone. He said it was an accident. What does it matter how the accident happened, it happened. I still don't have any recollection about it, but I'm happy I didn't suffer more than a concussion."

They all nodded their head in agreement.

"Now, we have more pressing matters. Jakar will be arriving in the office around five; we do a short tour and have dinner. Darrell have White-Chocolate prepare some summary financials to show Jakar. We are going to need his assistance in securing this last piece of financing."

"I'm on it." Darrell responded. Darrell and Charles left the room and as Big Mike was leaving I stopped him.

"Close the door, I want to chat with you in private."

He closed the door and turned and faced me.

"How you doing?"

"I'm alright?"

"How's Adriona?"

"I thought you….."

"It started to come back to me in bits and pieces a few days ago."

"Aye Shane, I am ashamed, I'm sorry, I never wanted to hurt you and what took place was an accident."

"I believe you…. I'm going to tell you what I remember and I want you to fill in the rest."

"I can do that."

"I arrived at your place met your woman Adriona, a beautiful sista. She let me in your home while you were grocery shopping. You came back just when she asked me to leave, and accused both of us of a ten minute affair while you were away. That is how long I was in your home before you arrived."

"Ay dog."

I put my hand up for him to hold off on any responses.

"Then you demanded that I leave your house, and when I didn't you tried to force me. Can you tell me what happen after you grabbed me?"

Looking dejected and shameful, Big Mike did just that. He told me how my leg hit his banister rendering me helpless hurling me down the stairs, and how he tried to hang on to me to prevent my fall. When I hit the bottom of the stairs there was blood coming from a gash on the top of my head. I was out cold.

"I was in shock. Adriona had to pull me out of it. I thought I had killed you. She called 911, and wanted to come to the hospital too, but I made her stay at home."

"Man, what is up with you?"

"I'm sorry Shane, not in a million years would I wish to hurt you."

"I know that Big Mike. I'm talking about you and your lady friend."

Big Mike could not look me in the face when it came down to his behavior regarding Adriona.

"I don't know Shane. I love her, and the thought of losing her or her being with someone else drives me insane."

"Why are you entertaining such thoughts? Has she given you reason to?"

"No, she is the most caring and faithful woman you will ever meet."

"So, why so possessive?"

No answer

"Big Mike, if you attempt to keep a strong hold on Adriona, you will lose her. And, if you don't let her go when she wants to leave, it will end tragically. Let me ask you something, and I want you to be totally honest. Know I will never judge you."

"Go ahead."

"Have you ever hit Adriona?"

"No!"

"That's good, but I do think you are on the verge of crossing that line. She is frightened of you which is not good. You want your woman to respect you, but never to be afraid of you."

"You're right! What should I do? I'm out of control, but I don't want to lose her."

"You need to find professional help."

"What?"

"Yes, I will help you find a competent and confidential Psychologist.

Big Mike and I continued our conversation and he opened up even more about his insecurities and his relationship with Adriona. How he wanted to start a family with her and take care of her the rest of his life. How he dreamed of our kids playing together and us taking family vacations together. As close as Big Mike and I were, that day our friendship grew closer. He trusted me to help him with this situation, and couldn't stop apologizing for the incident that occurred at his home. I promised him what took place at his home would never be revealed through my lips. I did tell him to truly make it up to me. He would have to bring Adriona over to the house for dinner to meet Kendra and the kids. He agreed.

Big Mike and I left the private office and returned to the trade room. The market was near its close. The office was emptying. Charles, Big Mike, Darrell, and I remained and waited on the arrival of Jakar.

****

Jakar was truly impressed with our office space on Wall Street, excitement and amazement would be an understatement in describing Jakar's mood when he visited Wall Street. Our conversations with him and his associates were genuine and jovial. After our tour of the offices, we settled in the trade room arranging chairs in a circular fashion in the middle of the room to talk business. Our main concern was securing another fifty billion to keep us in the race for Blue Sky. Jakar had been kept up to date on our progress and was not concerned so much about Titan Industries offering up a twenty five percent premium to shareholders which would cash us out from the Blue Sky deal with a significant profit for our efforts.

"We are not walking away from this deal. The twenty five percent over the market value doesn't interest us. The goal is the complete ownership of Blue Sky, the same as Titan." Darrel said.

"A four billion dollar return on a fifteen billion dollar investment is nothing to thumb your nose at!" Jakar returned.

"We are not thumbing our nose, but we are in this deal to close it, and the only way we know how to close is a complete takeover. Anything less would be considered failure." I expressed.

"And we are not into failing. It's not a good feeling." Charles added.

Jakar sat back in his seat and looked at his associates. "These guys are intense."

"Is there any other way to be when you are passionate about something?" Big Mike interjected.

"I guess not, and I guess that's why you guys are playing with the big boys on Wall Street." Jakar responded. "Is there some place my friends can spend some time while we finish up our discussion?"

"Yes." I told Charles to take them to the conference room and turn on the flat screen and let them watch whatever. Charles escorted Jakar associates to the conference room.

We continued our conversation. "It is a question of legacy. We not only want this for us, but for future generations to aspire to. Just as Reginald Lewis was the first African-American to control a billion dollar company in Beatrice International, which inspired a host of African American to careers on Wall Street. We would be the first to control a company with more than one hundred billion in market capital. Can you imagine the impact on young impressionable African Americans?" I said.

"And, with your partnership we will show how Africans and African Americans have come together to be a formidable power in the world of business and commerce." Darrell added.

"I understand where you are coming from. I really don't expect anything less from you guys....Now, how much are we talking.

"Fifty billion." Big Mike replied.

"Does that include the twenty five percent premium Titan is offering?"

"No."

"So, we are really talking seventy five billion to stay in the hunt?"

"Yes."

"What's the payback period?"

"Five to ten years." Charles responded as he walked back into the room.

"Okay that is not bad at all. How is that payback accomplished?"

"Blue sky is a cash cow. It has over thirty billion in cash sitting in a reserve, and the net cash flow on annual basis is close to five billion." I answered.

"There are also some possibilities of selling off some intellectual properties that are truly undervalued in the market place, but would bring a substantial price." Big Mike added.

"Sounds like you have a handle on this," Jakar said.

"We have analyzed this company inside out, no one knows this company better than us, not even Titan." Darrell rejoined.

"Okay...." Jakar paused for a thoughtful moment. "I may have a private group of people that have such a sum of money. "My bankers in Africa are too scared, just as you are finding out with your bankers here in America. This private group of investors is big on anonymity. These people operate outside the rule of law!"

The words gave everyone reason to pause. There were many problems with taking money from a private group where we cannot identify or verify the source of its funds. We were not only opening ourselves up to another SEC investigation, but possible criminal investigation. Darrell was the first to speak?

"I think that might present some unique problems for us."

Jakar shrugged his shoulders as if to say, it's your call. You asked for my help and this is what I can deliver. No one else spoke. Finally, I broke the silence.

"If you would make that arrangement on our behalf, it would be greatly appreciated." I stood to shake Jakar's hand, and he did the same.

He drew me in close and whispered in my ear. "You are the chosen one. We all must follow your lead."

We wrapped up our conversation and went to get Jakar's associates from the conference room. Harlem was our destination for dinner. Jakar said he and his associates wanted some soul food so Everett's was the place. The food was excellent, so was the service. We took in some drinks at Jillian's which was packed on a Friday night. Jakar and his friends couldn't get enough of the female patrons at the bar. We shut the place down and had the car take Jakar and his friends back to their hotel.

The next morning Darrell, Charles, and Big Mike showed up on my doorstep requesting a sit down. Kendra showed them to the parlor while I was getting the kids ready for breakfast. Once I had Miles and Monique set for breakfast I joined them in the parlor. I knew they were concerned about me moving forward with Jakar on securing the financing we needed to close the Blue Sky deal. Darrell was the first to voice his concern.

"Do you think it is wise to move forward with Jakar's proposal?"

"Darrell we have talked to numerous investors and bankers for the last several months with no success. If we want to have a chance at Blue Sky, we have to move with Jakar." I said.

"We had no other option!" Big Mike added.

"We ALWAYS have the options to do the right thing?" Darrell responded.

"The end will justify the means. " I said.

"If we are caught in a violation, we could be in serious trouble." Darrell said.

I know he was alluding to jail time, but the way I looked at it, all businessmen at some time bent the laws or broke them for the greater good of their mission.

"In business sometimes you have to get your hands dirty." Big Mike exclaimed.

"You don't have anything to say Charles?" Darrell asked.

"I see both sides of the argument, and I'm unsure."

"If I thought this would come back to bite us, I wouldn't have authorized Jakar to move forward. Worst case scenario, they find out, our sources of funds come from a foreign entity we can't identify, and we lose the deal. As long as we have acceptable deniability, the only party at risk is Jakar and he is not a citizen of the U.S., so the most his punishment would be is a ban from U.S. markets and the U.S itself."

"Shane is right!" Big Mike added.

"Are we sure, we want to go down this path?"

I nodded in the affirmative along with Big Mike, and then Charles added his approval.

"Alright I'm down." Darrell acquiesced.

We all stood and gave daps to each other, then they all joined us for breakfast.

****

The following Monday morning we were back in the office early as usual. Jakar flew back to Nigeria that morning and we expected to hear back from him in about a week's time. Time was running against us, so we set up a face to face with Big Red at his headquarters in Texas in two weeks' time. We had a lot on our plates, and we were becoming master jugglers – media, constant communications with GPG and Titan, Big Red, other Family members of Red that were trying to play us against Titan to increase the buyout price.

Of all the family members, Big Red had the largest share of ownership at thirty percent and the others combined controlled just about 25%, together they controlled the company. The real problem for Big Red was some of the family members were really in name only from marriage, second and third cousins who weren't vested in the company personally. They had never work in the company, and were the offspring of Big Red sisters and brothers, even nieces and nephews. They didn't have an appreciation for the generations that came before them and what had been sacrificed to build Blue Sky into the oil giant it had become.

I understood this; I made it my purpose to know the history of the family and the company, every detail from the most irrelevant to the relevant. I knew some hard decision were made to get Blue Sky through rocky hard times on more than one occasion and some of the decisions were not entirely to the letter of the law and that was putting it graciously. There were some who viewed the Red Family in the infant stage of Blue Sky Oil as pure criminals. Some of that sentiment was pure jealousy of tough minded businessmen in the pursuit of the American dream. As far as I was concerned Black Street was following in that mode in our pursuit of the American dream.

Around lunch time the receptionist rang my desk. "I have a Mr. Brendham here to see you."

Initially I didn't catch the name, then it popped into my head. I was anxious to meet this man who was at my wedding, our happy hour celebration, and called himself Brendham. "Please take him to the conference room and I will meet him there."

"Okay." She hung up the phone.

I hung the phone up, then gestured for Charles and Big Mike to come over and tapped Darrell to join us. I said one word. "Brendham"

"Where?" Big Mike asked.

"Conference room."

"What are we waiting for? Let's go!" Charles said.

"Wait, should we just send Shane in first?" Darrell asked.

"I thought about that, but if I'm being watched, all of us are being watched and together we need to see what this guy has to say."

We agreed to go talk to Mr. Brendham together. Entering the conference room I recognized the face of Mr. Brendham- ordinary, brown skin, conservative low cut, a narc suit, not any distinctive features that would cause him not to look ordinary. He definitely was the man I sighted on a couple of occasions. Mr. Brendham sat the head of the conference table which immediately made me think he was taking a position of power. I didn't care what he thought or how he saw himself in delivering whatever information he had for us. He got off to a bad start in my mind trying to play a psychological game by sitting at the head of the table. Big Mike and Darrell went to the left side of the table, Charles and I went to the right. They all took a seat, but I walk beside Mr. Brendham and stood there without saying a word.

"Oh, excuse me. I didn't mean anything by…" Mr. Brendham stood.

"It's okay." I said cordially and gestured for him to a seat next to Charles, he did. When he sat down, I thought fuck him. I didn't like him. I didn't say another word; I just studied him, as he did me. Darrell picked up on our analysis of each other.

"Well, Mr. Brendham we received your note and are bemused by your message."

"Yes, why would the government be watching us?" Big Mike added looking directly at him.

"Correct me if I am wrong, but you are the four who orchestrated a takeover of the fixed income trading desk at GPG?"

"Define takeover." Big Mike said.

"Okay… if you gentleman want to play this game I will go along just this one time."

"We're not playing a game. We think you are," Darrell replied.

Mr. Brendham paused showing his patience waning. "You all replaced all the white professionals on the trading desk with all black professionals at GPG and to your tribute quite successfully."

"That is not quite true." Charles said.

"Okay, we are playing semantic games. Look, I'm trying to do you all a favor and warn you that the combination of your all black philosophy and the success you've had at GPG and the takeover of World Textiles makes you threats to what they see as the fabric of American life."

"If it is true that we are being watched, what doesn't add up is why? We are not doing anything illegal, and we haven't hurt anyone." Darrell rejoined.

"It's not about being legal or illegal. You have the potential to be a disruption or an agent of change in a direction they have no wish to travel." Mr. Brendham paused. "Do you understand what I am telling you?"

"Disruption? We are just trying to live the American dream." Darrell answered.

"American dream…." He chuckled. "The American dream for me and you is very different than the American dream the government hopes for other Americans."

"What, that doesn't make sense." Charles questioned.

"It makes plenty of sense. You and I were never intended to create or control wealth and power domestically, especially internationally, but what makes you even more of a danger is your consciousness about your history, your American predicament as a citizen and your desire to change the condition –economically for your people.

"And that is bad?" Big Mike asked.

"I never said it was bad. I'm just saying with the power you are developing with a pro black philosophy, there isn't a more dangerous combination without knowing what your true intentions are."

"What do you mean are true intentions?" Charles asked.

"No one knows your intentions and with your move to take over Blue Sky and your financial connections to Africa –this is looked upon as troublesome." Mr. Brendham looked directly at me.

"What branch of the government agency are you with?" I asked.

A surprised Mr. Brenham answered, "FBI, but I'm retired.

"So, what's in it for you bringing this information to us?" I asked.

"Compensation, but I can help you with the FBI and CIA."

"I thought you said you were ex-FBI?" Big Mike asked.

"I did, but you could bet your last dollar that both agencies have you in their sights, especially since the recent visit of Jakar Akoni to your offices here on Wall Street."

"Do you have a card?"

He pulled from his wallet four business cards and gave each of us one. We thanked him for his time and his efforts to deliver this information to us personally. His card read "Louis Brendham, Federal Bureau of Investigation, Senior Field Agent, and had a phone number. We had the receptionist escort him out of the conference room where we stayed after Mr. Brendham's departure.

"What are you thinking Shane?" Big Mike asked.

"I'm thinking I don't trust Mr. Brendham. I'm not saying I don't think there is some validity to what he said. It's just that all the dots are not connecting for me."

"Like what?" Darrell questioned.

"If Mr. Brendham is retired, how does he know we're being watched? How does he know about Jakar's visit, and how do we take his word that he is retired and wants to help us? Why us?"

"Maybe he is watching them watching us?" Darrell added.

"It's still hard for me to swallow that we are being watch by our government. We haven't broken any laws. We are just living the American dream." Charles interjected.

"It's like the man says, the American dream is not the same for black folks. The most they ever wanted us to aspire to was buying a home and working a job the rest of our life…that was our piece of the American pie. Now, you have Black Street about to take over a multi-billion dollar company, and the threat is we have the potential for domestic and international power and influence. We have the potential to connect with our brothers across the sea and awaken over forty million black folks who have been a part of the walking dead for over four hundred years." Big Mike stated.

"You don't think you are putting a little too much on it Big Mike?" Darrell asked.

"Why the hell are we being watched? Putting too much on it? Not putting enough on it!"

The conversation between us got more thought provoking and threatening as we left no stone unturned pondering the reasons why the government had a watchful eye on us. Given the history of our country it wasn't far-fetched to think the government had an interest in us. Many African Americans with some power and influence in our community in the past Martin Luther King Jr., Malcom X, Black Panther Party, and host of others have been followed, wire tapped , and their organizations infiltrated and torn apart from within by American governmental agencies. This situation was getting real, real fast!

Since we changed our focus and vision for Black Street beyond just making money, we had been more active in the community- speaking to community youth organizations and schools located in the community of Harlem, and we had organized a non-profit headed up by Kendra's friend Vernon for the purpose of developing life skills and financial literacy programs for the youth in the Harlem community. Every time we went to speak the buzz was tremendous. It felt like we were some rock stars coming to perform. We were always dressed in business attire with our array of brims from Ice's house of hats. This attire gave us a little more street credit because most of the youth thought our hats were cool. Some said the hats made us look like some upscale street hustlers which we didn't mind coming from them as long as our message penetrated. We slowly started changing the image of a brim from a street hustler to a Wall Street Investment Banker.

Our status in the community lent credence to Mr. Brendham's theory. I still wasn't comfortable with him or the situation we found ourselves in, and I let it be known.

"We need to find out more about the man, Mr. Brendham." I said.

"How do we do that?" Darrell asked.

"Don't know, but I will find out."

We left the conference room to resume our day and refocus on Blue Sky.

Big Red

After our face to face with Mr. Brendham, my mind raced for a few days for answers and understanding. I didn't talk to Kendra about it because she had enough on her mind with the twins. Since I really didn't have a grasp on the situation, I felt there would be no purpose to the conversation, except adding worry to my wife's life and that's the last thing I wanted. So my first call was to my mother. She had been back and forth from the West Coast to the East Coast more than a few times visiting her grandchildren, and had talked about closing her business down and moving to the East Coast to be closer to me and the family. I encouraged her to do so, but it was hard for her to leave something she had built from the ground up so she remained on the West Coast.

When I called her, it was about 5:00 pm east coast time. I caught her in the office. The trade room had cleared out for the day and I was able to speak freely.

"Hey mom! How are doing?"

"Good son. How are you?"

"Fine."

"How are Kendra and the kids?"

"They are well. Miles and Monique are already having growth spurts."

"Yea, kids grow like weeds son. Make sure you take time to enjoy them. I know your schedule is busy with this Blue Sky deal, but always take time out for your family."

"I do mom."

"That's good."

"So, why have you blessed me with your voice today?"

"How did you know I had something on my mind?"

"I know my son!"

"That you do!.... Well, I have a situation here that is a bit troublesome, and I need to know the best way of going about handling it."

I filled her in on the Mr. Brendham news from my first sighting all the way to the first meeting in the conference room. She really didn't know who I should turn to in this situation, but cautioned me to be discriminating about who I trusted with this information, and the less people who knew the better. When I hung up with her, I was feeling no better. I was determined to find out just who Mr. Brendham was and if there was some concrete evidence behind what he had laid on me and the others.

On my way home on the subway the notion of being watched overwhelmed me, and paranoia seeped into my psyche. Were they watching me as I rode this subway? I looked around at the people riding the subway, couldn't tell one from the other, a FBI agent or a finance professional. Strangely though, when I thought about the prototype that worked on Wall Street and the kind of person that worked for the FBI and CIA there wasn't much difference in dress and demeanor. That was scary. I wondered whether our business phones were tapped, maybe my cell, or even my home phone. All my conversations heard by some third party entity that saw me as a threat. A threat against what?–like Charles said against wanting to live the American dream. What the hell! I became angered.

I got off the subway a couple of stops before mine, and walked to the House of Hats. I thought to myself, the only person I know who would have connections to get the kind of information I needed or tell me how to go about getting the information was Ice. When I entered the store he was in the back leaned over talking to this sista who was thick as molasses. He saw me and pulled up on his rap.

"Homeboy what's happening? I haven't seen you in a taste." He said as he walked to join me in the front of the store.

"Yea, I've been a little busy."

"A little? Man I've been reading about you and your crew all over the paper. Sounds like to me you got them white boys running scared on Wall Street."

"I don't know about them running scared, but I'm holding my own."

"Yea, you doin that shit my man!"

"Hey, Ice what time you close."

"In about an hour, what's up?"

"Wanted to talk with you about something."

"Oh, homeboy we can talk now."

"In private." I said.

Ice got the attention of the young lady still standing in the rear of the store. "Ms. Lady, I'm going have to get at you later. I need to rap a taste with my boy here, but don't be a stranger. I like your body temperature," Ice said to the young lady as she approached the front of the store.

She smiled as she passed by and exited. Ice followed behind her blew her a kiss as she hit the sidewalk, then locked the door behind her, and change the open sign on his store to close. He came back toward me, pulled two chairs from behind the counter and offered me one. There was a burning question I just had to ask Ice that was more important than even Mr. Brendham at the time.

"What did you mean by you liked that sista's body temperature?"

"Hot baby boy. You married and everything, but you saw the body on her. Was it hot or not?"

"Oh, it was most definitely hot."

He gave me a pound for being in agreement with that assessment. After I got that out the way I didn't hesitate getting right into it, as I did with my mother. I trusted Ice, just as much as I trusted Big Mike, Charles, and Darrell.

Once I was done bringing him up to speed on the Brendham situation, he asked me.

"You need some intel on this guy?"

"Yes!"

"I got some homies in DC with relatives that work in some of those buildings around the capital as janitors and grounds keepers they could get their hands on some information about this Brendham Kat."

"That would be great!"

"It's going to cost you Shane. I'm not going to charge you, but the brothas I know will want some doe to do this solid."

"Not a problem, you let me know their number and I will bring you the cash."

"Okay, I will contact them, and I will get back to you and let you know what's what."

We gave each other a pound, and I departed in a little bit of hurry. Once I looked at my watch, I saw that I was over an hour late getting home. I hailed a cab to get home.

I eased into the door quietly, so Kendra and the kids would not hear me enter the house. I had hoped to get way with pretending I had been home already. As I crept through the house toward the kitchen I saw my children seated at the dining table inside the kitchen area, then I saw Kendra and Darrell standing side by side talking while they were preparing food. When they saw me, Darrell abruptly stopped his conversation with Kendra which I thought was an awkward moment, but I couldn't let it go by without a comment.

"Don't stop talking on my account." I approached my kids to give them kisses and hugs.

"Nobody stopped talking on your account." Kendra responded dismissing my statement nonchalantly. "Now, where have you been? You are over an hour late. We've been waiting on you." Kendra said.

"I stopped by the House of Hats to talk with Ice."

"How is he doing?" Kendra asked.

"He's good! It was good to touch base with him. I hadn't seen him in a while; we're going to have to have him over for dinner to meet Miles and Monique."

"That sounds like a good idea."

"Matter of fact, I'd like to set up a dinner for our close friends and family."

"What's the occasion?"

"No occasion just wanting to share some time with close friends and family. What do you think Darrell, sound like a good idea?"

Darrell had been silent ever since I walked in the room. "Yea, yea… good idea." He replied.

Kendra walked around the bar and gave me a hug and kiss. "You are the best. I really got lucky when your mother walked into my boutique and started ranting and raving about her son and all his potential. She wasn't lying – handsome to boot!" She planted another one on me.

I smiled." Let's eat!" I said. We all sat and ate dinner.

After Darrell left, I sat with the twins in the family room and turned on the world news as I played with them. Kendra joined us, when she finished up in the kitchen. I thought to myself, Kendra smoothed over that awkward moment quite effectively. I've always said that Kendra was a better diplomat than I, and in that moment she was her best. We sat on the couch as a family, and I looked into my wife's eyes, and asked myself would she deliberately try to deceive me? She looked back at me with those big brown eyes and gave me the most genuine warm smile. With all the other issues I was dealing with in my life, I needed home to be my sanctuary. I trusted my wife, and to question her about Darrell would only cast doubt where I didn't want doubt to be. I thought about Big Mike and his reaction to me when he found me inside his home with Adriona, and how hurtful and wrong his accusations were. I wasn't going to make the same mistake.

****

Our trip to Texas was approaching quickly, we hadn't heard from Jakar, and we didn't bother with phone calls because we didn't want to give an impression of desperation. But, we did want the financing in place before the trip, so when we spoke to Big Red our words would convey confidence and a willingness and readiness to move forward. Without that financing we feared our words although sincere would be hollow. There were actually reports in the media that Black Street lacked the financial power to take over Blue Sky. An actual headline read "Too Big to Swallow, Black Hole for Black Street" giving the inference that we were out of our league in our pursuit of Blue Sky.

We were in a holding pattern until the financing was secure. I sensed restlessness amongst us all. The trade room banter, jokes, and personal analysis became more frequent.

Soul Train had this girlfriend for six months and the word was he hadn't hit it yet. Everyone was giving him a hard time and suggested he drop her and find another. Even Maria laid into him about this woman. Evidently his girlfriend was extremely jealous and possessive and would blow up his personal line on the trading desk when he didn't pick up his cell. By mistake this young lady called Charles's line, and he didn't like her tone.

"He's off the desk."

"Well, where the hell is he." She replied.

Charles took a deep breath, and repeated himself." He's off the desk." Then he hung the phone up.

When Soul Train returned to the trading desk, Charles had some questions for him.

"Your lady called on my line."

"Sorry about that, I'll make sure that won't happen again."

"What's up with her?"

Soul Train just shook his head in disgust. "Don't know." He mumbled.

"How long you been with her now, six months?"

"Yea, six months," he said subdued.

"Please don't tell me you still haven't hit that yet?"

Now everyone in hearing distance is paying attention to Charles and Soul Train's conversation.

Soul Train shakes his head no. Maria adds her two cents. "She's going way past Steve Harvey's ninety day probation. She got you on the hundred and eighty day probation."

There was laughter around the trade room.

"You must be getting some on the side from somewhere else?"

Soul Train again shook his head in the negative.

C-Walk couldn't help himself. "What the fuck Soul Train?"

"You are a got damn millionaire, and you mean to tell me for the last six months you have been drrryyy! Charles drew out the word dry in a dehydrated voice. "I can't believe you are drryy! How are you making it in a six month drought!

Soul Train finally cracked a smile.

"I don't see a damn thing funny about being drryy! Charles continued. "Especially when you have enough money to fuck a Halle Barry look alike."

The room erupted with laughter.

Then the whole room serenaded Soul Train: "*How dry I am, how dry I am, nobody knows, how dry I am!*" Laughter ensued and Soul Train joined in.

That was the best bit of levity we've had in the trade room for months.

In the midst of our laughter my personal line rung. I picked up. It was Jakar. I signaled for Darrell to pick up my line.

"Shane you have a commitment of seventy five billion towards purchase of Blue Sky. Fifty billion will be wired to your Nigerian account in Lagos, and the other twenty five will be wired once you have secured the purchase."

I thanked Jakar and told him we would be in touch. I hung up the phone and Darrell tackled me in my chair. Big Mike and Charles knew what had taken place from Darrell's reaction and piled on like I had scored the winning basket with no time left on the clock. Everyone else in the trade room just stared at us. We all rose to our feet, and made the announcement.

"We just secured the seventy five billion needed to keep us in the hunt for Blue Sky!"

The trade room burst into a roar and hugs and pounds gravitated through the room. Maria ran up to me and jumped into me with her whole body. My natural reflex took over, I grabbed and hugged her, but it felt inappropriate the closeness of the hug held no limits, her arms draped around my neck and my arms around her waist, she congratulated me. Lost in the moment we finally corrected our posture. Everyone was so busy, no one really noticed the moment, except Charles. When Maria left me to congratulate others, I looked around to see if anyone had taken notice, and Charles and I locked eyes and he smiled a devious smile. I shook my head to disavow the actions between Maria and me.

****

Darrel and I arrived in Texas the following Monday morning. We checked into our hotel rooms in Downtown Dallas. We rented a town car and used the GPS to find our way to Blue Sky's headquarters. When we reached their headquarters, both Darrell and I were amazed at the massive layout. There was an eighty story glass building erected in the center of the property reminiscent of the Lincoln monument with surrounding buildings around the perimeter of the property campus style. Darrell and I parked in the visitors parking right outside the main building. We walked into the massive glass building and were met by security who talked with a southern drawl.

"How y'all doin today? How can I help ya?"

"Mr. Johnson and Mr. Jackson to see Red." Darrell said.

"Okay let me take a look at my clip board." The security guard checked his clip board behind this long marble security desk. "Yea, I got y'all down here. Let me give y'all security passes." He handed us two badges with our names on them, Darrell Johnson and Shane Jackson. "Now what you do is take the elevator on my right." he pointed in the direction of the third elevator lobby on his right. "Take the elevator all the way up to the eighty first flo and the gal up there will sho you to Red."

"Thank you!" I said.

Darrell and I took the elevator up, exited on the eighty first floor. Just as the security had said, we were greeted by a red head middle age woman with black rimmed glasses wearing a red dress. Her skin was pale white. She was attractive.

"Hello, Red has been expecting you. Please follow me."

We followed her without a word. She led us to a conference room filled with people. At the center of the room was a large oval table made of finished oak wood, and at the head of that table sat Red surrounded by men and women in business attire. There were a row of seats lining the wall directly behind the conference table filled with professionals also. The seats around the table were filled all except two seats that were at the opposite end to where Red was sitting. As we entered Red welcomed us and offered up the two vacant seats that were closest to the door. Darrell and I took the seats offered. Then to our surprise someone other than Red without introduction led the meeting. She was a young white, blonde, attractive, physically fit, mid-thirties same age as me, and as she spoke there was a strange familiarity of her look and voice.

"As Red has already said, we welcome you both to our great city of Dallas and hope your trip was comfortable and your accommodations here in Dallas are suitable."

"Our trip was fine and on the advice of your staff our accommodations at the Regent is more than befitting." Darrell responded.

She continued. "I know you are a bit taken back by this overwhelming showing by executives and staff, but we all are aware of the seriousness of the situation with Blue Sky and all of us have sincere dedication, loyalty, and love for Red."

"Overwhelmed is an understatement. It was our understanding this would be private meeting between us, Red, and a few key executives that were shareholders in the company." Darrell came back.

As she explained everyone in the room was a shareholder and was a part of Blue Sky's management team. It bothered me that she was so familiar. Yet I couldn't place her, and more than her look it was the tone of her voice resembled someone I knew. Her voice was strong, confident, and even authoritative with a sharpness to it that gave me the impression she didn't mince words. Not knowing her name or the others at the conference table bothered me. Then, she hit me with it through the course of her dialogue with Darrell.

"Does Mr. Jackson have anything to add about his expectations of this meeting or is he a deaf mute?

"What?" Darrell vehemently exclaimed.

Snickers permeated around the table. I patted Darrell on the arm to calm himself, and rose from my seat with a smile. I knew exactly who this woman was. A blast from my past, it was Susan a classmate from my days at Darden, my Ivy League undergrad work. We along with Tim and Karen raised two hundred and fifty thousand dollars in capital for a young hip hop entrepreneur in New York-Calvin. I took the opportunity at that moment to deliver my argument in favor of Black Street buying out Blue Sky.

"Respect…" I started out. "Just as Red has felt a blatant lack of respect through the process of defending his company from takeover, I have felt the same way throughout my career and here today. For example, the absence of a proper introduction of myself and Mr. Johnson to all of you, when we entered this room, not even an introduction of our speaker before she addressed us, and on top of that to be referred to as a deaf mute. Aahh,… I thought more of Blue Sky management than to lower themselves to name calling. Now, putting all this into perspective, most of you deem this to be a hostile takeover as such I understand the animosity toward our visit and the number of people here to receive us. I am surprised an all-out physical attack has not taken place."

Big Red spoke. "I apologize for the way you have been received here, but it is hard to be civil to someone that wants to take your life's work and five generations of your family's work and sell it off like used goods in a garage sale."

"It is not our intention to do any such thing!" Darrell clarified.

"I see our misrepresented publically crafted reputation precedes us, but as Mr. Johnson has said our mission is not to buy and sell. We wish to own Blue Sky and manage the company in the spirit and dedication Red has over the years, just as his family did before him."

Susan interjected. "Is it your mission to replace all the white workers with black workers?"

"Again our misunderstood reputation precedes us. Let me take this time to explain our experience at GPG. GPG was my first job on Wall Street, and as a salesman on Wall Street I met a lot of people and had many associations. What I detected was a lack of black talent on Wall Street, and what I attempted to do was to show an all-black trading desk that could perform with the best of trading desks on Wall Street, therefore opening up the eyes of Wall Street to young talented financial professionals who happen to be black. Now, having explained that, as I look around the room, I don't see one black face, not even a face of color, and I am disturbed by this. I know this is not by design, but in any case my preference would be to have a more diverse executive management team."

"So, if you were to take over Blue Sky, you would be firing people."

"Okay, let's be realistic. Anyone who takes over Blue Sky is going to bring in their own people, and if I were to take over the company I would have some of my people put in strategic areas I thought necessary and prudent. Having said that I do believe Blue Sky to be a well-run and managed company, and I don't foresee any dramatic changes to the middle management structure."

There was silence. Red studied me, and then asked everyone to leave the conference room except Susan, and three other guys. Darrell and I remained in our seats.

"Come closer lets make this meeting a little more intimate, just between the seven of us. Everyone here has the authority to speak frankly and honestly about the concerns, hopes, intentions," Red looked towards Darrell and I, "and aspirations for Blue Sky. As you already know Susan speaks her mind, and I don't like to reel her in because her frankness is her greatest asset."

"Really, I think there is a line between frankness and inappropriateness!" Darrell expounded.

I could see Susan had hit a wrong chord with Darrell, but I put his mind at ease. I placed my hand on his forearm which was on the table. "How have you been Susan?"

"Good Shane." She responded sarcastically.

I looked at Darrell. "Susan and I have history. She was a classmate of mind at Darden where I did my undergrad work."

"Oh…okay that's the connection."

"Yea, we did a project together where we raised two hundred and fifty thousand dollars for an urban clothing and shoe designer. Do you remember that Susan?"

"I remember us losing a chance to take a tour of the New York Stock Exchange."

"You would just remember that!" I said.

"Okay, you two will have plenty of time to go down memory lane. What I want to know is why Blue Sky?" Red asked.

This was Darrell's original idea so I turned him loose. His presentation was precise, informed, insightful, passionate, and directional in the area of vision. I could tell everyone was impressed by Darrell's understanding and command of Blue Sky's business, products, markets, distribution, and their research and technology. He even surprised me with some of the details. When he was done, Red complimented Darrell on his knowledge of Blue Sky and its potential.

"You understand the potential for growth in this company more than my family members. I haven't yet had anyone inside or outside my company able to articulate its growth prospects so clearly, including myself. My family members should have heard your presentation. Maybe they would change their minds about selling and see this company has the potential to feed and give financial prosperity for generations to come, but they don't see it, so I am forced to sell." You could see the disgust and anguish on Red's face even at the thought of selling his family business. "I have one question for you Shane. Why Black Street instead of Titan Industries?"

"Well Red, you know Titan Industries –their plans for Blue Sky is just to gobble you up and make you a part of Titan Industries. The growth prospects that Mr. Johnson just spoke of would be done away with. Titan Industries is old school, they are a big giant looking to expand market share in the traditional market segments, but the innovative platform for research and development in your oil and gas exploration and refinement which would open up other non-traditional segments and expand market share in traditional segments is key. With Black Street Capital the Blue Sky name lives, instead of the twenty five percent premium on the stock price offered by Titan, which we are prepared to pay, we would like to pump that into your R&D to compete and ultimately sky rocket Blue Sky to the number one company in the oil industry."

Big Red remained seated not saying a word just looking at me, again studying me gaining more insight to the man who sat before him. He then rose; walked over to Darrell and I where we stood, shook our hands and congratulated us on a good presentation, but he said nothing else. Red left the room, and the other three men followed him out. Susan lagged behind. The three of us were left standing in the conference.

"How long will you guys be in Dallas?"

"Our flight leaves tomorrow." Darrell replied.

"Okay! Red will be in touch. Our receptionist will show you out. It was good to see you again Shane." She shook my hand and Darrell's and left the room and the receptionist promptly entered and escorted us to the elevator lobby where she initially greeted us.

Darrell and I made it back to the Hotel. We unwound in my suite reviewing the events of the day. We both were befuddled by the start of the meeting and the ending, and Darrell was not lost for words on Susan.

"Your so called friend Susan is a piece of work, and it seems Red thinks very highly of her. She is rude, a know it all, and condescending. If it's all the same to you when we take over this company please give me the pleasure of firing her to her face!"

I chuckled. “Susan is alright, you just have to get to know her. I used to feel the same as you when I first met her, but underneath that rough exterior is a caring person.”

“She could have fooled me!

“She fools most people, which can be an asset or liability.”

We ordered some food from room service watched some world news and then to my delight from channel surfing we tuned in to an episode of Sanford and Son. I’ve always liked the way Fred bragged about the empire he was leaving for his son Lamont. It didn’t matter that his empire was a junk yard along with a junky home. It was something he owned and would bequeath to his son upon his passing. I like the idea of leaving something for future generations, for your children just as Red’s parents, grandparents, and great grandparents did, but Red wouldn’t have that opportunity. At that moment I felt Red’s pain and I jumped up found a piece of paper and a pen, then put pen to paper. I wrote a heartfelt letter to Red about the lost opportunity to leave his life’s work to his children with the dreams of them carrying the torch and passing it to their children. I explained that was what I wanted for my children Miles and Monique. I shared my desire to continue in the tradition that his family had built and to memorialize the past generations who built Blue Sky into the international company. One thing I had learned about Red, he was an emotional man and he cared about preserving his family’s history and contributions.

Darrell questioned me as I was writing the letter. I didn’t utter a word until the letter was complete. I passed it to him.

He read it. “Jees man, I think you just delivered Blue Sky to us!”

There was a knock at my hotel door. I got up to see who it was and to my surprise it was Susan. I opened the door. She pushed her way in moving me to the side.

“Nice suite! She said as she moved to the main room where Darrell was folding the letter I had written and putting it inside an envelope. “Hey there how are you?” She looked back at me and whispered “I thought you were alone.” Then turned back around and gave Darrell the fakest smile you could give anyone letting him know his company was unwanted. Darrell looked to me, and I gave him a quick head gesture to give Susan and me some privacy.

On his way out he handed me the handwritten letter for Red. Once Darrell left the suite Susan's demeanor changed. I offered Susan a seat on the couch. She rushed me and gave me a hug and a quick kiss on the mouth before I could react.

"Whoa!... that was unexpected. "

"I'm not a predictable kind of gal."

"You can say that again."

"So, how have you been?"

"How have I been? On edge, what can you tell me about my chances with Red?"

"No mister, this is not a business visit. It's personal from one Darden alumni to another. How's Tim?

"I guess he's doing well. The last time I talked with him he was still at GPG."

"What do you mean the last time you talked with him. He is not a part of Black Street Capital?"

"No."

"Why the hell not?"

"It's a long story."

"I got all night!." She said emphatically.

She walked to the mini bar in the suite poured a drink for herself and me. She took her coat off and shoes, plopped on the couch in her white blouse and navy blue knee high skirt, then held my glass of wine up offering me a seat beside her. I took it, and as we drank wine I gave her the full story of Black Street at GPG and how Tim and I worked together before the betrayal. When I was done, Susan was flabbergasted at what I told her.

"I heard the rumors, but I didn't know the details to your motivation and how much Tim was involved."

"Who did you hear the rumors from?" I asked.

"Karen, she is an equity portfolio manager for a money management firm in San Francisco, and she used GPG for some of her equity trading."

"How come she never reached out to us?"

"From what she heard, you and Tim were running a Black Panther Party on your desk, so she didn't think you wanted to hear from her."

"That's nonsense. Just because we are pro black doesn't mean we are anti-white."

"Well, by hiring nothing but black professionals, you had to be anti-something?"

"Sometimes to accomplish a worthy mission, there can be collateral damage."

"Was your mission at GPG worthy?"

"In my heart Susan I think so, I made some mistakes and there might have been a better way to showcase black talented professionals, but that was the path I chose and I have no regrets. The experience has been fruitful."

"Well that's that!" She rose and walked toward the bathroom.

"Where are you going?"

"To take a shower I've been at work all day, and I need a shower. Why don't you order some dinner for us from room service?"

Before I could object she was behind the closed door of the bathroom. I thought about knocking on the door and somehow asking her to leave, but I didn't really want her to leave. I was enjoying catching up with her and something about her was attractive beyond her physical appearance. Her brashness and her non-judgmental acceptance of my Black Street story cast her in a different light. Susan was real, no cookie coating for her. I liked that about her, and I guess that's what I liked about her back at Darden.

Darrell rang my room to ask about dinner. I told him Susan was still here and that we were going to have dinner in the room. He was welcomed to join us, but he declined. Before he hung up, he asked, had she tipped her hand about which way Red was leaning.

"No, but I'm hoping before the nights end she will."

"Don't forget to give her the letter to deliver to Red." Darrell said.

"Will do!"

Just as I was hanging up with Darrell, Susan exited the bathroom with just her white blouse on which hung midway to her thigh. She had the top two buttons undone, and I could tell she had taken off her bra. My surprised reaction was revealed because I was hanging on to the phone and my mouth must have been open.

"Hang up the phone and shut your mouth before something flies in it."

I did just what she said nervously. There was a knock at the door. It was room service I had the bell boy bring the dinner in. He could not help himself from taking a gaze upon Susan. Her shapely and firm legs exposed, her slightly tangled hair hanging down shoulder length, her tan skin glistening through the opening of her shirt giving away hints of her firm cleavage that needed no assistance in staying upright. At that moment she was the epitome of sensuality. After the bell boy set the dinner table for us, I tipped him before he left the room. Susan sat at the table nonchalantly as I stood watching her survey the food on the table.

"Sit down; I'm not going to bite you." She said.

I took a seat directly across from Susan at the dinner table. I decided to ignore the lack of attire my dinner companion had on and to continue in the conversation of two friends catching up. Credit to the wine or her attire, but Susan got comfortable enough to start opening up about Red. She told me how he was her mentor, how she had worked at Blue Sky her whole career, and then she began to run down the company top to bottom –it's history and potential future. She contrasted Blue Sky to Titan Industries the pros and cons skillfully. She obviously knew the company and the space with which it operated very well. Red had trained her well, and she was much more insightful than I remembered her to be at Darden. Our conversation was so engrossing that her appearance faded to the background. We touched on topics ranging from the potential and aspirations of Blue Sky to her professional aspirations. Susan was being groomed to be the future CEO of Blue Sky. She revealed the other three men in the meeting at Blue Sky headquarters were the CFO, COO, and a Blue Sky Board member. She divulged Red had a deep seated hatred of Titan Industries and GPG stemming back generations of fierce competition between Red's Family and the Founder of Titan Industries and the Mackey Family. It had been GPG that help catapult Titan Industries over Blue Sky to number one.

History between Blue Sky, Titan, and the Mackey Family was tremendous. The conversation was truly beneficial, and I thought if Darrell were to be in on the conversation, he would have been equally impressed with Susan. Our conversation drifted back to our days at Darden after a while. She asked about Calvin the hip hop clothing entrepreneur that we helped in New York. I told her of the story about me contacting him to help me build my book at GPG my first year, and how he told me to fuck off because I slept with his girlfriend. She couldn't contain the laughter.

"You actually called him and asked for his help?" she said laughing.

"I didn't know at the time she told him. It was just a one night stand."

"Dumb move Mr. Shane Jackson. I'm surprised he didn't send some guys after you. He clearly had some connections to some unsavory street characters."

"Yea, but that wasn't Calvin's style."

"Let me ask you something." She asked.

"Go right ahead."

"We got much closer because of our experience with Calvin's store."

"I would agree."

"How come we never hooked up?"

From the moment she asked that question her attire came back into full view. I didn't really know how to answer the question, and I didn't really want to answer the question for fear of what was to follow my answer. "I don't know." I said unknowingly.

"I caught you on several occasions during and after that school assignment checking me out, looking at my body especially my butt."

"I was not!" Embarrassed by the commentary.

"Was too! You're just to chicken shit to admit it."

"Okay, I might have checked you out once or twice, but I was in college I checked out a lot of girls. That's what young men do in college –check out girls!"

She stood up and walked around the table where she would be in full view, then unbuttoned her blouse and let it drop down to the floor. My heart quickened at the site of her fit and toned body. She stood before me in nothing but a red G string, then she turned to give me a view of her derriere which was nice and heart shaped. I was speechless, my breath was taken away, then fear over took me; realizing how much I had let this situation get out of control. My thoughts and feelings went to Kendra, how could I, why would I, for fun, for pleasure, to destroy what I had with my wife was my biggest fear which I realized in that moment. I could lose Blue Sky to Titan Industries, I could accept Black Street going bankrupt, but to lose my wife and family, no! Not over a piece of ass. It wasn't worth it!

"I'm sorry Susan. I shouldn't have let this go on this far. I should have stopped you when you went to take a shower. I'm happily married and one thing I won't do is compromise my marriage."

"Oh… did you think you were going to get some of this? No, no ….

Susan walked away toward the bathroom. She re-emerged fully dressed. She thanked me for the dinner, and I thanked her for the conversation. I handed her the letter for Red.

"Good touch Mr. Jackson, I'll make sure he gets it."

I walked her to the door.

"You're a good man Shane. I wish you the best always, and it was great catching up with you. Your life has been the path less traveled, but you have made it work for you. Congratulations!" She moved in close and gave me a very tender kiss upon my cheek.

The next day Darrell and I flew back to New York.

Traitor in our Mist

We played the waiting game with Blue Sky. We continued to court them in subtle ways making our rounds on the business news media circuit playing up our intentions of running Blue Sky in the tradition of Red's family and praising Red for the well organized and managed company. Weeks turned to months and still no hint of the family's decision between Black Street and Titan. Our patience was challenged. We had increased our overhead in our pursuit of Blue Sky with the intention of marrying them into the Blue Sky Company once the takeover was completed, but the success of the takeover and the timeline had become indeterminable. It was a hard decision, but we needed to have some cut backs. We downsized personnel to our original size which we coined the fantastic eight. The layoffs were a morale downer, so I organized a dinner at my home to boost morale.

Kendra was great in helping me get the dinner together. Everyone from the office attended including Betty. Charles and Carmen had become an item and they attended the dinner together. Big Mike brought Adriona which was a treat for everyone. White Chocolate and Maria attended as did Soul Train, C-Walk, and Darrell who were dateless. The camaraderie was evident amongst us. We talked and laughed throughout the evening. Big Mike and Adriona were bombarded with questions regarding their relationship which they handled eloquently. Adriona was warm and pleasant, and the love between them was evident. Big Mike had told me in private they were in counseling sessions and it was going well, and he expected to announce their engagement in the coming months.

Carmen and Charles had a funny and peculiar relationship volatile at times and very loving at other times. When they arrived at my home, they were holding hands and very intimate in their interaction with each other, but by the time dinner was finished they were separated, socializing on opposite ends of the house at times giving snide looks to each other. Evidently Carmen was getting some attention from C-Walk that Charles didn't appreciate, and to make matters worse Carmen wasn't discouraging the attention. They had an argument over it and then to rub Charles's nose in it she deliberately flirted with C-Walk in front of everyone which sent Charles through the roof. I had to take him to the side and calm him down. I had never seen that side of him.

"What the fuck is she doing?"

"Making you jealous."

"Oh, if she wants to play that game, two can play that game. Where's Maria?"

"Don't drag Maria into your shit."

"Why, you want her all to yourself?"

"What?"

"I'm sorry man. I didn't mean that. I know you don't get down like that. It's …just that I love her so much….but she can drive me crazy at times. She's so beautiful and sexy. I see a lot of men checking her out when we have a night on the town."

"So what, that's just admiration and envy."

"I don't trust her that's why I keep my options open."

"So, what are you saying?"

"I keep me some trim on the side, so I don't feel like a complete idiot when I find out she's fucking someone else."

What the hell was it with us men? Here was Charles a multi-millionaire and a self-made man with the largest ego on the East Coast, and could realistically have his pick of the most beautiful women in New York. Yet he was worried about the faithfulness of his girlfriend, so not to be made a fool of, he was unfaithful to her, yet he loves her. What kind of sense did that make?

"You say, you love her, but you don't trust her. Charles there can be no true love without trust. If you don't trust her, leave that broad alone."

"I do love her! Man she makes me feel like no other woman has ever."

"How do you feel now?"

"Now?"

"Right now, this moment looking at her over their flirting with C-Walk." I drew his attention to the other side of the room. I thought her flirting with C-Walk to be very disrespectful and distasteful which made me lose respect for her.

"Like shit."

"Then, do yourself a favor, short that broad!"

"I'm not shorting her!"

I walked away from him in disgust. I heard him say again. "I ain't shorting her." People looked up around to see where that statement came from. Charles remained in the corner. I think I might have hurt his feelings encouraging him to short Carmen, but her behavior sure was encouraging the trade, which I knew, he knew.

I ended up in the parlor standing alone thinking about my conversation with Charles, regretting my comment. It was a bad choice of words. I thought I will apologize later. My thoughts were interrupted by White Chocolate.

"What's up Shane, great dinner party?"

"Thanks, you enjoying yourself?"

"Yea, this was a good idea. This will help morale."

"I hope so."

"What do you think our chances are to buy Blue Sky?"

"I think our chances are good!"

White-Chocolate shook his head in agreement, but I could tell he had other things on his mind. I didn't say anything else – I gave him time to get his thoughts together and tell me what he really wanted, when he was ready. We just stood there next to each other watching others at the dinner party. My eyes were drawn to Kendra, where ever Kendra stood, Darrell stood. I wondered was Darrell closer to Kendra than he was to me. From all indications one could make and argument in Kendra's favor. Then, I found my mind questioning how much Kendra and Darrell shared between them. Did Darrell tell Kendra about Susan being in my hotel room until late in the night? I had shared with him every detail of what happen that night with Susan. Would he.....then White-Chocolate spoke.

"You know what Charles said about me coming up short with my wife was not right." He said without looking at me directly.

"I know that and I asked him to apologize to you. Did he?"

"Yea, he did, but I saw the pity in his eyes. I don't want anyone's pity." He stated, again not addressing me directly.

"I can understand that." I responded not looking at him. We continued the rest of our interaction in this manner both of us talking into the parlor room air.

"It all starts with my wife. I think she's too much for me. I can't control her…… She's a beast in the bed. I can't keep up….. I feel like a teenage boy….whose fantasy has come true of sleeping with the girl of his dreams, but orgasms before the act is consummated."

Damn I thought. What kind of shit?..... And why in the hell would he tell me? We were cool, but not close enough for him to reveal his inner thoughts to me. I didn't know what to do, should I give my opinion, or was he just venting and needed an ear. I wasn't sure, so I stayed silent. He broke the silence.

"So, what do you think? What should I do?" He said looking at me directly and intently for the first time.

I very calmly and deliberately and gave my honest advice. "Go to the doctor get yourself a prescription of Viagra. Pray that the Viagra gives you a four hour erection, and for four hours you make love to your wife all over your home. Don't leave one room unmarked. When the four hour love making session is over, then get up, no cuddling and hugging and tell her you going to the gym to work out. Leave her ass at home. You leave and don't come back for a couple of hours giving her the impression you indeed went to work out……You understand what I'm saying to you?"

"Yes." He gave me a dap and moved on.

I surveyed the room and there was Charles standing in a corner with Carmen making out like he was at a high school house party. Then Big Mike and Adriona walked over to talk with me.

"You have a beautiful home, wife, and children. Thanks for sharing it with us." Adriona, then she kissed me on the cheek.

I looked to Big Mike praying the counseling had taken effect. He smiled and gave me a dap and a hug. We both laughed because he knew what I was thinking. We were joined by Kendra and Darrell.

"What's so funny?" Darrell asked.

"Nothing." I responded. "Just me and the Big Man sharing a moment."

"That's good!" Kendra said, and she hugged both of us.

Soon after, our home thin out- people saying goodbye and thank you to Kendra and me as they left. Hugs and Kisses were passed out showing appreciation and caring. Charles and Carmen were the last ones to leave. I pulled Charles to the side, away from Kendra and Carmen.

"I'm sorry about the short sale comment!"

"I know man, thanks for the apology.... Shane do you think all this money and attention we're getting from Black Street is changing us?"

"Yes."

"Me too."

We walked back to the women. Carmen said goodbye to me and kissed me on cheek and Charles did the same to Kendra. As they walked down the stairs I couldn't help myself.

"I still think the short sale is a valuable option!" I shouted.

Charles laughed and waved goodbye.

****

Early the next morning I get a call on my cell phone. It was Ice.

"Hey meet me at the shop in twenty. I got the info you been seeking."

I jumped up out of bed and threw some clothes on. Kendra asked about the phone call and what the rush was all about. I just told her I had forgotten about an early morning appointment I had, and I didn't want to be too late. I rushed out the door and drove to Ice's store.

When I arrived, he was waiting inside for me. He quickly came to the front door unlocked it, let me in, and then locked it behind me. He walked behind his register, and I followed him. Standing in front of the counter while Ice stood behind it, Ice reached for a folder underneath and laid it on top of the counter.

"It took some time, but my people in DC finally found someone with access to get the information you were looking for." He pushed the folder toward me.

When I opened it, I was surprised at what I was reading. The file included Brendham's picture, history, psychological profile, educational accomplishments, duties and responsibilities as a FBI agent. There were awards, retirement certification, pictures of relatives, and other information about personal and professional associations. The depth of experience and expertise this file referred to as Mr. Brenham talents was surreal. His profile fit the description of secret agent 007- he was trained in the mix martial arts, gun and explosives expert, and was on the counter terrorism squad for over 10 years.

"This dude is the real deal Shane."

"Yea, it looks that way."

"How are you mixed up with this Kat?"

"Don't really know yet."

"Are you in contact with him?"

"Yea." I said somberly.

"What does he want with you?"

"Don't know."

"Well the person who got this info has access, but he has a price, and its right here" he pointed down at the file. "It's going to cost us twenty five hundred."

"Not a problem, I will drop off the cash later today. Do you know how he got access?"

"Even though most brothas got no work in DC, we still have a few of the maintenance engineering jobs."

"Cool, do you think we can rely on him for more information if needed."

"As long as the green keeps coming his way, he ain't gonna have no problem. And, I made sure neither of them know who you are, so the buck stops with me."

"Appreciate that! I'm out and I'll make sure the cash makes it your way by day's end."

"Hey Shane, one thing before you leave, I have this lady friend who is a photographer and she would like to do a biographical pictorial of you and the fellas."

"Me, what for?"

"Are you kidding man? You are poppin! Do you know how much trim I get from that picture on the wall of you and me chillin out, brimmed out like two regular fellas." He points to a picture of him and me at a bar having some drinks.

"Really?"

"Really man! So, what do you say? This sista is from Harlem. I think she knows Kendra and has shopped in her boutique."

"That just might be kind of cool man. Bring her by the office on Monday and we'll go from there."

"Solid!"

Ice unlocked the door for me, gave me a dap, and I drove back home. The rest of the day my mind was preoccupied with Brenham. I had so many questions. If Brendham was telling the truth about the watch list, why was he revealing it to me? I still couldn't get it through my mind why the government wanted to watch us anyway. We weren't harboring any secrets nor had we any designed plans to blow anything up. I just aspired to be a businessman. Why in the hell would the government want to follow us around?

****

Later that night after Kendra and I put the kids to bed, I got a call on the cell phone from Big Mike. Kendra and I were relaxing on the couch.

"Big Mike, what's up?"

"There's a traitor in our mist." He said in a serious tone.

"What does that mean?"

"I can't tell you over the phone, you have to see for yourself. Meet me uptown 57th block in front of a restaurant called Alfini's."

"When?"

"Now!"

I hung up the phone with Big Mike.

"What does Big Mike want?" Kendra asked.

"He wants me to meet him in front of a restaurant called Alfini's."

"Why?"

"He wouldn't say. He just said there is a traitor in our mist."

"What does that mean?"

"I have no idea, but he says I have to see for myself."

"See what?"

"I don't know. That's why I have to go and meet him?"

"Eleven o clock at night? It doesn't make sense."

"I know, but a lot of things are not making sense recently."

"What does that mean Shane? Do I need to be worried about you? Will I have to come pick you up from the hospital again?" Her eyes teared up.

"Kendra,..." I hugged her. "I'm going to be alright, you don't have to worry about that. Let me go and see what's going on with Big Mike and when I get back, we will talk.

"Okay, be careful. I love you!"

"Love you too!"

I kissed her and grabbed my coat and headed out the door. It took me about a half hour to get uptown. When I arrived at the restaurant, I walked up the sidewalk leading to the restaurant. I turned around when I heard Big Mike call my name and honk his horn. He and Charles were sitting in his SUV curb side in front of the restaurant. I got in the back of the SUV and scooted to middle between the front seats so I could see both of them.

"Okay Shane is here! Tell us what the hell is going on." Charles said sitting in the passenger side seat.

Big Mike started the story off slowly. "Adriona and I came to have a nice dinner at Alfini's. We often come here; it's one of our favorite restaurants in the city."

Charles interrupted. "What the hell Big Mike, I know you didn't get Shane and I to come down here in the middle of the night to tell us about you and Adriona's favorite restaurant. Who is the traitor and, what is it that you have to show us? I don't have time for no bullshit!

"This ain't no bullshit! We got a serious situation on our hands that could jeopardize our company."

"Is it Brendham?" I asked.

"No!

"Then who the hell is it!" Charles retaliated.

"Yea, Big Mike why are you trying to spoon feed us?" I asked.

"Because it's difficult to tell you what I'm about to tell you."

"What the hell? Just tell us we're big boys!" Charles piped.

Big Mike was silent. Whatever was on his mind that he wanted to tell us was causing him some angst. His silence only made Charles and I grow more impatient. We grilled him some more about having us out here this time of night sitting in his SUV. Then, Big Mike exploded.

"Darrell's a faggot!"

Both Charles and I were silenced.

"What the hell did you just say?" Charles demanded.

"You heard me." Big Mike said somberly.

"What makes you say something like that?" I asked.

Now Big Mike had our undivided attention. Our patience grew instantly, giving him time to explain. He started in on his story, but this time he picked it up when he and Adriona were leaving Alfini's.

"We were waiting for the valet to bring the car around, when I spotted Darrell across the street going into a Bar. I tried to hail him down, but he didn't hear me. So, I turned to Adriona and asked her would she like to go over to the bar and have a drink with Darrell. She looked hesitant and unsure, so I asked her what's wrong. She asked me if I knew what kind of bar that was. I didn't quite understand what she meant, until she told me it was a gay bar. I started laughing saying my boy don't know what kind a bar that is, watch him come jetting out of there with the quickness. I thought man is he going to get it on Monday. He will be the laughing stock of the trade room, but as I waited to see him come scrambling out of that bar it didn't happen. The valet pulled up in the SUV, I asked him to pull it back and park it in front here. I waited some more trying to give Darrell the benefit of the doubt, but no Darrell. Fifteen to twenty minutes had passed. I looked at Adriona. She was quiet. I was angered. I felt betrayed. I took my anger out on her. How did she know that was a gay bar? Had she been in there before, was she bi-curious? I started turning into my old self."

"What the fuck does that mean, you started turning into your old self?" Charles asked.

"Let him finish." I responded.

"I caught myself and apologized to Adriona. I put her in a cab and sent her home. Once she left I wandered over to the bar and looked inside. She was right; it was a gay bar, not a woman in sight."

"Did you see Darrell inside?"

"Yes, and he's still in there. I haven't seen him walk out yet."

I was surprised by the revelation, but didn't feel betrayed nor did I think Darrell was a traitor. It was his private life. It was his choice to keep it private or make it public. Big Mike felt differently.

"What are we going to do about this?"

"There is nothing to do." I responded.

"What?" Big Mike asked surprisingly.

"Big Mike what do you want us to do? Go in there and beat the gayness out of Darrell. If he wants to get rim jobs and give blow jobs so be it." Charles said laughingly.

"Respect! Darrell's our brethren. No reason to be disrespectful and Big Mike there is no reason to call him a faggot. I got much love for Darrell as a brother and that love will not change or fade away just because he is gay."

"Shane, I apologize about the faggot comment, but you guys don't feel betrayed by this guy? We all have been boys for over a decade now. We've been through thick and thin together, and our friendship and trust has gotten us through. If he can keep this from us, what else could he be keeping from us?"

"Big Mike did it cross your mind he kept it from us all these years because he feared our reaction and the loss of our friendship?" I said

"I bet you that's why he and his mother don't have a closer relationship. That story about him not going in the military and not following the career path his mother wanted for him is just a cover." Charles said.

"We are his family and have been since our days at Jordan. And,….you know what? We should go over there and give him the support he deserves and let him know he has our love regardless."

That was just what we did. Big Mike had reservations, but Charles and I convinced him to join us. When we walked in the bar, Darrell was sitting at the bar talking to another brotha. I walked up behind him and tapped him on the shoulder. Big Mike and Charles were standing behind me. Darrell reacted shocked and seemed suddenly nervous. He stood up in front of us and began to speak in a shaken voice.

"I should have told….."

"No worries D, you're our brotha and that's all that matters to us." I interrupted.

He looked behind me to Charles and Big Mike, and Charles nodded his head to let him know he was with him, but Big Mike gave no indication.

"I wanted to tell you guys, but I thought.... I thought..."

"We understand." I said calmly patting him on the back.

The guy he was talking to gave all of us a crazy look.

Charles explained." This is our friend and he's having his coming out party."

Charles always found a way to bring humor to a situation. We laughed, but Big Mike wasn't laughing, and he looked uncomfortable. Darrell smiled, gave me a dap and a hug, then Charles, but Big Mike stood back, so Darrell respected his space.

"We'll see you later; I got to get home to the wife." I said.

"Yea, I got to get back to my caramel sundae, and we'll let you get back to your fudge bar." Charles added.

"Damn! Darrell, you know Charles he can't help himself."

"How about you Big Mike?" Darrell asked.

Big Mike didn't answer he walked out of the bar.

"He's going to need some time, but don't worry Big Mike will come around." I said.

Charles and I left the bar and caught up to Big Mike.

"You all right big man?" Charles asked.

"This ain't no damn joke, and Darrell's a faggot!"

"Respect Big Mike!"

"I'm sorry Shane, but that's just the way I feel."

Big Mike walked to his SUV got in and drove off. Charles and I walked to our cars and went home. When I arrived at home, Kendra was still awake on the couch watching television. I joined her.

"Who was the traitor?"

"There wasn't one." I said exhaustively.

"Then, what was Big Mike talking about?"

"Darrell is gay."

She paused. "Really?" She said.

"Don't even try it."

"Try what?"

"You knew Darrell was gay."

Silence.

I looked at her directly. "How long have you known?" I asked.

Silence.

"Are you going to answer my question?"

"Darrell started hanging out at the boutique a lot when we broke up. You guys were in the middle of building your trading desk, and he would stop by to see how I was holding up. His visits became more frequent which made me nervous because I wasn't aware of his intentions. I still loved you and wanted to get back with you. He made it clear he was strictly interested in a friendship. As our friendship and trust grew, he confided in me about his sexuality. I was surprised to say the least. He told me none of you were aware, and he asked me to keep his secret, and at that time I promised to do so."

"So, you didn't think it was prudent to tell me as your husband."

"I've struggled with it since we've been married. I wanted to tell you, but I didn't want to betray his trust."

"What does it say about a woman that is more concerned about betraying the trust of a friend than keeping secrets from her husband?"

Kendra was still. Her eyes were still and steady looking directly into my eyes. She couldn't produce the words to explain herself. As far as I was concern, there were no words.

"I pleaded with him to tell you, but he was afraid he would lose your friendship. I tried to assure him that would not happen, but he reminded me you dumped me because of my previous fiancé."

I just looked at her in amazement. Now it's my fault that she kept secrets from me. I didn't get it." So, it's my fault."

"No, I am not saying that."

"Then what are you saying?"

"I don't know." She said frustrated….. "Shane people look up to you, no one wants to disappoint you, and Darrell was scared. He didn't want to lose you; he didn't want to lose Black Street. I saw his fear; it was real. I didn't have the heart to risk your friendship with him because I really wasn't sure how you would react."

"I have clients that are gay." I responded.

"Shane you have a public persona and you have a private one and sometime the two can be worlds apart.

I paused.

She continued. "I should have told you."

"Yes you should have. There is a fair amount of uncertainty in my life with all that's going on, and what I don't need is uncertainty in my home? I can't deal with what I have to deal with out in this crazy world, and then come home and have questions of trust with my wife. You are the most important person in my life, if I can't trust you, I'm dead on arrival."

"I'm sorry,…but you are scaring me with all this talk of uncertainty in your life and dead on arrival. I want you to stop it." She falls in my arms on the couch crying. "You are the love of my life and you will never have to worry again about trust with me…..I am sorry Shane!" She said with sincerity.

"I love you and I do trust you!"

"Is there something going on I should know about?" she asked as her head lay against my chest.

"There are a couple of things and when I am sure what is taking place I will share it with you. I don't want you to worry unnecessarily, and at this point there is no reason to worry. I just have to sort some things out."

She understood. We fell asleep on the couch until the wee hours of Sunday morning until Miles and Monique woke us up. We spent the rest of the day at the park and playground, visiting in-laws, and shopping for clothes for Miles and Monique. I really enjoyed my family time; it was an escape for me. Playing and spending time with my wife and kids was euphoric and peaceful. I could have spent the rest of my life living out my days raising and caring for my children and loving my wife.

****

Monday morning I rose early and before I left the house, I called Mr. Brendam to meet up with me in a little coffee shop in Harlem on 125th street not far from the Apollo Theater. I got there about fifteen minutes early. I took a seat in the back of the coffee shop, but I had a clear view of the door. When Brendham entered he spotted me quickly, then walked and joined me at the small round wooden table. I had a coffee at the table waiting for him. I slid the coffee toward him. He grabbed it and took a sip.

"Black just the way I like it." He said as he looked me directly in the eyes.

I acknowledged his satisfaction with the coffee.

"Surprised to receive a call from you this morning, but glad to hear from you….Where are your partners?"

"Work." I responded calmly as I sipped my coffee."

Silence over took the table. "You don't like me much, do you Shane?"

I didn't answer the question. "How can you assist me with the CIA and FBI?" I asked.

"Okay, I see, what I said to you all at our last meeting resonated. For starters I could monitor through my contacts at the CIA and FBI what interest they have in your business and personal activities, and also identify if you are just a person of interest or has their view escalated to a threat of national security."

"Threat to national security?" I asked.

"Once you are designated in that category – the divide and conquer strategy is implemented-infiltration into your organization or creating friction between you and your partners will be imminent."

"Friction between us not possible."

"You mean Darrell being a homosexual didn't cause problems amongst you all?"

I knew then, I really didn't like Mr. Brendham. He was still watching us. "Why are you still watching us?" I said disturbed.

"Two reasons- First to show you I'm good at what I do, and if a retired old fart like me can get intel on you without your knowledge, how effective do you think the FBI and CIA can be? Second, to show you that you need my skill set as a part of your organization for intel and security purposes."

Everything he said made sense to me, but I still didn't trust him. There was something about him that didn't sit right with me. I knew I needed to talk it over with the fellas before I brought him on. Mr. Brendham and I continued to talk hypothetically about if we were to bring him into Black Street, how he envisioned his role. He described a small elite security force that would report directly to him with separate office space. A budget for salaries and miscellaneous expensed commensurate with their duties of gathering intel, security, and covert operations. It all sounded surreal to me! He even talked about training us in self-defense techniques, hand to hand combat, and weapons. As he got more into detail the more intense his voice became. This started to remind me of the novel *The Spook Who Sat by the Door*.

We ended our meeting with a handshake.

"Time is short, there are things you needed in place yesterday. I look forward to hearing from you soon. " Mr. Brendham said.

I didn't respond.

"By the way Shane, I'm honored by the opportunity to work with you."

I nodded, and then left the coffee shop.

Blue Sky

I made it into the office about two hours after the market opened. When I walked in there was a vail of silence that permeated through the trade room. Not much of a greeting from anyone, when I entered the room. Big Mike, Charles, and Darrell gave me a halfhearted what's up with a nod. Everyone else was silent. I sat down at my trading desk next to Darrell.

"What's up?" I asked him.

"Ask Big Mike." He replied.

His response said it all. Big Mike's discomfort with Darrell's lifestyle had made its way into the trade room. I turned around in my chair and looked in Charles direction. He looked up with uncertainty. I looked to Big Mike, who shrugged, as others did when I scanned the room. I surmised that most everyone in the trade room sided with Big Mike's sentiments. My patience was wearing. I had too much on my mind, too many things to resolve, too many issues in the forefront, my passiveness, my apologies, and compassion were betraying me. I tapped Darrell on the shoulder, stood and gestured for him to follow me. I did the same with Charles and Big Mike. We all walked in the private office. I closed the door behind us.

"We've all come a long way together! Now one of us has revealed a lifestyle that is contrary to what we believed. There is a cloud of uncertainty about our brotherhood. There needs to be a reckoning here in this room right now amongst ourselves. Now is the time to get it on the table, speak your mind, but keep your words respectful. When you lose respect, you lose perspective."

Big Mike spoke first. "I don't agree with his choice of lifestyle."

"It's not a choice!" Darrell rebutted quickly.

"Fuck that! It's a choice." Big Mike came back.

"I think it's a choice too." Charles joined in.

Darrell took a deep breath and exhaled.

"Does it really matter if it is a choice or not? Is that really the issue?" I asked.

No one responded.

"What is different about Darrell this day, then the days preceding us finding out about him being gay?" I asked.

No response.

"No answer, because there is no difference, he is the same man that we embraced and loved through college and the years proceeding. Only thing new is we have found out about Darrell's private life." I continued

"We found out that he is a liar," Big Mike shouted!

"I didn't lie about anything," Darrell shouted back!

"You just didn't tell us," Charles added.

"Which is the same thing as a lie!" Big Mike came back!

"Are you homophobic Big Mike?" Darrell asked?

"Hell no! What does that mean anyway?"

"It's a fear or discrimination of homosexuals," Darrell responded.

"Fear, discrimination- no, in disagreement to the lifestyle, yes." Big Mike said.

"I have to say I don't condone the lifestyle either." Charles added.

"This is why I didn't want to tell you guys. Two of the closest people to me now stand in judgment of me. Neither of you have the right. I will not apologize for who I am, and if you choose not to work with me going forward, then Shane can "cut me one" for my equity share in Black Street Capital."

"That's not going to happen. Whatever your objections to Darrell are, get over it. We have a lot to deal with and this shit right here is not worth falling out over."

"I don't know if I can move forward with a liar." Big Mike added.

"Big Mike what about your lies?" Darrell asked.

"What the hell are you talking about my lies?"

"What happen at your house with Shane?"

Big Mike did not respond.

Darrell continued. "As you said, not saying something is the same as lying."

Big Mike looked in my direction. I left it up to him. I kept true to my promise. Our secret would not be revealed from my lips. Big Mike put his head down ashamed of what he was about to expose. He started off with the history of his relationship with Adriona, how I found out about Adriona, his reaction, and our altercation that landed me in the hospital.

Charles eyes were buck wide with his mouth open. Darrell just had a blank stare.

"After all Shane has done for you, and you put him in the hospital. What the fuck were you thinking?" Charles drilled Big Mike?

"I wasn't, and I will never forgive myself."

"You were thinking, just not rationally," Darrell added.

"Big Mike and I have squashed that bit of history and we are moving forward. I want that for all of us with Darrell. Put this issue behind us move forward with our eye on the prize. We have more pressing issues."

"Like what?" Charles asked.

"I had a meeting with Brendham this morning."

"Without us?""

"Yes, I got some information on Brendham Saturday morning and by Saturday night we were dealing with this situation, and I met with him this morning."

"What happen?" Darrell asked.

"Well he is who he says he is, and he wants to work for us doing intel gathering and security."

"What do you think?" Big Mike asked.

I got questions from each of them which was a good sign. It meant they were refocusing on what really mattered.

"I think we might want to seriously consider bringing him in. I don't fully trust him, but I think there is some validity to what he has told us."

"Before we hire him, we need to have him show us proof of what he has told us." Darrell said.

"I agree! We make that condition a prerequisite to bringing him on."

"How do you know he is who he says he is?" Big Mike asked.

"Ice had a contact in DC that was able to get their hands on some confidential FBI files."

"How is that?" Charles asked.

"Brothas still have jobs with access just not through legal means!"

"Aha,…." Charles acknowledged with a dap.

"I say we move with that plan." Big Mike added.

"Not to get off topic but what about the others in the trade room? Some are not comfortable with Darrell after finding out he is gay?" Charles asked.

"Follow me!" I opened the office door walked into the trade room followed by Big Mike, Charles, and Darrell. "Can I have your attention please?" I announced. C-Walk, Soul Train, Maria, White-Chocolate looked toward me. "It has come to my attention some are uncomfortable with Darrell since he revealed he is gay. For those who feel you cannot work with him any longer because of his lifestyle, there is the door. I will have Betty cut you one today."

No one moved, no one said anything! I said nothing else. I walked to my desk and called Brendham. I gave him our prerequisite to bringing him on board.

The next day Brendham came into the office early with the documents we required. Upon his departure Big Mike and I escorted Brendham to the elevator lobby and as he entered elevator 1, much to our surprise the Mackeys' along with three Titan executives exited elevator 2 standing right in front of Mike and I in our lobby.

"Can we talk Shane?" Mr. Mackey asked.

The others were silent even Junior.

"Of course." Mike and I escorted them to the conference room. Once in the room Mike excused himself and returned with Charles and Darrell as the Mackeys and the Titan executives were getting settled in the conference room.

We sat on opposites sides of the conference room table somewhat reminiscent of my mediation hearing at GPG. I scanned the faces of the men who sat before me. Each Titan executive expressionless, but their body language said nervous and uncertain. The fidgeting in their chairs and their restless hands told on them. Junior I could read from a mile away –upset, though he was trying his best to cover it up. As for Mr. Mackey I couldn't get a read on him. He was calm and cool as usual.

"Shane we wanted to talk with you about a deal." Mr. Mackey started off. "It has come to our attention Red has made a decision about the future of the Blue Sky."

If Mr. Mackey would have made the visit alone, he would have had a better chance of bluffing me, but bringing along the others doomed his chances. I heard him out anyway just to measure the desperation. As he laid out his pitch it took everything to hold back the joy I felt inside. We had accomplished the dream. Blue Sky was ours for the taking. Mr. Mackey told us they had heard through the grapevine the offer was leaning toward Titan. He wasn't sure and the small probability of the offer tipping in our favor wasn't worth the risk in being left out of the deal. Titan was offering a 50/50 partnership in Blue Sky, executive management positions in the new merged company, generous salaries and bonuses. It all sounded good and wonderful, but it was all bullshit. Neither Titan nor GPG wanted us in on this deal. They wanted us out of the picture entirely and their bitterness over the World Textile deal was evident, especially Junior. Given the greed factor of Titan this was an act of desperation.

Once Mr. Mackey was finished with pitching Titan's offer, Darrell and Charles hit Mr. Mackey with questions requesting a little more color and details to the offer which Mr. Mackey was more than oblige to give. Big Mike and I kept quiet. I tried to keep my best poker face. Once the question and answer session was over. Mr.

Mackey asked for an answer to their offer. I took the liberty of answering for us all.

"At this time we will take the offer under consideration, but we will not be able to commit to any deal today."

"When can we have an answer?" Junior pushed.

"This is a decision that should not be done in haste, so we are going to need a few days."

"WE DON'T HAVE A FEW FUCKING DAYS!" shouted Junior.

Heads hung on the other side of the conference table. Mr. Mackey took a deep breath glanced at Junior then rose from his chair and extended his hand.

"We look forward to hearing from you Shane."

I rose and shook his hand, then called for the receptionist to escort them out of the office. We all shook hands, even with Junior, and they exited the conference room in single file with Titan executives bringing up the rear.

Darrell was the first to rush me, when they were out of sight, gave me the biggest hug. I almost fell over. "How did you know?" he asked.

"Their body language gave it away."

"Fuck man we did it!" Charles declared.

Big Mike sat back down with a euphoric expression on his face. Darrell's emotions started to get the better of him so I made him take a seat.

"I know we don't always see eye to eye, and I give you a hard time about some of your tactics, but I wouldn't want to be with anyone else in a fox hole in the midst of battle. I thank you for the friendship, your loyalty, for Black Street, and letting me be a part of your family." Darrell said. He then stood and gave me a dap and a hug.

Charles followed with a dap and a hug, then said. "You ain't all that."

Big Mike followed him." I knew you would lead us to heights only our dreams have reached."

"Give me a minute I'll be right back." I said.

I walked to the private office which had a bar, grabbed a bottle of champagne, and brought it back to the conference room with four champagne glasses. I set the glasses on the conference table before all of us, filled the glasses with champagne, set the bottle down, and picked up one of the glasses and the others followed. We all raised our glasses.

"To the brothas who came before us and paved the way to allow us to shine, and special thanks to Reginald Lewis for asking the question: "Why should white guys have all the fun"

We toasted and drank our champagne full of joy and excitement. We agreed not to tell anyone until the official offer came from Blue Sky which happened three days later!

****

We were having a quiet dinner the four of us going over the transition of Blue Sky at restaurant in Harlem. Charles mind was somewhere else. I asked him several times was everything okay, and he assured me everything was good, but he had the look of a man who just lost his woman. I knew the feeling! As we were finishing up our dinner my thoughts were confirmed. Carmen walked in the restaurant on a date with another man. She was looking exceptionally good – dressed in a knee high fitted black dress, black pumps, hair pulled back to show off her high cheek bones and caramel skin tone. What was most disturbing than her being out on date looking every bit of a ten, was who she was with- C-Walk.

"What the fuck?" asked Big Mike looking in the direction of Charles.

No response from Charles he stared at the table they were sitting at. They hadn't noticed us. We were in the rear of the restaurant tucked in a corner for privacy; we didn't want to be disturbed. We watched them, flirting back and forth and the heavier it got, the angrier Charles became, not verbally, but I saw veins flare up in his temple. He tried to keep his composure as much as possible. He finally spoke. "We gonna have to fire C-Walk."

"Done!" I saw C-Walk's dating of Carmen as an act of betrayal.

Darrell leaned over and whispered in my ear. "What grounds do we have to fire him?"

"Fuck him, he's gone!" I whispered back.

We finished our dinner, I paid the bill and then Big Mike, Darrell, and I got up to exit the restaurant. We walked right pass Carmen and C-Walk without a word. Their attempt at a greeting fell on deaf ears much to their surprise. Why they both were surprised showed how ignorant they both were to the gravity of the situation, but in my mind that fact wasn't lost on Carmen. I think she was using C-Walk to make Charles jealous, but she had no idea she was playing with fire. Once we reached the coat and hat check to retrieve our things we noticed Charles was still at the table sitting. He slowly rose up and made his way through the restaurant, he seemed to be loosening his belt buckle on his pants, then once he made it pass Carmen and C-Walk's table he released his belt from his pants with a single pull. He turned and wrapped his belt around C-Walk's neck from behind him and with a single twist and lift commenced to drag him out of the restaurant on his back as if he was hauling a sack of potatoes.

We all were in shock. Carmen screamed at Charles, but he paid her no mind and as he hauled C-Walk choking through the restaurant past us and out the front door. We followed. At the top of the stairs Charles used his belt to fling C-Walk down the stairs where he went tumbling recklessly. Charles advanced down the stairs with a singular focus of dispensing some more punishment. Big Mike, Darrell, and I followed him down the stairs with a mob mentally with the intention of teaching C-Walk a lesson. You cross one of us, you cross all of us and you will pay the price. Just as we got to him half dazed at the bottom of the stairs, I could hear Carmen screaming "NO, NO .. Don't do it!" From nowhere Brendham and four men jump in front of C-Walk shielding him from the onslaught.

"You can't do this!"

"Get the fuck out of my way Brendham!" Charles demanded.

"Shane you know, you can't do this." Brendham yelled.

I said nothing. I grabbed Charles and backed him off and sat him down on the stairs. I sat behind him and Big Mike and Darrell joined us on the steps. Brendham and his men got C-Walk to his feet.

"C-Walk you're fired. Betty will cut you one tomorrow." I said stately.

"You can't fire me!"

"I just did. Brendham see if he has his security card on him and confiscate it."

Brendham patted C-Walk down and followed my directions. Brendham and the four men with him now worked for us. We hired him and gave him a budget for staff and private office space. Brendham was our head of security responsible for overall security of Black Street and the personal security of each of us. So, his interceding was not a complete surprise. He was detailed and thorough. One or two of his staff mirrored us outside the office at all times. Something he insisted upon, when it was clear that our buyout of Blue Sky was imminent. We had monthly meeting with Brendham where he would update us on all material and pertinent issues concerning the security of Black Street, even personal issues that he felt needed to be addressed that would put anyone of us at risk.

He had mentioned to me in private about the tumultuous relationship between Charles and Carmen, and advised me to talk to him about just cutting it off. I got upset and told him to stick to more material issues not ancillary. He never spoke of it again. My comfort level with him mirroring me was not high and Kendra absolutely hated it.

She thought our private lives should be just that private, but when I disclosed to her about the file Ice was able to get his hands on. She acquiesced and tolerated the invasion for the sake of the kids. Kendra really cozied up to the idea when the announcement was made public about Black Street taking over Blue Sky and we had ten reporters out in front of our home looking to get a story. Brendham sent two men to the house to keep the reporters at Bay, so we could have some semblance of privacy.

Carmen came down the stairs and upon face to face with Charles the argument kicked off. The spectacle was almost comical. She didn't give a damn about the well-being of C-Walk, barely gave a glance his way, and when it was said and done, she left with Charles.

Everyone else left, Big Mike, Darrell, and I remained sitting on the stairs.

"What are we becoming?" Darrell asked.

No response.

He continued. "We are changing and not for the better. What we have to realize is with greater power comes greater responsibility. And, at this time we are on the road to abusing that power. First, we were about to beat a man up because who he was out on a date with, then we fired him because of his date. We are not gods!" he emphasized, then got up and left.

Big Mike stood. "We are Gods. When a man reaches his peak of potential he becomes God like. Shane, never think you are less than a god; you have just taken a mortal form." Then he left leaving me alone to my thoughts on the steps of the restaurant.

****

It took several months to close the deal and transition our management team in place at Blue Sky. We had some frivolous law suits we had to get through from some minority shareholders and Titan Industries who tried to block the buyout. Darrell was named CEO, Charles was CFO, Big Mike was Lead Counsel, Betty was Senior Vice President of Human Resources, and I put Susan as our COO which came as a surprise to everyone, even Susan.

Susan was more than qualified to be COO, matter of fact I would have been comfortable with her as CEO, but that was a job made for Darrell. All were curious why I didn't take an active day to day roll in the management of Blue Sky. Day in and day out job in the corporate world didn't appeal to me. As Chairman of the Board I would be able to see and have input to the overall strategic planning of the company and I was satisfied with that. My new role gave me more time at home with Kendra and the kids which I found to be gratifying. I took to fatherhood much more than I anticipated. With the birth of my children, I came to believe to help in the development and growth of a child, especially your own was a human experience all should have the opportunity to participate in.

Miles and Monique were growing up getting to the age where their questions were abundant and Miles wanted to see and spend more time with his Dad. I never knew mine, and I for damn sure was going to make sure Miles knew his. Miles was 4 years old now, so we enrolled him in the breakfast program in Harlem sponsored by Black Street for young black males. I taught a class on money and financial literacy. I used popular culture to articulate the fundamental principles of money. I would use the triumphs and downfalls of known celebrities in popular culture to emphasize my points. Other workshops and classes would emphasize history and the principles of development to become a man- from Boyhood to Manhood.

The Breakfast program was six days a week before school and on Saturday mornings. The program was free for all enrollees and they would receive a complimentary breakfast each morning along with their morning class. The Breakfast Club became so popular that there was a waiting list to get in. We also had parents outside the Harlem community that wanted their sons to be a part of the Breakfast Club. The demand increased rapidly as word travelled through surrounding communities about this unique program targeting young black males. We saw the need to expand the program and immediately set up Black Street Foundation, a nonprofit with sole purpose of funding the activities and programs for the Breakfast Club. We set up a board of directors and full time staff with the intentions of expanding the Breakfast Club to other communities in need. The news was met with great enthusiasm, but had its critics because of the exclusive nature of the student body, young black males.

I wasn't surprised at the criticism. Anytime you target a population even for good purpose there are some who cannot get past the exclusionary factor, even in the face of success they continue to be critical.

We had one other public criticism when the community was fighting for more services and organized a march down the street in which the Breakfast Club building was located. Some of the students and I watched as they marched with signs and t-shirts that articulated their position. One lady paused and asked why we weren't participating. She had a cigarette in one hand and a beer in another. I responded. "I don't believe in Marching. We don't teach that principle here to march with your hand out asking for something. The ideas we coveted were to learn how the game was played, educate ourselves on the rules of the game, then play to win. That is the American way! To teach our youth any other way, we feel, puts them at a disadvantage."

The lady looked with dismay and disagreement. "If it wasn't for marching you wouldn't have any civil rights and your black ass wouldn't be able to walk through the front door of a white owned restaurant."

"Well, to speak frankly I don't think that is altogether a bad alternative. If you look at the history of our community, black owned businesses were better off before civil rights. Once black folk had the right not to shop within their communities we broke our necks to give our dollar away. We essentially self- destructed by destroying our markets within our community and killing the power of capitalism within our community. Now instead of controlling and participating in capitalism, we fall victims to it. For example look at you, you have a cigarette in one hand and a beer in another, and you are marching for more services in your community, but all they do is flood our community with beer and cigarettes. If one of these stores were to put a big sign out saying Sale on Beer and Cigarettes, we wouldn't see you marching one more step until you went and got some more beer and cigarettes.

The lady was dump founded, the expression on her face told it all –she was speechless. Some of the students laughed, but I pulled them all back inside the building. I don't know if I was right or wrong in telling the lady that, but I think sometimes our efforts are misplaced and the emphasis should be on empowering ourselves not asking for anyone to empower us.

My time at the Breakfast Club became a big part of my life, especially with my son being there with me. I did take Miles on business trips with me and allowed him to sit in on meetings with me. I thought the experience at times were immeasurable, and would give him not only a sense of how capitalism and business commerce worked, but give him insight to people – how they react and interact.

As if my life couldn't get any better, my mother finally moved from Los Angeles to New York. I bought her a brown stone only five blocks away from us. She was retired and now enjoyed spending her time with her grandchildren.

Back to Africa

Since the takeover of Blue Sky, the market capitalization remained stable. There were no big moves to the upside or downside of the stock price. We all took that to mean the markets found the buyout to be neutral. They had no real issues with the new management and a lot of the mid-level management positions remained the same except for the finance area where we placed White-Chocolate and Marie VP of Financial Planning and VP of Financial Analysis. I was long overdue for a visit to the main headquarters in Dallas. I took a red eye flight out in the Blue Sky corporate jet which was the 2009 Challenger 300 had a white exterior with blue and gray stripes. The interior seated 10 passengers –six placed club seating, three placed divan seating, all covered in tan leather. There was tan wool carpet throughout, forward galley, microwave oven and an expresso machine, high gloss sapele fig cabinetry, and brushed aluminum hardware. This was the first time I flew in a private jet. Sitting in this aircraft felt unreal, like I was dreaming living another man's life. I flew with one security personnel, Tiger and one attendant, an older lady, brunette, with caked on makeup to hide her more evident features of maturity. She was pleasant and polite, and for the most of the flight she left Tiger and I alone to our reading and conversation.

Brendham controlled security personnel, but I had handpicked Tiger as my personal security. I knew Tiger ever since he started his first day a GPG as the building security guard. We talked sometimes about sports and politics, when I came to and from work. He was diligent and a hard worker. I remember when he got married and when he had his first child; he now had two children, same as me. He saw me and the family at a restaurant, and asked for a job reference. With a larger family the pay at GPG wasn't cutting it. His wife had some health issues with the second birth and his insurance didn't cover the extra cost. I made Brendham put him on his payroll and train him. Brendham's people were well paid I think each were well into the high five figures and Brendham himself was pulling down six figures. I always got the feeling Brendham resented that I forced Tiger on his payroll. Tiger felt the distance between him, Brendham and the other security personnel which caused him some concern. In the quietness of our private flight he revealed as much to me.

"Brendham is quite the character don't you think?" Tiger asked.

"What makes you say that?"

"It's just a feeling I get about him."

"What kind of feeling?"

"A feeling of a soulless man, he is without a soul."

"Why do you think that?"

"It's the coldness in which he treats his personnel. The lack of caring and sometimes respect in his communication with us. His attitude permeates throughout the department which I think is counterproductive, and could possibly jeopardize the security of Black Street."

"I appreciate you sharing this with me, and your concerns haven't fallen on deaf ears. One thing to know about Brendham is, he is by the book and has a military and FBI background. So, his demeanor can be harsh, but I find him to be fair."

Tiger didn't say much on the subject after that. We chatted some more about sports and family, then I took to my reading until we arrived in Dallas.

Darrell had a car pick us up from the airport and take us to our hotel which was in downtown Dallas. My appointment with Darrel wasn't until one in the afternoon, so I slept in, woke up around 10:00 am and worked out in the hotel gym. The car picked me up a little after 12:00. I made it to Darrell's office about a quarter to one. He was in his office hard at work looking every bit the part of a CEO of a multi-billion dollar international company. His office looked the part also; it was about one thousand square feet, hard wood floors, oriental rugs place under his desk and sitting area of his office. His desk was made of polished oak large enough for six people to eat a grand meal. The office had a wet bar, a private bathroom, and an area for receiving guest furnished with a black leather couch and a coffee table.

"Hey you made it!" He said when I entered his office.

"Yea, the corporate jet is nice!"

"Yea, I enjoy that ride from time to time myself."

He got up and gave me a big hug. "How are Kendra and the kids?"

"They are great! Kendra says hello, and wants to know why you don't return her calls?"

"Just trying to get my head around this huge company!"

"I know, but take some time to call the ones who care about you!"

"Yea, you're right. I will call her today!"

"She would like that!"

I could tell by Darrell's body language he was anxious to talk business. We quickly moved on from the small chat and sat down on his couch next to the bar. Darrell wasted no time unloading his concerns. First and foremost was the continued interference by Titan Industries with their fifteen percent interest, they were trying to pressure us to place some of their executives on our management team, and they did manage to get a seat on board, but we took them to court and were able to establish giving them a seat on the board would be a conflict, given Titan was in direct competition with Blue Sky. The judge agreed with our position and ruled Titan could only be an investor with no management ties to Blue Sky.

Darrell knew this, so his concern about Titan was in my opinion a little overblown.

"Shane I am telling you they have people on the inside of this company. Either they were here before our takeover, or they have been able to turn a few in their favor."

"Do you think it's anyone amongst your management team?"

"Not my immediate team, but maybe mid-level. I had a conference call with some Titan executives and one let it slip about a third quarter operation mishap which will cost the company in the area of two million dollars. Now, there is no way they should have known this fact because it hasn't been made public yet, so there is a leak."

"What do you think their intentions are?"

"I don't think it is to sabotage the company, but maybe just bring it down enough so the stock price suffers enough the market turns against us and labels management as incompetent. Then, our investor base might force us to sell to recoup their investment if they feel the principal is threatened."

It made sense. If Titan could declare Black Street put in place a management team ill prepared to take over a company of Blue Sky's size, they could bring into question, not only, our ability to maintain the company, but to grow the company. The possibility of panicked investors backing out and forcing us to sell could become real. Even our African connection was not a friend to losing money. My concern began to grow.

"Get tighter security on all operations from the plants to shipping. They might not try to sabotage the whole company, but to sabotage some part of our operations could feed into their plans."

"Done!" Darrell replied. "Now, I have been thinking about our expansion possibilities, and I think with our Nigerian friends we can make a go on Africa."

"I think that is a great idea. Jakar could be a great help in opening up some doors for us."

"Can you give him a call and talk to him?"

"Yes."

"If he is amenable to the idea, lets setup a conference call with the three of us. I have some possibilities for exploration, refinement, and shipping."

"You've given this some thought already haven't you?"

"Yes, and I'm telling you Shane if we pull this off, our market capital could double!"

"You're talking two hundred billion in market cap?"

"Or more!"

"Anyone else in on your thoughts?"

"No, wanted you to talk with Jakar first before I shared with anyone else. All this doesn't work without his buy in."

"Okay."

We finished up our meeting on some minor issues. Later we had a visit from Charles and Big Mike. We talked and laughed as time slipped away from us, we didn't come up for air until after 5 o'clock.

"I have dinner reservations for us at 6pm."Darrell announced.

"Let's hit it!" Big Mike said excitedly.

****

Darrell had made the reservations at a small restaurant in downtown Dallas not far from the hotel where I was staying. It was an upscale soul food restaurant called Serena's. The restaurant had an intimate setting. All the seating was booth style, lighting was dim, and ambiance was reminiscent of the 1920's. All personnel from the hostess to the busboys were dressed impeccably in black and white. I was impressed with the attention to detail. There were black and white photos of the Jazz Greats from Louie Armstrong to Billie Holiday placed around the restaurant. They had a small three piece band in the corner playing some jazz standards from the bebop era. The band was playing "Take the A Train" when we walked in.

We were greeted by the owner herself Serena. She was elegant and refined. She seated us toward the back of the restaurant. Tiger took a seat at the small bar in front of the restaurant.

"We are expecting more company." And, just as Darrell completed that sentence in walk Maria and White-Chocolate.

They looked good. I was glad to see them. White-Chocolate greeted me with a heartfelt hug and Maria did the same.

"It's good to see you Shane. How are Kendra and the kids?" White-Chocolate asked.

"They are well. Thanks for asking."

Before we all took a seat, in came Carmen and Adriona. "Hey Mr. Jackson how are you doing? How is my girl, my niece and nephew?" Carmen asked.

"Good." I gave Carmen a hug and kiss on the cheek.

Adriona didn't say a word as she approached me, hugged me, gave me a kiss on the cheek, and then said in the softest of voices "Thank you."

Big Mike stepped in closer to embrace and greet her. I patted him on the back.

"Let's all take a seat. I have these two booths reserved." Darrell said.

"Before we all do that I have an announcement to make." Charles said.

"What's your announcement?" I asked.

"Carmen and I are engaged to be married!" He declared.

There was a moment of silence, until Darrell broke it by congratulating them both. Everyone else followed with their congratulatory gestures, and then we all sat down. Darrell and I along with Maria and White-Chocolate occupied one booth while Charles, Big Mike, Carmen, and Adriona sat in the adjacent booth. The news of the pending nuptials between Charles and Carmen came at a surprise to me. I hadn't talked to Charles or Big Mike since their move to Dallas, but I wouldn't have been surprised if Big Mike had made the announcement instead of Charles.

I knew Charles days of chasing skirts were not all behind him. There were rumors of him with some of his female counterparts at Blue Sky which Darrell had brought up in our afternoon meeting. I tried to get his attention when the waitress brought the menus to our tables, but he was too engrossed in conversation with Carmen. As we were ordering our food two others joined us much to my surprise and pleasure – Betty and Susan.

"Can a white girl get a seat at your table your high and mighty black Nubian King?" Susan asked sarcastically standing and looking down directly at me.

"Some things never change!" I said.

Darrell moved out and I followed. I hugged Betty, then Susan. Susan slid in the booth. Darrel and I stood talking with Betty. She looked good. I inquired about her son and life in Texas.

"Shane, I have family out here, and it's been nothing short of a blessing. My son gets to play and go to school with his cousins."

"I'm glad things are working out for you!"

She kissed me on the cheek. "Darrell is doing a great job running Blue Sky!"

"Thank you." Darrell expressed

"I know." I responded softly.

Betty joined Charles and Big Mike's table. Darrell and I sat back down in our booth. I slid in first, next to Susan. Susan and Maria were engaged in conversation. Our orders came to the tables. I had the red beans and rice, cornbread, collard greens, and fried chicken. Just then a white gentleman dressed in a blue suit, white dress shirt, and blue tie joined Charles and Big Mike's table sitting next to Betty. He looked to be about mid-forties, medium build and height, a good looking man. I saw Betty introducing him, but I couldn't make out what she was saying. Susan saw me observing Betty and this man, so she leaned over in my ear and whispered. "That's Betty's fiancé… are you going to fire her?"

I turned and whispered in her ear. "Fuck you."

She leaned back in my ear and whispered. "You could have."

This whole exchange between Susan and I was being watch by everyone at the table including Maria who was giving both of us a very weird and disapproving look. I finally got to my meal, it was superb. I ate every last bite-but I should not have – my stomach was tight. My movement was limited. All I could do was sit somewhat slumped down in the booth. I felt like a weight was on top of my belly weighing me down. The call for desert came, I passed. Susan and I began to chat again more civil now.

"How's Red?"

"He's fine, enjoying retirement, travelling, and spending more time with family and friends."

"Family and Friends are important."

"How's your family?"

"Good!"

"Do you have any pictures to share?"

I pulled out my phone and thumbed through pictures of me, Kendra, and the kids.

"Wow, your wife is strikingly beautiful. I wouldn't have gone for me either with something like that waiting for me at home."

We both laughed. She continued. "You have some great looking kids too! You have done well for yourself Shane. Don't take this the wrong way, but I'm proud of you!"

"I hope you don't take this the wrong way, but I am proud of you too, and I know you will do great things at Blue Sky. I've always been impressed with your business acumen since our undergrad days!"

"Alright cut the bull shit!"

"No, bull. Initially I just thought you were spoiled. After I got to know you, I understood the brashness to be boldness and confidence that as a woman in a male dominated society you needed to succeed, and succeed you have. Red saw in you the qualities I knew you possessed back at Darden."

"Okay now I'm going to cry." She said playfully.

She pushed me with her shoulder that made me sit up straight. Betty and her fiancé walked over to our table, and she introduced Tommy to all of us with a look of trepidation. She shied away from eye contact with me as she stood there. After we all greeted Tommy, they returned to their table.

I leaned over to Susan and whispered. "Does she really think I would fire her because of who she's going to marry?"

"She is not sure what you will do or how you will react!" She whispered back.

I asked Darrell to excuse me. I got up from my table and walked over to Betty and asked for a minute in private with her. We walked to the back of the restaurants near the bathrooms.

"Do you really think I would fire you because your fiancé is white?"

She was silent. Still hesitant to let her eyes meet mine.

"Come on Betty. You know me better than that. What happened at GPG with Emmy was more paranoia on my part than anything else." Her head was still down like a school girl in trouble talking to the principal. "Betty!" I said stoutly. "Look at me!"

Her head rose and our eyes finally met; her eyes were watery. "Ever since I've known you, you have been pro black, and you have done so much for me……I just don't want to disappoint you."

"Betty, first being pro black doesn't make you anti-anything else. Second, you could never disappoint me. It is I who's honored by your friendship. I want for you what you want for yourself- joy and happiness and if you find that in Tommy then I share in your happiness."

Betty hugged and kissed me on the cheek. She walked back to her table. I followed until Maria met me on the way back, grabbed my arm and asked to speak to me. We walked back to the very space Betty and I had just been.

"So, what's up between you and Susan?" She asked.

"Nothing, our friendship has been one big trip since we met in undergrad."

"Did you fuck her?"

"Maria, come on."

"I didn't think you would do her."

"Is that what you wanted to talk to me about?"

She was silent…"No, not really, not at all…I really wanted to thank you for talking with Dexter?"

I had a puzzled look on my face.

"My husband, White-Chocolate!" she emphasized.

"Oh!" I had been calling him White-Chocolate for so long I had forgotten his real name.

"I'm glad my little pep talk helped out!"

"It did more than help. It saved our marriage."

She moved in close slowly which made me uncomfortable, put her arms around my neck and hugged me tight. I returned the hug slightly lifting her off the ground. I placed her back down and she walked back to the table with me in tow.

We left Serena's around 10pm. Charles and Big Mike put Carmen and Adriona in cabs and sent them home. Big Mike, Charles, Darrell, and I walked to the hotel flanked by Tiger. It felt good to have us all together again. In the darkness we walked, talked, joked, laughed, and reminisced. Once we reached the hotel, we made our way to a little smoke shop inside the hotel.

"Cubans," Darrell requested.

"Yes!" Charles responded.

Darrell bought cigars for all of us. We sat, talked and smoked cigars.

"So, engaged uh?" I directed my question toward Charles.

"Yea." he responded irritably. "What, am I supposed to ask your permission? You not my got damn daddy!"

We all were taken back by his response. We looked around at each other in amazement then laughter over took Darrell, Big Mike, and me. I mimicked Charles.

"You not my got damn daddy." I said in whinny voice. "Where the hell did that come from?"

Charles chuckled. "Carmen says we all follow you like your Moses leading us to the promise land. I told her, it's not like that. We are just all very close. We're like brothers!"

"Sounds like she doesn't like Shane?" Big Mike added

"No, she likes Shane. She just thinks we put him on a pedal stool."

"She sounds a little salty." Darrell joined.

"Ah maybe, but I love her."

There was a silence. Charles looked around at all of us and our looks said it all – Really?

"I do. I love that woman."

"How about the other women you fool around with?" Darrell asked.

"That's just some side trim, no big deal. I don't give a shit about those women."

I knew he truly cared about Carmen, but Charles being ready to settle down is what I question. I did not want to sit in judgment of him. I understood his attitude and his behavior. As businessmen we always weigh the risk versus the reward, and obviously Charles thought the risk was worth the reward, but many men have miscalculated that risk and lost the ones they truly loved. I conveyed my sentiments to Charles.

"You've never cheated on Kendra?" Charles questioned.

"No!"

"Darrell is not going to drop a dime on you to Kendra." Charles said.

"I know that, but I haven't. There is no reward big enough for me to risk losing Kendra. That is a simple analysis for me."

"You haven't been put to the test yet that's all!"

"Yes I have."

"By whom?" Big Mike asked

"Susan and Maria."

"I knew Maria would test you, but Susan, I'm surprised! What happen?" Charles asked.

"She came to my hotel room in Dallas after Darrell and I made the pitch to Red."

"Oh shit!" Charles got excited.

I continued. "She undressed before me…

"What?" Big Mike gasped.

"I basically apologized for letting it go so far and she left."

"Did she have body?"

"Yea,.." I shook my head yes.

"Okay I guess it's my turn." Big Mike announced. "Adriona and I are married."

"Aaaah my boy!" I jumped up and gave Big Mike a dap and a hug. "Why didn't you tell us?"

"Everything just happened so fast. We went down to the county courthouse in Dallas one day and got married. Nothing we really planned, but something we knew, we wanted to happen."

"Congratulations Big Mike." Darrell said, then gave Big Mike a dap and a hug.

Big Mike held the handshake between him and Darrell. "I want to apologize for the disrespectful words and the way I treated you when I found out you were gay."

"I accept and appreciate the apology Big Mike." They hugged once again.

"Come here Big Boy!" Charles and Big Mike dapped and hugged. "Congratulations!

As we sat around I thought about the discussion Darrell and I had about expansion into Africa. Nigeria was about eight hours ahead, so 12:00am our time made it 8:00 am in Nigeria. I pulled out my phone and made the call to Jakar much to the dismay of the others.

"Who is he calling this time of night?" I heard Charles ask.

"Jakar, hey how are you?

"Jakar?" Big Mike questioned.

"I'm good Shane?" Jakar responded." How is everything in the states?"

"Very well my friend, very well!"

"What can I do for you?" He asked.

"Blue Sky is looking to expand its operations into Nigeria, and we were hoping you could give us some introductions and help pave the way."

"My brotha, I will be more than willing to do that. Your success is mine and I think it to be a grand idea."

"I will have Darrell give you a call tomorrow morning. It will be early evening your time. He has all the specifics of the expansion, the strategic plan and outlook."

"I look forward to hearing from him."

"Thanks Jakar!" I said

"It is my pleasure Shane. Talk to you soon."

I ended the call with Jakar. "It's done. He's expecting your call tomorrow." I said to Darrell.

"Expansion into Africa?" Big Mike questioned.

"I'll let Darrell fill you in." I said.

Darrell took the next hour laying out his plan of expansion into Nigeria. I could see Charles and Big Mike were impressed by what they were hearing. Concern came over their face once Darrell shared with him his fears of Titan possibly having some inside people working to adversely affect the operations of Blue Sky. They both looked to me.

"Darrell's going to tighten security around some of the critical operational areas of Blue Sky, and with this move into Nigeria we can grow the company and pay back investors and silent partners, and then run Blue Sky ourselves." I told them.

They received that bit of information well.

****

Our trip back to Africa was several months in the making. It took multiple conference calls, video conferences, cutting through the red tape, and kickbacks, but we got it done. Jakar really came through for us. He worked tirelessly in opening doors for us that were usually closed to foreign companies. A large part of our investor base being Nigerian was a key factor in Blue Sky getting proper permits for land purchase and oil exploration. The news of Blue Sky's venture into Africa took the market by surprise. We kept our plans for Africa just amongst us-Darrell, Big Mike, Charles, me, and Jakar. We emphasized to Jakar the utmost importance of keeping this private, and to keep the number of people in the know to a minimum. This way we were able to avoid Titan getting any hint to what we were up to, and it worked.

Titan knew nothing until they saw it in the papers. I got a call from Mr. Mackey at the GPG offices requesting a sit down. I obliged, but divulged nothing. The entire meeting he pushed for information, while I answered each question but never with what he really wanted to know. It was like a game of poker both of us were adept, no real winner emerged.

When we arrived in Africa, we were heavy with family, friends, and security. Brendham had some objections to the trip, but acquiesced once he was convinced the trip would go forward as planned. He mentioned since the announcement of the Blue Sky's oil exploration activities in Africa the government surveillance and activities concerning Black Street had picked up. He thought a trip to Africa was too much to pass up, so Brendham came with his family and four of his security personnel. He left Tiger behind much to my dismay, but his reasoning was Tiger was good for domestic security, but security in a foreign country took more of a seasoned veteran. He was the head of my security, and I had come to trust his judgment, so I didn't question his explanation. My main concern was the safety of not only my family, but for the entire Black Street entourage. Jakar had security personnel also that Brendham coordinated with which gave me more comfort.

I brought my entire family including my mother, Kendra's parents, and brother. Big Mike brought his wife Adriona, Charles brought Carmen, but Darrell came alone. To him this was much more of business trip and he wouldn't have too much time to sight see and socialize. He was focused. We had about ten others who were close friends that had never been to the Mother Land and saw this trip as their opportunity.

Jakar had a big reception for us when we arrived in Nigeria. He had a band playing with dancers all dressed in traditional garb as a welcoming party for us in the Lagos international airport. It was a special day. All of us were in awe at the very sight of the greeting. When done, Jakar gave us an official welcome speech. They made us feel like this was a real homecoming. We were escorted to a fleet of black SUV's that took us to our hotel in downtown Lagos. The hotel, a five star hotel, very modern, upscale, private, and the service was top notch.

Kendra was beaming with the biggest smile from ear to ear. Her happiness was contagious and made its way through our whole group. We settled in our room. Miles and Monique were exhausted. Their bodies would have to adjust to the time change, so we put them to bed for a nap before dinner. It gave Kendra and me some time alone. We sat together on the couch in the front room of the hotel suite with the lights dim and Fela playing in the background.

"I want to buy a home here." She said softly.

"Really, you want to live here?"

"In the summer months when the kids are out of school."

"I would like that and it would be a good experience for Miles and Monique."

"We could get a big enough space to house the entire family, my parents, your mother, and any friends who come and visit."

"Sounds like a good idea! Do you know where you would want to buy?"

"Victoria Island, where we were married."

"I thought you might say that; that is a beautiful place."

"I've yearned to go back there, since we left."

I laid my head on her lap and kicked up my legs across the couch. She stroked my head lovingly. Before I knew it I drifted off to sleep.

The next morning Darrell woke us early. We were meeting with businessmen who were helping to handle the logistics for the operation out of Nigeria. Big Mike, Charles, and I along with Brendham toured the exploration fields and the new refinery which both were completely staffed by locals. What I realized that day was Jakar was becoming an even more powerful man in his home country because of this partnership and relationship with us. With Blue Sky operating in Nigeria now, nothing was off limits to us. We had access to government officials, influential businessmen, and people of great prominence in the country. Our tour by some dignitaries we had not met before.

After the tour I had time to talk with Jakar in private at his request. We travelled with his security to his home in Lagos. I notice Jakar always travelled with a least two security guards and his home was guarded like Fort Knox with over ten men guarding it. His home was not much to see from the outside, stucco exterior with a dull earth tone color to go with its dull design and rectangle shape, but once inside, he spared no expense marble floors, spiraling stair cases, plush carpets, leather and tiger skin furniture, updated kitchen with fine oak cabinets, and a family room which could match the finest sports bar with at least 10 fifty inch wide screen flat televisions all around the room. The raised back leather chairs stuffed with enough cushion to feel like a bed. I fell in love with them. He offered me tea as we sat in the family room, and as usual he was more than forth right with me about his thoughts.

"Shane, you have exceeded my highest expectations of you. I was right when I pegged you as an up and coming star in American Capitalism. Your move to Blue Sky was nothing less than genius."

"Blue Sky was Darrell's idea, not mine. He deserves all the credit for that move."

He shook his head with a smile as he sipped his tea, as if he didn't believe me. "Yes." He paused, looked at me and took another sip of his tea. "How did you come upon this Brendham man?"

"Well, it was as you said. I was put on the radar of the American government intelligent agency because of my history at GPG and Black Street's takeover of World Textiles, and Mr. Brendham revealed that information to me."

"And, now he works for you?"

"Yes."

"How did he come to you? Meaning how did you meet him?"

"Well I thought I spotted him a few times following me, and thought my mind was playing tricks on me until he walked in my office and introduced himself."

"When was the first time you thought you spotted him?"

"Here in Nigeria on my first visit, at my wedding."

Jakar didn't respond immediately, he thought for a moment. "When he came into your office he told you the American government was tracking you."

"Yes."

"And, he has a military background and is and ex-FBI agent.

"What are you getting at? You don't think he is retired?"

"Shane in the Art of War, it states the most dangerous agent is the double agent. Your government has a history of infiltrating organizations they think is contrary to American interest."

"Contrary to American interest? I am the manifestation of the American dream."

"Yes, you are my friend, but as I told you when I first met you, your philosophy and approach of inclusion of African Americans and now Africans can be troublesome to some in your government."

"Why should I worry about that? I have broken no laws."

"It is not about the law. There are dues that need to be paid Shane, so your philosophy of inclusion can be spun the right way and not in a way that would label you a racist or an exclusionist. I know that may sound crazy, but we live in a crazy world."

"Who do I owe dues to?"

He looked at me. He couldn't believe I asked the question, but he knew the question came from an honest place. He answered. "People of influence in communities, inside and outside the political landscape, opinion molders, media, and other powerful people. These were some of the people with us today. I am constantly in contact with political figures and other influential people in Nigeria, and you need to do the same in America or you will be headed for more trouble than you can ever image. It's coming Shane, you must prepare for it! With Blue Sky, its coming!"

I understood having people of influence in my corner was important and essential for the long term survival of Black Street Capital, but my singular focus had been on Blue Sky for so long I hadn't taken the time to focus in that area, and the media coverage of my image and others at Black Street had been a mixed bag of tricks some good and some bad. I appreciated Jakar's words of warning and thanked him for his concern. I understood his concern was not only for me, but for himself as well.

Jakar's comments about Brendham were discomforting, but I trusted the information I had gotten from Ice's source in D.C. I had decided, I would have Ice double check the in

After thanking Jakar for his concerns and perspective, we sat without anything more to say. To break the silence I brought up the desire to purchase a home in Africa! He smiled widely.

"Ah, my brotha you want a home in the Mother Land."

"Kendra and I have talked about it, and we would like to spend our summers here with family and friends."

"That is a fine plan! When would you like to start looking?"

"Give us a couple of days, we have plans to take the family and friends sightseeing, but after that our schedule is more flexible."

"I have the perfect broker for you. Abeni my daughter; she has been in real estate for ten years and knows Nigeria like the back of her hand. I take it; you want to look in Victoria Island."

"You read our minds."

"Doesn't take much, if one had attended your wedding!"

Jakar was right our experience there was special and by buying a home there somehow I think Kendra and I wanted to share the experience with our children. We finished up our tea, talked some more business, and watched a bit of soccer. After a couple of hours I was back at our hotel.

****

A few days later our whole entourage headed to Victoria Island to help view and choose our home away from home. Kendra and Abeni had viewed numerous properties on line and Kendra narrowed it down to about five homes she wanted to tour. From what she told me, she had a lot of input from our mothers. When we arrived the weather was beautiful on the Island, sunshine and a clear blue sky. The sands and the water on the beach were calling us, so we split up into two groups, those who wanted to go directly to the beach and those who wanted to view the homes.

I opted for the beach with the kids, along with most of the men. I wasn't concerned about the purchase of the house. It was Kendra's for the choosing. When we settled on the beach, my children played in the water and sand by making sand castles with moats. The castle walls were high and solid protecting it from any external threats. As I watched my children erect this castle my thought went back to Jakar's words and how any trouble or threat that came my way was also a threat to my family. A frightened feeling came over me that made me want to hug my kids. My reaction to the feeling drew looks of befuddlement as I grabbed them and hugged them tightly, covering their faces with endless kisses. I turned and looked at Darrell, Charles, and Big Mike relaxed on the beach in shorts sitting in beach chairs taking in the warm sunshine.

I approached them and took a seat beside Darrell.

"Does your mother still work on the hill?"

"Yes. Why do you ask?"

"I want to meet her?"

"Why?"

Charles and Big Mike were listening in.

"It's time for us to avail ourselves to some people outside our circle with influence and who are opinion molders."

"And, you think my mother fits that bill?"

"Don't know, but I do think she can get us introductions to people who do fit that bill."

"Shane, I haven't talked to my mother since I graduated from college?"

"Is that when she found out you were gay?" I asked.

"That's when I told her, and her reaction to me coming out was so irate and disrespectful it kept me from telling anyone else."

"So, what you told us in college about a schism between your mother and you had nothing to do with your career path?" Charles asked.

"No, that had nothing to do with it." Darrell responded. "She tried to reach out to me when I became CEO of Blue Sky, but I never returned her call."

"It's time to return her call." Big Mike joined.

"I don't know.....too much time has passed." Darrell said.

"That's your mother, it's never too late, and her calling could be a sign she had a change of heart. The perception and thinking of the world is constantly evolving, and likely so has hers." I said.

"Maybe…."

Darrell agreed to call his mother when we got back to the states. A few hours had passed with us on the beach before the others joined us. The women came back with unadulterated happiness. According to Carmen, Kendra found the perfect house for us on the island. Kendra's smile stretched from ear to ear as she described the house. She wanted me and the kids to come with her right then to see the house.

I was game, but Miles and Monique weren't keen on leaving the water and sand. We convinced them with promise of a quick return. Abeni drove us back to the house Kendra had fallen in love with. I hadn't seen anything this beautiful in my life. The home fit perfectly on the five acres of land –pine trees, vibrant green plants, and narrow cobble stone paths running throughout. The property was located at the top of a hill that overlooked the beach and was indirect line of the sea breeze. The house was a sandy earth tone made of a sturdy clay structure, highlighted by mahogany doors, windows panes, and a roof with red tile which gave the home a Spanish Villa appeal.

The interior was just as breath taking. The walls were similar neutral tone, like the exterior. The home was one story and opened up to the landscape and scenery with floor to ceiling windows throughout, a huge French door in the family room. It had fifteen foot vaulted ceilings, and five spacious bedrooms, four and a half baths, and a large custom modern kitchen with marble floors. One other appealing aspect to the house was its guest house located about an acre away from the main house. The guest house was circular in diameter and provided the same openness to the landscaping as the main house. It had two bedrooms, and two baths, built like a suite at a hotel. The color was a darker earth tone, and had dark brown wood for its doors, trim and roof.

"Impressive!" I told Kendra.

"Can we get it?" She asked.

"It's your call. You want it, buy it." I said.

"You think the kids like it?" She asked

Miles and Monique were running around the entire house yelling, jumping, and skipping calling dibs on their bedrooms of choice. Miles was trying to reserve for himself the master bedroom, but I had to be the bearer of bad news and let him know if mom decided to buy the home this would be our bedroom. He quickly chose another. It was clear where the kids stood on the purchase of the house.

"I think the kids have already voted." I said. "Write the check babe and buy the house!"

She hugged me with a big smile and turned to Abeni. "We'll take it!"

****

We stayed behind after everyone else returned to the states to get settled into our new home. My mother stayed along with Kendra's parents and her brother. This gave me more time with Jakar. We met at least three times a week for the month and a half we stayed in Africa. We would talk at least an hour just about life lessons- goals, faith, vision, drive, and family. Jakar often emphasized family and how in times of turmoil and doubt family helped recharge us and lift us up to overcome the greatest of obstacles. I appreciated those words and others he shared with me during my time in Africa. Jakar was quickly becoming a trusted mentor. My time in Africa drew us closer, and I looked forward to our meetings.

Once Jakar questioned me about the Art of War by Sun Zu. I had read the book, and knew of some of its principals, but I had little or no command of its philosophy. Jakar challenged me to not only re-read the book, but to master the concepts between its pages. I had every intention of putting his request to practice, but between Blue Sky, family, and setting up our new home in Africa, it got put on the back burner.

About two weeks before we were schedule to return to the States, I got a call on my cell from Tiger.

"Brendham just fired me!" Tiger's tone was a mixture of anger and confusion.

"What?" I said surprised.

"I didn't think you knew about my firing and when I asked Brendham did you know, he said he only gave you information on a need to know basis, and you didn't need to know about my firing."

"Did he give you a reason?"

"He made some jive ass excuse about my experience and you becoming more international in your business and personal affairs."

I thought for a moment. Brendham had mentioned his concern about Tiger's readiness to perform his duties in a time when things were becoming more complex and intricate, but to dismiss him without consulting me when I personally picked Tiger, he had stepped out of his lane. Mr. Brendham had some explaining to do!

"Tiger sit tight; I will be back state side in a couple of weeks. I plan to have a sit down with him and get to the bottom of your dismissal."

"Thanks, Shane….one more thing, Brendham is beefing up security personnel and a lot of them look like ex-agency types and mercenaries."

I thought Tiger's last comment was interesting. Was the government surveillance and activity on Black Street stepping up to warrant more security? Was Brendham getting ready for some kind of physical conflict? I needed more info, and I needed it from Brendham. I reiterated to Tiger to wait for my return and to speak to no one about his dismissal.

Back Home

On my return home, I met first with Tiger face to face. I told him to meet me at the same coffee shop that I met Brendham in Harlem. We sat and talked over coffee and some pastries.

"Tell me more about these additional security personnel Brendham has brought on board."

"Well, I don't know a lot more than what I told you over the phone when you were in Africa, but before my dismissal I noticed a lot of closed door meetings that didn't include me, almost like they were circling the wagons."

"That's peculiar?" I said aloud.

"Shane, I've been thinking about this whole situation day and night since Brendham fired me. First, Brendham comes to me with some lame excuse about not accompanying you to Africa because I was needed in New York. I figured at the time he wanted to make the trip and give his family the experience of Africa, so I didn't question it. Second, some of the new guys would make snide comments about me being your shoe shine boy and a lot of other derogatory terms that need no repeating. I didn't make much of it at the time because I thought it was nothing more than jealousy. It's clear to me now there are lines being drawn between you and Brendham. Brendham is on a power trip and anyone in his department that has more of an allegiance to you will be terminated. I was his first casualty and probably his only one because the rest of the team is his drones."

I listened carefully as Tiger talked about closed door meetings and what he described as the newly acquired drones. He became curious and did some snooping and digging of his own. He uncovered the files and information on the newly acquired. He described some as having disciplinary reprimands in their files, and a couple had even been fired from the agency. As he revealed more to me about the background of some of these individuals I became more disturbed and wondered was Brendham running a rouge unit out of Black Street. Freelancing his skills and abilities to the highest bidder without disclosing this to us and turning what we thought was purely an expense for Black Street into a profit center for himself.

The thought of Brendham stealing from us, angered me beyond belief. If I was a cartoon character, you could have seen the steam blowing from my ears. Now I questioned this whole notion of the government having me under surveillance and Black Street being public enemy number one. The only thing that kept me from losing it was the file retrieved from the agency by Ice's contact. I needed to get back to Ice's contact and see what else he could dig up. I shared with Tiger the uncovering of the government documents by a contact in D.C. I assured him I would have Brendham give him his job back. I wanted Tiger to be my eyes and ears over there now. He assured me he was up to the task.

"Until I can determine what game Brendham is playing be careful." I told him.

My next stop after meeting with Tiger was Ice's hat shop. As soon as I walked in he greeted me with warmth and brotherhood.

"Youngblood, back from the mother land?" He approached and gave me a dap.

"Yea, we made it back!"

"For a minute I thought you might not come back."

"Me too, Kendra bought a house, so we stayed a little longer than anticipated."

"You mean to tell me you own a piece of the mother land?"

"Yea, we got our piece of the rock."

"That's alright Shane…that's alright." He said with pride and admiration shaking his head in approval.

I changed the topic. "Need your help once again."

"Anything Shane, you name it!"

"I need your contact in DC to do a little more snooping around."

"What are we looking for this time?"

"Update on the government file on Black Street, and some more in-depth information on Brendham."

"You got it."

"Especially on the Brendham piece Ice, I need your contact to do some real digging on this cat."

"Is he causing you some grief?"

"That's yet to be seen."

I left the hat shop and went to our offices on Wall Street. We had reduced the office space back down to its original size when we first started Black Street Capital. The only person that remained in the office was the receptionist. She manned the phones and would handle the sparse visitors. Often the visitors got off on the wrong floor or needed directions to another Investment company in the building. I came into the office when I was home two to three times a week, so the receptionist had a cushy gig.

I quickly moved past the receptionist desk and got off the elevator. She tried to engage me in conversation, but my mind was too occupied by the idea of Brendham cheating us out of our money. I walked into my office, closed the door sat at my desk, looked out into the empty office space and for the first time felt alone. I got up and walked out of my office and entered the trade room. Immediately I felt comfort, then I stood in the middle of the room reminiscing about days past when we were all in this trade room trying to build Black Street Capital into the company we envisioned. I missed my comrades, a part of me wanted to be in Dallas with Darrell, Charles and Big Mike helping in the day to day management of Blue Sky, but truth be told I really didn't want to do the day to day operational management that wasn't my purpose. Although the pursuit of Blue Sky was long and drawn out, I still enjoyed the process, and after taking Blue Sky over, I was ready to move on to the next challenge. I enjoyed the chase, but once the catch was made I was ready to move to the next new thing!

As I took a seat at the trading desk, the urge to re-enter the markets was overwhelming. I sat there and thought long and hard about what I wanted to do. The extra family time was great with

Kendra and the kids, but I still envisioned a life I wanted for myself outside of my family life. Darrell and the crew had Blue Sky well in hand and positioned perfectly for growth in the future, but I wanted something else that would put me back in capital markets. Berkshire Hathaway came to mind.

"That's it!" I muttered to myself.

Berkshire Hathaway was an investment company just as Black Street Capital was, but the difference was Berkshire was a publically traded company and Black Street was privately held. Berkshire strategy was to take significant positions in companies, then influence the company's management to increase shareholders' bottom line. They possessed a lot of power in the companies they owned making them major players not only on Wall Street, but in the international business landscape, and politics. Right then I made up my mind. All the pieces were in place already in Black Street Capital to make it a fully functional investment company again, but instead of focusing on one company at a time to buy, sell, or hold. Black Street would focus on several companies at a time and purchase them with the intent to hold them as a part of our portfolio effectively making us another Berkshire.

At my core I was an investor. With this new strategy I could invest in many companies influence the vision and objectives of those companies domestically and internationally which opened up the doors to wield more political influence and power. Now that was appealing to me. I started truly feeling that I found my purpose my mother spoke of. I think another integral part of my purpose was my community. Giving back through the breakfast club had been truly satisfying, and educating youth about money and finance also happened to be a passion of mine. Just as Mr. Roberts did for me at the age of 15, I wanted to do for the youth in our community. It was settled in my mind. It was clearest and most confident decision I had ever made, except for the decision to marry Kendra.

I became so excited over the idea; I shot an email to Big Mike, Charles, and Darrell for a conference call the next day. I didn't mention my worries about Brendham. I thought it prudent to wait and see what Tiger would come up with and what Ice's guy came back with. As I wrote the email I remembered I owed Brendham a visit. So, I shot him an email requesting a meeting with him after work in my office. It didn't take long for any one of them to get back to me. Darrell set up the conference call for all of us at 8:00 am the next morning, and Brendham replied he would be in my office around 6:00 pm.

The rest of the day I caught up on emails and returned calls. As the day slipped by I was tempted to start making calls putting things in place for Black Street's new venture, but I held back because I wanted to get the fellas input before I moved forward. Before I knew it the receptionist informed me she would be leaving for the day. I continued to go through my emails. I thought it would take a good two weeks to go through all of them. I came up on an email from Mr. Mackey requesting another sit down with me. Given the conversation between Darrell and I about a possible leak at Blue Sky, I replied and agreed to the sit down.

As soon as I finished my reply to Mr. Mackey, the phone rang on the trade desk. It was Brendham in the lobby. I buzzed him in from the trade desk. He entered the trade room and I offered him a seat adjacent to mine.

"Thanks for coming to meet me on such short notice. I just want to speak….." he interrupted me.

"Shane, I know why you asked to meet with me. I had to fire Tiger for the very same reasons he couldn't make the Africa trip. Black Street and you are becoming bigger than I imagined. In order to keep you and everyone else secure we need top notch professionals who have the experience, expertise, and knowledge- domestic and internationally. I will not compromise the integrity of my unit with someone who doesn't meet those qualifications, and Tiger doesn't measure up! This is my final word on this matter and I will not change my mind."

I was offended by his tone, content, and demeanor. Sitting in front of me looking like a black Anglo-Saxon dictating to me about what he wasn't going to do, when in fact he worked for me; that was something I wasn't going to tolerate, but I remained calm and cool.

"Tiger will report for work tomorrow morning 8:00 am sharp. You will re-instate him, giving him back all his original responsibilities and duties. You will provide him with additional training and education to bring him up to the level you expect from your personnel. Do you have any questions?" I looked directly into his eyes.

Clearly disturbed but understanding who was boss, he responded solemnly. "No."

"Do you have any updates for me on government surveillance or activity in regards to Black Street?"

"No."

"Okay, Mr. Brendham going forward instead of emails and phone calls for my updates lets meet face to face once a week ….make it Friday after market hours. You will come here to give me a briefing in person." I looked him again directly in his eyes.

His eyes tried to avoid direct contact, but were drawn back to mine. I detected a slight tremble in his eyes, not derive from fear, but more homegrown from anger." Sounds good to me."

"Okay!"

I stood up to shake his hand and dismissed him. He rose also, grasped my extended hand and shook it.

"Once again thanks for coming out on short notice."

As he walked off I gave him a firm smack to his back side like a high school football coach sending one of his players onto the field to make a play. The backside smack caught him off guard and before he could respond I returned to my seat and turned my back on him. It was a demeaning gesture, but I thought he needed to be taken down a peg or two. Although hesitant he walked out without any other words exchanged between us.

****

The next morning I was in the office early enough to make my 8:00am conference call with the fellas. I laid out my vision for Black Street Capital going forward. I had everyone's support. They were excited for me and the vision I laid out.

"You set us up nicely here at Blue Sky, but we all know your passion is in the markets and I think Berkshire is the perfect business model for Black Street. We will be bigger than US Steel." Darrell said.

"If I have it my way, we will own a good piece of US Steel!" I replied.

"Congrats Shane, I know you will make us all proud with the new venture."

"I haven't done anything yet Big Mike."

"But, you will. We are all sure of that!"

"I want in!" Charles barked out over the phone.

There was a silence over the line.

"You're CFO of Blue Sky. How in the hell….we are just getting started?" Darrell retorted.

"I want to go back to New York. Carmen doesn't like it here in Dallas and neither do I. I'm cut from the same mold as Shane. I like the excitement of capital markets, and the strategy of buying companies and influencing management to maximize profits fits my expertise."

"How about you Big Mike?" Darrell asked.

"Adriona loves Dallas and I do too. I like my responsibilities here at Blue Sky as the head of the legal department. Even though I'm unable to practice law this gets me back to my first love, and who knows I might be able to get reinstated to practice law."

"I'm glad to hear that Big Mike! Charles, if you want to make the move back to New York and help me get started, I would welcome you with open arms."

"What the hell am I going to do about a CFO," Darrell asked with concern?

"I think White-Chocolate would be a perfect candidate for this position." Charles answered Darrell's question.

"I think that is a good suggestion, how about you Darrell?" I asked.

"Yea… he's a good one. Let me have a talk with him, but Charles don't go rushing out of here tomorrow. Because I know you, you will be on the red eye to New York if you could. Give me some time to transition White-Chocolate into the position."

"How long you need?"

"I need at least two weeks – that's standard. After that Susan and I, we can bring White-Chocolate up to speed."

"Okay you have two weeks! *I'm coming home, coming home, look to me cause I'm coming home*!" Charles sung with delight.

"We have other issues beyond the singing CFO; I think, I located the leak."

"Who is it?" Big Mike asked.

"They're in the marketing department, they confided in Susan thinking she would be in agreement with their actions."

"Fire them all!" Charles commented

"We can't just fire them. The information was given to quote on quote shareholders," Darrell said.

"Technically speaking they have not committed any crimes." Big Mike responded.

"How do we handle it?" Charles asked.

"I'm not sure." Darrell said.

"Isolate them, replace them, and wait them out."

"What do you mean Shane?" Darrell asked.

"Relocate them, and isolate them in a physical space away from headquarters under the guise of a special project, and make sure they are not privy to any material information about Blue Sky. They will all quit before you fire them."

"I like it!" Big Mike exclaimed.

"It just might work. I'll run it by Susan and get her thoughts."

We finished up the conference call with some smaller issues, and I purposely didn't mention the Brendham issue because I wanted to get back the intel from Ice's contact. I reminded Darrell we needed to be more politically connected. He mentioned some of Blue Sky's political friends who he had met and had dinner with. Most were local political figures, but there were a few on the national level with their hands out for donations to their charities and re-election funds. He also mentioned that Blue Sky had one of the most prestigious lobbyist firms in D.C. doing an excellent job of lobbying the interests of Blue Sky.

I wanted to add one more political figure to the roster, his mother. Darrell objected initially because he didn't see the reason. He thought I was trying to mend family fences, and he may have been half right, but my mind was thinking bigger. I wanted a close ally on Capitol Hill for one reason Brendham! From our meeting yesterday my comfort level with Brendham was dwindling and fast. I needed my own insider, not that I didn't trust Ice's man, but I wanted several sources to compare the information. I asked Darrell to set up a meeting in Dallas at Blue Sky headquarters next week with his mother, with trepidation he agreed. We ended the call on that note.

Later on that afternoon I had the sit down Mr. Mackey. We met in his office at GPG headquarters. As soon as I entered the building, I was greeted with warmth and respect from security and others who recognized me from my days at GPG. Before I began my meeting with Mr. Mackey I wanted to say hello to an old friend – Timothy. I asked the receptionist to ring Tim's desk. She informed me he no longer worked at GPG. I wasn't surprised at the news, but more surprised he lasted as long as he did after my departure even though they promised him the Managing Director position. Once sitting in front of Mr. Mackey, he wasted no time letting me know what was on his mind.

"Africa, a big move for Blue Sky you think the venture will be as profitable as you all envision."

Knowing Titan industries had people in Blue Sky that were compassionate to their efforts, I really didn't try to hide what was evident. “Yes, we think the move will prove to be a game changer. I was just out there and things are ahead of schedule and progressing nicely.”

He shook his head in agreement, but couldn’t hide his surprise with my candor. “Good to hear.....” He hesitated deep in thought. “I always wondered why you sent Michael to Africa. It was for capital for Black Street, so you saw your dismissal coming at GPG and you planned well, but there is no way you could have foreseen Blue Sky and Africa.”

“You’re right that was a natural fit and not my idea, but our CEO’s.”

“Darrell is good, and you all were smart to keep Big Red’s protégé Susan on.”

“With all due respect why did you ask for this meeting? I know it wasn’t to commend me on Blue Sky moves.”

“No… it wasn’t. You have a problem Shane in which Titan is willing to overlook if you can come to some kind of agreement of stock purchase in which Black Street Capital will sell forty five percent of their holdings in Blue Sky to Titan Industries.” He paused to gage my reaction. I was non-reactive. “Of course they would purchase the shares at market which would net Black Street a very sizable profit and leave you with fifteen percent of the shares outstanding.”

“Whatever problem I may have its not big enough for me to sell forty five percent of my interest in Blue Sky to Titan.”

“Shane I have come to you on behalf of Titan, but in confidence. We know the monies used to secure the purchase of Titan came out of Africa, and on its face there is nothing illegal about that transaction. If those monies came from illegal entities which would be considered laundered money, it would open you and Black Street capital up to SEC violations and possible criminal prosecution.”

My first thought was he was fishing, but he was fishing in the right pond. Second, if he could prove anything he was saying we wouldn’t be having this conversation, so I stone walled him. “I have no idea what you are talking about.” I said calmly.

"Shane, Titan wants Blue Sky and nothing will stop their pursuit. It would be prudent to consider the offer."

I changed the topic. "On my way in I asked the receptionist to ring Tim's desk and was told he no longer works at GPG."

Mr. Mackey paused. Once, he realized I wasn't going to consider his offer, he accommodated my question. "He was let go about six months ago."

"What happen?" I questioned him, knowing to question Mr. Mackey was a slap in the face to him, yet he tolerated the question.

"Life happened! Tim had no vision, drive, and was no good at building and sustaining relationships. All these things you know firsthand."

"And, you knew that when you offered him the Managing Director position."

"I know we are not about to replay history. What's in the past is best left there."

"Agreed."

We stood and shook hands, and then I left his office and the building. While walking Wall Street my mind wasn't pre-occupied by the initial conversation with Mr. Mackey, but it was Tim. Although I felt betrayed by Tim, in a weird way I still considered him a friend. The last time we spoke the words between us were conciliatory. I wanted to know how he was doing. Did he find another job? Did he leave Wall Street? I needed answers. I still had his number in my phone, so I called him. No answer. I left a message, but wasn't satisfied. An urge came over me to find out about Tim's wellbeing. I took a taxicab to his home.

I knocked on his front door hoping at the very least to speak to his wife Vivian. Upon my second knock I heard a woman's voice asking "Who is it?"

"Shane Jackson."

"The door opened and there was Tim's wife Vivian standing in the doorway. I remember her being a very attractive woman. She still was attractive, but her eyes and body looked weary and exhausted, even the warm up outfit she was wearing, a dull blue, was befitting her mood and tone.

"Hey, Shane how are you? Come on in."

"Good." I entered. The house was not in disarray or ill kept. There was no sign of the kids or Tim. "Where are the little ones?"

"They are not so little any more, but they are in school. They should be home in another hour."

"How about Tim, is he at work?"

She muttered something under her breath which was hard for me to make out, it sounded like she said. *"Don't we all wish?"* "No, Tim is home today. He's just upstairs let me go and get him."

She offered me a seat in the living room while she went upstairs to get Tim.

I waited in the living room alone about fifteen minutes before I heard Vivian and Tim making their way down the stairs. I heard them talking.

"You should have put on something better and shaved." She said in a loud whisper.

"It's just Shane." He whispered back.

"Yes, Shane Jackson who owns Blue Sky and who can give you a job at the drop of a hat."

"He's not here for that, and I don't want to hear any talk of that while he is here! I mean it Vivian!"

Then they reached the bottom of the stairs and the chatter between them stopped. They both entered the room with strained smiles.

"Shane, it's good to see you."

"Like wise." I said.

Tim greeted me with a handshake. We sat on the couch side by side, and Vivian took a seat in the chair opposite us. Tim looked depressed, exhausted, and unkempt. His jeans; dingy blue brown and wrinkled like he took them out the dirty clothes hamper and his t-shirt was sky blue and too small. He had grown a beard that needed some grooming, and he was in dire need of a haircut, and he was musty. There was an eerie quietness to the room after we greeted each other.

Vivian's eyes shifted between the two of us examining us from head to toe. The room was becoming uncomfortable. I had obviously come at a time of turmoil between the two. Her support, comfort, and patience she held when Tim was having his struggles on Wall Street before he joined my trading desk at GPG had faded. Now disdain and dissatisfaction emanated from her. I tried my best to cut through the tension.

"So, what's been happening?"

"Nothing!" Vivian blurted out. Obviously she could not hold her adverse feelings in toward Tim. She had reached her boiling point. Her eyes revealed her words before she could get them out. "Six months he's been out of work. The first month was okay he actively looked for work, when nothing came up he quit, and for the last five months he's been in this house sleeping, eating, and shitting that's all. He don't do shit! Although he's home, he's been an absentee father and husband."

"The doctor say's I'm going through depression." Tim said in a somber tone.

"Fuck that doctor!" She yelled out. It startled me, how bluntly she put it. She sat up in her seat to articulate her point. "You are a black man! You don't have time to be depressed. You have a family to feed. What do you think black men did during slavery? You think they went to masta and said…" she was animated to the point of being comedic. "I's depressed boss, I jus wanna sta in tuday and sleep and eat." Shaking her head as if she was the master listening to the slave's plea, "Okay Toby, you just want to sleep and eat today. Okay boy! That just fine, but before you go and sleep in today, you see the tree round yonder?" and she pointed toward the kitchen behind her; "I'm going to tie yo black ass to that tree and whip you until I put you into a permanent sleep."

I couldn't help it, the laughter blurted out of me. I hunched over and laughed uncontrollably. Tears rolled down my face. I wasn't only laughing at the skit she just performed, but the unreal situation that was unfolding right before me. It was unbelievable and that made it comical. I rose my head still laughing looking at her and her facial expression was filled with anger. I laughed even harder, then suddenly her expression loosened and her lips curled up to form a smile. I continued to laugh and she couldn't help but to join in. The laughter became contagious and Tim joined in.

"What you laughing at boy!" I demanded, and laughed even harder.

Vivian and Tim watched me make a spectacle of myself on their living room floor rolling around laughing my ass off.

When I finally settled down, I addressed them both. "You two are funny! I needed that laugh. I'm glad I came by when I did. I have an opportunity for you Tim."

"I told you! Vivian shouted. She ran and jumped on Tim's lap.

"At Blue Sky in Dallas, I will do whatever you need Shane." Tim said.

"No not at Blue Sky."

They both looked confused.

"At Black Street Capital, I'm getting ready to re-enter the market with the intention of picking up shares of companies so we can garner influence over management, and we deem a strong viable entity to add to our portfolio of Companies."

"Berkshire!" Tim responded.

"Yes,… I will need a micro economist and analyst which would be a nice fit for you."

"How much does it pay?" Vivian quickly rejoined.

Tim tried to quiet his wife but it was too late. She had spoken, and I didn't mind. I still loved Tim like a brother.

"Well given his experience. I think we could offer five hundred K plus bonus."

Once again there was silence, but this time it was peaceful and tears of joy followed. Tim and Vivian were overwhelmed.

"There is just only one pre-requisite."

"What is it? I will take care of it right away."

"You have to… take a god damn bath. You offend!"

We all got a laugh out of my last statement. I didn't want to ruin the moment between husband and wife so I called a cab and said goodbye, so they could celebrate the moment, and right when I was leaving their kids arrived from school, and they could see mom and dad were having a better day, then days past.

****

Two weeks later I was on my way to Dallas Texas for a meeting with Darrell's mother, and I brought my better half with me. Kendra and I had always made time for us when the kids were with my mother or her parents, but this was the first time we travelled without them which made Kendra a little nervous. I had planned a quiet romantic plane ride in the Blue Sky's private jet which didn't miss a beat.

Romantic music filled the passenger area with Teddy Pendergrass and Barry White's greatest slow jams –Turn off the lights, Greatest Inspiration and more. The cabin lights were dimed and a dozen red roses adorned the dining table along with a chilled bottle of white wine. We were served a three course dinner by the attendant Carol. After finishing dinner, Carol joined the pilot in the cockpit. I pulled Kendra to the back of the plane in a private room and sat her down on the leather sofa. I kneeled down in front of her gently caressing her legs, lifting her feet and began messaging her feet softly. I sensed some nervousness and tentativeness in her.

"What's wrong?" I whispered.

"What if someone walks in on us?"

"I will fire their ass!" I said jokingly.

"You are crazy. You can't fire somebody for that!"

"K are you uncomfortable with this?"

She hesitated and slowly replied "Yes."

I stood and took a seat beside her on the sofa and kissed her ever so gently on the lips. "Okay." I then swiveled her legs on my lap and laid her back and continued with the foot message. We talked the rest of the flight about the kids, our new home in Africa, Black Street, and our future. It was a good intimate conversation both of us sharing our hopes and desires for the future. More and more I got the feeling

Kendra wanted to make the house in Nigeria our home and the brownstone in Harlem our vacation spot.

She felt with the Blue Sky is expansion into Africa the opportunity was ideal for us to make the migration back to the Motherland permanent. But, my plans for Black Street threw a wrench into her desires, so she queried the possibility of relocating Black Street from Wall Street to the Business District in Lagos which I wasn't open to even considering. She wasn't upset. I think she was testing the waters, but I knew her persuasive abilities were unmatched. It was just a matter of time before she would convince me of the move. She knew it, and most importantly I knew it.

We landed at Dallas-Fort Worth International Airport about 9:00 pm. As we got off of the plane Darrell was waiting on the tar mac with a town car. Kendra came alive when she saw him standing by the car. She ran to him and gave him a hug. I thought that a bit much, but I understood he was a dear friend.

"Hey…you look great! Oh, it's so good to see you!" Kendra said excitedly.

"It's good to be seen! I see my boy has been taking good care of you…you are looking fly and fashionable!"

She stood back and twirled around. "You like it?"

"Yes." He replied.

Darrell reached out to me. We embraced along with a handshake. "What's up son? Didn't expect you here at the airport to greet us, but much appreciated."

"I didn't have much time in Africa to spend with Kendra, and I thought it might be nice to have drinks before I have the car take you to your hotel."

"Sounds good!" Kendra responded.

Kendra, Darrell, and I got in the back of the black town car. The driver loaded our luggage in the trunk, and we were off to drinks.

"Everything is set up for tomorrow around 9:00 am." Darrell said.

"Is your mother here in Dallas already?" I asked.

Kendra interrupted. "Your mother? I would love to meet her!"

"Ahh… I think that can be arranged Kendra." He said hesitantly. "And, no she is not in Dallas yet. She should arrive early tomorrow morning around 7:00 am. I have a car picking her up and bringing her to the office."

"Okay." I responded.

Kendra went on about meeting Darrell's mother for the next few minutes. "How exciting, your mother, a congresswoman. How does she look? Do you look like her? How old is she? Does she live in D.C.? When is the last time you saw her?"

"Fifteen years ago." Darrell spoke quietly.

"What?" Kendra responded surprisingly.

"I never really talked about my mother to you because I don't have a relationship with her. I'm sorry if I misrepresented myself in that regard."

"It's okay Darrell. I understand. If you are not comfortable about speaking to me about your relationship with your mother…."

"No, it's not a question of comfort with you. It's about my comfort level with my mother in general."

Kendra leaned over and kissed Darrell on the cheek.

I took a file out of my personal bag, I had been carrying since I got it from Ice, and handed over to Darrell. He opened the file and viewed the documents inside.

"Is this for real?"

"Yes."

"What's in the file Shane?" Kendra said in a concerned voice.

"Us babe, that is a file that contains private information, surveillance, and inquiries about Black Street, all its shareholders, relatives, practically anyone who is associated with us. Those are official government documents."

"So, Brendham was telling the truth that the eyes upon us have picked up since our acquisition of Blue Sky?"

"Yes, but there are still some things about Brendham that are causing me concern."

"What is it?" Kendra asked.

"I just don't trust him. He's trying to operate the security arm of Black Street independent of us."

"How can he do that when we fund his department?" Darrell objected.

"My sentiments exactly, so now he's required to have weekly face to face meeting with me giving updates on all activities and current events pertaining to Black Street."

"Good! Keep an eye on him Shane. I wasn't comfortable with him from the beginning."

I nodded my head in agreement. Kendra slipped a couple of the documents from the folder and was reviewing them.

"They have your "Breakfast Club" under surveillance. What is that about?" Kendra blurted out.

"The training of young black males has always been a threat!" Darrell responded.

"I'm hoping your mother can be an asset to us to win favor with some of these government agencies that see us as a threat."

"For a price I'm sure she will!"

"Mom's rolls like that?"

"Absolutely!"

We had a little laugh between us all when Darrell told the story about his mother trying to extort money from some PTA members for her favorable vote on some funding for their school district. We continued our conversation about Darrell's mother until the car pulled up to the curb of a downtown restaurant and bar. We got out of the car and headed in.

The restaurant was upscale and packed with people. The décor was a little bland for my taste, but elegant. The room was filled with chatter from its patrons and had a large bar in the middle. When we entered the restaurant, Darrell surveyed the restaurant and then a man stood up and waved him over to his table. He looked at us and said "this way." The man we walked toward was African-American, thin build, clean cut, no facial hair, wire rimmed eye glasses, dark skinned, and dressed in a pink polo shirt and khaki pants.

"This is my partner Clarence." Darrell introduced.

Kendra jumped toward him in a surprisingly excitable manner, and hugs this man as if he was a long lost relative. I stood back observant of everyone- the pleasing look on Darrell's face to Kendra's reaction, the elated smile on Kendra's face and her hands all over this clown, and the silly smile on this clown's face. I was non-responsive to the introduction. I shook Clarence's hand when Kendra finally let the man go. We all sat down at the table which was a semi-circle booth space. Darrell and Kendra sat across from each other on the inside and Clarence and I sat across from each other on the outer edges of the table.

Clarence looked directly at me. "The great and powerful Shane!"

I thought what the fuck is he talking about? This jackass doesn't know me. I kept my cool and smiled at his remark.

He continued. "I've heard a lot about you. I'm very happy I finally get to meet you."

I smiled once again in his direction without any direct response. The waitress came over just as Darrell and Kendra were giving me bemused looks.

"Can I get you some drinks to start off?" She asked.

"Just water for me." I responded.

Darrell ordered a bottle of wine for the table along with some appetizers, and informed the waitress we would not be having dinner. After the waitress took the order all eyes were on me. Darrell, Kendra and Clarence were all staring at, not saying a word.

I couldn't explain my reaction to Clarence. Darrell was my brotha. I knew he was gay, but I had never come face to face with a man he was dating. It cast a different light on Darrell's homosexuality. Maybe I was accepting in theory, but not in practice because I now had a feeling I really didn't know Darrell at all. The moment became awkward and uncomfortable for me. Everyone at the table could feel my energy and it wasn't positive.

"Shane, what is wrong?" Kendra questioned me, almost chastising me with her tone.

When I attempted to reply to her, I looked over and she had moved over separating herself from me and my backwards unexplained behavior. My attempt was short lived. I got up and walked away from the table. Kendra followed me. We ended up at the bar in the center of the restaurant.

"Darrell was right!" she confronted me.

"He came at me wrong!"

"He was just kidding, trying to break the ice with you. You barely even greeted the man when Darrell introduced him."

"He don't know me that well to joke with me like that!"

"I don't believe you!! Don't mess up this night for Darrell. It took a lot for him to introduce Clarence to us!"

Silence….. I just looked at Kendra directly in her eyes she was mad at me and maybe for good reason, but I wasn't happy with her siding against me at the table.

"I don't believe you…Are you with me or against me?" I questioned angrily.

"Shane…" she shook her head side to side "don't go there with me. Darrell is our family and the way you are treating his date is uncalled for." She said cautiously.

"Let's get something straight right now, that we evidently haven't gotten straight in the five years we've been married…. I would rather you agree, defend, or be non-reactive to me when issues come up in a public setting, then in the privacy of our home or in this case in the privacy of our room tell me how you think I was wrong or reacted badly."

"Are you that insecure Shane? Do you need someone to stoke your ego at all times?"

"You still don't get it. I want a united front with my wife. Right or wrong I want you to back me. I don't give a damn about what anybody else thinks. If you disagree, then lets disagree in private. I am the captain of this ship and right or wrong I will guide this ship. Now if you want off the ship then say so!" I was shouting about this time.

Kendra looked at me shockingly.

Darrell approached, "What is going on?" he questioned both of us.

Kendra was furious. Her tears were not just of sadness, but of anger. I had questioned her loyalty to me once again and this time I took it a step further by asking if she wanted to remain my first mate.

"I'm sorry I shouldn't have said that; I just-

I was interrupted by Clarence. "What's going on all mighty Shane?"

I didn't hesitate I grabbed him by his pink polo shirt right around the collar with both hands and flung him to the ground, and was going to punch his lights out if it wasn't for Darrell jumping on my back pulling me off him. Cooler heads prevailed when security came running along with our driver which was our security. Our security smoothed things out with the restaurant security and management.

Darrell left with Clarence and the driver took Kendra and me to our hotel. Kendra didn't say a word to me the whole ride. We checked into our room. She drew herself a bath while I sat in the front room of our suite and watched the world news in the dark. She emerged from the bathroom an hour later still no words, walked into the kitchen for a glass of water then she went to bed without saying good night to me. I continued to watch television until it started watching me and woke me about five in the morning.

I showered and called for the car to take me to Blue Sky headquarters. I arrived around 6:30am. Darrell was in his office. I went directly there to talk with him.

"Kendra alright?"

"Don't know." I said quickly and somberly.

"Are you alright?"

"Don't know" I repeated.

"I'm sorry about last night."

"I should be the one apologizing. You did nothing wrong. You just wanted to share more of your life with us and I prevented you from doing that, and for that I am sorry."

"Shane are we okay?"

"Yea man, it's just I saw you in a light I wasn't used to or comfortable with when I saw you with Clarence."

"You know I'm gay!"

"Yea, but it's different for me to hear you say you're gay, and me seeing you in a gay relationship, because my history with you is different than that….make sense?"

"Are you saying it is okay for me to be gay as long as you don't have to see me in a gay relationship?"

"I don't know what the hell I'm saying, and I don't want to talk about this shit anymore."

"What is going on with you?"

"Don't know, lot on my mind."

"This Brendham stuff?"

"Yea and a meeting with Mackey where he threatened me over the financing of our Blue Sky deal."

"How in the hell…"

"I know, but he's fishing. With our venture into Nigeria and our dealings with Jakar it doesn't take much too conclude our financing came out of Nigeria. If he is able to connect the dots and has evidence to the source of funds…

"How could they get that?"

"Bribes, misrepresentation, black mail, and all the above."

"By any means necessary!" Darrell commented.

"Right, we have to repay that money, making sure we don't put those sources of funds in a compromising position where they become threats to us."

"The Africa move will quadruple us in profitability and market value is estimated to triple. If this plays out as expected we could potentially repay those sources by year's end."

"Darrell that should be priority number one!"

"Done!"

Big Mike and Charles walked in Darrell's office to join us for the meeting with Darrell's mother.

"What's up Shane? Carmen and I can't wait to get back to New York!" Charles declared.

I greeted him with a dap and a hug. Big Mike and I greeted likewise.

"Your girl Maria almost lost her mind when she heard of your plans for Black Street. She wants in." Charles said.

"She knows the opportunity is in the Big Apple?" I asked.

"Hell yea! She almost had an orgasm begging me to talk to you about bringing her aboard."

"What about White-Chocolate?" Big Mike asked.

"What about him? He's as happy as a fat kid in a candy store with the opportunity as CFO of Blue Sky!"

"He's not concerned with his wife working in New York while he is working in Dallas?" Big Mike asked in a concerned voice

"I don't know. I think there may be some trepidation on his part, but many couples live in different cities and make that shit work."

"I guess so." Big Mike replied.

"Don't hire her Shane." Darrell interjected.

"Why not?" Charles questioned.

Darrell looked directly at me. "Don't do it." He reiterated.

"She's a top analyst, hard worker, committed and dedicated. She's got my vote to bring her on!" said Charles.

"Well, I say leave her here in Dallas at Blue Sky!" Darrell gave his opinion in the informal vote.

"I guess if she wants to go and her husband doesn't object, who are we to stand in her way? Like Charles says, she's more than qualified." Big Mike added.

"Well, we already have one more joining Charles and me in New York." I said.

"Who?" Charles asked.

"Tim!"

"Get the fuck outta here. Your black ass is full of surprises!"

"What made you do that?" Big Mike asked.

"Don't know really….." thinking "I believe everyone deserves a second chance."

"I don't think I will ever fully understand you. But, that was a good thing to do." Darrel rejoined, walked over and dapped me with a hug.

Darrell's secretary rang his phone letting us know his mother had arrived and she was waiting in the lobby for our 8:30 meeting. The Secretary showed her into his office where Darrell was seated behind his desk, Big Mike was flanked to the left of Darrell, and Charles and I were flanked to his right. Ms. Wilson was a small framed woman, looked to be in her mid to late fifties. She could have been older, but it's harder to pin point the age on black women especially when they get older. Dark complexion, brown eyes, conservatively dressed in a pants suit, and physically fit; she was an attractive woman, but her mouth, the language she used, didn't match her appearance which was quite alarming initially until we got used to her way of speaking.

"All you pretty ass niggas up in here, waiting on little o me! What can I do you for?" She took a seat in one of the two open chairs directly in front of Darrell's desk.

"Hello to you too mom." Darrell declared.

"You still practicing homosexuality?"

"It's not anything I practice mother. It's what I am."

"Waste of good nigga."

I leaned over to Charles and whispered. "She is something else!"

Darrell was clearly shaken by his mother's presence and her insensitive words toward him. I tried to take control of the situation and shift the conversation to the purpose of our meeting. I took a seat in the empty chair next to Ms. Wilson, but before I could address her she confronted me.

"So you are the HNIC!"

"Excuse me" I questioned her.

"You are Shane? Aren't you?"

"Yes ma'am!"

"So you are the HNIC?"

"I don't quite get what you are getting at."

"Head Nigga In Charge!"

"There is no HNIC amongst us." I replied.

"Okay, I'll play the game that way if y'all want to, but let's cut through the bullshit. Y'all need information and I'm in the perfect position to get it for you. As a congresswoman I have access and friends that could be assets to you in the operation and management of Blue Sky and Black Street. For my help it will cost you twenty five thousand."

"You are Darrell's mother." Big Mike cried.

"I wouldn't give a damn if I was Mary the mother of Jesus Christ. It would still cost you twenty five thousand and that's not an annual fee, its quarterly."

"What the fuck, that's an extortionist sum of money!" Charles declared.

"Watch your language!' I requested of Charles.

He looked at me and shrugged his shoulders, not knowing how to handle the situation.

"How do we know you can deliver what you say?" Big Mike asked.

"Right now, they got you all under surveillance, especially you Mr. HNIC." She looked directly at me. "And your African connection Dakar…

"Jakar." Darrell corrected her.

"Jakar, Dakar whatever the fuck his name is. He is of major interest and they are trying to dig into him in a major way. They have the SEC looking over every inch of your takeover of Blue Sky and this move into Africa has caused a major commotion."

"Why us," Darrell asked?

"Nigga wake up! Are you kidding? You four in this room are major international businessmen, who have the ability and money to influence commerce, business, and politics internationally. But, you are unknowns- no political affiliates, causes, or charities. All they have to go on is this Negro right here;" she looked directly at me again "who wants to hire nothing but niggas on white folks' dime."

"We have a diversified professional staff here at Blue Sky." Darrell declared.

"I think she's referring to our days at GPG." I commented.

"Damn right! I knew it was just a matter of time before I would get a call."

"It wasn't my idea." Darrell responded.

"I know that shit! It's this fine mutha fucka right next to me! Are you as half as good in bed as you look?"

That comment totally caught me off guard and left me speechless. Charles laughed and Big Mike laughed, but Darrell was upset.

"Mother don't embarrass yourself."

"I thought y'all were some real niggas. If I'm mistaken, I apologize..." She paused. "Look do we have a deal? I will and can deliver what I say. With me in your corner I can begin persuading political figures and pundits in your favor bring you out of the darkness into the light where you don't look threatening, but you look more like the American dream personified."

"Pay the woman!" Big Mike declared.

We ended our meeting with Darrell's mother with an agreement that she would work on our behalf to feed us information about government surveillance and simultaneously introduce us to people who were influential in the political arena and in the media realm. We agreed upon her number of twenty five per quarter for one year, just to make sure the money was being well invested. Before she left, Darrell and she confirmed plans for dinner.

"We still meeting for dinner?"

"Yes, mother. We have reservations at Jarrad's at 8:00 pm. It's an upscale barbeque restaurant in downtown Texas. I will have a car pick you up from your hotel around 7:00 pm."

"Okay, but look come alone, I don't want to see no shit that's going to ruin my appetite."

Darrell didn't react to her request, but none of us were stunned by the boldness of her request. She exited Darrell's office, and Darrell's secretary escorted her to the lower lobby where her driver was waiting for her. I tried to bring some levity to the sour note our meeting ended on.

"Darrell I think your mother wants to give me some of that!" I said slyly.

"Hey careful, no matter how far out there she is, she is still my mother."

"I know….I'm just saying if I was single, I might be tapping that ass tonight- mother or no mother….. She had a little onion on her!"

Big Mike, Charles, and I busted out in laughter and Darrell demanded we leave his office.

"Get out my office you heathens!" He shouted, but he couldn't help but to laugh too.

We left his office in a jovial mood. Right outside Darrell's office in his private lobby waiting was Maria. She approached us.

"Can I talk to you," She asked me directly?

"Sure,"

"In private," She requested.

"Okay."

I gestured that I would follow her. I told Big Mike and Charles I would check with them later. I followed Maria down the hallway into the elevator; her office was on the 60th floor of this eighty story glass tower. Maria had put on a little weight I could tell, but in all the right places. As always Maria was stylish and sexy in her work attire- black pumps, charcoal grey fitted skirt about knee high, and a very stylish button less white blouse with a high collar that crisscrossed leaving the keen eye with a treat.

We joined a few others on the elevator and got off on the 60thfloor. Maria led me to her office where she closed the door once we entered. She offered me a seat at the small conference table. She sat right next to me, turned her chair to face me, and I did the same.

"Blue Sky has been a great opportunity for me and Derrick, and his promotion to CFO is really a dream come true for him. It's a perfect fit, but VP of Finance for me, not so perfect. It's not my dream, my dream has always been Wall Street and through Black Street I fulfilled that dream, and .....Well.....if the rumors are true about Black Street Capital being players in the market again. I would like you to consider bringing me back into Black Street."

Her timidness and humility caught me off guard. I knew Wall Street was her dream, and she liked the excitement of the markets. She was like me a hunter, but I had never granted her request of an apology to her husband for my part in what happen in Puerto Rico, and I never thought she fully forgave me for that, but her sacrifice and contribution to the World Textile deal was invaluable. I looked at her with a smile not saying a word. She smiled back.

"I have Derrick's blessing, so don't worry about that....Shane I miss New York. I want to come home." She pleaded.

"Maria if you want in, you're in, no need for trepidation on your part."

"I love you!" She shouted and jumped up and as a reaction I stood, then she gave a no holds barred hug –tight and in close. My arms wrapped around her waist and her arms looped around my neck, she whispered in my ear. "Thank you so much!" Her body was inviting, firm and nice, and she smelled terrific. I couldn't help but to hold her a little longer than I should have. She seemed to not mind, then I stepped back. "I'm going back home to the Big Apple!" She declared.

We talked briefly of the timeline, and then I left her office and made my way to Charles's office where he was continuing in his transitioning of White-Chocolate to the CFO position. I entered as they were going over time lines. They both looked up.

"How did it go?" Charles asked.

"Maria said White-Chocolate gave his blessing, so who am I to stand in her way." I looked at White-Chocolate.

"Thanks Shane, her happiness is mine?"

"Alright I don't want you sulking late nights wanting your woman listening to "Distant Lover". Charles said jokingly.

"You got jokes!"

Just then I got a text from Kendra. "Hanging out with Carmen, We need to talk. Meet me at the Hotel at 5:00 pm. K."

Charles saw me reading the text on my phone. "Carmen and Kendra shopping?"

"Yea!" Hanging out was synonymous with shopping when those two hung out.

I spent the rest of the day at Blue Sky headquarters mostly with Charles where we hammered out some broad strokes for moving forward with Black Street Capital. By day's end Big Mike and Darrell tracked Charles and me down in the conference room we had high jacked. They wanted to go and have drinks just the four of us so we did. Around 4:30 I caught a taxi back to the hotel to meet Kendra.

I walked through the door exactly at 5:00 pm where Kendra was waiting in the front room of the suite. She did not look happy, matter of fact, she was dressed for a confrontation – warm ups, tennis shoes, and hair pulled back in a ponytail. Her look was almost laughable, but I dared not laugh. When a sista is in attack mode, you must tread carefully.

"I want to talk about that shit you said to me yesterday."

Damn she must have been boiling hot, because she cursed. I just shook my head for her to go ahead with her protest. She pulled her sleeves up elbow high.

"Shane I realize you have become a very powerful man, but don't ever threaten me with divorce because you will lose that fight, two kids and five years of marriage-you're smart, you do the numbers!"

I think she just threatened me! I thought to myself.

She went on. "I will give you the first time in our home where Vernon went on the attack. I should have had your back, and I apologized to you for that, but no one was attacking you at that dinner table with Darrell and Clarence. We just didn't understand that silly look you had on your face!"

Silly look, I couldn't believe she was using my own lingo against me. Kendra had really picked up some of my mannerisms and habits. It was almost as if I was in a confrontation with myself, just a female version. I found that to be awkward. She continued.

"Darrell looks up to you, he cares what you think! You don't think your reaction hurt him. He thought you were all good with him and his sexuality….you said as much!

I had no words in response. She was right. I did back him unconditionally.

Kendra didn't let up. "Darrell is like family and given he has no relationship with his mother he looks to us for support and you…you just….Aahh" she waved me off in disgust.

Another one of my gestures, my persona had rubbed off on her.

"I know you got people lining up to kiss your ass and stroke that enormous ego of yours, but I didn't know you expected me to get in line and kiss it too!"

"You don't want to kiss my ass babe. I damn sure like kissing yours!"

"You think this is funny don't you!" She declared as she rushed me un-expectantly.

She jumped on me in anger and fury. She was out of control swinging ferverishly with her open palms hitting me in the chest and on top of my head. In my attempt to move away from her I stumbled and fell to the floor. She jumped on top of me and continued with her tirade of blows. I turned over on my stomach trying to protect myself from the onslaught. She stood and pulled my overcoat over my head while I was laying flat on my stomach and attempted to pull me around the room. I tried to stand while she was pulling and lost my balance and she flung me back down to the floor. Then it dawned on me, my wife was trying to whip my ass, and thus far she was succeeding. I rolled and tried to get away, but when I stood my equilibrium was off and clothes ruffled, she charged once again laying me flat out!

"Have you lost your mind?" I shouted.

"No, have you lost yours threatening me with divorce," She shouted! "Do you know how much that hurt me?" The tears started to flow. "How could you say that to me? I love you! We have two kids together. We have made a good and special life together. You can be the biggest prick when you want to be. You know that?"

"I know, and I'm sorry. I should have never said that. I over reacted. I didn't mean it! I'd rather loose Black Street and everything else than to lose you and the kids. You and the kids are my life line, and without you my life is no more….. I love you K."

She let her defenses down and collapsed her head into my chest in a deep emotional cry. We lay there with me holding her for the next half hour – no words spoken just holding one another. I felt bad. To see her in pain and tears pouring from her eyes and to know the cause of pain was me pulled at my heart. Kendra rose her head up and sat atop of me.

"I have to get ready to go meet Darrell and his mother for dinner."

"Okay, I will change my clothes too!"

"No, I'm still mad at you" she made a fist and pushed it into my chest firmly – you hurt me, and you still have some issues to resolve with Darrell's sexuality. I will be going by myself, but we are meeting our friends at "Spot Light" a night spot for drinks and a little dancing around 10pm. I will meet you there!" She rose and headed for the bathroom.

I sat up. "How about a little love making session before you go?"

She stopped and turned toward me. "No, I forgive you, but I'm still mad at you!"

"That's even better you can release that anger on me in a different way."

"You just told a joke!"

"No, I was really being serious."

She wasn't having it. Kendra went into the bathroom took a shower and got dressed to meet Darrell and his mother for dinner. I sat on the couch and fell asleep watching television. She woke me before she left.

"How do I look?" She asked

My eyes half focused; “You look great” and she did. A beautiful caramel dress by Calvin Klein made out of a thin silk fabric. It didn’t cling to her body, but it moved with it which made for a very sensual look. I made another ditch effort for love making, but she brushed me off and told me not to be late to the Spot Light.

I fell back to sleep on the couch and didn’t open my eyes until I got a text from Kendra. “Where are you?”

I texted her back. “Your text just woke me up”

“I knew I should have given you a wakeup call. Hurry up and get down here. Luv u!” The “Luv u” was promising; she must have been softening up toward me. I hurried. Showered and dressed I called for a cab and rushed to the Spot Light.

The line to get in the Spot light was down the block. I texted Kendra to let her know I was outside the club, and she sent Charles to get me. As we walked in Charles introduced me to several people, he was obviously a regular at this spot. There were a couple of beautiful young women that approached us on our way to the table where our wives and friends were sitting. One was eyeing Charles and her hands knew their way around him. He had to stop her before she carried it too far.

“Is this him?” She asked as Charles stopped her hands from drifting to his private parts.

“Yes, this is my boy the one and only Shane.”

“Hello, with your fine chocolate ass!” she said seductively.

“How you sistas doing? Nice to meet you.”

“Shane, this is Shantel and Angie.”

Angie had a little more tact, but she tried to give me her entire resume. I had to interrupt her. “Sorry, but my wife is waiting on me.” And I pushed Charles forward through the club. “Are you banging Shantel?” I asked him.

“Like a screen door in a tornado!”

“Charles, there is nothing about that sista that says discreet. Be careful.”

“I got it all under control.” He said nonchalantly and continued through the club and led me to the table where White-

Chocolate and Maria, Big Mike and Adriona, and Carmen and Kendra were all sitting laughing, drinking and having a good time.

"What took y'all so long?" Carmen questioned.

"Fans, fans, fans. We got'um girl!" Charles returned in a quick cadence.

"Yea, fans, I believe y'all just got some big heads." She responded.

Kendra got up from her seat and gave me a hug, then showed me her cheek for a kiss.

"Aahh, that's crazy!" I said

She laughed, then pecked me on my cheek and showed me her cheek once again. I gave her a peck. She sat back down in the booth, and I slid in next to her.

"Is that all I'm going to get?" I asked.

"That's all you going to get now." She responded

We had everyone's attention at the table at this time.

"And tonight, I'm going to lay a blockbuster on you!... tonight!" I announced.

"Yea, well I 'ma have a block for you to bust too baby, so you better bring a whole lot of hammer!"

In my best Bill Cosby imitation I said. "Have hammer, will travel and go deeep into your crevice!" Kendra and I both bursted out in laughter and those who knew the scene from "Lets Do It Again" joined in. Those who had never seen the movie looked lost –that included White-Chocolate and Adriona. Big Mike explained to Adriona and told her he would rent the movie so they could watch it together.

The rest of the night went very well. We ate, danced, and drank. Kendra and I parted company with the others around 1:00 am. We went back to the hotel and had that blockbuster of a love making session.

Black Street

Six months later Black Street Capital was fully operational and had five percent or more equity stakes in six different companies. Charles, Tim, Maria, and I made up the nucleus of the operation along with eight other junior traders, analyst, and support personnel. We were aggressive and Wall Street quickly took note. Tim and Maria started a blog on our website that had become very popular with market players, economist, and businessmen. The calls started coming in for both interviews and commentary on market perspective and economic outlook. I was very happy for Tim and Maria; both were blossoming in their new positions at Black Street.

Along with the increasing popularity of Black Street we had our dissenters and haters; trying to discredit and sully our reputation. We were even attacked by some media outlets. There was one article by a reputable newspaper that read as follow:

> Black Street - Wall Street Raiders
>
> By Joan Sanders
>
> The business definition of a Raider is one that attempts a usually hostile takeover of a business corporation. Hostile takeover is an understatement for what Black Street does in the wake of its corporate takeovers. They take no prisoners, and management shakes in their boots once

their companies are in the crosshair of Black Street. They rape and pillage pension monies and other assets that are deem to have any value. Pens, Pencils, and paper are not spared from the aggressive sale happy Investment Company. They get in and out leaving nothing behind but rubble.

This group is led by Shane Jackson who is known for his resurgence of GPG's fixed income desk back in mid-2000. Shane while at GPG discriminated against all non-black candidates, and was dismissed for violating equal opportunity employment laws. Now he is under investigation by the SEC for Black Street's takeover of Blue Sky for alleged misappropriation of funds. Shane has been described as a self -made billionaire, but questions of character, racism, and a blatant disregard for the law has followed him his entire career. At thirty seven he is a Wall Street Tycoon, but the way in which he goes about doing business is likened to a street drug dealer that holds a community hostage through violent and unscrupulous practices of selling drugs to mothers and minors, then using his charisma to pursued leaders in the community to look the other way while decimating the community in which he resides.

It's not like Wall Street hasn't seen its share of corruption in its history, but when you have a giant gorilla in your mist, then animal control should be contacted to tranquilize and remove the beast from the community. In this case the responsibility belongs to the SEC. Let us hope for all of Wall Street's sake that they do their job and remove Black Street from our financial community!

Charles was the first to site the article while in the trade room and blew his cool, and I would have to say rightfully so.

"What the fuck? Shane you got to see the shit they're printing in the Journal this morning!"

"What is it?"

"Some woman is writing some bullshit about Black Street and you!"

Charles handed me the paper and I read the article quickly and was furious.

"What the hell is this? This is downright slander and defamation of character. Get Big Mike on the phone and have him take a look at this."

Charles called Big Mike and got him on top of it. Soon everyone in the trade room had read the article and everyone was piping hot. Word got to Darrell, and he called me on the desk.

"Shane, just saw the article. You alright?"

"Yea, first I've heard of an SEC investigation."

"Same here! Think there's any validity to it."

"Yes, from my last conversation with Mackey I think he has pointed the SEC in our direction, and given the information in the article about GPG, I'm sure he or Junior is the source for this Joan Sanders and given the tone of the article I believe it to be Junior."

"How do you want to handle this?"

"Just have Big Mike and your mother work on getting a retraction from the Journal."

"Nothing else?"

"No, it's desperation time. Titan Industries is forcing GPG to indulge in some dirty work. Their dream of taking over Blue Sky is becoming just that, a dream. Your work has been exemplary in tripling the earnings of the company and as you predicted the market value of Blue Sky has already doubled and given the analysis by Tim the upside looks boundless. We are positioned perfectly to take care of all our concerns."

"I'm in agreement."

Darrell understood exactly what I meant by taking care of all our concerns. We were in a position to repay investors plus a substantial return to Jakar's questionable source of funds. The threat by GPG and Titan had become a hollow one. Blue Sky had been gobbling up market share from Titan with the Africa move, and Titan shares suffered tremendously. Titan was not in a position to stop the loss of market share, but they were trying desperately to stay relevant in the oil exploration and refinery business.

Darrell and I ended our phone call, and then I overheard Charles cursing out some one on his line over the article in the Journal.

"Look bitch we pay you for a service, and got dammit you better start delivering. Now this article in the Journal practically calls Black Street a drug dealing operation and paints Shane as the king pin, and you better get your ass in gear and take care of this shit!..............I don't want to hear any excuses. We pay your ass to front run shit like this, so it should never see the light of day. What the fuck happen with this article?.......................first you heard of it? Bitch if we don't see a retraction and apology by the end of the week your ass will be cut off. I'm not fucking with you. Don't you try me, ya dumb bitch. You call me when this is done!" and he hung up the phone.

"Who were you talking to?" I asked Charles

"Ms. Wilson."

"Darrell's mother?" I questioned.

"Hell yea!"

"Why are you talking to her like that? You have to show some respect."

"Shane, I believe in communicating with a person in a language that they can understand, and that bitch is ghetto, so I talked to her in a way I know she hears and gets the message."

I couldn't object to his reasoning. And by the end of the week we received a call from the editor of the Journal apologizing for the characterization of Black Street and myself. A retraction was printed on the front page the following week. No one ever gets a retraction printed on the front page. Ms. Wilson was able to use her political connections and other relationships to push for the front page retraction, and then the Blue Sky PR firm threatened a lawsuit for defamation of character which got management's attention.

About a month later we added another company to Black Street's portfolio which caught the street by surprise. The targeted company was Titan Industries. The stock price had suffered so much that when we ran the numbers, we figured the company was undervalued by thirty percent. We also figured if we were to takeover Titan and liquidate the operations that overlapped with Blue Sky operations and merge the two we would stand to add seventy five billion in market capital to Blue Sky and dominate the world oil market. This would also add five to six billion in cash to the Black Street coffers. As soon as Titan became aware of our position through our SEC filings the call from Mr. Mackey hit my desk and the next day five SEC compliance officers paid our office a visit.

We set the SEC officers up in the conference room to begin their investigation, which they really called an audit, because contrary to media belief there was no evidence of wrong doing on our part in any of our deals, but they were determined to try and turn up something. We had our CPA firm handle all the inquiries and request, I found out later, the five that sat in our conference room was only twenty percent of the total staff working on our audit. There was another twenty working in the main office of the SEC. Most of the inquiries and requests were for the files and financial transactions with our African based investor group which wasn't surprising and had been anticipated, and Jakar had been prepped.

Was I worried about the audit? Yes and no. I knew we had our bases covered, but I also knew they had the ability to make things appear which I had no control over. So worried yes, but fearful no! The fear didn't really hit me until Brendham called me at my desk one day and asked for a special meeting that couldn't wait for our regular weekly meeting. I accommodated the meeting, but I requested the presence of Tiger. Tiger continued to be my designated personal security personnel, and he was my checks and balances when Brendham gave me reports. Brendham's reports toned down in its alert of continued surveillance by the government. Despite the article in the Journal, Ms. Wilson did a good job in opinion molding with political figures, pundits, and various media outlets, and her reports on the government were consistently accurate.

I took the meeting after market hours and I asked Charles to stay behind. Walking in the trade room side by side Brendham and Tiger took a seat in the middle of the room where I had four seats set in a circle. Charles and I occupied two of the seats adjacent to each other, and Brendham and Tiger took the seats opposite us.

"My audience for my briefings and updates is expanding." Brendham declared.

"Well, I thought since this was to be a special briefing that it might warrant some extra ears, eyes, and opinions."

Mr. Brendham shook his head in agreement.

"Well, Shane we've had some death threats."

"Death threats?" Charles questioned.

"Yea." Tiger confirmed. "There have been several. They started about two weeks after the escalation in stock price of Blue Sky."

"Do we know the source of the threats?" I asked.

"Not at this moment." Brendham answered.

"Any evidence of the threats being government sponsored?" I came back.

"We are not able to ascertain that information as yet, but we are working on it." Brendham said.

"Are these general threats on Black Street or are they more specific?" Charles questioned.

"General in nature to Black Street personnel, but specific to Shane." Brendham answered.

It felt like I had swallowed a brick that fell to the pit of my stomach when I heard Brendham say "specifically Shane". I couldn't fathom someone wanting to kill me. Why? Who? I had just started to understand and accept the monitoring by the government. I just chalked it up to the cost of being a businessman with power and influence, but to have death threats upon your life, that was a whole different ball game. My mind drifted to Kendra and the kids and the possibility of them losing a husband and father. I wasn't in fear of my life, but fear of my family's loss, and my fear turned to anger.

"You alright?" Charles reacted to my facial expression.

"Yea."

"I want to know the source."

"I'm working on it." Brendham answered.

"Find out!" I demanded.

"We will!' Tiger responded

I took a deep breath. "So where do we go from here?" I asked.

"Twenty four hour security for your family and the other principals of Black Street." Brendham responded.

"Who does the principals include?" Charles asked.

"You, Michael, and Darrel." Brendham answered.

"I think firearm training would be prudent at this time." Tiger added.

Guns! I thought, I know about money, markets, and economics, but guns couldn't have been more foreign to me. The thought of carrying and shooting a gun made me feel my freedom was being taken away and was something I didn't want to do, and didn't find appealing.

"Is that really necessary?" Charles questioned. He felt the same uneasiness that I did at the thought of guns.

"We might be getting ahead of ourselves with the firearm training." Brendham suggested.

"I think not, we have good intel that points to these threats being credible, and I feel it's better to be safe than sorry. I will be assigned to you Shane as usual and I would like to get started tomorrow if your schedule allows."

I agreed.

"Shit, don't leave me out. I want in on the training too!" Charles interjected.

We ended the meeting designating security personnel that would be assigned to each of us. There was a primary and secondary in case of sickness or absence, and coverage for the night watch. I approved all the plans going forward for our security, and increased Brendham's budget to bring on more security personnel.

The next day after work Charles and I along with our assigned security personnel Tiger and Melvin went to gun range. The building was non-descript in an industrial area, exterior painted flat white, but upon entering the building it look like something out of a James Bond movie- a warehouse with a medley of weapons on display in glass counter tops, hung on the walls behind the counter, and a state of the art indoor shooting range behind a sound proof and bullet proof glass wall. The warehouse was filled with women and men either purchasing firearms or testing their skills on the firing range. It almost looked like the people inside were getting prepared for a war. Tiger and Melvin were familiar with the facility. Evidently Brendham took all his new personnel here for fire arms training. Now Charles and I were the students.

Tiger and Melvin each enter the facility with a case which resembled a medium size suitcase. They flashed their identification and immediate access was given, and most of the sales force and customer service personnel knew them by first name. We went directly into the shooting rang. Tiger had reserved two spaces in the center of the range. Tiger and I occupied one of the spaces and Melvin and Charles the other.

Tiger opened his case and laid out four different guns in front of us. Then he went through the description of each emphasizing the pros and cons of each.

"This first on the left Shane is a 9mm automatic, this second one is a 357 revolver, third one is a 45 special, and the fourth one is a 38 semi. All these guns would fit on your person with a shoulder holster or a waist holster. Now the 38 is a beginner's gun light weight, not prone to jam, and well balanced. The others are more advanced, have a bit more power and if not held or shot correctly can result in some errant shots. This happens often to those who are not well trained on the use of these weapons. We will start with the 38 and work our way up to the others over time. The 38 is really the training gun, but I will give you some time today with the others and as we move forward your training time will shift from the 38 to more of the powerful handguns. Now, I want you to pick up the 38."

I picked up the 38 in my right hand the steel was smooth and cold. I turned the gun and examined both sides, always with the barrel facing the target or downward which Tiger was adamant at reminding me. The gun was not loaded. Tiger put the ammunition for each gun beside them. He showed me how to load, then unload the 38, and then watch me load it again. I armed the gun by pulling the clip back. Tiger was methodical and meticulous in his training of me, but most of all he had patience. Having never held a gun there was a slight tremble in my hands. Tiger understood and walked me through the firing process from start to finish. He covered hand position, aiming at the target, and squeezing the trigger before he let me take my first shot.

We had on protective goggles and ear muffs. My first blast from the 38 startled me as if I didn't know a bullet was going to fire from the barrel when I pulled the trigger. My reaction was almost comical. Both Tiger and I laughed aloud. The second and third shot calmed my nerves, but I missed my target on all three shots. Tiger adjusted my hands on the gun and lifted my head and arms, and directed me not to be so tense firing the weapon. There was some improvement in my next two shots, but I was far from mastering the 38. I would need a lot of work, and on the first day we spent over three hours at the firing range.

When we were done for the day I thanked Tiger for his patience and knowledge of firearms. Charles' experience with firearms matched mine for the most part. Our specialty was finance and investments, not guns and ammunition! We left the facility sharing our experience and tripping off the sense of power you got with shooting a gun. Charles was turned on by the feeling, but I had trepidation. I liked having power and influence, but the power to end some one's life in the palm of my hand was unnerving.

Tiger gave me the 38 with ammunition and a shoulder holster to carry before we left the firing range. I put the 38 and the ammunition in my bag. I arrived home worn out and frustrated from the day's activities. Miles and Monique were already in bed, and Kendra was in bed reading. I kissed her while she sat and read; then threw my bag on top of the chest that resided at the foot of our bed, and walked into the bathroom. I had heard the thud when I tossed the bag on the chest, but paid it no mind, but Kendra did. The 38 special fell out of my bag.

"Shane what is this?" She asked sternly pointing at the 38 lying on the floor.

Not knowing what she was referring to I answered. "What?"

"This gun that fell out of your bag!"

"Oh..that." I walked back into the bedroom and slowly bent over and picked up the 38.

"Shane,… why do you have a gun?"

No response, I just sat on the foot of the bed with the steely gun in my hand staring down at it. I had the same question for myself. What was I doing with this gun? Has my life come to this, and why? Seeing my uncertainty and frustration Kendra slowly moved over and sat behind me, wrapped her legs around me and caressed her arms around my neck, then she whispered.

"What's happening?" and she kissed me very gently across my neck and cheek.

I took a deep breath." Death threats." I half mumbled.

"Death threats?" Kendra responded frantically. She swerved around in front of me, now sitting on my lap facing me looking me squarely in the eyes with concern.

"Yea, Brendham and Tiger have gotten information that confirms there have been death threats levied at Black Street, but more specifically toward me!"

"You! Why?"

"That's what's so bothersome, I haven't a clue, unless it's just some crazy person full with jealousy, envy, or infatuation. It just doesn't make any sense. At this time there is no evidence it is government sponsored, but even that wouldn't make sense. What reason would the government have to eliminate me? I am not a threat, nor is Black Street."

"You are a black man with significant power and influence and with real economic and political ties to Africa. On the one hand the surveillance is understandable and to a certain extent is expected given the history of our government, but death threats –this is not the sixties." Kendra said in deep thought.

"I have to find out the source of the threats. Tiger and Brendham say they're working on it, but I may have to employ others with different resources to uncover the information."

"What about Ms. Wilson, Darrell's mother?"

"Darrel's got her on it. We are waiting to hear back from her!"

"What other sources do you have?"

"Ice has some connections in DC."

"Ice?" She questioned.

"Yes, that's how I was able to confirm the information I was getting from Brendham."

"Oh..Okay. I have to say it Shane."

"What?"

"I'm not comfortable with a gun in this house."

"Nor am I, but if it comes down to protecting my family, I don't want to be caught empty handed. Until we know if the threat is real, I think it better to err on the side of protection."

Kendra looked deep into my eyes and could see the struggle I was going through with having the gun, let alone having it in our home. She laid me back on the bed and stretched her body on top of mine and kissed me tenderly. It felt nice and assuring!

****

Several weeks had passed since the news of death threats, and we still couldn't substantiate the source of the threats, and according to Ms. Wilson there was nothing on the government's radar regarding death threats. But Tiger, adamantly pressed for us to keep up the firearms training, and even took it upon himself to add Ju Jitsu; he was a black belt. Despite the distractions Black Street and Blue Sky moved aggressively forward with our plans. With Blue Sky's increase in market capital the debt market was a perfect vehicle to payback investors in Blue Sky. Issuance of bonds didn't require any liquidation of shares owned and with Blue Sky's triple A rating, the interest rate was much lower than what was paid back to investors.

Black Street's pursuit of Titan heated up. Charles was leading the charge aggressively buying up available shares at bargain prices. Titan tried to match by offering a buyback of shares, but given its loss of market share to Blue Sky which affected their bottom line, financing for the buyback was next to impossible. We used some of our contacts in the media and other political and market pundits to leak negative financial and market information about Titan. Some of the news stories stretch the truth a bit, but nothing out of the ordinary for regular articles or news stories, so the media ran them. Our full court press against Titan didn't sit well with some of the Titan executives, so they scheduled an impromptu visit to Black Street headquarters.

Around 3:30pm, Charles, Maria, Tim, and I were still in the office going over our Titan strategy and Tim was updating us on economic data trends, when the receptionist alerted us of some visitors from Titan Industries and GPG. Without question I knew the GPG representatives were the Mackeys and I assumed the same executives from Titan that paid us the first visit to our office. Immediately Charles was ticked off.

"I'm tired of these mutha fuckas dropping in on us. What the fuck?"

"I understand your frustration, but it's nothing more than a power play on their part. They feel they have the upper hand when they can drop in and demand a meeting. So, lets not take them out of their comfort zone. Meetings with them will reveal more about them than it will about us."

We all agreed to take the meeting. We set four chairs in the middle of the trade room and two chairs opposing them. Tim and Maria remained seated at the trade desk behind us. They entered the trade room led by Mr. Mackey. Junior tagged behind his father, and was followed by two Titan representatives I had never seen. They didn't look the executive type. Charles and I stood and greeted each of them as they walked to the center of the trade room. Turns out the two with the Mackeys were part of the Titan Family that founded company, Abrahams and Lincoln. I thought right away upon their introduction this meeting was going to be short on substance, and big on emotions. We offered them seats in the chairs set out for them.

"Thanks for meeting with us on such short notice." Mr. Mackey started off.

Charles was quick with the rebuttal. "More like no notice!"

"As I said we apologize for coming without calling ahead."

"What can we do for you?" I asked.

"You can stop buying our stock!" One of the family members blurted out.

Charles and I didn't respond. Charles followed my lead in remaining calm with open ears, and the rant began.

"You already own Blue Sky, what the hell do you want with Titan Industries! We are in the same industry what sensed does that make for a diversified portfolio. I don't know what you are trying to pull, but it won't work. You are out of your league. I will see you in hell before you wreck what my family has worked generations to build." said Mr. Abrahams.

This guy was worse than Junior, he let it all hang out. He lost his composure, sense of dignity, and respect. He was foaming at the mouth; spit accompanied every word that came out of his mouth. I suspected Charles was holding back his laughter while I was holding a poker face. When I glanced over at him, a sly smirk was displayed on his face which threw this guy into a rage.

"You think what I'm telling you is funny, you black mother fucker!"

I didn't react. Charles body jolted, but he followed my lead. I could hear Tim and Maria adjust in their seats, but they stayed seated. I just stared at the four men, and a few moments later I saw shame creep in to Abrahams eyes when he looked down and away. Right then, I felt his desperation and knew he was a defeated man. His family owned a collective thirty five percent of the outstanding stock. We were up to twenty five percent and counting. Without access to capital their hopes of accumulating more shares through a buyback program was quickly slipping away. The door was wide open for us to take over Titan and merge it with Blue Sky effectively reducing the Titan founding family to an insignificant minority interest.

Mr. Mackey understood the dynamics of what was taking place, so he tried to keep the meeting together and on track. "Shane, can we strike a deal? "

Now we were getting somewhere. They were about to show their hand. "What kind of deal?"

"Titan will sell its fifteen percent interest in Blue Sky to Black Street at market, and in return Black Street will discontinue with efforts to takeover Titan Industries."

Charles and I both knew the fifteen percent interest in Blue Sky was bank financed and upon liquidation of those shares the loan would have to be repaid. Even with the capital gains tax deferred on the profit from selling the shares, it wouldn't allow Titan to gain a majority share in their outstanding stock, and Mr. Mackey knew we knew that. His offer was really Black Street doing a favor for Titan Industries and why would we do that? We wouldn't.

"I will give your offer consideration. Can I call you tomorrow with our answer?"

Mr. Mackey knew what our answer was, but my response allowed him to save face in front of his clients which he appreciated. "I will look for your call tomorrow?" He stood, and the rest of us followed suit. We all shook hands and they left the office.

Charles embraced me and we both had a good laughed! Maria and Tim looked confused.

"Are you really going to consider the offer?" Maria asked.

"Maria, the offer was ridiculous. The numbers don't add up. There is no way Titan can gain a majority share of its company." Charles responded.

"So, we won!"

"Hell yes! We own Titan!" Charles declared.

"Holy shit!" She rushed to Charles and gave him a hug, then me, then Tim.

We had a small celebration just the four of us. It was good to see a smile on everyone's face. Our accomplishment was unprecedented. Black Street had taken over the top two oil exploration and refinery companies – unthinkable! Tim and I had a moment while Maria and Charles were getting their coats ready to hit a bar for drinks.

"Thanks man, I………"

"No need, you were a big part of this, and your research and analysis was top notch allowing us to accumulate shares of stock at rapid pace. You carried your weight Tim.

"Thanks man!" he hugged me.

"Ain't that cute? Come on lets go celebrate!" Charles commented.

"I can't join you. My daughter is in a play tonight. I got to hop."

"Well, celebrate with your family, and give the wife and kids a kiss for me." I said.

"Will do!" Tim left the office heading home.

Charles, Maria, and I took the celebration to a bar down the street. The bar was filled with suits. It was packed. We maneuvered our way through the crowded bar. We order some shots and carved out a small niche at the bar. Maria was getting a lot attention at the bar from the surrounding suits, but she paid them no mind.

"I want to make a toast." Maria declared, "To Black Street the illest company to ever hit Wall Street!" She downed her shot. Charles and I followed. "Bartender another round!" She shouted. "You two were some cool mutha fuckers in that meeting with GPG and Titan. I wanted to kick that white man in the nuts when he called y'all some black mutha fuckas! But, I chilled because y'all were so chilled."

"The only reason why I didn't make a move was because of Shane. He was in total control."

"I felt the same way as both of you, but I knew they were a defeated group, so there was no point reacting to the rant that stem from anger."

The next round of shots came and Maria quickly downed hers. Charles followed, but I milked mine a little. It was clear to me where Maria and Charles were headed-inebriation, but I wasn't going there. They both went a few more rounds while I continued to nurse my second.

"You better try to catch up homeboy!" Charles said.

"I'm good."

"Shane,... you are a party pooper." Maria was feeling the alcohol. "But, I ain't mad at you. You're a boss ass brotha!" She moved closer, put her hand around my waist and pulled me closer and whispered. "Thanks for bringing me back. Love you always." Then I noticed Charles was directly behind Maria very close. "Ah... someone is being bad back there..ha, ha,ha," then she looked at me, "but it feels good." She whispered sensually in my ear.

I backed away, finished my drink, gave Maria a kiss on the cheek and hug, then a dap to Charles. "I'm out!" I declared. As I walked out of the bar I called Tiger to pull the car around front to pick me up. Once outside, Charles caught up to me.

"You leaving now, right now!"

"Yea and you should do the same."

"We both can do her tonight!"

"Don't shit where you eat! Put Maria in a cab and send her home, then have Melvin take you home to celebrate with your beautiful wife."

"Ah shit, just like Maria said, party pooper!"

We both got a chuckle out of that. Tiger pulled up to the curve in the black SUV. I got in the back and rolled down the window. "Send Maria home!" I emphasized.

Charles went into his rendition of Tupac's Temptations along with a little dance shuffle on the side walk:

Tell me baby are you lonely? Don't wanna rush ya
I can help ya if ya only, let me touch ya
If I'm wrong love tell me, cause I get caught up
and the life I live is Hell see, I never thought I'd see
the day when I would calm down, you ain't heard
I've been known to clown and Get Around, that's my word
See you walkin and you lookin good, yes indeed
Got a body like a sex fiend, you're killin me

Tiger and I pulled off laughing before he was done. When I looked back he was walking back into the bar. I thought, temptations, lord knows I've had my share of them since Black Street. The closest I've come was with Susan and Maria, but I often question myself about how far I allowed them to go to tempt me. I was attracted to that line between right and wrong, good and bad. I liked the rebel role; I reveled in it in business. My business life teetered on that line daily, and I have crossed it many a day and never losing a day's sleep over it. Was I a man without conscious? I didn't think so! As I once told Tim all men have their line in the sand, it's up to the man to define his own line, and be willing to deal with the consequences of his decisions! I drew my line in the sand at my family. I wasn't willing to jeopardize my family for no one or a moment's pleasure. I knew if Black Street was lost forever, returning me home a broken man, my family would make me whole again. Family was eternal in my mind, and home was where my family was, and I liked going home!

About a half hour later I arrived home. Kendra had put the kids to bed and was lying on the couch in the family room watching her guilty pleasure "Hip Hop Wives". I took off my coat and joined her on the couch. She didn't hesitate to wrap her arms around me and show me love. I really loved that about her. We celebrated this victory in silence, but in the comfort of each other.

Game Changer

6 am in the next morning I was in the office sitting down with Charles mapping out how we were going to finalize the takeover of Titan Industries. We now owned about twenty five percent of the company and were looking to take it up to a fifty five percent. We estimated in two weeks' time we could reach our goal. The stock was taking a dive and sellers of the stock were numerous with Black Street the only buyer. Investors were fleeing the burning house. Typical Wall Street over reacting to bad news which seem to be coming out at a record pace on Titan in the light of Blue Sky's tremendous success. Both Charles and I worked the phones with Big Mike and his staff on the logistics for the takeover of Titan. As promised, I made a call to Mr. Mackey.

"Hello, Shane I appreciate the call. I wish you the best with your Titan purchase. Hope I don't sound condescending, but I'm proud of you. You have exceeded my wildest expectations. I knew you were a special talent, and thank you for the courtesy of the call."

"You're Welcome"

We ended the phone call. Mr. Mackey showed class in the face of defeat which I knew then was the trait of a successful man.

Once I completed the phone call I was anxious for Charles to free himself up from his calls before anyone else arrived for work. I wanted to address a pressing issue that I needed some closure on.

"Did you hit it?" I asked.

"We set you up." He said with a devious look.

"What do you mean you set me up?"

"Maria knows you will not jump in that pool, but she thought you might jump in the pool if you knew I wanted to swim in the pool, and the only way I would ever get a chance to swim in that pool is with you."

"What the fuck were you thinking?"

"She came to me with it!" He pleaded.

"Damn that! Stop thinking with your lower head and use the head above your neck. She manipulated you, and then through you she tried to manipulate me. I don't like that shit! I ought to fire that bitch as soon as she brings her ass into this office."

"Man, you're over reacting!"

"Bullshit, I don't know who's who in my life and I'm getting tired of it. You supposed to be my brotha – If some chick comes to you with some freaky fantasy about whatever, you're supposed to run it by me first to see if I'm down with it or not, not play it out to see if you can catch me in her web of deception."

I was furious with Charles, and he knew it. The pace of my breathing quickened, my stare was deep and penetrating, examining and questioning. Just then, Maria entered the trade room. Without hesitation I rose from my chair with purpose toward her, grabbed her by the arm and firmly escorted her out of the trade room followed by Charles. I raised my free hand toward him letting him know this was going to be private conversation between Maria and me. He stopped and returned to the trade room. I led Maria into the private office and closed the doors behind us. Once inside I released Maria's arm. She turned to face me in shock.

"What the hell Shane?"

"That's what I should be asking you. What the hell are you trying to pull?"

"What,…" she acted like she had no idea what I was talking about.

I just stared at her without words.

"Oh, you talking about…last night. Ah,… I was just a little lit and just messing around with you and Charles."

"That's bullshit! Charles told me about your plan!"

"OH, he told you." She responded softly. Lost for words she couldn't continue to speak.

We just stared at each other without words; studying one another until my expression changed and fear over took Maria.

"Clear out your desk and take yo ass back to Dallas."

"Noooo!" She screamed. "Come on man, don't send me back….Okay I fucked up, but it's just……..no matter how hard I try I just can't get you out of my system." She pleaded then paused. "Alright, I should have never dragged Charles into my shit, and I apologize for that, but you send mixed signals."

"What the hell are you talking about mixed signals? I'm not sending you any signals!" I declared.

"Oh, come on Shane. I see you checking me out when you think I'm not looking, watching me walk across the trade room, checking out my ass, eyeing my legs, and other parts of my body. The hugs between us are not regular Shane, its more there and you feel it just like me. Who the fuck you think you foolin? You want some of this and you deny yourself the pleasure of having it!"

"So mutha fuckin what, if I check you out from time to time, and you got damn right I abstain from crossing the line. I love my wife, and I'm not jeopardizing that for nothing in the world, especially not a piece of ass!....Look, I'm not mad at you for being attracted to me, I knew that when I decided to bring you back to Black Street, but for you to connive and plan to get me in a compromising position using Charles…."I shook my head in disapproval. "I can't trust you anymore, and I want you gone. I will tell Darrell to expect you back."

"I'm not going! I'm not leaving you!" And she walked out of the office and straight into the trade room.

A couple of minutes later I walked into the trade room. When I entered, she was sitting at her desk crying, and Charles was consoling her. Others had arrived for work including Tim who was curious about the water works displayed by Maria. Once I sat at my desk Tim came over and asked me what was going on. I told him Maria would be returning to Blue Sky. He asked me why and I told him she missed her husband. He didn't pry, but I could see he wasn't buying that story.

Soon after Tim returned to his desk, Charles walked over and took a seat next to me.

"Don't do this to Maria, she's good people." He said calmly.

"I don't know that to be true."

"How can you say that? She's been with us from the beginning."

"Charles we are carrying guns, death threats continue to roll in, the government is watching us and for all we know they could have plants inside Black Street. I don't trust anyone anymore and she just gave me a reason not to trust her."

"You trust me?" he questioned.

I paused. "I trust you because I know you. You think with your loins, not with your head sometimes, but I know your heart. You would never do me harm intentionally."

"Ay yea and u know that!" He stood to embrace me.

I stood and we embraced. He whispered in my ear. "I'm truly sorry Shane, and just for the record I sent Maria home in a taxi. I went home to Carmen to celebrate, and it was a hell of a celebration." We laughed together. Maria approached.

"I just want to apologize to the both of you. I should have never done what I did…... My feelings for you Shane are complicated and confusing, but one thing I do know is I don't want to lose your friendship. I put my desires for you, before what you needed from me, and I promise it won't happen again."

I couldn't believe she was testifying before everyone in the trade room. I felt a little embarrassed for her and me. She continued.

"Please don't send me back to Blue Sky. I'm sorry!" She pleaded. Tears fell from her red eyes like a waterfall.

She reached out to me and I grabbed her hand, pulled her in close for a hug. Her cries were heavy and heartfelt. I truly cared for Maria, and she was a big part of Black Street. She had made sacrifices for me I would never forget. My heart couldn't stay harden against her any more than it could toward Charles. They were a part of my Black Street family for better or for worse.

The emotional rollercoaster finally came to a stop later that morning. Black Streets takeover of Titan Industries had hit the news wires. It was the hot topic of the day; how Titan Industries was defenseless against our attack and how the lack of financing from banks and private money left Titan a naked prey to Black Street. Most media outlets just reported the facts, only a few used borderline derogatory language in describing Black Street's inevitable takeover. Ms. Wilson had done a good job of cleaning up the perception of Black Street with the media.

The buying was fast and furious. Charles was a madman scooping up large blocks of shares of Titan. Tim, Maria, and myself were preparing the companies we would use for the due diligence effort in vetting Titan to ensure there were no surprises in their books or any preventive stock measures that would inhibit our takeover or sabotage the company. The day was long and exhausting. By day's end it was just the three of us – Maria, Charles, and me. We called it quits around 5:00 pm, and decided to go for drinks, but this time instead of Wall Street pub, we opted for a Harlem favorite, Julians!

I had Tiger pulled the SUV in front of the building. Charles called for Melvin, but he had left earlier in the day because of sickness, so Charles and Maria rode with me. When we arrived at Julian's, it was packed. Tiger let us out in front and left to park the car. We went directly to the bar, but we put our name on the waiting list for a booth, our stomachs were grumbling at us after the long up and down day. Once we got our drinks it wasn't long before they seated us at a booth. We sat with Maria sitting between the two of us and recapped the events of the day. When the morning drama came up Maria became teary eyed and apologized once again to both Charles and I. I had moved on and told her she should do the same. There was no reason we ever had to speak of it again! We drank to that.

As I looked around Julian's I saw Tiger seated at the bar surveying the room. He was on constant alert never seeming to be relaxed. I actually appreciated that about Tiger. He had picked up a lot since I had him put back into Brendham's unit. His instincts were sharp and attention to detail was unmatched. I almost thought we should put him on the due diligence team that would be combing through Titan's books. Detecting that my eyes were scanning the room Tiger walked over.

"Everything ok?" He asked the table.

"We're good. Would you like some food?" I asked.

"No, thanks

"Why don't you sit and join us?" Maria asked.

"Thanks for the offer, but it's better I maintain a view where I can see the whole room and the table you are sitting at." He returned to his seat at the bar.

Our food arrived which was just some appetizers. I didn't want to eat too heavy before I went home because I knew Kendra would have dinner when I arrived. We chatted and laughed while we gulped down the appetizers. When we were done, we walked up to Tiger at the bar and he escorted us through the crowd. As we approached the door a young lady came up to me. She was holding a magazine with my picture on the cover, and she wanted my autograph. I had done an interview for a small publication called Harlem Business, but hadn't seen the finish product the girl was holding it in her hand. She was black, stood about five feet five, black hair, and a darker shade of brown, strangely attractive, dressed for the night life – tight dress and high heel shoes, but one thing I noticed was her nose ring. It was peace sign made of diamonds.

Tiger stepped outside Julian's while I signed the young ladies magazine. Charles and Maria watched, giving me a hard time calling me Denzel and asking for autographs themselves. When I looked out to see if Tiger was pulling up with the SUV, he was still standing outside like he was surveying the block east and west, then his attention was drawn up on top of the building across from Julian's. As I approach the doorway to exit Julian's Tiger turned and ran toward me yelling "BACK INSIDE". He dove toward me, and his force pushed me to the ground. My backward momentum forced Maria and Charles to the floor too. Lying on top of me Tiger wasn't moving, when Charles helped me move him and turned him over, there was a hole in the middle of his face where blood was profusely pouring out. In disbelief and scared I looked at my chest, it was soaked with Tiger's blood. Screams rang out from the surrounding women who saw Tigers face. He had been shot through the back of his head and the bullet exploded out the front of his face. Tiger had been shot by a rifle with a silencer. A bullet obviously meant for me. As Tiger lay dead on the floor of Julian's, panic and fear spread through the restaurant, and people wanted out of Julian's immediately. They rushed toward the front door where they were met with a hail of gunfire that blew out the store front and injured many. People began to run to the back of the bar escaping out the rear exit.

Both of us severely shaken, Charles and I pulled Tiger's body out of range of the gun fire toward the middle of the bar behind some chairs and tables for cover, Maria followed. The gunfire stopped, Maria took out her phone and called 911. I looked toward the front of Julian's, then the back. People were rushing out the back of the restaurant. Then, I heard someone yell "they're coming". I looked out in front of Julian's and two men were approaching from across the street one white, one black, both wore black over coats with dark shades, and they were carrying assault rifles. I took out my semi-automatic .38 from my shoulder holster and armed it; Charles did the same with his .45. I searched Tiger and took his .9 mm and his .38 revolver which I handed to Maria.

"We got to get out of here!" I told Charles and Maria.

They both shook their heads in agreement. We were all stunned by Tiger's death, but quickly realized if we didn't get out of there we would be next. I pulled Maria behind me. She was trembling. I told Charles to follow as I made my way toward the back of Julian's. Julian's back door led out to an alley. I approached the door with caution even though patrons were streaming through the back door. I paused and tried to sneak a peek out the door using others as cover to see if it was clear for us to exit. Multiple shots were fired at the door wounding more patrons. I dove back inside of Julian's.

"What the hell are we going to do?" Charles yelled.

I didn't know. Both Maria and Charles were looking to me for direction. I squatted and moved toward the front to get a look back into the front of Julian's. The two men who were approaching were now inside Julian's casing the place with their rifles in the ready position. We could see the enemy out front, but they couldn't see us so we had an advantage. Trying to get out the back way would be a sure way to end all our lives!

"We go out the front way!" I said.

"No, lets' stay put and wait for the police." Maria pleaded. "I called 911!"

"We stay here; we're dead before the police arrive! They're hunting us down!" I stated.

"I don't hear any damn sirens anyway! And, I ain't going down without taking some of them with me!" Charles declared.

Charles and I agreed; I would take the shooter on the left, and he would take out the shooter on the right. We both crouched behind the doorway into the restaurant left to right. My heart was beating hard. I thought it may pop out of my chest. I counted down from three with my fingers, when it was time, I jumped into action focused on the shooter on the left, never taking my eyes off him as I quickly walked toward him through the door way. Charles did the same on his target. I squeezed the trigger and bullets shot out the barrel of my .38 in rapid succession hitting the shooter in the chest before he could react. The shooter on the right reacted to my shots and turned his rifle toward me, but Charles shot him in the arm sending his shots errant. Charles then put three shots to his mid-section sending him lifeless to the floor.

I was sweating heavily and my senses were heightened. I felt the blood running through my extremities and the hair on my arms and head felt like they were standing at attention. I trembled from the shock of what Charles and I had done. I looked at him and it was like looking in a mirror – heavy sweating, trembles, and shock. Then, we heard shouts and Maria came running out from the back of Julian's.

"They are coming!" She yelled as she ran straight to me.

"Let's go!" I commanded.

We made haste to the front of Julian's. Charles covered our backside.

"We have to make it to that corner store at the end of the block for cover!" I told them.

"Let's go, I don't think our luck is going to hold up in here!" Charles declared.

We exited Julian's through the blown out store front window, and ran down the street toward Ace's convenience store. The shooters located in the back of Julian's had made their way to the front, and on site of us fired their weapons. Charles and I fired back. We tried to shield ourselves in the doorways of closed establishments along the block. Ducking in and out of doorways, Charles and I tried to lay down cover fire for each other as we progressed down the block.

We finally reached the end of the corner which was no small task, but if we wanted safety we had to make it to the Ace's. Crossing the intersection diagonally I knew would be a dangerous proposition, but we didn't have another option. We proceeded into the intersection laying down constant fire toward those down the block heading toward us. I led followed closely by Maria with Charles bringing up the rear. New shots rang out coming from three men approaching from the north side of the intersection. I returned fire and hit two of them, and I made it to the cover of the convenience store, but when I looked to see only Maria by my side. I panicked, then to my horror I saw Charles lying face down in the middle of the intersection motionless. There were three shooters on the opposite corner of Maria and I-two were down, one was ducked behind a parked car.

"Nooo!" I yelled. I pulled the .9mm from the small of my back and reloaded the 38, then Maria tried to hold on to me to stop me from going to get Charles, but I forcefully pulled away from her and charged the intersection both guns blasting. The shooter behind the car came out charging the intersection also from the opposite side. I shot him in the leg and shoulder, then one of his bullets hit me in the left shoulder spinning me right, then another bullet coming from the north end of the intersection hit me in my side near my rib cage sending me spiraling down to the ground. But, I continued shooting in the direction of the first shooter as I was falling and took him out with a head shot. I found myself lying right next to Charles where both of my weapons had escaped my hands. I was hurt, bleeding from my shoulder and stomach. The shooter from the north end approached fast. He was coming in close for the kill shot. All I could do was brace myself as best I could, and as he approached I heard two shots fired, and then blood squirted from the shooters head and chest. When he fell, I saw Maria behind him, gun extended with smoke coming from the barrel.

She saved my life. She ran up to me. “Can you move?” She asked.

“Yea.” I moved to pick up the guns I dropped. Then we both moved to check out Charles who still wasn’t moving.

“We got to get outta here Shane!” She rose up with gun in hand. We saw a black tricked out Escalade blasting music approaching, oblivious to what just had occurred in this intersection. Maria pulled a jack move on the brotha.

Gun pointed at him from the front of his SUV, he stopped on her command. She moved to the driver’s side to confront him. “Get yo bitch ass out the car!” He saw blood on her face and clothes and didn’t hesitate to relinquish his vehicle. She pulled the SUV alongside of Charles and me, and then got out to help me put Charles in the back of the Escalade. I climbed in the back with him. She floored the SUV leaving a cloud of smoke and the smell of burnt rubber behind us.

“We need to get Charles to the hospital.” I said as he lay across my lap.

“Does he have a pulse?” Maria asked looking back at me.

I tried his wrist, nothing, then his neck, nothing, his body was limp……. I pulled him close and held him tight. My head fell backward.

“Shane does Charles have a pulse?” Maria asked urgently again.

Silence! When I pulled my head back forward, tears were streaming down my face.

“Oh nooo!” Maria cried and her eyes reddened, then tears fell as she drove.

I coughed, and then I coughed again and again. Maria turned to me with grave concern. “Shane you alright?” I coughed again and again. The coughs became more violent and uncontrollable, then the next cough I spit up blood. Maria looked back again and when she saw the blood, she lost it. She screamed my name “Shane!” I coughed once again. This time blood spewed from my mouth and sprayed the back of the passenger side seat. I felt dizzy and my sight became blurred. Maria was talking to me hysterically, but I couldn’t hear a word she was saying. Tears rolled down her face; her eyes filled with terror. Then everything went black, and my head fell to the side of the back seat window. I heard muffled sounds of tires screeching, than a crashing sound, and a big bursting sound.

****

Darkness, stillness, calm, unknown were the only words to describe my state. I couldn’t see anything or feel anything. A dark cloud engulfed my entire body. Time was immeasurable and irrelevant. The depth of my understanding of what had happened to me was null. Obviously I wasn’t dead because I recognized my consciousness, but it wasn’t in a current state. It was in a subconscious state. My thoughts ran rapid, I played and replayed the events of the day over and over in my mind, but they seemed unreal. I wasn’t convinced of their gravity. Thoughts of Charles were painful, too much to accept, so I forced the thoughts away. I tried my best to stay in the dark grey areas of the cloud that I found myself engulfed in. The mind play went on for what seemed like an eternity.

I started hearing voices around my body, close to my head, by my side and down by my feet which startled me initially. I didn’t know some of the voices, but I did recognize others. I quickly determined the voice by my head talking to me in a very soft and gentle voice was Kendra. Other voices that faded in and out were my Mom, Big Mike, Darrell, Carmen, and White-Chocolate. As soon as I heard White-Chocolate my thoughts turned to Maria. How was she?

Did she make it? I had a hard time making out the words that were spoken around me; they were muffled, unclear, slowed, and fragmented.

"Maria….bruised…concussion….difficult to walk." Those were just some of the words I could make out from White-Chocolate's voice.

Then I heard Carmen speak in a mixture of words and cries. "Charles…..funeral…….Saturday 2:00pm……..going home."

I tuned out after the funeral news on Charles. The cloud now served as my hiding place to rest my mind and to find some semblance of peace. I didn't want to leave the cloud; it was my escape, my place of solace and tranquility. As I said before time was immeasurable, I don't know how long I tuned out (later I found out 3 days), but I tuned back in when Kendra's voice sounded stressed and uncontrollable.

"You…..what…….hell you talking about!"

"I'm…….giving you…….if ….husband…..doesn't come…….coma…..next few days……unlikely he………come out."

"Get…..out of…..room!" Kendra shouted. "Get …..hell……..!"

Then I heard Darrell's voice. "Shane…….make it!"

Big Mike's voice tried to reassure Kendra. "Shane…..strong."

I couldn't pick up anymore of the conversation between the three. It was as if they moved away from me. The next thing I knew Kendra's voice was by my head speaking tenderly. Her voice was clear and words recognizable, emotional, sincere, and loving.

"It's time for you to wake up baby. You've had your rest, and lord knows you needed it. Miles and Monique need their Daddy, and their new sibling coming is going to need Daddy. Yes we're going to have another child. And, I need you baby, we have a lot of living and loving to do before either of us leave this life time. Come back to me Shane!" She pleaded with sounds of sniffles. I've never loved anyone the way I love you." Then it happened, I felt her get in bed with me, her head across my chest and her arm wrapped around my waist tightly.

My sense of time returned, feeling slowly returned to my extremities. I fidgeted a little under Kendra which startled her. She rose; darkness engulfed the space we occupied. She spoke “Shane!” I moved around in the bed and tried to focus, but darkness prevented me. I tried to respond to her, but my mouth was dry and my throat was sore, so I reached my hand out to her. She grabbed my hand fiercely dropping to the bed caressing her face it. I felt the wetness on her face. She trembled. I tried to sit up, but was too weak. I felt her kissing me all over my face almost frantically, and then she lifted her head to get a good look at me. The lights were dim in the room, and my vision was blurred, but slowly Kendra’s face started to come into focus.

“Baby can you hear me?” she asked.

I responded slightly nodding my head.

“Oh Shane!” she embraced me. “I thought I was going to lose you.” She kissed me on the cheek.”

I pointed towards the water in a pitcher at the foot of my bed. She quickly poured me a glass of water. I sipped the water. My sore throat only allowed trickles to move through my body. It felt like I was swallowing a hand full of small needles. The pain was excruciating. Kendra reacted to my pain.

“Take your time Shane, just a little at a time. Your body has gone through a lot. I’m going to call the nurse and get a doctor in here to examine you right away.”

I held her hand before she could ring for the nurse. “I……..lo..ve….you.”

She kissed me gently on the side of my face. “I love you too! She rang for the nurse and before I knew it the room was packed with doctors and nurses checking monitors, examining all my body parts, and taking blood. This went on almost nonstop for the next few days. Everything was checking out normal as far as I could understand. I was on a tremendous amount of drugs, and didn’t have all my faculties about me.

Kendra took charge. In my weakened state I was in no condition to talk to anyone. Kendra limited the number of visitors and even kept Big Mike and Darrell's visits to a minimum. My kids' visitations were limited, but for a different reason. Kendra thought, and I agreed Miles and Monique seeing me in a fragile state might be a frightening sight for them at their age. To see Dad who they saw this towering strong and unbreakable figure reduced to a feeble specimen of himself was unfathomable. So, Kendra just told them Daddy was sick, but would be getting better and back to his old self. My mother was the only one who wouldn't adhere to Kendra's limits, and Kendra didn't even try to enforce it upon her.

My mother sat by my side, rubbed my hand and face, and I smiled at her. Tears flowed from her eyes. Kendra left the room to give us some privacy. My mother spoke in a very emotional tone mixed with anger and angst.

"My son....I love you and I am so proud of you as a father, a son, a man, a businessman, and husband. I raised you with the expectation that you would do great things, and you have done nothing less. You have exceeded my wildest dreams for you......... For someone to try and hurt.......I will have them killed!" I patted her hand to calm her. She continued. "You have a beautiful wife and children! Take them and go far away, live the rest of your life and enjoy the fruits of your labor. I don't know why someone would want to..." Her voice cracked."......kill you, nothing is worth your life, but your family, so dedicate the rest of your life to them. Please my son, I'm pleading with you,....no one will hold it against you or think badly of you. You owe no one anything! You only owe it to your family to be there. Your kids are young...... You have accomplished more in your thirty seven years than people accomplish in a lifetime."

I heard every word my mother said. All her words were heartfelt and touching. I knew she meant every word, but deep down she knew I wouldn't run! Even in my current condition I wouldn't run! I patted her hand once again trying to comfort her. She knew right then my answer. My mother bowed her head in my stomach and cried. I had never seen my mother cry and maybe as her only child and a single parent, she never allowed me to see her cry, but on this occasion she didn't hold back.

My mother left after she composed herself and kissed me on the forehead. As my mother was exiting the room Kendra came in. I saw them embrace each other in passing. I almost thought my mother wasn't going to let Kendra go, but she eventually did. Kendra approached the side of my bed, stood beside me and grasped my hand. I took my free hand rubbed her tummy and smiled.

"Yes! You heard me?"

I shook my head yes.

"It's a boy Shane. Our family is growing." She paused. "We need to talk about how we are going to move forward. I know it's difficult for you to speak at this time, and the doctor said it would be several days before the swelling in your throat will allow you to speak. I will tell you what I think the best course of action is and you just nod in agreement or disagreement."

My main concern was rest and getting healthy. Whatever Kendra had in mind I didn't anticipate too much objection on my part.

"I want us to leave the states; take you back to Africa where you can recover and get proper rest without any of the stresses of Black Street or Blue Sky. Only Darrell and Big Mike will know our whereabouts, and your mother and my parents will be travelling with us. I have hired an outside security agency while we remain State side. When we arrive in Africa Jakar has arranged for security personnel for us. I have not kept Brendham in the know. I felt if your gut was telling you he wasn't trustworthy, and then he wasn't. Darrell will keep him busy with Blue Sky security until you guys decide what to do with him. Big Mike is going to transition back to New York to run Black Street Capital until you return." Then she looked for my approval.

Without hesitation I gave it to her by nodding I was in agreement. Since the time I met Kendra I was always impressed by her business savvy and prowess. In a lot of ways she had better business acumen than I, and if something were to happen to me she was more than capable of running Black Street, and she would have the help of Darrell and Big Mike.

"One other thing we need to discuss."

I nodded for her to continue.

"The police have been anxious to question you about what took place at Julian's. The doctors and I have been keeping them at bay until you regained some of your strength. They have questioned Maria, and others, but they think you're the key to getting to the bottom of what happened. You will have to speak to them before we can leave the states."

I nodded once again.

****

About a week and a half later my throat had healed enough for me to speak. My voice had changed, it sounded strained, very similar to the way Miles Davis sounded after his accident. The changed alarmed me. I didn't like it, until Kendra said it made me sound sexier and the unfamiliar pitch and tone didn't scare my kids. I stayed in the hospital just a couple of days after my voiced returned. During those two days I had more test and visitors; mostly family and friends, but I did have a visit from two FBI agents.

Kendra had security personnel posted inside and outside my room. The federal agents were detained at the door by security before they were allowed to see me.

"We were scheduled to question Mr. Jackson today. Are we still on for this time?" They asked Kendra.

She looked at me sitting up in bed, and I gave her the go ahead.

"Please come in!"

The agents entered and security provided them two chairs by my bed on the right. Kendra came around to my left and sat on the bed beside me. The questioning started off with introductions of agent Nelson and agent Thompson both Caucasian men. They asked me all the standard questions to validate who I was – my name, where I was born, how old I was, my social security number, my mother's name, and the names of my wife and children. Once they established I was who they thought I was, it got interesting.

They queried me all the way back to my undergrad years and my relationships with Tim, Susan, Karen, and Calvin. They wanted to know about the project we worked on together to expand Calvin's Hip Hop Apparel business. They even mentioned almost in passing the escapade I had with Calvin's girlfriend in New York before I enter grad school. I found that to be quite weird. Then, we questioned them about their line of questioning.

"This case is complicated. There are a lot of moving parts!" Agent Nelson said.

Complicated, moving parts, I didn't like his response. I had a question. "Why are the Feds involved with this and not the local police?"

"We have taken over the case because your involvement with Jacob Brendham!"

"My involvement!" I said excitedly. Kendra rubbed my back to calm me. "He is the head of my security. There is no other involvement or grand scheme beyond his duties as security personnel." I said calmly.

Both agents shook their head and continued their questioning. They focused in on my relationships with Big Mike, Darrell, and Charles and our graduate days at Jordan. How I brought them on at GPG and attempted to turn the entire trading desk black.

"What was the purpose of that?" Agent Thompson asked.

I paused, still under appreciating the line of questioning." Simply put, opportunity."

They both looked at each other. "You didn't think there was equal opportunity for blacks at GPG." Agent Nelson asked.

"No I didn't."

"Was there any evidence of that?" Agent Thompson questioned.

"Lots of evidence all anyone has to do is look at GPG's history, their management, and culture of their business environment."

"But, they hired you!"

"I was the exception, not the rule!"

They finally moved on from that topic into Black Street Capital and our acquisitions of World Textiles, Blue Sky, and Titan Industries. Now, some of the details of those purchases were for public consumption, but other aspects were strictly for insiders and never left the walls of Black Street's trade room. When we brought Brendham aboard he swept the trade room for bugs and found several, so I knew the information came from some of the government bugs. Now I became reserved with my answers because I didn't know if they were the enemy or allies.

"What happen between Maria and City Manager Espinoza in Puerto Rico?"

Yea and fuck you too! I wanted to say, but I played it cool. "I don't know what you are referring to. If you have questions about Maria, you need to ask her."

They looked at each other. They knew I was being deceptive. I didn't care what they thought. They continued to drill down on the Blue Sky and Titan Industries, then all of sudden they shifted.

"What happen between you and Big Mike, when you ended up in the hospital with a concussion?"

I never told Kendra what really happen and she just acquiesced to believing I had an accident. "That was just an accident!" Kendra responded.

"Accident?" They knew Kendra didn't know the truth of the situation. "It had nothing to do with Big Mike's abusive relationship with Adriona, and you Mr. Jackson trying to protect her?"

They had Big Mike's place bugged. How in the hell did Brendham missed those bugs; unless he was still working for the government? Kendra looked at me in dismay. I answered. "No!"

They took some notes and moved on. "Did you know Charles was having affairs all over New York City and possibly having an affair with Maria?"

"No."

"Did you and Charles ever have a threesome with Maria?"

They didn't give a damn that my wife was sitting right there. Kendra didn't react at all to the questioning. "No."

They were fishing, and to progress their fishing expedition even deeper they questioned me about the altercation in the restaurant with Darrell's partner Derrick.

"I will not dignify the question with an answer. What took place in the restaurant had no bearing on who is trying to kill me."

"Maybe so Mr. Jackson, but at this time we cannot leave any stone unturned."

"So, are you trying to say Big Mike or Darrell might have tried to have me killed?"

"What we are saying is we don't know, and until we do, everyone is suspect. Especially those you might have crossed in a business deal, had a personal altercation with, slept with their mate, or had a simple disagreement. I know the questioning seems harsh and unwarranted, but agent Nelson and I have over forty years of combined experience on the bureau, and we will find out who is behind this."

I thought to myself there is a high probability your agency is behind it. You might want to start your investigation there. Then I followed up with this question. "Charles had taken out a couple of the men who were after us. Maria and I together took down at least three. Who were they?"

Both agents paused and looked at each other, then agent Nelson spoke. "Three were guns for hire and we know nothing more about them at this time, but two of them were agents."

"Agents!" Kendra barked.

"Ex-agents Mrs. Jackson, that were let go from the agency for disciplinary reasons."

What the hell was going on! Now fear entered my consciousness and I wanted out. I wasn't in any condition to defend myself or my family and despite beefed up security around me. I wanted to implement Kendra's plan right away. I really didn't think the Feds were going to get to the bottom of this any time soon and why would they when some of their own were involved even though they were ex-agents.

I looked in Kendra's eyes and the same fear that filled my heart occupied her eyes. We concluded the question and answer session with the agents, and they left the room. Big Mike and Darrell came in as agents Nelson and Thompson left.

"You two don't look good!" Darrell exclaimed.

"Two of the attackers were ex-FBI agents." Kendra said.

"What!" Big Mike was furious. "So, it was just as Jakar said. The government is behind this."

"Kendra said ex-agents!" Darrell explained.

"What's the difference? They were a part of the government and for all we know they are still, but just not in an official capacity. What are we going to do Shane?"

I didn't have an answer. I felt fatigue and weak. Before I could attempt to answer Big Mike, Kendra stepped in. "We are keeping to the original plan."

"You mean cut and run! That's the plan Shane!"

"Big Mike...." I began

Kendra interjected. "Shane is not one hundred percent, matter of fact; he is not even thirty percent. It's a miracle he is even here with us. You try taking a shot to the abdomen and one in the shoulder with poison tips and let's see how you feel. Don't ever talk to him about cutting and running. He deserves better than that from you!"

"Shane ...I didn't mean it like that; its' just that we lost Charles, and we can't let that shit slide."

"I'm not going to let that slide. Give me some time. Kendra will be in touch. I have to secure my family and recover, and then we will get to the bottom of this. I promise you!"

Big Mike gave me a hug, then Darrell. "I'll be in touch." Darrell whispered.

They left the room. Kendra was still angry with Big Mike. I don't know if it was from what he said or what was revealed during the questioning regarding my concussion. I didn't ask her either.

Recovery

Several months had passed. My recovery was coming along. The change of environment to Africa suited me well. The house was a Godsend, therapeutic in its setting and tranquil in its design. I didn't give it much thought when I first viewed the home. I just knew, if Kendra loved it, I loved it. But, now in my weakened state my gratitude for her purchase was abundant. Kendra took care of my every need. She fed me in bed, bathed me, cut my hair, and administered the best messages a man could ever wish for! She could have hired a nurse to care for me, but she wouldn't relinquish that responsibility to anyone. My mother offered her help in the care of me, but Kendra wouldn't have it. I detected something heavy on her mind she wanted to share with me, but I gathered she was waiting for my full recovery.

As my recovery progressed we took walks along the grounds of the property with the kids. It was a good feeling having family in our home. I was about seventy percent recovered and was feeling stronger as the days went by. Kendra was showing by now and started to slow down because of the pregnancy. Our nights were quiet when the children went to bed and usually my mother and Kendra's parents retired early. Kendra and I used this time to connect, talk about how we were feeling, what we were feeling, and the future. Kendra used this time to also voice her concerns.

"What happen between you and Big Mike at his home?"

I told her the entire story.

"Why didn't you tell me?"

"I promised Big Mike it would stay between just the two of us."

She took a deep breath. "I understand." She paused. "What is going on between you and Maria?"

"Nothing."

"Have you slept with Maria?"

"No."

"Why did the agents ask you about a threesome between you, Charles, and Maria?"

"There was an incident where Charles and Maria were drinking heavily. They presented to me the proposal. I declined."

She studied me. She then leaned over and gave me a gentle kiss upon my lips and snuggled under me. "I knew Maria was attracted to you and cared about you when she came to the house and vehemently defended your contributions to the community. But, I know you, and you would never allow something like that to come between us."

She was right!

"What about Charles?"

"Charles?"

"Yes, was he out there fooling around on Carmen like those agents said?"

"Why would you ask me about Charles?" I paused and looked at her sincerely. "Whatever was going on with Charles was between Charles and Carmen, and I would surmise given what we know about Carmen, anything Charles was involved in she knew."

Kendra nodded her head in agreement. We lounged downstairs for the next couple of hours cuddling and smooching like young lovers, and then we carried ourselves to bed.

As my strength returned Kendra allowed some visitors to come and see me at the house. The first was Jakar. He had been chomping at the bit to pay me a visit. Kendra put us in the study off the family room, Jakar looked good. He was excited to see me and as expected wanted the intimate details and what had taken place in America and the death of Charles. I filled him in on all the details up to the point of the question and answer session with the FBI agents.

"Two of the perpetrators were ex-agents?"

"Yes!"

"I wasn't surprised when you told me your government had you under surveillance, but to target a legitimate businessman is a bit much even for your government. What does Brendham have to say about all this?"

"Brendham has been kept out of the loop."

"Why?"

"Trust!"

"I can't disagree with that move. He has a far ways to travel to regain your trust, but be assured you will need him to get to the bottom of this!"

"I agree!"

"Remember Shane; keep your friends close, but your enemies even closer."

"Yes." I replied thoughtfully.

"How are you feeling?"

"Better, gaining my strength back, able to play some with the kids, I would say I'm about seventy percent. Kendra has me on a steady diet of fruits and vegetables and a heavy dose of herbs and minerals!"

"Kendra is a good strong woman, and is a testament to you as a man. Only a strong secure man picks a woman that is his equal. Darrell and Big Mike both give her much praises in this time of crisis."

"She is more than I could have ever wished for in a wife, friend, and partner!"

"Aahh!...I hear congratulations are in order?"

"Yes, our son is expected next month."

"Now, I don't wish to be out of line, but it would be appropriate to give your new son an African name seeing he will be born on the Mother Continent."

"I think that is a good idea, but the final word will come down to Kendra."

"I've already lobbied her and she is excited about the idea."

"Then, so am I."

"Smart man, I know why men and women who work with you find you to be a great leader because to lead you must know how to follow."

"I appreciate the compliment."

Jakar and I talked for another hour or so until Kendra entered the room and ended Jakar's visit. As he left out, he promised to keep in touch. Kendra and I thanked him for his assistance with the security personnel guarding our home and guarding Kendra and other family members when they ventured out for shopping or sightseeing. He offered additional security if needed. Jakar and I shook hands, and he hopped into his chauffeured pearl black range rover with tinted windows.

Next on the visitors list were Big Mike and Darrel which was a pleasant surprise. I talked with both by phone only a few times, and neither let on about their visit. We sat in the study and strategically talked about how to move forward with our business and how to track down the culprits of Charles' death. Kendra joined us in the study.

"Shane, you're looking like your old self, a little thinner, but you're looking good! Big Mike said.

"Thanks I'm starting to feel like my old self."

"Yes, the doctors have said he should be fully recovered in just a couple of months." Kendra added.

"Well, that is good news!" Darrell joined in.

"Alright gentleman, how about an update," said Kendra? Then, I will leave you men to talk amongst yourselves."

Darrell started off with Blue Sky. "Blue Sky's stock price took a hit initially because of Charles' death and the assassination attempt on Shane, but rebounded as we absorbed Titan Industries and the African operations continue to bring in large returns. As of market close yesterday Blue Sky market capital was just a tad above half trillion."

"Got damn!!" I expressed. I stood and embraced Darrell. "Good job!" I told him.

"Well I can't take all the credit. We have a great team at Blue Sky, and Big Mike did his thing to close out the Titan deal."

"Well, we had to drag a few Titan family members with us across the finish line, but they were just hanging on for dear life. You and Charles finished them even before they knew the game was on!"

"Yea, that was all Charles. Once we set our sights on Titan, Charles went after them like a raging bull!"

"I miss my brotha!" Big Mike iterated.

"Me too," I agreed.

The conversation changed right there on a dime toward how we were going to handle the perpetrators who killed Charles and tried to kill me.

"I want to find them and kill them all!" Big Mike sounded off.

"What about just bringing them to justice?" Darrell asked.

"I agree with Darrell. We shouldn't take the law into your own hands." Kendra let her opinion be known.

In deep thought of my departed friend all eyes were on me waiting for my response. I was just about fully recovered and in my quiet moments alone I had been replaying everything that happened back in my mind. There were some things that were not fitting together right in my mind.

"I'm in agreement with Big Mike, KILL THEM ALL!"

"Shane!" Kendra pleaded.

"Yea!" Big Mike showed his gratitude for my agreement.

Darrell sat down flabbergasted at my response. "Why?" He asked.

"Charles' security Melvin was out sick on that day. Just a coincidence, I'm not buying it!"

"What about the FBI investigation?" Darrell snapped back.

"Feels like they are investigating me more than, they are trying to find the perpetrators."

"They are too busy doing shit to find shit! Excuse my language Kendra." Big Mike rejoined.

She nodded to assure Big Mike it was okay. "I'm going upstairs to get some rest." Kendra announced.

The pregnancy was starting to wear on Kendra and all this talk of revenge and tracking down the culprits ourselves was more than she could handle. I went to her and gave her a hug and kiss. "Are you okay?" I asked softly.

"Yea, just a bit tired. We'll talk about this later- just you and me huh?"

"Absolutely!"

She gave me a kiss and left the study.

I turned to rejoin Darrell and Big Mike where they were standing in the study, Big Mike uttered. "Melvin is our starting point!"

I agreed, but Darrell was reluctant and both Big Mike and I knew it. We still pushed ahead with a plan we thought would give us the best chances to uncover who was behind this attack. After a couple of hours of discussion and planning, Big Mike and Darrell had some other news that they had saved to discuss with me in private, not in front of Kendra.

"White-Chocolate resigned as CFO of Blue Sky, and Maria resigned from Black Street Capital." Darrell stated.

"He's concerned about his marriage and the safety of Maria." Big Mike expounded.

No verbal response from me, I sat in silence with understanding.

"They travelled here at the insistence of Maria to talk with you before they travel to Cuba." Big Mike explained.

"They are here in Africa," I asked?

"Yes, they are staying at the A Hotel where we are staying. They are awaiting our arrival back to the hotel where we told them you would be accompanying us!" Darrell said.

"It's getting a bit late, but if they are expecting us – absolutely!"

I excused myself, walked up stairs and explained the situation to Kendra, and not surprisingly she knew of White-Chocolate and Maria's travels to Africa and expected me to meet with them.

"I am not particularly happy with her feelings towards you, but I'm indebted to her for saving your life. A long time ago I realized the man I married was a very powerful figure many women would be attracted and allured by. I found that to be threatening, but how I overcame that fear was belief in our love and you as a man!"

She rose from the bed kissed me tenderly and sent me off with her blessing.

Big Mike, Darrell, and I left my home escorted by five security personnel. The Archaic was about a fifteen minute ride from the house down by the beach. We arrived in three black Range Rovers with dark tinted windows. Jakar's security men were impressive, thorough, and professional- not a group of men you would ever want to cross. They secured the perimeter and the hotel lobby, before letting us out of the SUV. Big Mike and Darrell led me to White-Chocolate and Maria's room. Three security personnel posted up in the hotel lobby and two outside the room. We knocked and waited a minute or so before we heard White-Chocolate's voice.

"Who is it?"

"Hey it's me, Big Mike and Shane," Darrell replied.

White-Chocolate opened the door stepped back and allowed us to enter. Big Mike entered first, then Darrell, followed by myself. White-Chocolate greeted us all with a handshake in the entrance space to the room. Emotional and shaken, when he spoke, his voice quivered with freight and uncertainty.

"I'm sorry for what happen to Charles……and you, Shane. I love Maria more than I love life itself, and if I were to lose her I don't know what I would do," he hesitated. "As her husband it's my responsibility to keep her safe, not you…Shane. She's my wife!" He cried out, and then burst into tears. Big Mike, Darrell, and I just stood there looking at him, giving him time to compose himself. "I'm sorry…..I didn't mean to …"

"No apologies needed." Darrell interjected.

"I understand where you are coming from." I spoke directly to White-Chocolate. "You're a good man, and I owe you an apology from when I showed you and Maria a blatant disregard by asking her to get information from Espinosa for the World Textile deal. You stayed with Black Street despite my behavior. You are a bigger man than me because I would have gone ape shit if someone would have requested that of my wife. With all that has taken place I now realize my arrogance in that request, and I ask for your forgiveness in that matter. I want nothing less for you and Maria than happiness. I respect your decision to take your wife somewhere you feel is better for her well-being –physically and mentally. I'm sorry that she got caught up in this, but know this, if Maria hadn't been there, I might not be standing here before you and for that I am eternally grateful!"

White-Chocolate was silent. He held out his trembling hand, I grasped it. He pulled me in with conviction and held me tight with both arms. I embraced him tightly. He squeezed me tighter and tighter as the seconds ticked away, and then whispered. "She is the bedroom waiting for you."

White-Chocolate released me, and I walked to the back of the suite toward the bedroom where Maria awaited. I lightly knocked on the bedroom door.

"Come in." I heard Maria call out behind the closed door.

I entered the room. Maria was standing back from the door in the middle of the room. The room was cream, dimly lit, the bed was unmade, and luggage sat in the far right corner behind Maria, some half opened. Maria was in jeans, white button down blouse with her hair pulled back in a ponytail. She looked good, but I could tell she had been crying. I closed the door behind me and only took a couple of steps inside the room.

"I finally did what you asked of me." I said

"What is that?"

"Apologize to White-Chocolate."

A hint of laughter from her. "I'm surprised your ego allowed you to acquiesce to my request."

"With all that's taken place my ego has fled, maybe never to return."

"I hope not." She paused. "How are you doing?"

"I'm getting better!"

"I'm glad to hear that." She paused and fiddled around with her hands nervously. "We lost…." She broke into tears before she could finish. I stayed where I stood. After a few moments she composed herself. "We lost…Charles."

"Yes," I nodded my head in agreement.

"When you started coughing and spitting up blood, then lost consciousness, I thought I lost you, and at that moment I had never been more terrified in my life. I wanted to join you!" She took a deep breath. "I don't know if I lost control or gave up control of the SUV." She broke down again.

Her revelation quieted me. I didn't know how to react. In that moment I felt sorry for Maria; she was clearly conflicted and confused. She had a man madly in love with her in White-Chocolate, but she felt a connection to me that was so deep and real to her she tried to kill herself at the thought of my death. All this was unfathomable to me.

She continued. "I felt, if I couldn't be with you in this life, I could be with you in another-"

"Maria White-Chocolate loves you! Go with him, take some time to get your thoughts together, spend some time getting to know him better, and I guarantee you that you will find in him what you think you've found in me."

She acknowledged my sentiment, then switch topics. "Does Kendra hate me?"

"No, Kendra doesn't hate you. She's thankful you saved her husband's life."

"She's a boss bitch! When you were down, she stepped in and ran shit!"

"I know she would appreciate those kind words."

Maria walked toward me slowly not saying a word, her eyes fixated on me, then halted just a step short of face to face. She looked into my eyes, both of us silent. Examining me closely, she didn't find what she was looking for. Tears rolled down from her eyes. Maria took the half step closer and came face to face, raised her arms, put them around my neck, then pulled herself up to hug me tightly lifting herself off the ground. She buried her head on the side of my neck.

"Please hold me." She pleaded.

I obliged her request, and just as her husband's hug got tighter and tighter as the seconds passed, so did hers. I reciprocated the affection.

She whispered." If I had it all to do over with you, I'd do it all again! No regrets!" She then let go of me and me her. She turned around and slowly walked back to the spot in the room where she first stood when I entered the room. As she turned to face me, tears were streaming down her face.

She was saying goodbye. I turned and exited the room where Big Mike, Darrell, and White-Chocolate hadn't moved from the spot I had left them. We said our goodbyes to White-Chocolate and left the room. I was mentally drained after that. Big Mike and Darrell went to their rooms and I went home. On the ride home I reflected on my relationship with White-Chocolate and Maria. I started off wrong with both of them when I asked Maria to get closer to Espinoza for information. Ever since that time, the relationship between all three of us had been on a downward spiral if we knew it or not, and to know I was the cause of so much pain in their lives broke my heart.

Kendra was in bed asleep when I arrived home. I changed into my pajamas and slipped into bed behind her, cuddled up, and fell fast asleep.

****

The next day Darrell flew out with White-Chocolate and Maria, and much to my surprise Big Mike had travelled with Adriona and planned on staying in Africa for a while. Little did I know what Big Mike had in mind when he stayed. Each morning he took me through a rigorous regiment of cardio and weight training. I could barely keep up initially, but as the days rolled passed, I got better. With Kendra's strict diet she had me on and Big Mike's workouts I was feeling better than I ever had!

Adriona really took to Africa which gave her and Kendra plenty to talk about and share. Kendra was really excited about having her third child in Africa. We decided on a name for our third addition to the family which was inspired by our friend Jakar. Our chosen name for our son was Fabio a Yoruba name which meant gift from God. Fabio came on schedule, weighing in around nine pounds and twenty seven inches in length. Now Miles and Monique favored their mother, but Fabio was the splitting image of his father, dark in tone, penetrating brown eyes highlighted by beautiful lashes, full lips, and a set of pipes on him that was heard all through the hospital on his arrival to this world.

Kendra delivered like a champ, and was up moving around only two days after Fabio's birth. Miles and Monique were amazed at the sight of their little brother and wanted to help their mother feed and take care of him. But, everybody had to fight for time with him because the grandparents were well positioned to jockey for time with their new grandson. Late nights was my time when I could just look at him and enjoy his peacefulness. I used Fabio as my confessional. I confessed how I needed to return to the States, but how fearful I was to return; the possibility of not returning from the States to see him grow up and be a man. How I couldn't let Charles' death go in vain, and the guilt I felt about White-Chocolate and Maria

I don't know if Kendra was listening to my confessions to my son, but in a way I hoped she was. I needed her to know how I was feeling and what I had been thinking without it being a burden on her; and my greatest fear, that she might consider my human fears and sorrows as weaknesses. We had talked and agreed the family would stay here in Africa for an undetermined period. I convinced her I had no choice but to return to the U.S. She knew my return was inevitable, but for her own good selfish reasons she wanted me not to go.

We decided to have a celebration of Fabio's birth, which would allow for some friends to fly into Africa to take part in the celebration- Carmen and Darrell specifically. We had a cook out! Jakar and his family attended along with some other neighbors we befriended since our arrival. The birth and celebration of our son was the highlight of our stay here thus far. Everyone was happy, almost as if they didn't have a care in the world. It was great to be happy, and not attached to fears and worry, even if only for the moment. The joy on Kendra's face was priceless. I wished time could stand still! When I saw Carmen, I saw an emptiness that was trying to masquerade itself in the celebration.

Carmen saw me looking at her and casually made her way toward me. Without a word she gave me a hug, and following the same pattern as others her hug got tighter as the seconds ticked by. A little uncomfortable, I looked around for Kendra to save me from the moment, but when I met Kendra's eyes, her look said, be compassionate and understanding, so I hugged Carmen. When I did that, her hold became firmer, and I felt her body pulsating from the emotional cries making their way through her body manifesting themselves in the form of tears streaming down her face. I tried to release her when she calmed down, but she would not relinquish her hold. I tried to comfort here by re-establishing my hug.

"He loved you." She spoke softly in my ear.

"I loved him too!"

"He would have followed you into a burning building. He respected and looked up to you as a man and a husband. He wanted for us what you and Kendra have. He told me what took place between you, Maria, and himself, and the advice you gave him before you left. That night probably was one of the most romantic and satisfying nights we spent together since our honeymoon. Thank you for that." More tears flowed. "I miss him Shane. He wasn't perfect, but he was mine, and I know in his own way he loved me, and I him."

"Charles truly loved you!"

"I know you going to do what you got to do, but you make it back here to be with your family. My girl needs you!"

"I will be back!"

Carmen kissed me on the cheek and as casually as she walked toward me, she walked away. Big Mike approached.

"Is she okay?"

"I think she will be alright."

Big Mike pulled out some Cuban cigars, gave one to me and he took the other.

"Lets walk." He requested

Big Mike lit our cigars and we walked the property away from the others, followed in the distance by security.

"Are you ready?"

"Yes!"

"It's just you and me. Don't count Darrell in."

"Why do you say that?"

"Darrell is comfortable. He likes the status he has attained as one of the top CEO's. He's got his significant other, looking to get a domestic union and, Clarence, his mate hates your guts! Although he says, he's down. His heart is not in it, and if his heart isn't in it, then mistakes could be made, and we can't afford mistakes. This is life and death shit! You hear me Shane?"

"Yea, I hear you."

"When we leave for New York in a week, send Darrell back to Texas that's what he wants anyway."

"You sound a little bitter toward Darrell. What's going on?"

"Every time I talk to him he makes me feel like he wants to sweep Charles death under the rug and move on."

"I don't get that vibe from him."

"That's because you haven't been around him as much."

I told Big Mike I would have a talk with Darrell to see where his head was, but I emphasized we needed to continue to trust in each other and that we were all family. Big Mike and I returned to the party. I looked for Darrell, and found him in the kitchen with Kendra preparing some food platters. I walked in and kissed Kendra on the lips, nice and short.

"Awww….. Shane you've been smoking those Cuban's with Big Mike."

"Yea."

"Please get some mouth wash before you see the kids again."

I laughed. "I will!" I walked around to the opposite side of the preparation table where the refrigerator was open and helped myself to bottled water. Then, I turned and asked Darrell a question.

"Why didn't Clarence make the trip with you?"

The question caught him by surprise. “Ah, he wasn’t really feeling well and the long plane ride, doctors advised against.”

I looked at him and could tell he was lying. I directed my attention toward Kendra standing next to him, and she was focused on him with a look of disbelief. She urged him with her look to come clean.

He returned a look of resistance toward Kendra, and then acquiesced, “Alright, he didn’t want to come. He doesn’t particularly like you.”

“And, I don’t particularly like him either!” I rebutted.

“Shane!” Kendra pleaded.

I kept my focus on Darrell. “How do you feel about Charles’ death?”

“What kind of question is that?” Darrell demanded.

“It’s the kind of question that needs to be answered.”

“I think it was wrong and dirty! Our brother is gone.” He looked directly at me. “What are you getting at?”

“Do you think we need to go after the people who killed Charles?”

He hesitated, looked at Kendra, and then spoke. “I think we should leave it to the police.”

“You mean the FBI; the people who are ten months into their investigation and haven’t got a shred of evidence, except that two of the deceased were their own. Is that the people you are talking about? Huh?” I barked.

“Shane calm down.” Kendra said.

“You know these people who killed Charles tried to kill me, and if my family and I are in danger you know you and your little butt buddy are too!”

“Shane! You apologize that was uncalled for!” Kendra pleaded.

Darrell was smart. He knew if we didn’t find the culprits ourselves, they wouldn’t be found. His attitude upset and hurt me deep, so I tried to return the favor with an insult of him and Clarence. I couldn’t half believe, I said it myself, but there was no way I was going to apologize right or wrong. Darrell was shocked. I was shocked. How could he dismiss the life of our brother Charles? His death demanded retaliation and the FBI left the ball in our court, and I for one was going to make damn sure the killers were tracked down.

"When Big Mike and I leave for New York, you can go back to Texas and carry on with your work at Blue Sky. Big Mike and I will handle this situation ourselves."

Now Darrel was mad. I left him out. Over the years Darrell has had opposite views than the rest of us, but when push came to shove, we all move in the same direction and this time shouldn't have been any different, but I wasn't up for any dissenting views, when in my mind the path was crystal clear. Darrell left the kitchen and so did I. He left for his hotel and I went back and joined the party. Later that night Kendra tried to approach me, but I wasn't up for a discussion.

The following week leading up to my departure back to New York, the atmosphere in the house was subdued. Kendra didn't mention my spat with Darrell and kept her focus on family, especially with the baby. I enjoyed my mother and Kendra's parents. Big Mike and Adriona were constantly over the house. Adriona became aunt Adriona to my kids, and her friendship with Kendra grew closer. Kendra invited Adriona with Big Mike's blessing to stay at the house with her and our family until Big Mike and I returned from New York. I hadn't seen Darrell all week, and I didn't ask Kendra about him and she didn't mention him.

On the day of our departure back to New York, the whole family came to the airport to see us off. We had arranged for a private flight. We had also arranged for one back to Dallas, for Darrell, which flew out earlier that day. We were travelling with ten security personnel handpicked by Jakar. They loaded the plane, then boarded. Big Mike and Adriona said their goodbyes. Teary eyed and words of support and love made for a moving moment. I was mobbed by Miles and Monique. It broke my heart to see them crying. I promised them Daddy would return soon. My mother was emotional and made me promise to return to them. I got hugs and kisses from Kendra's parents and Carmen.

Finally, everyone stepped back and Kendra stepped forward with Fabio. I kissed him tenderly on the forehead and said goodbye to him and promised once again Daddy would return. Kendra passed him off to Auntie Carmen. She jumped on me straddling her legs around my waist with her feet crossed behind me. Her arms were wrapped around my neck firmly; she kissed me passionately which caught me off guard. Her mother pleaded. "Kendra!" Her mother's plea did not deter my babe one bit she was laying one on me before I got on that plane. The warmth of her mouth was eternal, and I was missing it before I even let it go! She came up for air then gave me two tender pecks, then went back for more. Monique hollered "Mommy, Daddy that's embarrassing!" Nothing was stopping Kendra until she was good and ready to relinquish the kiss. Staying straddle across my waist she spoke to me passionately with conviction.

"Be careful, you watch Big Mike's back and he will watch yours! Trust your gut. Your gut is what got you here. Trust it to see you through this situation. I'm only a phone call away, if you need me." She paused and looked into my eyes. "You made the right decision to send Darrell back to Dallas. His mind is not there, so he would only put you and Big Mike in jeopardy."

Now that surprised me! She saw it on my face. She continued." I love you, you are my man, my husband, and the father of our children, and just as a side bar I want at least two more." She smiled." You have never broken a promise to me in the ten years we've been married. I want you to promise to come back to me, so we can live the rest of our lives together making more babies and living the lives intended for us by God! I want you to promise me!

I hesitated. As Kendra said I had never broken a promise, and I had never lied to her, but deep down I wasn't a hundred percent sure I could deliver on this promise. If I broke the promise to my mother and my children, Kendra would explain to them I did my best to try and make it back, but who would explain to Kendra. Just the thought of it broke my heart. "I promise." Then I broke down.

Kendra got off me, turned me around so no one could see my tears, buried her head in my back, and then gave me the slightest push towards the gate. I walked through the gate and onto the plane without looking back.

Get That Mutha Fucka!

We arrived, under the radar in the wee morning hours at New York Kennedy airport. We made sure our private chartered flight was booked in the flight manual as a cargo flight originating from London. No grand greeting at the airport and no awaiting caravan of black SUV's to escort us through the city. We rented four, four door sedans from various rental car companies. We rode two to three deep per car, never four to a car. Riding four deep would be asking to be pulled over by the police. We didn't stay in our residences in New York. Big Mike arranged for us to stay in a house outside the city limits. When we arrived, we arrived at a massive compound surrounded by security gates and a security post at its entrance. Big Mike entered the security code and we assigned one of our security team at the front post.

The road from the entrance extended about a half mile before you reached the entrance to the house which had a circular drive way and five guest units behind it. The main house had five bedrooms, four baths, a chef's kitchen, theater room, arcade, gym, and a den with a flat screen television. The floors in the bedrooms had plush red carpet while the other rooms were either marble floors or hardwood floors with throw rugs. All of the walls were painted a pearl white which illuminated the rooms. Each guest unit on the grounds had three bedrooms and two baths, with a den and modestly decorated which would have made the pickiest guest happy. Big Mike assigned all the rooms. I had one master bedroom and he the other. He assigned five security personnel to the main house and the others to the guest houses.

I entered my room and on top of the king size bed there laid a large case. I walked over put my only luggage bag down beside the bed, and then open the case. When I opened it, to my surprise, the case had two .9mm hand guns with two clips each, one .38 semi-automatic, and one automatic rifle with scope, and a rocket launcher. It was like something out of Scarface. Big Mike walked in shortly after I examined the case.

"To your liking?" He asked.

"Yes." I spoke calmly.

He walked out of my room back into his own. I felt fear enter my body looking over the artillery on the bed. I pulled a lot off in my thirteen years of business, but this was something entirely different. It was going to need my utmost attention to detail, and understanding of all the players, and their mind sets. Their purpose and mission would be imperative to singling out who was behind the attack. Our search was not only for the perpetrators, but the person who mastermind the attack.

I unpacked, took a shower then and fell asleep until about 12:00 pm in the afternoon. I hadn't caught up with the change in time zones yet. When I woke up, I washed up, got dressed and went down stairs. I found Big Mike dressed and eating a good looking breakfast in the kitchen- fresh fruit, eggs, toast, and orange juice.

"I saved you some. It's over on the table there." He pointed behind him on the table next to the stove.

"Thanks!"

I walked over, filled my plate and sat next to Big Mike.

"Where is everyone?" I asked

"They are checking the grounds, and relieving the first shift of security at the front gate."

"Okay!" I stuffed my mouth with some pieces of juicy mangos.

"Here's your new cell. It's a cell and a two way radio, so we can communicate with each other instaneously if need be. The number to my cell and our security personnel is already in the memory of your cell, same as mine."

I picked up the cell examined it briefly. "Good deal!" I scooped some eggs into my mouth along with a bite of toast.

"What's our first move?"

“I want you to track down Melvin. Here’s an address on him.” I reached in my pocket and handed him a Brooklyn address. “I don’t know if he still lives there, but check it out and hit me on the cell. I’m going to go into Harlem to check on some intel.”

“From whom?”

“Ice.”

“Okay, he’s been a reliable source of information?”

“Yes!”

Big Mike and I left the house at the same time. I travelled with four security personnel –two in the same car as me, and two trailing in a separate car. Big Mike did the same. After about twenty five minutes we arrived in Harlem and to Ice’s hat shop. The two security guards and I entered Ice’s shop. When we entered I didn’t see Ice behind the counter, there was a young lady very Afrocentric in her dress with an afro standing behind the counter. I approached and her big brown eyes along with her genuine smile greeted me warmly.

“Welcome to Hats on Kats!”

“How are you my sista? I’m looking for Ice.”

She looked puzzled. “I’m sorry, but no one by that name works here.”

Just as she finished her statement I hear someone walking from the back.

“What’s happening Shane?”

It was Ice. He walked up and greeted me, then introduced me to his daughter Octavia.

“Hello, Octavia it is a pleasure to meet you!” I shook her hand.

“He was asking for someone named Ice.” She told her father.

“Yea baby girl, that was the nickname Daddy used to use.”

“I apologize, I…………”

“No need. Shane, come in the back so we can rap a taste.”

I asked Ice if it was it okay for my security to remain in the store while we talked. He was okay with it. Ice and I walked through the back door into his private office. He sat behind his desk and offered me a seat in front of his desk.

"You travelling with the African connection?" He chuckled.

"Yea, they are my security while I'm in the states."

"They look like some serious Kats!"

"That they are! They give me a good sense of security."

"Hey, congrats on the new edition to your family."

"Thanks!"

"You really thinking about making Africa your home?"

"That's where Kendra wants to be, and I want to be where she is!"

"You don't have to say another word. Kendra is worth following to another continent!...Okay lets get down to business."

Ice reach down in his desk drawer and threw some files on top of the desk before me, then gave me the short version of what was in the files.

"The government got you under surveillance, been watchin you and your family in Africa. They got yo address in Nigeria, and names of other family members livin with you. What I don't know is, were they behind the hit against you and Charles. The water is muddy. I'm sorry about that, but I still got my man's head to the grindstone on it."

I kept listening intently. I did open up the files and began to peruse them for information while Ice was giving me the update. He continued." Now ya boy Brendham. We know he is ex-FBI and has been freelancing ever since his retirement. All of his clients have been corporate and mutha fuckas with a lot of doe. And get this one of his corporate clients is GPG!"

"What?"

"There is a list of all his clients in the file."

I looked through his file and found the list, and as sure as I was sitting there I saw GPG on the list. "How did you get this list?"

"The government has Brendham under surveillance too!"

"Why?"

"Don't know!"

I thanked Ice and told him I would be in touch, and to keep his guy digging for any information he could get his hands on pertaining to this matter. I reached in my coat pocket, pulled out an envelope full of cash and placed it on Ice's desk. He picked it up looked at its contents.

"Why so much?"

"Because I will have to call on you again, and I will need you to deliver on a timely basis."

I walked out of his office back into his store where my security was waiting. I said good bye to Actavia, and we left the store. While we were getting into the car, my cell rang.

"Shane, Melvin still lives here. His neighbor says he usually gets home around 3:00 pm, which is about a half hour from now." Big Mike said.

"Okay, you hold up there. I'm on my way we're just about fifteen minutes away."

When we arrived, Big Mike had two men on opposite sides of the block at each end. One car parked at the end of the block with one man and Big Mike in a car with a driver parked midway into the block on the right side. We pulled up behind Big Mike's car, and I had my other security drive ahead and park on the adjacent street. I used the two way radio to communicate with Big Mike.

"Where does he stay?" I asked.

"1412 just up ahead from where we are parked on the left hand side."

There were a few people out on the block just hanging out and few kids playing stick ball in the street. As we waited for Melvin to arrive home, my mind drifted watching the kids play, to my kids and how much I missed them already. I hadn't been gone more than twenty four hours. Big Mike broke radio silence.

"We are on!"

I looked up and there was Melvin exiting his car walking toward his front steps. I jumped out of the car and called out. "Melvin!"

Big Mike stepped out of his car right after. Melvin looked at me, then Big Mike, and without words he ran down his block. Big Mike and I chased after him. The residence watched in awe of the whole episode. When Melvin approached the corner full speed much to his surprise, he was knocked flat on his butt by one of our security. We picked him up. The cars met us on the corner; we threw Melvin in the trunk and took off.

We drove back to the compound where we were staying, unloaded Melvin and brought him into the main house. Big Mike went to the right side of the television room pushed a button on wall behind a picture and the wall with the mounted flat screen opened up. Through the doors was a damp and dark room made of dingy grey finished cement. Nothing was in the room, no chairs, pictures, shelves, windows or tables. Big Mike instructed security to bring a chair in the room. We sat Melvin down in the middle of the room. We dismissed a few of the security guards from the room and three of the highest ranking security personnel remained with Big Mike and me. I stood in front of Melvin to his right and Big Mike to his left, the three security men took up positions behind him, left, right, and middle. I began my questioning.

"What happened to you the day Charles and I got hit?"

"I was sick. I called Charles and let him know that morning I wasn't feeling well."

"If that's the case, why the fuck were you running when you saw us?" Big Mike barked out.

Beads of sweat began dripping down from his forehead. He clearly was shaken and clearly lying.

"Hey, look I......I just thought since y'all got hit when I wasn't around... you would blame me! So, I ran when I saw you."

"You still on payroll?" I asked.

"Yea,..." he nodded. "Yea."

"How in the hell are you still on our payroll, and on sight you start running from your employers?" Big Mike demanded.

Melvin didn't have an answer, at least not a reasonable one. He fumbled and mumbled incoherently. I stopped him.

"There is a chance for you Melvin, but you have to give us what you know. Now if I hear anymore bullshit from you, that's it, I'm throwing your black ass to the dogs.

Then, Big Mike made a call. The door opened and in there were four security guards standing in the doorway with four full grown vicious and angry Pitt Bulls tugging at the chained leashes they were on. Big Mike and I stepped aside making sure Melvin had clear view of the dogs.

"What the hell!" Melvin pleaded.

"If you don't start telling us the truth, I'm going to lock yo ass in this room with these Pitt Bulls and let them eat yo ass alive!"

"Alright,..Alright, I will tell you what you want to know."

"Okay, get to it!" Big Mike demanded.

"Lee ordered me to call in sick that day you and Charles got hit. I didn't know at the time what was going on, but Lee mentioned I wouldn't want to be around y'all on this day. I didn't question him at the time, but when I heard what went down, I knew Brendham must have ordered the hit."

"Why?" I asked.

"I don't know."

"You a god damn lie!" Big Mike shouted.

"I'm telling you the truth. I just follow orders, nothing else. I'm not a part of Brendham's inner circle."

"Who is?"

"Lee."

"Where can we find Lee?" I asked.

"I don't know where he lives…"

"Let the dogs loose on this mutha fucka Shane!" Big Mike suggested

"No, no…I do know where he will be around 8pm tonight."

"Where?" I asked.

"Moonbeam."

"What is that?" Big Mike demanded.

"Upscale strip club in Upper Manhattan."

"How do you know he will be there?" I followed up.

"He's sprung on this blond stripper that dances there. He's there every Wednesday around 8:00 pm filling her g-string with money."

"If you are lying, you got an appointment with those dogs." Big Mike gestured for the security to take the dogs away. He told one of the other security in the room to get some rope and tie Melvin down to the chair. We walked out the room and toward the kitchen. Once we reached the kitchen we conferred with each other.

"What do you think?" Big Mike asked me.

"I think, he's told us what he knows. We need to get to this Lee character right away."

"Upper Manhattan, upscale strip club, could bring a lot of attention to us."

"Yea, but that's a chance we have to take."

"We could find him there, then track him home, then take him."

"If he is in Brendham's inner circle, he is more seasoned than Melvin, and would spot us tracking him immediately, and possibly escape and alert Brendham. I think our best bet is to take him inside the strip club."

"We will have to bring Melvin with us."

"I know he will have to point him out to us. I'm hoping we can keep the confrontation to a minimum, but if it escalates, we will have to move quickly to get him out of there."

Big Mike nodded in agreement. He then went back into the room where we had Melvin locked up and filled him in on the plan. We had a few hours to kill before leaving for Moonbeam, so we ate and watch some television. I wanted to call Kendra, but I knew my focus needed to be where I was because my intuition and every being of my body was on alert indicating things were about to get very real!

We left the house with all our security personnel and Melvin around 8:00 pm. We figured by the time we arrived, Lee would be well into trick mode; stuffing dollars in this blonds G-string. We stayed consistent with our riding arrangements with no more than three to a car. Once we got to the spot, I thought it best that Melvin and I along with one of our security enter the establishment. We didn't want to cause too much attention to ourselves when we entered.

I warned Melvin before we went in it would be in his best interest to cooperate with us and not alert Lee to our presence.

We entered the club. It was indeed upscale, full bar, kitchen, stage made of clear glass equipped with three golden stripper poles with mirrors in the rear. Instead of Moonbeam they should have call this place the Gold Rush. Every woman in the place with the exception of a few, were attractive blonds with shapely figures. The club was crowded with patrons, but most were young white professionals in their Brooks Brothers suits which didn't give us good cover, so I stayed in the back of the club hidden in the cut. I instructed Melvin to go to the bar where he would have a better view of the entire club to spot Lee. He was saddled with the task of luring Lee outside where Big Mike could grab him, and we could take him back to the house for questioning.

Melvin looked nervous. He went to the bar and ordered a drink. He turned and surveyed the room. His facial express indicated; he hadn't spotted him. He continued to survey, then two strippers approached him and he shunned them away angrily and nervously. I thought he wasn't going to be able to pull this off. The bartender brought him his drink. He took a couple of sips which seemed to settle him. Then it happened, he perked up and was peering toward the stage at the seats down in front. There was a blond dancing on stage in front of a brotha. It was him, Lee. It had to be him. This wasn't a popular place with the brothas. I saw Melvin take his drink and walk toward the gentleman sitting in the front seats tipping the stripper. Melvin took a seat next to the man. I watched them closely. The man was upset. He seemed to be chastising Melvin. I quickly turned to my security and sent him to the other exit in the club. It didn't look like Melvin could get a word in. Lee was angry. What did Melvin say to him?

I saw Melvin get up and leave the man. The man never gave Melvin a second look. He continued to rain dollar bills down on the blond. Melvin walked to the back of the club where I was standing.

"What happen?" I quickly asked.

"He got mad!"

"Mad at what?"

"About me being here."

"What?" I said in disbelief.

"Yea, he asked me what the fuck I was doing here, and to get the fuck out of here."

"Oh, I see." I nodded my head. "He's embarrassed. He's sprung on a stripper. "The blond on stage, is that the one you were telling us about at the house?"

"Yes."

"Alright, when she leaves the stage from what direction will she re-enter the club?"

Melvin pointed to the left next to the exit where I had a man posted.

"Okay Melvin, I want you to go over there and wait for the young lady. When she comes back into the club, you tell her, you got a friend that has a thousand dollars for a lap dance from her. You got it?"

He agreed. Melvin walked over and sat at the table next to the exit across from my security. The girl was still fishing dollars from Lee, and when the song finished, she exited the stage. About fifteen minutes later she re-emerged from the direction Melvin had pointed out to me. Melvin grabbed her arms and whispered in her ear. They both then headed in my direction toward the back of the club. When they arrived, I told Melvin to leave us. One thing was consistent that cut across color lines- money, especially women who shook their money maker for a living. She moved in closer and put her arms around my waist. I didn't resist because I wanted her in close so I could tell her what I needed her to do for a fee, and I wanted to look like a patron interested in a private dance. I saw Lee scanning the club looking for her, so I was direct.

"I got one thousand dollars for a lap dance." I whispered in her ear.

" Lets go!" She tugged at me.

"It's not for me."

"Who is it for?"

"Lee."

"Lee? Why you buying him a lap dance?"

"The thousand is not only for the lap dance, but I need you to take him in a private room where there is no club security, get him comfortable in a compromising position, then we will take over from there."

"We?...Is Lee in some kind of trouble?"

"The less you know the better. I just need to talk with him in private. Now, are you interested?"

"For a thousand dollars hell yea!"

Just as I thought. "Now, is there a private room next to an exit where we can go out undetected?"

"Yes, there is private room not far from the dressing rooms with a private exit for the dancers. There is no security in the room or at the door. The only people who will see you exit will be some of the dancers."

"Okay! I must impress upon you that included in your payment is the price for you not alerting Lee that we wish to talk with him."

"I completely understand. I don't know him like that!"

"Cool."

I handed her the money. She gave me directions to the private room she would be in, and then warned me I wouldn't be allowed in the private area without a dancer. I thanked her for the warning and told her I would give her ten minutes to get Lee comfortable."

"All I need is two minutes once we get in the room." She walked away headed straight toward Lee. She sat down beside him and rubbed his head. After a short exchange they both got up and walked into the VIP private area where one security guard stood. I quickly waved my security over. Updated him on the plan, then called Big Mike to let him know I was sending Melvin out, and to pull the two cars around the back of the club in the alley. I waved Melvin over and told him to go out to the car.

I hailed down two dancers to take us to the VIP area for a lap dance. We casually walked past the security guard by the entrance.

The VIP area was large and expansive, dimly lit with red lights. The floors were clean covered in a black and white ceramic tile. The doors were labeled VIP with a number. At the other end of the room I saw an entrance to the dancers' dressing room. The girl said they would be in VIP room 10. I steered the dancers we were with to the other side of the room. When we approached VIP 10, one of the girls spoke out.

"We can't go in that room it's already occupied."

"They're expecting us." I replied.

I pointed to my security to take the lead at the door. He put his stripper behind him, and my stripper was behind her and I was behind her. He looked at me and I gave him the signal to open the door. He barged into the room. I pushed the dancers in the room right behind him. We found Lee in the room with his pants and underwear down by his ankles. As he stood up surprised by our rude entrance the stripper fell back on her backside. Before Lee had a chance to react my security hit him with a haymaker directly in the nose splitting it open. Blood gushed from his nose against the walls, on my security and on the stripper. Everything happened quickly; all the strippers realized what was taking place and panic set in. I worked quickly to calm them down.

"Quiet, if you stay quiet and cooperate, there is five hundred in this for each of you." I told the other two strippers.

They both agreed to the deal. I took another thousand in cash and gave it to them. They helped my security get Lee's underwear and pants back on.

Lee was out of it, slumped back in the seat. Lee was in and out of consciousness. My security threw him over his shoulder, and I directed one of the strippers to check outside the door to make sure the coast was clear. She gave the thumbs up, and we hustled Lee out of the VIP room through the dressing room entrance. We hurried our way through the stripper's dressing room past a few onlookers and out the exit into the awaiting car in the alley.

****

An hour later a conscious Lee found himself in the same interrogation room, we used for Melvin. Hands and ankles tied down to a chair in the center of the room, and surrounded by the same five men. Big Mike took the lead on the questioning of Lee.

"Tell us what you know about the hit on Shane and Charles?"

Silence.

"We can make this easy, or we can make this hard, but I promise you, you will tell us what we want and need to know before you leave this room."

Lee spit in Big Mike's face. Big Mike quickly retaliated with a right hand punch into Lee's nose that was already broken hurling Lee backward in the chair onto the ground, and hurting Big Mikes hand.

"Aahh shit!" Big Mike held his hand.

"Excuse me Shane," one of the security named Kuto approached me while the other two security set Lee back upright in the chair.

"Yes?" I acknowledged him.

"Let me do this for you. I guarantee we will get all the information you wish, and the suffering will be his alone."

Kuto did an excellent job in the strip club, so I agreed.

I stepped aside and allowed him to take the necessary steps to extract the information from Lee that would lead us to who ordered the hit. Kuto worked methodically. He first pulled one of the other security, said something to him and he left the room. He then bent down in front of Lee and began taking his shoes and socks off while talking to him.

"My employer is in need of some information you have, and I will make sure you provide that information even if I have to take you to within an inch of your life." He spoke calmly.

Kuto stood as the other security re-entered the room carrying a full size duffel bag. He set the bag on the ground. When he opened it, Big Mike and I looked at each other in amazement. Inside the bag was an arsenal of torture –a mallet, a machete, large heavy duty cutters, a long pointed steel rod, and various other instruments reminiscent of a surgeon's utensils. He laid each instrument of torture out before Lee. While Kuto was surveying what lay before him, the other two added duct tape up and down the legs and arms of Lee to secure him to the chair more tightly.

In a calm slow motion Kuto picked up the heavy duty cutters from the floor and walked over to Lee's right side. He put his left hand on top of Lee's arm took the cutters in his right hand and straddled the open cutters around Lee's pinky finger. He looked Lee dead in the eye and cut the finger off. Blooded squirted out onto the floor from his finger. Lee let out an excruciating scream.

"Aaahhh!" Lee's breathing got heavier. His eyes bulged.

Kuto didn't say a word he immediately straddle the cutters around Lee's index finger, and then he waited for Lee's breathing pattern to normalize. He looked him once again in the eyes and without words cut off his index finger. Blood again spilled out onto the floor. Lee belted out one louder than the first. Kuto without hesitation straddle Lee's middle finger.

"Ask me a question!" He screamed.

I was numb to the torture Kuto was putting Lee through. I wanted answers and revenge on those who tried to take my life and had taken the life of Charles. I was a different man now. I felt dirty and gritty without remorse; ready to dispense punishment on who ever got in my way, and at that moment I knew I had the right men around me. I looked toward Big Mike. There was no regret in his face, just a matching menacing look.

Kuto looked at me. I began my questioning.

"Why did Brendham order the hit on Charles and me?"

"He was following orders?" He said breathing heavily.

"Whose orders," I demanded?

"I don't know. He never told me."

"That's bull shit!" I shouted.

"I don't, I'm telling you the truth. Brendham is private like that!"

"We are not fucking with you. You better come clean about everything or you will get more of the same." Big Mike barked out.

Kuto moved back to the luggage, pulled out the long pointed steel rod. He took out a blow torch and heated up the tip. Lee looked nervously. Kuto studied the tip as it turned red, and then he moved the blow torch flame down the rod from the tip heating more of the rod. Once he was satisfied with the intensity of the heat on the rod, he approached Lee and pointed the rod directly at his left eye. Kuto move the rod slowly towards Lee's eye, Lee shut his eye lid and tried to bend his head back, but one of the security held it in place. Kuto stopped the rod about a half inch away from Lee's eye.

"Okay, okay! Please, please tell him to stop!" Lee pleaded.

I touched Kuto lightly on the shoulder. He backed off.

"Tell me everything!"

He took a deep breath. "Brendham's been on to you since you sent Big Mike to Africa to recruit investors for your transition from GPG. "

"What the fuck!" Big Mike exclaimed.

"Yea, we are contracted by the company Garvin, Pratt, and Green. Matter of fact they are one of our largest clients next to Titan.

Now all this just became real and even more unbelievable.

He continued. "The Mackey's put us on your trail, when you started up Black Street Capital. We got on your payroll and kept tabs on you for them. There was a little bit of a fall out when you started buying up Titan shares. They blamed us for not having intel on that takeover. Brendham tried to explain you had lost confidence in him and you were relying more on Tiger. That's when the order came down."

"GPG order the hit?"

Lee nodded in agreement.

I felt fire ignite my body. I was beyond angry. I was enraged, ready to go ballistic on GPG. Bomb the whole god damn headquarters and blast anyone trying to escape from the building, just pick them off one by one like a sniper. I believed what Lee had told us, but I had to keep my head about me. I had additional questions.

"Was there any government involvement?" I asked.

"Not that I'm aware of. You were under government surveillance, but you weren't seen as a security threat initially. Your status did get elevated when you took over Blue Sky, especially when you had Titan in your crosshairs."

"How do you know there wasn't any government involvement?" Big Mike rejoined.

"We had intel that pointed toward the government knowing there was going to be the attempt on your life and turning a blind eye to it."

"Who did Brendham get to carry out the order?" I asked.

"Mercs, ex-government agents that were contract killers."

"Will Brendham be in the office tomorrow?

"Yes."

Lee answered other questions pertaining to some details that needed clearing up, and I wanted the names and addresses of each man responsible for Charles's death. I intended to hunt each of them down. After finishing up with Lee it was close to midnight, I retired to my bedroom. Sleep didn't come easy. Tomorrow was judgement day and payback would be a mutha fucka. My state of mind was unstable filled with rage, uncertainty, violent thoughts, revenge, and retribution. The consequences of the actions I was about to take didn't register. I wanted to call Kendra, so she could bring some sanity to the situation and talk me down off the ledge I found myself on, but I didn't want to be talked down so the call was never made.

The next morning I woke at the crack of dawn. Big Mike and I along with four security guards including Kuto, headed to the Black Street Capital office on Wall Street. We arrived right when the market opened. We left Kuto and one other security in the receptionist area. Tim and few other professionals were in the trade room. To say Tim was surprised and pleased to see us would be an understatement.

"Ah shit!" Tim got up and almost ran to me, then hugged me tightly.

"What's up Tim?" I laughed. It felt good.

"Man…I tried to come and see you, but I couldn't get past your wife's security. I tried calling, but all your lines had been changed. I even went by your house, but security outside the house wouldn't let me get near it. Big Mike and Darrell calmed me down when I wasn't able to check on you and assured me you were recovering well."

"Tim it's all good! I appreciate you checking on me. How's your family?"

"They are good. Tiffany's as worried about you as I was, and she will be elated to hear you came into the office today. "

"Tell her I said hello."

"I will," he nodded his head.

"So, what you got going on today?"

"Just some cleanup on Titan shares, and we are looking at some up and coming companies in the Tech industry."

"Can I have the office for a couple of hours?"

He looked puzzled, but he quickly responded. "Yes,…yes."

"Thanks Tim!"

He looked at Big Mike, and Big Mike gave him a reassuring look. He took a second look at both us, and then a weird look appeared on his face. It looked like he was reacting to our dress. I looked at Big Mike's attire, then mine. Both of us were dressed in blue jeans, black t-shirts, boots, trench coats, and black sniper hats. I realized we weren't dressed for a day on Wall Street, but more for what we were there for –interrogation and some dirty work. I tried to give him a reassuring look, but I don't know how well it worked.

Tim sent everyone home, and then grabbed his brief case and coat, shook my hand and Big Mike's hand and exited the trade room. I didn't hesitate. I called Brendham immediately while Big Mike called Kuto and one other security into the trade room.

"Hello," Brendham answered his office phone.

"Brendham, Shane."

"Shane, I've been trying to contact you! What the hell is going on! Your wife…"

"Brendham calm down. I'm in my office. Come by and I'll explain everything," I said very calmly.

"I'll be there in thirty minutes!"

"See you then," I hung up the line.

Thirty minutes later Brendham walks into the trade room alone wearing his Brooks Brothers suit and tie along with an overcoat. He looked like he grayed more since the last time I saw him. Self-assured and confident he was bold in his declaration, as he entered the room.

"Shane, we have lost precious time in tracking down the culprits of the heinous act against you. I hate to say it, but your wife has hindered the entire process, and it will be a miracle if we are able to track down the perpetrators!"

I was silent, and so was Big Mike. When he finished his rant about bringing him up to speed on what has taken place since my hospital stay and where the hell had I been. I cordially and quietly spoke to him.

"Have a seat Brendham."

Kuto got up from his seat and brought a chair for Brendham to sit on."

"I see you got yourself another Tiger." Then he sat down in the chair, and right when his butt hits the chair, Kuto grabs both of Brendham's arms behind him and in seemingly a millisecond he had tied both arms with a plastic zip ty. "What the hell is going on here Shane?" Kuto searched him and took a .45 semi-automatic off him.

"Brendham you're getting slow in your old age, and to think I had you as the head of my security."

"You are making a grave mistake," he emphasized!

"No, you the mutha fucka that made a grave mistake," Big Mike shouted!

"We know. The jig is up," I exclaimed.

"What the hell are you guys talking about? Are you on drugs?" he demanded.

"No, but you must be on some kind of drug thinking you could fuck us over and get away with it," Big Mike declared.

Brendham then calmed down looked directly at me. “What’s going on Shane? I am totally at a loss. You are like a son to me. When I came to you, it was out of concern and love. All I’ve ever wanted to do was to protect and teach you how to survive down the road you were travelling, and somehow….. We lost our way.”

“Like a son, love and concern, those are peculiar words coming from a man who was hired by GPG to track Big Mike into Africa and to keep a watchful eye on Black Street Capital,” I said.

Brendham eyes were not reactive, his body motionless just the breath from his lungs slightly moving his chest in and out.

“Who gave the order,” I asked softly.

Silence, he wasn’t going to give up the information easily.

“Take him back to the house with Lee and Melvin. Wait for me there,” I instructed Kuto.

I saw Brendham react, but ever so slightly to the names of two of his security personnel.

Kuto and the other security took Brendham down the stairwell onto a side street where the other guards were waiting for them. Before Kuto left I instructed him to get all the information he could out of Brendham by any means necessary!

I made the phone call that Big Mike and I knew was our next move.

“Hello, may I speak to Mackey Sr?”

The operator connected the call.

“Mackey here,” he said in a familiar tone.

“Hello Mr. Mackey.”

“Shane my boy, how are you?”

“Better sir.”

“We were worried about you! Didn’t know how to get in contact, and heard your wife whizzed you out of the country, but given the situation I don’t blame her.”

“Yes, she did what was best for me and our family.”

“Yes she did! You have a good woman in Kendra.”

“Thank you! Well, I don’t want to take up too much of your time on the phone. I’m in my office.”

"Yes, I can see the number. Glad to hear your back at work."

"Can I get some time with you today?'

"Well my calendar is pact this week."

"I think I have some good news for you to bring to your Titan clients. I'm thinking of a compromise on the Titan takeover."

"Shane why don't you come by right now!"

Just what Big Mike and I wanted to hear. We left the building on foot. We arrived at GPG's headquarters about twenty minutes later. GPG had building security but it wasn't tight. There were no metal detectors, so that gave Big Mike and me confidence to walk in packing heat. Past the building security, up the elevator to the top floor, past the receptionist, we were escorted into Mr. Mackey's office by his secretary. She closed the door behind us. I locked it as Big Mike moved closer to Mackey with a menacing look. Uneasy Mr. Mackey stood "What …." Big Mike punched him dead in the chest a powerful blow sending him tumbling to the ground on his back gasping for air. I walked over to his desk and turned up the volume on his flat screen television on the wall of his office. Looking down at Mr. Mackey on the ground with Big Mike's foot on his chest, I asked him the burning question.

"Why?"

"Why, what, Shane, I don't know what you are talking about."

"Why did you kill Charles and try to kill me?"

"What? That is preposterous! Who told you such a thing?"

"Brendham works for you, am I right?"

He was thinking. First time I've seen Mr. Mackey at a lost, confused, and scared. I took my .9 mm out and armed it. Big Mike did the same. I placed my foot on Mr. Mackey's neck.

"Okay, yes Brendham works for me, but I put him on Michael when he was travelling through Africa, and when you established Black Street Capital, I had him watching you. I never told him to get in your employ. He did that on his own. And, I did not try to kill you nor did I kill Charles. I'm a businessman, and I might do a lot of things some may consider illegal or stretching the law, but I am not a killer. I draw my line in the sand there! Shane I respect you. I even like you, and we play hardball in the field of business, but I would never take your life it would be like taking the life of my son. I wouldn't do it!"

"This mutha fucka is lying! Let's finish him Shane, " Big Mike demanded.

I wasn't as sure as when I walked in Mr. Mackey's office. My cell phone rang. I checked it. It was Kuto. Something told me to answer, so I did.

"What's up?"

"Brendham broke down."

"What did he say?"

"Mackey Junior and an Abrahams."

"Okay," I paused to think.

Big Mike anxiously bumped me. "What's going on?"

"Get a location on Abrahams and call me back."

"Okay."

I put the cell back in my jacket. "What's going on Shane?"

"Junior and an Abrahams are responsible for Charles death."

"Junior," Big Mike said puzzling.

"Not my son," Mr. Mackey pleaded. "No, Shane I beg of you, not my son. I will take his place. Take my life for his."

"Get up!" We lifted Mr. Mackey up into his chair. "Now listen to me, is Junior in his office."

"I don't know Shane."

"Look old man, we'll kill both of you," Big Mike exclaimed grasping Mr. Mackey's shirt.

"There's an explanation Shane. My son wouldn't do that. It's not in him. He couldn't live with something like that over his head. My family doesn't deal in death."

"Call him and tell him to come to your office."

"Please don't kill my son." Tears rolled down Mackey's face.

I felt his tears. My mind drifted to my two sons Miles and Fabio. If their lives were in jeopardy in front of me and there was nothing I could do about it, it would bring me to tears. Big Mike wasn't feeling or hearing any of it.

"You better make that call or I'm going to kill you right here and now!"

Mackey made the call. "Junior come to my office." He hung the phone up.

I stood beside the door and Big Mike stood beside Mr. Mackey behind his desk with his gun pointed toward Mackey's head. Five minutes later Junior entered the office casual and carefree, but all that was about to change. He saw Big Mike with a gun to his father's head and panic set in.

"What the fuck?"

He didn't see me behind him by the door. He heard me close the door and turned, and I punched him dead in the face. Bloodied his nose and he staggered. I didn't stop my assault on him. I threw another over hand right to his jaw that sent him plummeting to the ground, kicked him in the stomach, and then stomped him in the face with the heel of my boot. I bent down and grasped him by his blood stained ruffled suit, brought him to his feet and flung him across the room.

"Wait,… wait….What the hell is going on Shane?" Junior held his hand up pleading for mercy.

"You and Abrams put a hit out on me and Charles, and you and your daddy are going to pay for it!

"Hell no! I did no such thing. Whoever told you that is a fucking liar," he screamed. He looked at his dad. "I didn't do it dad," he cried.

"I know son, don't worry. Shane is a reasonable man. He knows the truth when he hears it,"

"Bullshit! He's going to kill us!" Junior cried out, "fucking asshole!"

"Shane, I believe my son. I spoiled, pampered, and coddled my son too long when he was young and that has led to his obnoxiousness, brashness, and privileged attitude, but one thing I know about my son; he is no killer as I've told you before."

I paused, looked at Mackey Sr., Junior, then Big Mike. Big Mike was steady, finger on the trigger ready for whatever. I thought, then realized Brendham was not the type of man who would follow or take orders from the likes of Junior, Mackey Sr?, yes. I believed Mr. Mackey when he said he had nothing to do with the plot to end my life. I believed Junior by default.

"Shane as it stands my son and I have some minor bumps and bruises that will heal in a day or two. I understand your reaction to the death of your friend and the attempt on your life. If you leave us now with no further harm to me or my son. We will forget this ever took place. You have my word."

Mr. Mackey was a man of his word, and he would be able to keep Junior quiet. I think that played a large part in my decision. When Kendra and I had dinner with Mr. Mackey and his wife, she found Mr. Mackey to be pleasant and likable. Kendra had the best judgement of people of anyone I've ever known. I gestured to Big Mike for us to leave. Without questioning or showing any resistance he followed my lead. We rode the elevator down in silence. Once we exited GPG headquarters Big Mikes spoke.

"What's our next move?"

"We head back to the house, see what progress Kuto has made with Brendham, and we focused our sites on Abrahams."

"Yea, he's the mutha fucka we want!"

I nodded in agreement.

Taking Care of Business

Back at the house Big Mike and I entered through the front door and were greeted by primal screams. I surmised it was Mr. Brendham. The shrieks had a hint of indignity and self-righteousness being ripped from the very essence of its physical presence. I walked toward the stairs headed up to my room. Big Mike questioned me.

"You don't want to see what progress Kuto has made with Brendham?"

"No, when he gets what we need come get me. I'll be in my room."

"Okay," Big Mike walked off toward the sound of painful yelps!

I started my ascend up the stairs to my room, overcome. The episode with the Mackeys had given me a different perspective. In our need to avenge the death of our friend and brother Charles, we were on the verge of killing two men with no connection to his death. Nothing was black and white only shades of gray. I wasn't the law and I wasn't God, but deep down I wanted someone to pay for Charles's death. I wanted someone to pay for trying to kill me, for putting the worthless scum Brendham in my life. I wasn't sure I was on the same page as Big Mike anymore. I needed to talk with someone. I needed to talk with my wife. I took my cell out as I sat on the bed, and before I dialed the number, Big Mike appeared in the doorway.

"Not a good idea."

"What?"

"Calling Kendra."

"Why?"

"I'm torn just as you are Shane. Doing the right thing is not always clear and concise! But, if I thought for one moment the law would do the right thing and bring to justice those who perpetrated this act of violence against you and Charles I would acquiesce and let them do their jobs,…" his words turn to anger " but they ain't doing shit because they're too busy into shit! Didn't you say Ice's file had evidence the government has Brendham under surveillance too?"

"Yes."

"Then, they're watching all this shit go down, and they knew about the hit on you and Charles. It's up to us to set this straight and fuck where the chips fall." He paused and looked me directly in the eyes. "If family don't lookout for family, then how can the family feel protected? I know you got Kendra and the kids and I want to have kids with Adriona and start a family of my own. As much as this is about the death of Charles, it's about protecting what we built-Black Street, our legacy, and our freedom. We shouldn't have to live outside the country we were born. Our kids should be able to roam and play in this world wherever we wish. We have worked for that right and black folk who came before us worked for that right! Shane, we are Black men in America! Nobody is going to fight for us; we have to do it for ourselves."

"Agreed!" I had no rebuttal for what Big Mike had just laid down. I didn't know if I wanted to make the sacrifice of possibly not seeing my family again, but I also didn't want to run and hide, and Big Mike was right government eyes were upon us.

Just then Kuto walks up.

"It was Abrahams who gave the order without the knowledge of GPG. We got a location on him."

"Okay, give me a minute and I will come down," I said.

Big Mike and Kuto left. I called Kendra.

"Hello?" an uncertainty in her voice.

"It's me Babe," I said somberly.

"I started to worry; it's been two days and I hadn't heard from you."

"I know and I apologize, but we switched out our cells for these new ones, and it has been non-stop since we got off the plane."

"I was just worried. Are you okay? You don't sound like yourself."

"I'm better now that I've heard your voice."

"Should I be worried about you Shane?"

"No need. How are the kids?"

"Miles and Monique are fine making new friends and enjoying their grandparents, and our newest edition he has sprouted a little more since you left."

"How are you?"

"Missing you! I want you to make it back home; you hear me!"

"Loud and clear." I sang gently. *"I'm coming home,..coming home,... tell the world that I'm.... coming home."*

"You still got humor through all this. That's a good sign." She paused. "I know you and Big Mike are doing what you have to do, but.....I'm not sure...

I interrupted her. "It's going to be okay. I love you, and I will be home soon." My voice drifted as I was trying to end the conversation.

"Shane," she shouted. "I loved Charles too, and Carmen is like a sister to me, but I don't want to lose you."

"It's bigger than me!"

"Nothing is bigger than your life! You have a family waiting on you," she cried.

I could hear the sniffles and sobbing.

"I'm going to finish this and then I'm coming home."

"I beg of you, please come home now. It's not worth your life. I beg you!"

"I love you. Kiss the kids for me," I hung up the line.

I went down stairs immediately into the room where Brendham, Lee, and Melvin were being held. Upon entering the room my focus was on Brendham a defeated man. Drenched in sweat and blood, trembling as if he was in subzero weather all his fingers from his left hand were cut off, his shoes were off his feet which resembled ground beef, and his right eye was completely burnt out filled with blood. I looked down on the floor and saw the steel rod bloodied about an inch from its tip. Big Mike and Kuto along with three other security were in the room with the detainees. I stood in front of Brendham.

"Please kill me Shane. Don't make me suffer like a dog."

"Damn that! You will keep suffering until you help us get this Abrahams!"

"I gave you his location." He pleaded.

"You and Lee will have to make the trip with us."

"I'm in no condition to travel," Brendham said.

"You don't have a choice. It's either travel with us or stay here and let Kuto torture you some more and then you can plead with him to kill you."

Brendham understood he had a better chance of survival coming with me. Abrahams was held up in a swanky hotel for the weekend in downtown Manhattan. He had been on edge and nervous ever since his attempt to kill me wasn't successful. When Brendham didn't know my whereabouts, he had a nervous breakdown. Brendham assigned two security personnel to guard him 24hrs a day. At the time Brendham thought it was an overreaction on his part, but Abrahams was convinced I would retaliate, and he was right. Time lapsed and Brendham removed the 24hr security at Abrahams' request. Sometimes when you are constantly surrounded by security personnel, it can leave you feeling like a prisoner of your own circumstance. I indeed knew the feeling.

"Clean him up and get him and Lee ready to go," I told Kuto.

We left the house about an hour and a half later. This time we rode three to a car- Kuto, me, and Brenham in one car, Big Mike, Lee and one guard, and three security guards in the last car. The rest of the security stayed at the house babysitting Melvin. We arrived at the swanky downtown Manhattan Hotel "M" around ten thirty pm. The hotel was in full swing, it looked like a formal affair. When we entered the hotel, we got our fair share of stares. We stood out like a sore thump! The lobby of the hotel was lavishly designed bright white walls garnished with vibrant color paintings, plush velvet purple circular oversized chairs that resemble love seats. A black grand piano in the center of the lobby, elevated by a small white marble stage in which a very accomplished pianist was playing classical music, Bach's Mozart concerto. The hotel was only five stories high, and from the lobby you could see the walk ways with outside railing that led to each room in the hotel. People crowded the lobby socializing with drinks in hands, enjoying the music, and giving glances of disapproval to who they felt didn't fit in.

Big Mike, Kuto, and I along with Brendham and Lee made our way through the crowded lobby to the elevators. Abrahams was on the fifth floor- room 501. When we exited the elevators on the fifth floor, we made a quick left turn and were facing 501. Brendham knew the plan- we would follow his lead, and he would get Abrahams to open the door by telling him he had some urgent news about me. We patched up Brendham best we could, but he still looked a wretch. He couldn't stop sweating and trembling, the eye patch with sunglasses covered his missing eye, but there were some remnants of the blood around the eye upon closer examination. Brendham was dying right before our eyes, but I didn't care. He was going to carry out this last order from me, if it killed him or not!

Brendham stood square in the middle of the door. I stood to his left out of sight from the peep hole and Lee, Big Mike, and Kuto stood to his right out of sight. Brendham knocked twice.

"I didn't call for room service," Abrahams yelled from inside the room.

"It's Brendham."

"Brendham?" He questioned

"Yea, open up. Got some news on Shane," he knocked again. "Come on open up!"

"Why didn't you call first? I have a guest."

"I didn't have time for that, I need to speak to you in person. This mutha fucka Shane is in New York!"

"Fuck!" Abrahams said in frustration.

"Alright give me a minute."

Both me and Big Mike looked at each other at the exact same time, and we pulled our nine's out and armed them, Kuto did the same. Big Mike put his hand on Lee's shoulder from behind with gun in the other. I held my gun down with both hands on it, crouching down slightly, and then directed Brendham to move closer to the door. About fifteen seconds passed and Abrahams still hadn't opened the door. I directed Brendham to knock again.

He did. "What's the hold up?"

"It's open," Abrahams called out.

What the fuck I thought. This bastard knows I'm outside this door waiting on him, and that Brendham has betrayed him. I said to myself "I'm going to kill this mutha fucka! If this is how it's going down, lets get it over with." I took a position directly behind Brendham and put my left hand on his left shoulder, then directed him to open the door and enter the room. When Brendham opened the door I pushed him through the door and into the room. I heard the cock of the shot gun before I saw Abrahams. This cat started blasting. His first shotgun blast hit the wall of the hallway Brendham and I was navigating through. There was a bathroom up ahead on the left and Abrahams was standing in the back right corner of the front room in the hotel suite.

As I continued to push Brendham forward into the room pass the shotgun hole in the wall where dry wall dust filled the air, I laid down some fire into the corner where Abrahams was standing. Abrahams cocked his shotgun again and let another blast go this one hit Brendham in the chest and sent him back into me; I spun and lunged forward letting Brendham's lifeless body fall to the ground. All the while keeping my finger pressing down on that 9mm trigger sending gun fire in the direction of Abrahams where one bullet caught the edge of his shoulder making Abrahams whence and scream out. I quickly took cover in the bathroom on left. Big Mike charged in with Lee ahead of him and Abrahams quickly turned and sent shotgun fire in their direction. Big Mike returned fire while pushing Lee into the den which led to Lee's prompt demise when he was shot in the abdomen by Abrahams' shotgun fire. Big Mike kept his finger on the trigger and darted to the right once he passed through the hallway where there was no cover. I kept a steady firestorm from my.9mm from the bathroom. Abraham's attention was averted toward me allowing Big Mike clean shots to Abraham's chest sending him backward against the wall and dislodging his shotgun from his hands. Big Mike stopped shooting. I reloaded with another clip and came out of bathroom.

As we stood over him, Abrahams was sitting against the wall with two bullet wounds in his chest bleeding out. In the face of death Abrahams was abusive and indignant.

"I knew that god damn Brendham would sell me out to save his ass….fuck the both of you, take the company my family built from nothing to an international power, the both you can go to hell and kiss my ass before you get there!"

"We ain't gonna kiss nobody's ass, but we are prepared to see you in hell," Big Mike declared.

Both Big Mike and I pointed our guns directly at Abrahams who had a look of terror on his face. We simultaneously shot him multiple times, his blood spewing out on both of us.

Kuto ran to us. "We must go!"

Big Mike and I still standing over Abrahams, Kuto nudged us both. "It's time to go!"

We snapped out of it and quickly walked out the room to people staring up and pointing at the room. Kuto let off fire down in the lobby over the reception desk to give a good scare to the onlookers in an effort to divert attention from our faces. Screams from the lobby rang out and people frantically exited the hotel. We quickly made it down the stairs out the lobby and into the awaiting cars. As we pulled off we heard the sirens. We were well out of sight once the police arrived on the scene. The drive home was quiet and somber, not cheery or mission accomplished. Big Mike and I shared a car for the first time since we left Africa. He sat in front with Kuto driving.. Big Mike turned and gave me a dap with his fist.

Once we made it back to the house I released Melvin and put him on a plane back to his hometown Chicago. I also sent our security back to Africa on a chartered flight that night, except Kuto and two others. I was mentally exhausted and physically tired. Both Big Mike and I rested in the family room, me on the soft couch, Big Mike on the oversized love seat. With the sports channel playing on the flat screen we fell asleep. In a deep slumber I was slowly awakened by a funny smell. I tried to focus my eyes, but the glare from the television hindered my vision. I looked where Big Mike slept in the love seat, but my vision was blurred. Then I saw the outline of a man rising up behind Big Mike and at the moment when I attempted to yell to alert Big Mike, a bag slammed over my head, and the smell that had woke me up was strongly present inside the strong cloth bag and before I knew it, I was out!

****

I awakened with a terrible headache. I had lost all sense of time. I had no idea how long I had been out, what day it was, and even the time of day eluded me. I tried to clear my head and when I focused in on my whereabouts, I was sitting on a cot, in a single room, concrete floors and walls with a toilet and sink, no windows except the one on the door. I was clearly in some kind of holding room being detained. I stood, walked to the door and look out the small window. Outside I saw a white narrow hallway with similar doors to the room I was in. I couldn't see either end of the hallway. I had never been inside such a place, but where ever I was, it wasn't ordinary. I stepped back and examined the room more closely. It was big space about one hundred fifty square feet, fourteen foot ceilings, a speaker above the door and cameras on each side of the room. The room was drab and cold, but clean; sterile clean.

I sat back down on the cot. I wondered about Big Mike and our three security men. My mind was full of questions. Were they in this same place as me? Were they even alive? Were the people who grab me the police? Was this the end of the road for me? These unanswered questions put fear in my heart. My legs and hands trembled. I stood and rubbed my hands together trying to calm myself. I thought pacing would help me control my nerves, but I felt my whole body begin to shake. I looked up at both cameras in the corners of the room, and new I was being watched. I didn't care. I was afraid of the unknown. Would I ever see my family again, my wife and kids, my mother, and my friends? Was I going to jail? Was I in jail? Who was I being held by, the authorities or some other organization that might be related to Abrahams or the Titan Corporation? After what I had been through, I left all options in my mind open which didn't work to my advantage just made me more nervous and afraid.

I wanted to talk to someone to help settle my nerves. The depth and girth of what Big Mike and I did in New York hit me big time. The torture and death became real. Although I knew the reason for our actions, justification for taking the law in our own hands became problem some. My emotions started to get the best of me. Tears began flowing down my face in rapid fashion. Sounds emerged from mouth reminiscent of moans and groans. I bowed my head in my hands just trying to get a hold of myself, but I couldn't. Soon my entire body was trembling and I was sobbing relentlessly. I laid back down on the cot, and several minutes I had cried myself to sleep.

I was exhausted mentally and physically. I slept what felt like for days. Since there were not clocks in the room I was being detained, I had lost all consciousness of time. When my eyes would finally open after deep sleep, it was only for some blurred moments before I fell back into that deep slumber. My dreams haunted me. I tried to escape them, but they came at me with a vengeance – Charles's death, Brendham's and Melvin's torture and demise, and Abraham's death. It became too much and awoke letting out a yell which took to position of sitting straight up on the cot. I looked around nothing had changed, but I felt my stomach grumble, and I realized I hadn't eaten since I been in here.

I walked toward the door once again to look out the small window, nothing had changed. My thoughts shifted to Big Mike. I wondered was he having a difficult time in here as I was assuming he was in the same place as me. I went back and sat down on the cot. Then, the possibility of me never getting out of there hit me. I hadn't been read my rights or spoken to by anyone. What if they had staged my death, and passed a body off as mine to Kendra and my family? "Kendra would know me." I told myself, but not if they presented a burnt body, so burnt not even my mother would recognize me. These types of thoughts race through my mind all the possibilities of how to fake my death and keep me locked up inside this room forever. The thought of not seeing my wife and kids terrified me. I realized in that moment just how powerless I was, and not even the biggest ego in the world could save me from this situation. I had to try to get back to right mind before my thoughts drove me crazy.

I paced around the room for several minutes just trying to calm my mind. I was getting weak and dizzy from no food or water, and just as I was about to drop on top of my cot two men one black and one white in blue suits open the door and entered the room.

"Mr. Jackson please turn around with your back toward me. " The black man said.

I did as I was told.

"Put your hands behind your back."

I complied. He approached and handcuffed me. Right when the handcuffs went on a part of mind rested. I knew know that I was in the custody of some type of legal entity. Just knowing brought me slight bit of comfort, but what awaited ahead still was very menacing.

They walked me outside the room and down the hallway. I tried to see inside the adjacent and opposite rooms to see if I could spot Big Mike, but they were moving me too quickly and my sight was blurry from fatigue and lack of food. When we got to the end of the hallway, the lead officer looked up in the camera showed his badge, and we were buzzed through the closed door. We walked another 100 feet, and they led me into another room with large mirror window which I immediately thought this was the room where the questioning went down.

The black officer led me to a chair at a table in the center of the room. He took the handcuffs off, and helped me sit down in my weakened state. He and the other officer left the room leaving me to myself. I sat there half-conscious wondering what's next. After about what seem like five minutes a different man entered the room – white male, grey suit, slim build, with graying hair. He sat on the table in front of me a glass of water and small package of crackers with a pitcher of water in hand he watched me down the glass of water in just an instant, and he refilled the glass several more times to see instant replay after instant replay.

"You might want to slow down just a little." He said.

I looked at him, but I had no response. I just kept on jugging water. Once I had my fill, I started in on the crackers. He left the room momentarily, and returned with a chair which he put opposite me and sat in it. Then from his pocket he placed a few more cracker packets on the table. I quickly obliterated them.

"How are you feeling?"

"Better."

He paused. He looked at me intently. "I have some questions for you, and we can do this the easy way or the hard way. It's up to you the way this thing goes."

I nodded my head letting him know that I understood what he was getting at.

He started slowly.

The questions were ridiculous. They ranged from my association with Jakar, Blue Sky's operations in Africa, our influence on the political landscape around the world, and my humble beginnings at GPG. All the questions were in regards to terrorist plots and a racist mindset by me and my inner circle. My answers to all those questions: RIDICULUS! My answers were not pleasing to the interrogator, and agitated him to no end. He became emotional and started foaming at the mouth screaming at me, then declared that I was a murderer, thief and scum of the earth. He accused me of stealing Blue Sky, Titan Industries, cheating on Kendra, having a design and desire to overthrow the government, and using my breakfast program for Harlem youth as a recruiting tool to execute my plans. I listened and responded: RIDICULUS! His tirade went on for at least 20 minutes. I tried to play it cool even when he laid out the charge of me being a murder. He finally paused looked at me in disgust, then rose and slapped me across the face. My instinct and I retaliated by charging him, and before I knew it, I was face down on the ground with this guy's knee on my back with my left arm pinned behind me. The two officers that led me into the room re-entered. The officer that had me pinned told them to take me back to my holding cell.

Once back in my cell, I thought to myself "these idiots think I'm a terrorist". What could be more insane than that? There was nothing in my past that could lead one to think I was a terrorist or harbored plans to overthrow the government or was there? Jakar warned me when we first met that my strategy to create opportunity for other black professionals at GPG would be seen as a threat to America, especially as my power and influence grew not only domestically, but internationally. I dismissed it as non-sense, but now it was real. My success had become my enemy or at least fuel for those who opposed me. As I sat in my cell and contemplated how the hell I was going to get out of here, my mind had no solutions. It was apparent now that the government was holding me and Big Mike. What were there plans for us? We hadn't been charged with anything, for now it looks like they were just holding us for questioning. If this was the case, they were breaking the law. They could not legally hold us more than 24 hours without charging me and Big Mike. It was apparent these guys were operating outside the law, or had some kind of authority over the law if they deemed Big Mike and me terrorist threats.

My mind at this time was swirling with all kinds of thoughts, but when those thoughts moved to my family I began to panic. The unknown became very worrisome to me. I missed and needed my family. I wanted to talk to Kendra to make sure they were okay and not under any duress. I had to lay down to calm my nerves and before I knew it I was asleep. I slept for several hours. When I opened my eyes, the entire room was pitch black. I raised my hands and couldn't see them before my face. About 5 minutes a later two to three men bust through the door, the room is still pitch black, so I just felt hands on me. No instructions or words they just dragged me out the room and down the hallway which was pitch black also. It wasn't until they pulled me through the door that exited the confinement area, did I realize these guys had night goggles and were dressed in army fatigues. They were relentless in dragging through the entire space way beyond the room they put me in the first time. They took me down in an elevator to an entirely different part of the building.

It was drab down there. It was all cement with tradition jail cells, but all the cells were empty. When we reached our destination, it was 30 x 30 room surrounded by grey cement from top to bottom, there was 10 x 10 wooden board in the middle of the room with restraints, and the seemed to be slightly slanted downward about 10 to 20 degrees. At first sight of this contraption I knew what was ahead for me and my impulses took over and I started to resist vehemently. I heard myself shouting "What the Fuck" repeatedly as the three men forcefully strap me down on the board with my head on decline to my feet. My heart started pumping blood through my body faster, my mind was swirling trying to find a way out, my hands and feet struggle to break loose, but to no avail. The three men stepped back, but I don't think they ever left the room. My focus shifted from them onto a man that entered the room. This was the same man who questioned me the first time.

"We tried it the easy way the first time. I think this time we will try something different."

I had no response, but I couldn't take my eyes off him. This man was calm and collected and very methodical. First thing he did was walk around the wooden plank checking the shackles on my feet and hands. Once he was satisfied, he slowly took a white cloth from his pocket and laid it across my face. My heart beat quickened. I had heard about waterboarding as form of torture, but I knew nothing about it. To tell you the truth, I had no idea what was to come next that's just how clueless I was about this technique.

When he started slowly pouring water onto my face over my nose and mouth filling them with water, I gaged almost immediately. He paused, and took away the cloth from my face.

"We can continue down this road or we exit off this road immediately. It's up to you"

The gagging left me short of breath. I was trying to catch my breath and answer him at the same time. I wasn't trying to be hero, and I was willing to answer any questions he asked. I wanted to exit off this road immediately. "Exit" is all I could muster up. He gave me some time to compose myself as best I could, then he started in on those dumb ass questions again, and once again I gave him the same answers as before, and he turned livid. He quickly placed the cloth back across my face and commenced to waterboarding torture. He kept the water slowly raining down on my face only giving me breaks only to breathe three or four full breathes, before he repeated the process. I felt like I was at the bottom of the ocean without breathing gear taking in water desperately trying to swim to the ocean's surface to catch my breath, but it was beyond my reach. I was drowning. I felt like I was dying over and over again. I had chest and arm spasms, desperate and hysterical pleas for him to stop. He paid me no mind. It got to the point where I wanted to surrender to it all. The feeling of dying was unlike anything I've experienced in my life and not anything that I wanted to repeat. I pleaded and begged. He finally paused. Then the words came out "I'll tell you what you want." I don't know how coherent the words were, but I was ready to spill the beans about the murder Big Mike and I committed and confess to any other charges he put in front of me. I was a broken man, devoid of ego, pride, spirit, and any ray of light. I just wanted the torture to stop.

They unstrapped me brought a chair in the room and sat me right side up. Once I had some semblance of normalcy. He went in on those ridiculous questions, but this time I gave him everything he wanted to hear. By the time I was finished Black Street was a terrorist organization with plans on over throwing the government. We had connections from Africa to the Middle East into Europe. Blue Sky was being used to wash money to fund all our terrorist plans. I implicated everyone no one was untouched, not even the dead – Charles. When I implicated him and slandered his name, it hurt me the worse. Charles was dead, no way to defend his name against my absurd assertions.

Afterward they took me back to holding cell. Once there I just stood in the middle of the room staring at the ceiling, not all there, trembling and shaken to my core, tears rolled down my face. Soon I dropped to my knees, and I cried long and hard. I couldn't stop; it was like I wanted to purge this entire experience, but that was impossible and I knew it, so I cried even harder. I wanted to see my family just one more time, but I wasn't sure that would happen, so I cried harder. I cried myself to sleep in the middle of my cell.

I don't know how long I slept, but I didn't move from the middle of my cell, until someone entered my cell. It was just one guy. He asked me to stand and follow him. He wasn't coercive or abusive. His demeanor was very calm. I did as I was told. He led me back into the room where they initially question me, but this time when we entered the room Big Mike was in there sitting at the table. I entered the room slowly. A big smile came over Big Mike's face when he saw me. My guide let me enter the room by myself while he stood at the doorway. Big Mike approached excitedly, but became cautious and concern when he saw my face. He assisted me to the table and helped me take a seat.

"What did they do to you? Got damn it!" He said angrily.

I patted him on his shoulder. "I'm okay."

I didn't have many words for three reasons: One was because I knew they were listening, two l was drained and tired, and three I was embarrassed about the lies I told about Black Street Capital just so they would end the torture. Big Mike didn't press me. He gave me a very caring reassuring look. He put his hand on my shoulder this time, and just nodded his head in an affirmation.

Big Mike and I sat in that room patiently for over an hour, without much conversation between us. I actually laid my head down on the table after a while just feeling exhausted. When Darrell walked through the door with his mother and Mr. Mackey, Big Mike nudged me, and my head rose slowly and focused on them. Their reaction to me was the same as Big Mike's – concern. Darrell didn't approach us directly. He walked over to the back corner of the room, and then gestured Big Mike and I over. Seeing that I was having a hard time rising up from my chair Big Mike assisted me. Once we made it over to Darrell his look of concern turned to anger.

"Hey, what did they do to you?"

I smiled.

"He's okay." Big Mike answered.

"The hell he is! Somebody will pay for this!"

"I'm alright', I finally came back. Then, I asked looking over at Mr. Mackey and his mother. What was this about?

"They are here to help us." Darrell answered.

"Mackey," Big Mike questioned.

"Yes, despite y'all kicking the shit out of him and his son, he has decided to help. Matter of fact when I called him, there was no arm twisting on my part he was more than willing to give his assistance."

"Okay, lay it out for us. How do we get out of this," I asked?

"Well, we have already bargained a deal with the help of my mother, Mr. Mackey, their political contacts and others."

"Other contacts, like whom, "Big Mike asked.

"Ex CIA and FBI: now look, we had to put some money in the coffers of some of these people. "

"What was the price?" I asked.

"Hundred Mil."

"So, we bought our way out," Big Mike declared.

"No, not really, the money helped, but without my mother and Mr. Mackey asking for the favors from their friends, both you and Shane would be rotting in the worse prison known to man!"

"Prison is no place for a man or a woman," Big Mike commented.

"What's the move from here," I asked.

"Big Mike and you have to listen to a little grandstanding by my mother and Mr. Mackey, then the agents will come back in and ask you every question under the sun and you must answer openly and honestly. No question is off limits, and then we all go home."

Big Mike and I looked at each other, and then we looked at Darrell.

"I've answered most of the material questions. Their main focus is on Black Street, and you Shane. They want to know what makes you tick and what motivates you. They already know Black Street operations were above board, some bending of rules, but none more than any other multi-billion dollar global company."

When I heard Darrell say that, I knew what spewed out of my mouth from the torture, they recognize as pure fiction. Big Mike and I nodded out heads in agreement.

"Hey, just one other thing," Darrell said. "I should have been with you guys. We're family and family sticks together even in disagreement. I'm sorry!"

"No, you were where you should have been. If it wasn't for you, all of us would be rotting in jail,…thank you," I said!

I gave him a big hug. Knowing he just delivered me back to my family. Big Mike did the same as he understood how big of a deal this was, and Darrell came through for us. Big Mike and I returned to the table and sat back down. Darrell's mother was up first and she did not disappoint. She ranted and cursed to an Oscar performance, but Mr. Mackey was entirely different.

"Shane, I understand why you and Michael did what you did, and to be very honest I might have done the same thing at your age. Friend dies, attempt on your life, and no one to turn to for justice, so you take justice in your own hands, that's how America was built. A few Americans who were being mistreated and couldn't get justice took upon themselves to fight and give their lives for what they believed was right. I'm sorry about the loss of Charles, and I'm sorry for my family's participation no matter how small. Knowing and not telling anyone to stop a crime makes my son culpable. I thank you for sparing his life! Shane, deep down I have always been in your corner, and in a lot of ways you reminded me of myself. I was never envious when I saw you create your own investment company, just proud. I hope you consider me a friend, because I do you!" He stood and approached. I stood and met him on the left side of the table. He embraced me firmly with his arms wrapped around my shoulder and the other under my arm, and I returned the embrace. "I'm proud of you son," he whispered in my ear.

"Thank you," I whispered back in his ear.

After Darrell, his mother, and Mr. Mackey left the room, four agents entered the room, two left with Big Mike and the other two stayed with me. For the next six hours they drilled me from everything starting with my undergrad work at Darden to the shooting of Abrahams in his hotel suite. After it was over I was exhausted, but relieved. It was like a confession to a priest. When you profess all your sins and the priest absolves you of those sins, you have a clean slate in which to start over with. I wanted that, I needed that. A clean slate, no looking back just forward, it was too much baggage to carry and to bring back with me to my family would be nothing more than a burden on us all.

When I left the room and met Big Mike, Darrell, and others in the lobby, I felt like a two ton brick had been lifted off my back.

"I'm ready to go home!" I said.

"I thought you might be ready to get out of here. I have our private jet waiting to take us to Nigeria. We leave as soon as we can get to Kennedy," Darrell said.

To say I was elated would be an understatement.

"Do you want to call Kendra," Darrell asked handing me his cell phone.

"No, I want to surprise her!

"She made the call to me after she talked with you to put all this in motion. As I told you before, you have a hell of a woman!"

"I know I can't wait to get home to her, but I'm going to need a few days to rest before we depart. I don't want Kendra to see me this way."

The rest was needed and very therapeutic for me. I talked by phone to Kendra every day and her words were healing. We talked about me, her, and the kids, and how we wanted to move forward as a family. My desire was no longer to compete, conquer, build, influence, and control. I just wanted to give. Give to my wife, my kids, my mother, my friends, and whoever needed my help. Giving in such a way that I had no expectation of receiving in return, I was now void of ego, selfishness, and a need to feed either one. When you are taken to the edge of death and brought back, you become acutely aware of your humanity. Your testament to your life flashes before you and all your accomplishments means nothing if you haven't advanced humanity, and I hadn't. My soul for the first time was alive, and Kendra heard it in my voice.

"This is the man I've been waiting to stand up. The man your mother told me about."

I could hear her cries through the phone.

"I miss you.,,, I'm coming home." I said softly.

****

When we arrived to board our private jet, there in the anchor area was Kuto with our other two security guards. I was very happy to see they were safe and sound and on their way back to the mother country with us.

"Are you okay," Kuto asked?

"Yes, everything is good and now even better that I see you are safe."

We embraced and boarded the plane. Once on board my excitement grew with anticipation of seeing my family again. Although I had been gone less than a two week it felt more like six months. I wanted to plan something special for my return.

"I need a piano player," I spouted out on the flight in mid-air.

"Ah hell no, we are not going through that again," Big Mike retorted. "You have not lost your woman. Kendra is at home waiting for your return. She will be happy enough just to see yo black ass!"

"I second that emotion," Darrell confirmed.

"I know a pianist," Kuto answered.

"My man," I responded.

"No,..no…no," both Big Mike and Darrell objected.

"Shane, you can't sing man," Darrell pleaded.

"Yea man, since singing ain't your thing, maybe you should just write a poem."

We all laughed. But, I didn't care what anyone said, my mind was made up to serenade Kendra!

Thirteen hours later, early in the morning we landed in Nigeria. We took a taxi cab into Lagos and held up in a hotel to shower, get some clean clothes and eat. Big Mike and Darrell, despite their objections, pitched in to make my plan to serenade Kendra come to fruition. Kuto's friend, the pianist came and met with me at the hotel. We talked about the music I wanted. He was familiar with it and able to play it. Everything was coming together nicely. I arranged with my mother to get Kendra and the kids out of the house for an hour or two. We had the piano transported to the house, and I had a little time for setup and rehearse.

My mother executed her part to the letter. When I arrived, I was just overwhelmed at the sight of my home and knowing I would see my family soon. We set the piano right in the middle of the property on the green grass by the trees. It was a beautiful sunny day. Adorned in white traditional clothing with some sequence, I was clean and sharp. The shirt was long and oversized which hung nearly to my ankles with the same white sequence pants underneath and sandals. The mic and speakers were set up and the piano player in position. We practiced a couple of times through, but my voice didn't get any better, and a few sour notes made an appearance, but I wasn't bothered by any of it, and the pianist was polite and kind.

Kendra and the family finally pulled up. Miles and Monique raced to me screaming "Daddy, Daddy, Daddy." It was a great feeling to hear them and see them running calling for me. I almost melted and broke down right there. I bent down and picked them both up, kissed and hugged them. Kendra approached with the baby along with other family members, but they kept a distance because they knew what was in store. I put the kids down and they stayed by my side hugging each leg. I looked toward the pianist to start. I gave it my best shot:

Here we are on earth together,
It's you and I,
God has made us fall in love, it's true,
I've really found someone like you

Will it say the love you feel for me, will it say,
That you will be by my side
To see me through,
Until my life is through

Well, in my mind, we can conquer the world,
In love you and I, you and I, you and I

I am glad at least in my life I found someone
That may not be here forever to see me through,
But I found strength in you,
I only pray that I have shown you a brighter day,
Because that's all that I am living for, you see,
Don't worry what happens to me

Cause' in my mind, you will stay here always,
In love, you and I, you and I, you and I, you and I
In my mind we can conquer the world
In love, you and I, you and I, you and I

I got through it without breaking down. Kendra rushed to me with tears in her eyes, baby clasped to her chest. She me the baby, then hugged and kissed me like she hadn't seen me in thirty years. My lady, my wife, my friend, my partner, my woman, and my broad, I couldn't have made a better choice in a woman to spend the rest of my life with. Tears streamed down my face, I was overwhelmed with emotion. My mother came and hugged and kissed me in the little room that was available for her to squeeze in because Kendra and the kids weren't letting go.

Big Mike and Adriona had reunited together over on the side. They joined us by the piano along with Darrell.

"I'm sure glad you didn't get on your knees and beg this time," Big Mike declared.

"I know, that was a little embarrassing," Darrell added.

"My man is good beggar," Kendra rebutted as she caressed my face. "Don't you ever stop begging me baby!" She kissed me.

"I won't!"

THE END

Made in the USA
Middletown, DE
02 June 2019